Best
Transgender
Erotica

Best
Transgender
Erotica

edited by
Hanne Blank & Raven Kaldera

Circlet Press
Cambridge, MA

Best Transgender Erotica
edited by Hanne Blank and Raven Kaldera

ISBN 1-885865-40-6
Printed in Canada

First Printing January 2002

```
                ALTERNATIVE CATALOGING-IN-PUBLICATION DATA
                          Blank, Hanne, editor.
       Best transgender erotica. Edited by Hanne Blank ands Raven Kaldera.
                     Cambridge, MA: Circlet Press.

   23 short stories about transsexuals, crossdressers, and others who can't
                          be so rigidly defined.

       1. Erotic fiction, American. 2. Short stories, American. 3.
   Transsexuals--Fiction. 4. Transvestites--Fiction. I. Title: Transgender
                                erotica.

                       813.083538   —dc21
```

Distributed to the book trade by SCB Distributors, Gardena, CA
(800) 729-6423

For sales to individuals, specialty stores, and mail-order catalogs, please
contact Circlet Press at (617) 864-0492 or write to:

> Circlet Press, Inc.
> 1770 Massachusetts Avenue, #278
> Cambridge, MA 02140
> http://www.circlet.com

Table of Contents

Introduction   7

How   13
    Hanne Blank

The Gay Science   19
    Charles Anders

Small Considerations   29
    R. Gay

Wild Ride   43
    Raven Gildea

Teenie Weenies, Inc.   51
    Matthew Kailey

Tangaroa   61
    Allison Lonsdale

Pinkeye   77
    Simon Sheppard

Evolution   85
    M. Christian

She'll Always Own A Piece of Me   93
    S. Naomi Finkelstein, a.k.a. Max

The Audit   101
    Dominic Santi

Doppler   115
    Todd Belton

No Charity   127
    Corbie Petulengro

Up for a Nickel   139
   Thomas S. Roche
A Dance of Queens   157
   Sacchi Green
Mars Conjunct Venus   171
   Magdalene Meretrix
Mallrat   177
   Sam Kling
Becoming   187
   Alex Gino
The Coldest Light   195
   Gary Bowen
As The Sparks Fly Upward   207
   Raven Kaldera
The Velveteen FTM   223
   N. D. Hailey
Wanting That Man   231
   Karen Taylor
Walt   241
   Ian Philips
The Essence of Magic   259
   Stacey Montgomery Scott

Introduction

Transgender erotica... what does that even mean to us? For decades now, what's passed for tranny smut—erotica and pornography focusing on transgendered people—has been written about transfolk by people who are not us, who don't know us or love us, outsiders who may not even have met or spoken to an actual transgendered person in their entire lives. Transfolk have been pictured as cardboard cutouts with improbable anatomy who will fuck and be fucked by anyone, anything, anytime, in any way, as if in a no-holds barred sexual dream where once gender norms go, so does anything else, no matter how unlikely, exploitive, or even abusive.

There has always been something extremely pathetic in the way that we've been pictured, the extremism of traditional transgender-focused porn so objectifying and depersonalizing that it seems to many like it's intended in some ways to punish those who transgress the male/female gender binary: The forcibly cross-dressed husband relegated to a humiliating half-life, the transsexual who is deemed too freakish to ever have a real relationship, the she-male hooker in ratty nylons and crusted makeup, the raped and murdered victim in the alleyway about whom no one will care tomorrow. Traditional trans-focused porn hasn't given us erotic role models or even a notion of what our sexual possibilities might be like, it has only given us warped, grimy peep-show windows through which to gawk at the sideshow Half-and-Halfs. *See what happens,* thunders the unspoken voice of mainstream tranny-porn subtexts, *when you blur the boundaries between male and female? See what happens when you cross that line?*

This book, just in case you're still wondering, ain't that kind of tranny smut. In this book, you'll find transgendered people as they

7

really are, or in some cases as they might be hundreds of years from now or in mythical, magical worlds of the imagination. These are our stories. Like magicians with a tablecloth, these stories whip the gender-binary ground out from beneath our feet with exuberance and chutz-pah, leaving transpeople and their lovers standing, revealed in all our strength, sexiness, and pride.

When we, the editors, first got together and began to plan this book, we had quite a few very definite thoughts about what we want-ed for a book like this… and what we didn't. First and foremost, we wanted erotica that was both sex-positive and trans-positive, both of us poised to ditch anything that resembled the scenarios mentioned in the opening paragraph of this introduction. (And, yes, we did get some.)

Beyond that, we each brought our own perspectives, curiosities, intrigues, tastes, and issues to the book, each of us coming at trans-gender issues, and transgender sexuality, from different backgrounds, experiences, and points of view. Raven Kaldera is an intersex FTM shaman/activist, parent, educator, herbalist, writer, and organic farmer married to an MTF transsexual. Raven is happy to be able to announce that he has hopped into bed with just about every kind of differently-gendered person you can imagine (no, really, it was all research, hon-est). Hanne Blank is a bio-grrrl power femme writer and historian who first discovered the joy of transgender at the age of 18, when she devel-oped a searing (if unrequited) case of the hots for an ultra-glamtastic drag queen. She has been life-partnered to an intersexual for many years and has a longstanding fascination with gender, gender perform-ance, gender politics, and the nexus of power, gender, and sexuality, topics she has explored extensively in academic and non-academic writing as well as in her personal life.

So we're two very different people, but we definitely share some passions—and goals. One of them, brought to life in this book, is to provide some images of transgender sex that are truly transgender in nature. "Traditional" transgender erotica stars mostly "she-males," male-to-female pre-operative or non-operative transsexuals who are often required to fuck like men in the pages of cheap porn mags. In our experience, this is neither realistic nor terribly fair, and certainly underestimates the complex realities of MTF (male to female) lives. And as for erotic material featuring FTMs (female to male transfolk), well, there wasn't even enough that we had anything about which to complain. Until very recently, erotica featuring FTMs was almost com-pletely nonexistent, except for occasional exceptions such as Gary Bowen's short-lived but steaming ezine *Roughriders* and the recent inde-pendent porn film *Alley Of The Tranny Boys*. Of course, when some people today are still shocked to hear that FTMs exist at all, the relative scarci-ty of FTMs in smut is hardly a big surprise. But there is also a social and gender-political reason for the general erotic invisibility of FTMs, one we find it important to explode.

Our sexual culture, by and large, runs on stereotyped femininity and fetishizations of the phallus. Picture your typical het-boy-focused "girl-girl" porn for an excellent example: Over-the-top makeup, big hair, long nails, silicone tits that don't lie down even when their own-ers do, and, of course, the perennial presence of a few down-market dildoes that reassure the (presumably male) viewer of the necessity of some sort of dick in the proceedings. As long as both the stylized fem-inine and the prominent phallus are present in some degree, the image easily becomes one of sexual interest and intrigue, at least according to the typical gender-political map of our Western cultural sexuality. No wonder "she-male" porn, highly cosmetically feminized but cock-focused, is so popular. And no wonder that FTMs and butches, those with neither the stereotyped aspects of femininity that signal sexual femaleness nor the God-given schlongs that command recognition of sexual maleness in our culture have long been considered the sexual bottom-of-the-barrel, zeroes in terms of attractiveness.

But we know better. And so, we'd be willing to guess, do many of the people who will read this book. You can well imagine our delight when we began reading through the submissions for this book and found that we had been literally deluged with erotica starring FTMs of all shapes and sorts and flavors—so much of it that we couldn't use even a fraction of what was sent. It seems that transmen and the peo-ple who lust after them are finally getting around to reclaiming their sexiness and heat. And it's about time, because honey, you just can't put all those boys on testosterone and expect them not to be fantasizing something.

Thus, this book contains quite an array of FTMs and those who want them. Karen Taylor's "Wanting That Man" explores the dynamic of going from dyke to straight man, while M. Christian's "Evolution" turns the whole concept of sexual preference on its head. Surprisingly, though, most of the FTM tales we got were from gay-identified trans-men; stories such as Nico Damon Hailey's "The Velveteen FTM", Matthew Kailey's "Teenie Weenies Inc." and several others thrust them-selves into transfag territory.

At the same time as we had a wonderful surplus of good FTM tales, we had a desperate dearth of stories involving male-to-female trans-sexuals in actual sexual relationships. A few starred them as hookers or rape victims, or involved with impersonal zipless-fuck sex, but few authors seemed willing to delve into what it was like to function in a non-objectified way as an out-and-proud transwoman—thus it is our true delight to bring forward the work of several who do. Stacy Montgomery's "The Essence of Magic," Thomas Roche's "Up For A Nickel," and Corbie Petulengro's "No Charity" accept no apologies and brook no equivocation: These women are gutsy, gritty, tender, fierce, and they don't mind letting you know that if you can woo them into your bed and your life, you'll never regret an instant.

But wait, we hear you crying, there's more than one kind of transwoman! Some of you probably bought this book specifically looking for, well, a different kind of girl. Don't worry, they're here, too... but perhaps not in the ways you might expect. In our call for submissions, we actively discouraged writers from submitting any exemplars of the time-honored forced-feminization transvestite story. Raven, having read through a friend's massive collection of forced-fem smut, had determined that there were only about ten plots evident in the four hundred or so stories he'd skimmed, and that was only if you counted minor details: Mom forcibly feminizes Son, Aunt forcibly feminizes Nephew, Hubby squeals, "Oh no, please don't throw me into that briar patch!" as Wifey forces him to don a negligee and stockings, and so on. Hanne had read quite a few similar tales, and we both found them just a little too facile, not introspective enough to be interesting, way too repetitive, and did we say way too repetitive? So we discouraged people from submitting forced-fem and crossdresser stories unless they were damned sure they'd gotten an angle on the genre we hadn't seen before. Once again, the maxim "ask, and ye shall receive" proved true: Keri Gino's "Becoming" and Charles Anders' hilarious and touching "The Gay Science" bring us the erotic magic of high-femme crossdressing while giving the cliches a well-deserved rest.

Then there are those stories—like R. Gay's "Small Considerations"—that speak to the uncharted territory between any of the established gender signposts and what it's like to live there, a gender without a country. Every year we meet more and more such people, who proudly proclaim that they're both, or neither, or Something Else Entirely, or I-don't-know-and-neither-do-you. Some of the stories, particularly Allison Lonsdale's "Tangaroa" and Magdalene Meretrix's "Mars Conjunct Venus," take gender fluidity to a level where only another world will hold them. But then Todd Belton's "Doppler" comes along and plays out the possibility of seamless, fluid gender shift in a world that seems so everyday that you may find yourself simultaneously wondering why it doesn't really happen that way in real life and reeling from the implications of what it would mean if it did.

These implications—what it means to have gender be fluid, changeable, definable only in context or in the moment—are among the many reasons transgender sexuality is seen as so threatening by so many people. To put it simply, whether due to nature or nurture or simple lack of exposure, most people on this planet only want one sort of gendered person when it comes to their sexual desires. Those who are both, or neither, or nearly-one-but-not-quite, or say they're one but look like the other, confuse those boundaries, making what once seemed clear-cut and simple into a distressing and ambiguous series of judgement calls. If you find yourself wanting people who don't fit into the male/female binary, you also find yourself questioning your own sexuality. This bothers a lot of people, especially when it happens in the time-honored manner: all of a sudden someone finds out that the hot number they've just been drooling over used to be a... or still has a... or wants to be a... oh, no, I can't be attracted to that! For some people, even finding out that someone they know has a transgendered partner can trigger similar feelings of shock and even betrayal—"I thought I knew you!" Sometimes those internal wars of transphobia and homophobia can trigger hostility and even violence: Our very presence undermines world views right and left.

In this way, creating a book like Best Transgender Erotica is an act of resistance. Refusing to apologize for our vitality, for our right to live as full human beings in bodies and identities that do not conform to the expected binaries—and to love and lust after people who challenge the so-called "norms" in these ways—is a way of homesteading the frontier of our collective experience of human possibilities. Taking back our sexuality and expressing it in literature that knows and resists (sometimes defiantly, sometimes manipulatively, always consciously) the predatory colonization of the deeply inculcated gender binary and the whole scheme of sexual expectations that go along with it, while simultaneously celebrating the crucial and often subversive power of sexuality, is a way of casting a vote of confidence in our collective future.

That said, we don't require that everyone who reads this book have an identical sense of ideas or priorities about gender or sex or even sexuality—as if we possibly could! We certainly don't require that you completely relinquish the use of the gender binaries by which most of us tend to run our daily as well as our erotic lives. Instead, think of this introduction as a psychic customs house: If you're carrying any assumptions about who and what you think is in this book, this is the place to drop them. They're not likely to survive the experience if they go inside. Don't worry, we'll return them to you on the way out again... if you still think you'll fit into them.

Enjoy.

Hanne Blank and Raven Kaldera
January 2002

We lead off with co-editor Hanne Blank's meditation on certain aspects of the fine art of being partnered to a person of non-conventional gender, a world of intensity packed into a bite-size chunk that explodes in your mouth and your mind. Hanne has been partnered for years with an intersexual, and she knows all about questions, and questioning... and the fact that sometimes, the questions are much more important than any answers one could ever give.

How

Hanne Blank

E ven when the words remain silent, curled under the tongue, the question still hangs there, expectant like a teacher's arched eyebrow. I try to ignore the police-car lights in your eyes that try to pull me over, want to drag me off the road and take me back to the stationhouse for questioning, perhaps to tell me of the error of my ways. A love not built to code agitates, shocks, confuses. As usual. And when you ask, silently or not, I am the only one of us who is not surprised.

Eir hands on my cheeks, smooth and sure, stroking the panic out of me, wordlessly reminding me of a language I already spoke. The shimmer of minnows in my belly when we kissed and e tugged the shirt from my waistband, the feel of such soft hands. My astonishment, my delight, watching eir body emerge for the first time, for me, in a cool grey afternoon light that made eir long curves glow like silk carved in marble. The wonder of it underneath my lips, underneath the hands that fluttered from nervousness, the fear that I could not be adequate, not worth the myth, not worth the tenderness of the long eloquent hands that nestled in my hair. I did not know how, then, either.

You've seen me with my lover and you are dying to know. The questions fall like rain as soon as my lover steps out onto the porch for a chat with a friend, spattering me with needy ignorant concern. Medical and concise, the MD inquires about diagnosis, about hormone levels, nodding as sagely at my answers as if I were telling him something that mattered. Tourguide, I narrate as the story rumbles, one more time, down the same winding street, pointing out the exotic obvious until we reach the point where we began, the corner marked by a signpost with the one-word question I will not answer.

15

I kiss the corner of eir slack-tired lips, the taste of sex still smeared across my chin, my mouth. Together we've soaked right through the towel we put across the bed in case of heavy weather, sweat and lube and come and tears that spattered eir chest as e lay below me and I came, and came, eyes flooding with the astonishment of finding eir long slow satin between my legs again. We lie baptized in one another, weary, still hungry, stirring our torpid bodies slowly, unforgettably forcing fingers into ruthless, reptilian need. My slack-jawed wonder at the song of eir body, the rough gasp that made me bite my lip as I writhed, filled beyond a simple fuck, speechless at the terrible strength that fucks me hard, fucks me tender, fucks me true.

I might tell you, I think, if the if the circles of your eyes did not seem as thin as coins, one side curious, prepared to flip to show judgement stamped in righteous silver on the other, In God We Trust. I lack the strength to give you an answer that lies between the indelible lines of your Law. It is hard enough to live that answer, to hover roundly just at the tips of fingertips, enigmatic, obvious, never knowing if those hands would crush or caress.

E growls, low in eir throat, and I flex my hands against eir thighs, pulling em harder against me. Having called em into me I must endure it, shivering, knowing that I, my thighs and lips have brought this to be. As it was in the beginning. Rhythm drowns panic, friction muffles my unworthiness as e moves beyond me, into me, pleasure and pain flowing muddy side by side halfway up my spine, not mingling until they reach the delta. Long hair brushes my shoulders, tender webs immobilizing my arms as e rides my body, writhes my body, eir mouth opening so that I scream into the pillows, teeth sinking hard into softness. Sated kisses enumerate the rough rings of bruises across my shoulders, until with sudden awful desperation I blindly find eir chest and bite, hard, hard enough to leave my mark, hard enough to make myself cry, and I marry em always and again.

Don't think I don't know what goes on in the secret bedrooms behind your eyes. You strip us both, hold us bare in the sterile fields, prodding and lifting, checking, worried. "Thank God," you think, "that there can be no children," and we hear you, surrounded by your unavoidable need to know that all is quiet, all is well, all is safe and normal and smells of whole milk and *Gray's Anatomy*. We escape when you sleep, and are our own children, new and unmatched, giggling on the grass, drinking tea from cracked cups, licking chocolate and tangerine from one another's lips, insolent, embraced by the sea and the fire.

I am terrible, crashing down, and e is helpless, caught in desire. Trembling, e moans, singing soft anthems of wishing it were always so, that always my wanting would make it so. Seeing my thirst, e offers me tears, and blood, and the wetness of want, and the endless arching damask of eir peerless skin. Magnificent, I dine. Each hand a mouth, each tooth a finger with which to caress, my tongue a slender song, silver questions across the banner of eir body, answered in the old speech. E is beyond me, no body, no hands, no chains strong enough to anchor em to ground. Beggar at my own banquet, I cringe with momentary fury at this beauty I am given and can never take, that is always newer than the fruit itself, no matter how much juice runs down my chin. Finally I have no choice but to cradle em in *exhausted arms, shaking with love as I let em cry the release of being taken, both of us so soft in the moments when there is nothing left to fear.*

You always ask, and I wonder if you notice that I always change the subject. The question hangs suspended, untouched, swirling, unheeding, the same question we ask the fish, the birds, the sky. You want to know how we do it, what goes where, what happens at the freak show after lights-out time, who does what to whom and how, with what, what it looks like, what it looks like, how that mutant flesh must feel, inside, above, around me. You want everything and anything, titillated, terrified, curiosity choking you back to three dumb letters or none at all. Silent, watchful, your eyes travel the length of my beloved, and then return to me, demanding to know how.

It's a pity you don't ask for a blessing instead. If you did, perhaps I'd tell.

Cross-dressing is a highly subversive activity. It turns you into a shapeshifter, and often (as our protagonist discovers) brings you into the realm of the Sacred Trickster, who can do almost anything in the name of educating through chaos... and get away with it. However, sometimes subversion collides with heartless social reality and other people's repressions, and compromise can be a bitch. So can the tricksters we hold so dear, particularly when we forget that even the seemingly invulnerable have their own vulnerabilities, and we see all sides of the equation in this hilarious tale of dressing up and being dressed down.

Beware: If you look into Charles Anders' panties, those panties look also into you. Charles is the author of The Lazy Cross-Dresser, *a style bible for slack T-girls published by Greenery Press. Charles has also written for* Anything That Moves, Black Sheets, *and dozens of other magazines and anthologies.*

The Gay Science

Charles Anders

I. Running Gag

Crinoline encased Belle's head. She worked her mouth up and down along Penelope's cock shaft and swirled her tongue the way "J," the Sensuous Woman, advises. Belle considered herself a pretty good little cocksucker, but two things impeded the rhythm of her head between Penelope's parted skirts. First of all, for fear it might be their last blowjob, Belle didn't really want Penelope to have an orgasm while driving. Second of all, Penelope occasionally had to reach under Belle's neck to change gears.

"Fuck!" Penelope yelled, jerking the wheel of her Miata. "I thought I told you to look for the Charlotte exit! Now we're going to end up in fucking Winston-Salem unless we can find a way to double back."

Belle let go of Penelope's cock and started to explain that she couldn't really have been watching for the I-40/I-85 split at the same time as she was sucking Penelope's prick, now could she?

"Did I give you permission to stop sucking, bitch?" Penelope swatted Belle's exposed nape, and Belle wrapped her lips around the latex-covered cock again. "Shit. We'll just have to cross the median strip. Keep an eye out for cops, will you?" Belle tried to nod, but it got lost in the general bobbing motion.

The next thing Belle knew, the car was lurching wildly. Then the road was replaced by something bumpy and uneven. Finally, another lurch and the sound of tires in pain as Penelope floored the gas pedal. Belle deep-throated Penelope a little more than she'd expected and had to battle her gag reflex for a moment. The blow job resumed its graceful tempo about the same time the sirens started up.

"Fuck," Penelope said. "You were supposed to be watching for cops. At least you'll have lots of opportunities to polish up your lackluster fellatio in jail, huh?" Instead of slowing down, Penelope stomped the gas again using the full pivoting power of her six inch stilettos. "Hold on, bitch," she yelled before driving through the drive through lane of a Hardee's at 90 miles an hour.

"That Waffle House isn't built to code!" You could tell Penelope ran a major building contracting firm. Belle heard tires screeching, sirens and shouts, and remembered Penelope's spare frock, artfully draped over the license plate. "There should be at least a 50 foot clearance behind the back wall."

Belle felt an impact—no more than a nudge, really—then more acceleration. She knew better than to sneak another glance at the chaos outside of her perfect little universe of fellatio. "I say unto you: One must still have chaos in oneself to be able to give birth to a dancing star," Penelope cackled. Then the domme's tone changed to one of discovery and the car swerved 180 degrees again. "Oh, what luck! Greensboro's last remaining drive-in is having a revival of Deep Throat!"

Belle heard more screeching, as if in a last minute tailspin, then seemingly only a second later Penelope was ordering two tickets. They parked among dozens of identical Japanese subcompacts, then nestled while Linda Lovelace swallowed hard overhead. Belle felt Penelope tap her on the head. "There's something wrong when a blow job goes on more than twenty minutes and nobody's ready for their close-up." Belle went to work with renewed vigor, and lots of tongue, per "J's" instructions.

II. Beyond Good and Ugly

To think that just a few months earlier, Belle had lamented the absence of a Bad Influence in her life. "It's not enough to be a submissive sissy slut conceptually," she bitched to her pedicurist Magnus. Magnus buffed and tutted sympathetically. "I need somebody to push the envelope, to unlock the hidden potential for—"

"Synergies? Connectivity?" Magnus said wryly.

"Oh, sorry. Was I talking consultant-speak again?"

"Just a little." Magnus grinned and reached for his file.

Then Belle joined the Sissy Reading Group and fell under Penelope's thrall. Her and all the other SRG members, actually. It seemed to amuse Penelope to watch them all vying to impress her. They met in an upstairs room at the local queer community center— eight or nine anorexic men wearing thrift store lace, frayed nylons and way too much theatrical makeup. (Belle wore a peach chiffon number, ankle socks and six inch pink stilettos to the first meeting, plus approximately a metric ton of rouge.) Belle stared at Penelope throughout the first half dozen meetings, barely able to keep from drooling. The group leader always outshone the other sissies—a typical outfit involved a power suit of some sort with short skirt, topped off by subtle make-up and a neat hair-twist. As the leader, Penelope found it hilarious to have them read Nietzsche, her favorite author.

The other SRG members all tried so hard to impress Penelope that Belle felt totally eclipsed. "So, like, Nietzsche rejects a Manichean dualist worldview, ya know, but still he buys into a like totally binary genderscape," offered Fifi, carefully showing her pink miniskirt (which matched her nails and shoes) to good advantage. Fifi, evidently a pastel kind of gal, wore a lime-green latex top over a conical bra... and lots and lots of maroon eyeshadow. At Fifi's remark, Penelope smiled and yawned.

Belle longed for Penelope week after week until finally the teacher broke the ice. Another student, Maria, had stayed behind to ask a tricky question about Nietzsche's conception of the feminine. Probably Maria just wanted to flirt with Penelope. Belle remained in her seat, unable to think of a question, but also unwilling to leave the two of them alone. She snapped out of her daze when Penelope turned to her and barked: "Belle! I need something to occupy me while I talk. Come over here and bend over. And don't straighten up until I tell you."

Barely able to believe what she was hearing, Belle nevertheless stood where Penelope had indicated and flattened her torso across the desk's surface. Penelope hoisted up Belle's skirt and pulled down her panties. Belle heard the fritz sound of teeth tearing a wrapper, followed by a squirting noise. Then Penelope set about simultaneously broadening Belle's sphincter and Maria's mind.

"Nietzsche's conception of the feminine is... uhhhh... predominantly one of violence." Incense flowed within a private shrine that Belle had never known existed within her—it felt searing but also hypnotic, beautiful. "Woman is violated by the very people to whom she must spend her life atoning, but in turn her main attraction for men is the capacity for revenge," Penelope said, while the sensations continued to sweep Belle away. Then Penelope stopped explaining Nietzsche and womanhood, and the incense blew away.

Belle felt so proud that she'd taken all of Penelope inside her until she turned to see a Penelope holding up a single latex-covered finger. "Damn, girl," Penelope said. "You seriously need to strengthen your PVC muscle." Belle nodded without understanding.

Belle stayed bent over, since Penelope hadn't told her to straighten up. She knew somehow waiting for instructions would save her a lot of grief. Waiting paid off: Belle heard Penelope behind her, felt something brushing her buttocks. Penelope crossed in front of Belle as she slipped the lipstick tube back into her purse.

"Give it a minute to dry. Then pull up your panties and get your ass home, girl." A slap to Belle's thigh, then Penelope was gone, arm in arm with Maria. Belle was left wondering if she was allowed to straighten up. She eventually decided that the order to "get her ass home" included verticality.

When Belle got home, she spent half an hour trying to position her ass so she could read the lipstick scrawl in the mirror. Eventually she was able to make it out: a phone number and the quotation, "she who is evil is most evil in solitude."

Belle called the number and met Penelope for coffee, both of them dressed to the nines. They met a good hour's drive from home, for Belle's comfort and to minimize the chance of meeting someone who knew them "en homme." Then Penelope took Belle home and whipped her for what felt like several years. Belle spent the rest of the weekend on her hands and knees cleaning Penelope's one-bedroom apartment. After that, the two of them got together regularly and got into tons of trouble.

After the car chase incident, there was the Krispy Kreme foot job. Belle felt something nylon-covered snake under the plastic table before her, and up her skirt. A mouthful of warm cruller fell out of Belle's mouth as she gasped. The lone woman behind the counter cleaned the coffee maker without once turning around (and Belle was watching, terrified) as Penelope worked her foot up and down along Belle's panties.

Belle sucked Penelope off in the cineplex ladies' room, in a cemetery, on the roof of the venerable Carolina Inn in Chapel Hill, in the Duke University botanical gardens, under the pool table at a very heterosexual-male sports bar, and behind the Southern Baptist Tabernacle Church. At 3 a.m. one Wednesday morning, Penelope tied Belle to a billboard on I-40 and left her there. Belle spent two exhausted, terrified hours concocting an explanation before Penelope showed up again. In short, Belle had never been happier in her life.

III. Man And Girlyman

Nietzsche writes: "An easy prey is something contemptible for proud natures. They feel good only at the sight of unbroken men."

Belle lived in fear of Penelope growing bored and deserting her. Belle purposely wallowed in this fear because it could blot out all the other fears—arrests, physical injury, public humiliation, job loss—that clustered under the category of "getting caught." As long as Belle feared losing Penelope more than anything, nothing else could frighten her. Nothing. Or so Belle thought.

Until Little League. "It's an exhibition game," Penelope said in an uncharacteristically cajoling voice. "And I know what an exhibitionist you are. You'll love it."

"So I'm going to service you behind the bleachers? In a pinafore, maybe?"

"No, we're going to go dressed as normal guys and behave incredibly well." Penelope had a rhino-sized dildo up Belle's ass, and she had a way of slowing down her thrusts every time she spoke that had Belle straining to catch every word in the hopes that being a good listener would get the Happy Train moving again. Belle's eyes were fixed on Penelope's fleur-de-lis wallpaper and the edge of her thick red carpet. "It's the first time I've had custody of Benny when there's been a game. This is one of those crucial tests of fatherhood I read about in a Robert Bly book."

"But…" Belle had to exhale as Penelope eased in a little, "…we've never done anything as Pete and Bill before."

Penelope pressed on. "It won't kill us this once. I need moral support, dammit!"

"I've never met Peter," Belle bleated. "I don't want to know Peter! I want you!"

"Fine. As Penelope, I'm ordering you to go to the Little League game. As Bill. With Pete. OK? Now shut up before I gag you." Penelope slapped Belle, more angrily than playfully.

Could Penelope give an order to Belle that would be binding on Bill? It made Belle's head hurt to think about it. She tried asking Magnus for advice, launching into her diatribe before he'd even gotten her shoe off. "—dragging me to some sort of pre-pubescent phallic brandishment to punish me for being a size eight! Why me?"

Magnus took a deep breath. "It sounds like she wants to deepen the relationship."

"I feel like I walked into a foreign film in the middle. That isn't the relationship I signed up for. Magnus, you're a sports fan, right?"

"I remember once telling you I had played tennis when I was twelve."

"That makes you way more of a sports fan than me. Can you go to this thing? She just wants a man to go on her arm. I'm terrified of losing her, but I can't do this."

It took all sorts of inducements, including buying a year's worth of weekly pedicures in advance and a promise to recruit every other SRG member as new clients, but eventually Magnus agreed to go watch the game with Penelope. When Belle received instructions on the meet, she passed them on to Magnus and breathed deeply.

The afternoon of the game came and went, and Belle sat by the phone and checked e-mail every thirty seconds. After a week, Belle resigned herself that she'd never hear from Penelope again. So, when it arrived, the e-mail startled her. "I suppose I shouldn't be surprised that we couldn't break out of our old paradigm," it read. "My place. Tuesday. 8:30. Dress slutty. Don't be late." Wednesday morning was a big presentation, but Belle didn't care. She spent the rest of the weekend churning with sugar-dusted fear. She had failed her mistress— stood her up, even!—and now she was going to be punished! Could life be any more exciting? Belle could hardly guess what penalties skipping a Little League game merited (she woke up Sunday night sweating at a scenario involving a Wiffle bat) but she had faith in Penelope's inventiveness.

Belle assembled her trashiest look yet for Penelope. A latex miniskirt showed off her pink panties, while on top she wore a black bustier that left her bare in back. Ballet boots and latex gloves completed the look. She walked the block and a half from her parking spot to Penelope's place in a tizzy, nearly twisting her ankle rushing off the sidewalk.

Penelope didn't smile when she greeted Belle. Instead she held out a ball gag immediately. Belle started to say something, then just opened her mouth as wide as she could. "Your safeword is the theme from 2001," Penelope whispered. Then she positioned Belle in front of her big oak table, legs strapped to the table legs and arms tied to the chandelier. That had the effect of keeping Belle quite securely rooted (if bent forward a bit precariously) while simultaneously adding to her distress, since struggling too much might bring the chandelier down and piss off Penelope further.

If Belle had questioned whether she'd pissed Penelope off, the basket of binder clips, the sort Belle used for hundred-page reports, made it plain. Penelope yanked the bustier down until Belle's nipples were exposed, and pulled her panties out of the way. Soon binder clips clung to every sensitive spot on Belle's body, including her armpits. Belle sobbed through her gag. "When you were boring male clay, you used to fantasize about forced femme, didn't you?" Belle heard the whooshing sound of a flogger a second before she felt a biting pain on her back. "Of course you did. It's what every sissy dreams about—a knowing dom, usually a woman, transforming her into her fantasy against her will. If only someone would take charge, shave me, give me a makeover, and leave me no choice about it, I wouldn't have to be responsible for my own desires that scare me so much." Penelope laughed and Belle felt more lashes.

"That's why I try to get you gals to read Nietzsche. Actually read him, not just ransack the Cliffs Notes for ways to get into my panties." Penelope changed floggers to something that felt more wiry and stung way more. "Then maybe you wouldn't waste time waiting for someone else to transform you into what you want to be. Maybe then you wouldn't just view me as someone who can give you what you want, instead of a real person. You managed to feminize yourself, so why not form your own identity while you're at it?" Belle had no answer, even if she weren't gagged.

Penelope tired of her own diatribe and began quoting Nietzsche with every stroke of her flogger.

"What is the seal of attained freedom? No longer being ashamed in front of oneself."

Thwack!

"There is not sufficient love and goodness in the world to give some of it away to imaginary beings."

Thwack!

"Only those who change constantly remain akin to me."

Thwack!

"Two pains are easier to bear than one!"

Belle whimpered and struggled to recall the 2001 theme. She remembered an ape throwing a bone at a baby in space. No, wait! Belle hummed a low note, then up a major fifth, then up another fifth, as loud as she could. It worked. Penelope had the clamps and most of the straps off by the time Belle hummed the final triumphant ascending scale. The gag came off and Belle's tongue lolled.

"This will be our last meeting," Penelope told Belle. "Magnus, get her out of here."

Belle looked over at the big red velvet chaise lounge. Magnus was slowly swinging his legs over and standing up. He came over to the table she was leaning against and lightly touched her bare shoulder. He offered his arm and Belle took it, then they walked to his car in silence. Belle realized that she'd have to get her car later. And that she was crying.

"Were you there the whole time?" Belle asked once she was strapped into the passenger seat.

Magnus nodded. "Penelope and I thought it'd be wise, to keep things from getting out of hand. She's one tough woman." His voice throbbed with admiration.

"So you two hit it off at the game, huh?"

"We're just friends. For now, at least."

"Why couldn't she just be happy with our fun? Why get all heavy on me?"

"Too many Germanic thinkers?" Magnus shrugged. Belle laughed a little. Magnus looked downright handsome by the dashboard light. "Seriously, I think she felt used. I mean, you told me you just wanted a Bad Influence, and I think she wanted someone she could go to baseball games with. It happens. But maybe she's right, and you should be your own Bad Influence."

"Maybe." Belle reflected for a moment. They were driving along a quiet street. "Would you like me to suck you off?"

Magnus shrugged again. "Why not?" Belle didn't hesitate. She crouched over Magnus' lap and unzipped him. It felt odd to fellate in a stationary vehicle. His cock seemed smaller than Penelope's but felt warm and silky in Belle's mouth. "There," Magnus said, stroking Belle's head. "You are a slut, after all. I haven't even bought you dinner."

Belle laughed until she choked.

What is it like to live in that liminal space of "not quite"? Not-Quite-This and Not-Quite-That? How do those who love you learn to cope with and desire it? This emotional, beautiful tale delves into those betwixt-and-betweens with grace and insight, even venturing into the often hotly contested ground of how one defines sexual preference while living in a liminal gender state. When, in this story, the narrator's lover hits a point of frustrated bewilderment, and cries "So you don't want to be a woman or a man, but you only want to be with a woman and not a man?" it forces each of us to confront the ways in which the nature of things we do not understand can throw a wrench into our comprehension of the things we think we do.

R. Gay is a twenty-something writer in the Middle West. She has an object of unrequited affection who is the inspiration for most of her stories as of late. She is a lovely shade of brown but only mentions this because people tend to assume otherwise. As such, she is not fond of assumptions. Her work can be found past, present and future in Moxie Magazine, Clean Sheets, Scarlet Letters, *and the anthologies* Does Your Mama Know?, Love Shook My Heart II, *and* Herotica 7.

Small Considerations

R. Gay

I have a constant craving for my best friend, Blake. Under normal circumstances, I would covet his soon to be ex-wife. Yet he is so indescribable that I find myself, awake at night, imagining what it would feel like for him to rub his salt and pepper beard against my navel. But I can't let myself cross that line. It is too complicated. Masculinity gets in the way... his, and mine. Such a small consideration, he always tells me. Not small enough, I reply.

His shoulders... they're broad, the muscles tight and sinewy. His legs render me speechless. Strong, lean, tanned to the hem of his shorts and disturbingly pale just above there. And when he crosses his legs, I can see the muscles of his thighs flexing beneath his slacks. He runs, eight miles a day. The best time to get thinking done, he says. I prefer to think within the comfort of my couch. A cigarette helps the effort. We have little in common beyond our mutual attraction. At the same time, we have a lot in common, but I rarely allow myself to see that.

Blake has the kind of body I've always wanted. In my mind, I have dissected the most enviable parts of his anatomy. Half of one of my bathroom walls is covered in black and white collage of the person I have become. His arms, another guy's torso, and the calves of that Dutch model, my cunt the only body part I really want to keep. I've carefully pasted all these body parts together, and the resulting image looks exactly how I sometimes feel, scattered, incongruous, awkward.

At times, I think that Blake knows more about me than I know of myself. We met seven years ago, during our senior year in college as we turned in our theses. Mine was a wordy treatise on gender and lesbian

31

identity in mainstream films. His was an exposition of deception and betrayal in Hamlet. Standing in front of our advisor's door, we quickly exchanged documents, scanned, and muttered the requisite approval. Later, I found him at the water fountain, letting the thick stream of water splash across his eyes. And I felt an uncomfortable twinge between my thighs as he stood, turned towards me and smiled. It was a slow, almost lazy smile crawling from the center of his lips to the corners, until his mouth opened widely enough for me to see and instantly adore a charmingly imperfect set of teeth.

We went out for drinks that night to celebrate the end, or perhaps it was the beginning of something... neither of us were certain. We told each other almost everything about our lives. At some point, he covered my hand with his, and I didn't move away. I just slid my fingers between his, and held on. He hated poetry and trusted in the superiority of women and understood why Raymond Carver is brilliant. He believed in music as the closest he'll ever get to God and he believed in the necessity of soul mates and he didn't even blink when I explained that I was a raging feminist lesbian type person out to deconstruct notions of gender. In fact, he wanted me to tell him more. I tried, but could only get so far, because I didn't quite have all the answers, myself, particularly when I found myself squeezing his hand tighter, locking my ankles around his, wondering what it would be like to take him home and continue the conversation over breakfast. And as we exchanged phone numbers somewhere between nightfall and dawn, he told me I was not quite. Not quite what, I asked nervously, cracking my knuckles and he rubbed his chin slowly. I'm not sure yet, but I'll let you know, he finally answered. When I walked home, those words kept bouncing around my mouth as I muttered them repeatedly. And I was scared. In a few hours, he had managed to put into words what it had taken me twenty-two years to voice.

We've seriously crossed the line once, Blake and I. Three months ago, he needed a ride home from the airport so I offered to be his chauffeur for the evening. And when I saw him standing in the baggage claim, watching the same green suitcase travelling around and around the carousel, I was in awe of his profile. I could see the gentle creases in his forehead, the sharp slant of his nose, beard, neatly trimmed. I hid behind a bank of phones, watching has he twisted his wedding ring and shifted his weight from foot to foot and concluded that it was his overt masculinity that kept me silent and hidden.

When he turned towards the exit, I stepped from behind the phones and smiled. He waved me over and I jogged towards him. He stretched his arms outward and it only seemed natural to bury my face against his armpit as his arms wrapped around me. I could smell sweat, the lingering scent of cigars and deodorant, his cologne. His beard tickled my forehead, and before I could stop myself, I raised my head, he leaned down, and brushed his lips so lightly against mine, that my back arched and I clasped my hand around the back of his neck, kissing him in an entirely inappropriate manner.

I pulled away first. I had to. Because if I didn't, I would have to admit certain things about myself, and so would he. Welcome home, I whispered. He brushed his thumb across my chin, and stared at me. I have to go to the bathroom, he said gruffly, and I nodded, following. As we stepped into the last stall, my throat tightened, and I shoved my hands in my pockets to stop the trembling. He set his briefcase down and leaned back against the wall. I felt an overwhelming need to say something, but the silence between us was so fragile, that I was afraid that my words would create something irreversible. He began loosening his tie, but I shook my head, took my hands out of my pockets, and carefully untied the loose knot, letting his tie dangle about his neck. Slowly, I began unbuttoning his shirt. I love the feel of his shirts, sharp, almost slick against my fingers, as if they are made of some mystical material, not a cotton-polyester blend.

He rested his hands against my shoulders, curling his fingers into my back as I pulled his shirt apart and began kissing the dark base of his throat, the muscled arcs just below his nipples. I was intimately aware of his wedding ring pressing through the thin material of my sweater, but I chose to ignore it. The ability to commit adultery was another one of those things I don't care to admit about myself. But then I told myself that they were separated, soon to be divorced. Adultery was a small consideration under such circumstances. Tentatively, I let my tongue slip past my lips, drawing a thin line of saliva between his nipples. I was fascinated by them, light brown, thick and hard, swelling as I flicked my tongue against them then suckled them into my mouth, my lips pressed against his chest. I heard a groan circling in his throat, and I placed two fingers against his lips. His hands slid lower, to the empty space where my breasts used to be. I instinctively leaned into him, but then pulled away. I was not ready for him to touch me there, and I don't think he was either.

Let me touch you, he said softly. I shook my head, sliding to my knees, as I traced the muscles of his stomach with my tongue, letting my tongue play briefly inside his navel. Inhaling deeply, I pressed my forehead against the cool brass of his belt buckle, enjoying the quivering sensation of his cock beneath his slacks, against my cheek. He had no way of knowing how much I fetishized this very act of dropping to my knees before him. I have imagined the possibilities so many times in so many different ways that I closed my eyes as I loosened his belt buckle and undid his slacks, pulling them around his knees. I licked my lips and moaned softly as he pressed his fingers against my scalp. Holding his cock in one hand, I brushed my lips across the head, but then I stopped, and pounded my fist against the tiled floor. I can't do this,

I said, staring at the toilet. I expected him to curse, shove me away, but he nodded and began straightening his clothes. Later, in the car, my sweaty palm gripping the emergency brake, he covered my hand with his, brushing his fingertips across my knuckles until we pulled into his driveway. I stared out the window as he gathered his things, but before I pulled away, he said, *You think too much. I have to,* I answered, thinking how weak those words sounded.

We haven't discussed it since, but when I see his lips, I remember and I hope he does too. We've been avoiding each other lately, communicating rather cryptically, through postcards, sending and receiving up to three or four a day. The lady at the card store thinks that I have a paramour in some far-flung corner of the world. Every morning, she smiles and shows me what's new, asks about my paramour, tells me that its nice to see a young person keeping the art of manual correspondence alive. It would take too much effort to explain that I am sending these cards to a man who lives seven miles away from me. And it would take too much effort to explain why I'm more comfortable filling postcards with tiny print rather than picking up the phone, or meeting him for lunch. Some days, there aren't enough postcards in the world to tell Blake all the things I need to say. And I wrote that earlier today, on one of my cards. But then I tore it, and flushed the brightly colored shreds of paper down the toilet.

Instead, I will send him two cards, hoping he'll read them in the correct order, explaining my well thought out plan for killing a coworker, and the mailman who feels the need to read Blake's postcards before dropping them in the mailbox. I caught him today, because I was home early from work, so this message is in part for him. These mundane details will mask my loneliness, my hunger, my doubts, my fears.

My life is so full of irony these days that I can almost laugh about it all. I've put so much time, energy, and money into reassembling myself that I have lost sight of what it is that I am looking for. I do not want to want this man or any man for that matter. But God do I want Blake. And I constantly berate myself for that want. Why put myself through all these changes, only to end up with a man? It seems like I'm taking two steps forward, five steps back. But then I tell myself that it is not about whom I want to be with, but who I want to be. And then I imagine the expressions on my friends' faces were I to tell them that I am in love with a man—the chagrin, the shock, their open disgust in the face of my betrayal to the Cause. I will send a third postcard to Blake today, explaining all of this to him. I need him to understand what I cannot understand myself. And then I will wait until tomorrow's mail arrives, and pray that he writes back. Because if he doesn't...

The night before his wedding, Blake and I went to the seediest bar we could find, Jake's Bait, Tackle, and Beer, and slapped a hundred dollar bill down on the bar. Keep the beer and whiskey flowing, we told the bemused bartender, who crumpled the money and tossed it into the cash register. We smoked cigars, chastised ourselves for a general lack of imagination, and rocking back and forth on his stool, Blake sulked about his impending nuptials.

"It should be you and I tomorrow," he slurred.

I laughed, taking a shot of whiskey, as I twirled myself around on my barstool.

"Never let liquor speak for you," I told him.

He set his mug down and planted his hands on the sides of my stools. "I'm speaking for myself here. I want to be with you, marry you, whatever."

I crossed my eyes and tried to focus. "Barefoot and pregnant has never been my color."

"I don't need you barefoot and pregnant. Although you have delightful toes."

"Blake, just stop," I told him. "Nothing good can come of this conversation."

"We will not know that until we have this conversation."

"I don't do men. I don't know how to explain that in simpler terms."

Blake began tracing watermarks on the bar. "That's rather hypocritical, don't you think?"

"Come again?"

"You're all hung up on my manhood, as it were, when in the grand scheme of things, it's a minor detail."

"That's easy for you to say. You know what you are."

"I know what you are too."

"I'm a little more complicated than not quite…"

Blake chuckled. "You remember that?"

I nodded. "I do."

"Have you ever considered that I welcome those complications?"

"You're straight."

"Not quite."

"And I'm not."

"Really?"

"You're too clever," I whispered.

"I'm not trying to be."

"You aren't ready for me."

Blake slammed the palm of his hand against the bar, and I jerked my head upwards. "You do that all the time, you know… deciding how other people feel, what other people want."

"I'm making a decision for me. Respect that."

"If you let me in, just once, I might surprise you."

"That's a chance I'm not willing to take. I like things as is."

Blake rubbed his forehead. "And you can watch me marry someone else tomorrow?"

I wanted to cry. I wanted to let him in. I wanted to grab his hand, and run out of that shit hole, and drive all night to Vegas. I could feel my heart falling apart, ripping at the seams and floating away from my center, at the thought of him, in a somber tuxedo saying I do to someone else. But I was equally terrified by the thought of me, standing across of him in a tuxedo of my own, two hundred guests staring at us, murmuring in confusion. "I don't have a choice," I finally replied.

Blake took another sip of beer. Patting my back, he said, "You're a better man than me."

In that moment, I wished I could record those words. And in that moment, I knew that I would always be in love with Blake, even if I couldn't allow myself to be with him. I wanted to steal away to the parking lot, and slide into the back seat of his car with him. I wanted to fumble with his clothes, just to feel the smooth of his skin against my hands. I wanted to straddle his lap, ignoring the roof of the car putting pressure on my neck and the bright street lamp exposing us to passersby. I would ride his muscled thigh, and grasp the thin of his neck skin between my teeth. I would circle the base of his cock with my fingers, and move him inside of me. I would kiss him the way I've never dared to kiss anyone, tasting whiskey and cigars on his breath, and my head would swim and I would feel slightly nauseous. But I would hear him moan, and press himself against me, and raise his hips to fill me. Nothing else would matter.

I want to write this on a postcard as well. I want to tell him that I'm ready. But a man can only be patient for so long. Its probably too late for us. The postcard I'm writing is full, and now I'm filling page after page of my favorite notebook, with a letter that can never end because I am putting to paper my every thought. There's a knock on the door, and sighing, I remove my glasses, push my chair away from the desk, and drag my feet to the front door. I'm not expecting anyone, so I am irritated. I peer through the eyehole, and bang my forehead against the door. Blake is standing on my front porch. Wincing, I open the door, and he hands me a stack of postcards.

"It would cost me a fortune to send you all these," he says. "So I am delivering them in person."

He looks tired, worried. It is an expression I have seen on his face once before. For my twenty-sixth birthday, I treated myself to a mastectomy. I never wanted to completely alter my body. But I needed something more streamlined... more masculine than the soft curves of my chest. So I went through a year of therapy and warned all the people in my life of my decision. It was Blake who took me to the hospital. I wanted to go alone, but he insisted. And afterwards, when I was groggy and high on opiates, the nurses told me that Blake had spent the entire time pacing the waiting room, harassing anyone in a medical uniform for information. I tried to laugh, but the throbbing beneath my stitches forced me to smile instead, so hard, that my cheeks ached. I heard a light knock on the doorframe and Blake stepped into my room, hesitating.

"You can come in," I said hoarsely.

He cracked his jaw and approached the bed. As he sat down, he covered my right hand with both of his, and the one thing I remember is how large his hands were, and how small and pale mine was. His hands were warm, and I could imagine our hands melding together. I could feel his pulse against my thumb. I wanted him to hold my hand forever... hold all of me between his hands. He surveyed my body anxiously, his eyes lingering on my chest. "How are you feeling?"

I raised my left hand limply. "Couldn't be better."

He squeezed my hand tighter. "Are you sure?"

"I hurt, Blake. I hurt everywhere, but I've never felt this good."

He exhaled one silent sob, resting his head on the edge of the bed. "I've never been so scared."

"It's a routine surgery. Women have been re-arranging their chests for years."

"You're not just any woman," he said wryly.

I turned, staring out the small window. "Truer words."

"Never spoken."

"How long can you stay?" I asked.

"Forever?"

"But seriously."

"I'm not leaving until you do."

My heart pounded so hard, I feared that my stitches would tear. "You shouldn't say things like that."

He drew a finger along my jaw line. "Today, you don't make the rules."

I tried to protest, but I was so tired and sore that I nodded, and let my eyes fall shut.

Eight weeks later, I felt confident enough to face the world. I had needed time to learn how to live in my new and not quite body. I invited Blake over for dinner, and wore a form fitting white T-shirt, jeans, my feet bare. When I passed by the mirror and saw the outline of my new body, I giggled aloud. It was an odd thing, finally being able to recognize myself in my reflection. When he hugged me, and I could feel his body against mine with nothing in between. I shivered so hard my toes curled.

"I've missed you so goddamned much. You look fantastic," he said, and I could feel his beard tickling my ear. It was a curious sensation that traveled along my earlobe, down the side of my neck into the pit of my chest. We held each other for too long, as we often do, and blushing, I pulled him into the kitchen, taking the bottle of wine he handed me. He sat at the table, stretching his legs, and I bit my lower lip, looking away. "Can I see?" he asked shyly.

"See what?"

"Your body. I want to see your body."

I shook my head, concentrating on the stew I was preparing. "What you see is what you get."

He smiled softly. "I will wait."

I reached across the stove and turned the fire down. "No one can wait forever."

"I can."

I clenched my fingers into a tight fist. "You don't have a choice."

Blake stood and crossed the short distance between us. He brushed his lips across the back of my neck and slid his hands down my arms. I wanted to let myself fall into him, move to the side, have him take me against the cabinets, my forehead held to the ceramic counter, as I screamed his name and all the nasty things I wanted... needed him to do to me. "What's stopping us now?" he demanded.

"The same things that have always stopped us."

He stepped back, and sat down. "Right. How dare I forget."

I began ladling stew into two bowls. "You're angry."

"I'm frustrated."

My gums hummed with tension. "I'm sorry."

He sighed. "I know you are. And I do not want to pressure you or create more crap in your life, but frankly this all pisses me off. I do not know how to make myself into someone you can want."

But you are the person I want, I could have, should have said. "You can't."

"So you don't want to be a woman, or a man, but you have to be with a woman and not a man? It makes no sense."

"I don't expect you to understand. It makes sense in my head." I was intimately aware of the coarse denim against my thighs.

"Can I crawl in there for a few hours?"

"I wish you could. I want you to," I said, cursing inwardly at the slip.

"Aha! Progress."

"Don't read into that, Blake," I said sharply, setting his stew before him.

He pursed his lips and nodded. "Smells good."

I wanted to sit on his lap, wrap my arms around his neck and drink wine until we stumbled into my bed and simply slept, together. I wanted us to feed each other and feed upon each other. But I took my bowl, and sat across from him, moving pieces of celery around with the edge of my spoon. He caught my eyes, once, and I tried to share with him all my thoughts. I tried to hand him the key to deciphering my desire with that one look. He cocked his head to the side, as if the message he received was incomplete. And it probably was.

Looking at his hands, I notice that his wedding ring is missing, the only remaining evidence, a pale band of flesh. I rub my eyes and take the postcards. Blake has very neat handwriting. Each letter is small and deliberate, making complete words elegant. Part of me wants him to leave, so I can soak in my bathtub, carefully poring over each note. But a bigger part of me wants him to stay so I can give him the pages and pages I have spent all day writing. We go into my office, and he sits on the futon. I can hear the sound of his knees cracking.

"I've got something for you too," I stutter. He arches his eyebrows as I hand him three postcards and my notebook.

He pats the empty space next to him. "Let's read together."

It is the little gestures like this that make me love this man so much. The way the word together sounds so natural coming out of his mouth, as if it is the way we have always been meant to be. I swallow, hard, and sit, close enough that our arms brush. We are silent for what seems like hours. I try and memorize each message, as if these postcards will fade away the moment I set them down. I wonder if he is doing the same. He moves his lips when he reads and I am comforted by the hushed sound. Finally, he sets my notebook down and turns to me. It is darker outside but I can see arcs of tears resting on his lower eyelids.

"I don't know what to say," he says.

My heart falls. "I've shared too little, too late."

"Not at all."

"I didn't realize I said that aloud. I guess I don't know what to say either."

Blake gently caresses my face, and I lean into him tentatively resting my hand against his thigh. "Seven years is a long time to wait," he whispers.

"It had to be this way."

"I understand that."

I let the postcards fall to the floor, and we watch as they float midair and then scatter across the room. I inhale deeply and grab my inner lip between my teeth. Straddling his legs, I place my thumbs against his forehead and drag them along the contours of his face; the sharp of his cheekbones, his jawbone, the deep cleft in his chin, finally resting the pads of my fingertips against his upper eyelids.

"You act like this is the first time you've ever seen my face," he tells me.

"It is."

He nods knowingly, and I move my hands to his shoulders. Inching forward, I press my forehead against his and he wraps his lips around mine, pulling them into his mouth. I can feel his tongue moving across the thin ridges of my lips. I part my lips. I want to feel his tongue with mine. The muscles of his stomach tense against my chest, and his hand slides down my back, grabbing a handful of my T-shirt. I am nervous. My hands tremble as I slide my fingers across his cheeks, trace his earlobes, and slide them beneath the collar of his shirt. His skin is warm, slightly damp. I can tell that he smoked a cigar earlier as the stain of tobacco rolls down my throat. I clench my thighs around his, and deliberately pull his shirt apart, the buttons flying in every direction.

Blake's hands are under my T-shirt now, fingers crawling along my spine. I tense and my breath quickens as he wraps his hands around my ribcage, his thumbs arching upwards towards my chest. I can hear the sound of his thumbnails against my nipple rings. And then he hooks his thumbs inside the rings, gently tugging them away from my chest. I kiss him harder. My lips hurt as I try to pull his mouth into mine.

"I want to see your body."

I circle his wrists with my hands and pull them away from me. His lips stop moving, and his eyes are haunting, the crest of disappointment almost spilling out of him.

"I need this," he says hoarsely.

I need it too, but I do not say this. Instead, I ignore the butterflies in my stomach and the doubts in my mind, and pull my shirt over my head, throwing it to the side. Blake's shoulders slump with relief. I sit perfectly still. He pushes me backwards and I plant my hands against the thick futon mattress, my back sharply arched. No one has ever seen me like this, and if I think too much, I will simply pass out. I do not know how to make myself comfortable with such exposure. He kisses my shoulders and rubs his cheek across my breastbone. For moments, we sit like that, my breathing ragged, his calm, steady. He is waiting for me, and before I can stop myself, I can feel a tear trickling down my cheek, falling onto his face. Blake wipes the tear with one finger, brings that finger to his mouth to taste. He stares at my chest long and hard, then slowly, so slowly its almost painful, he feels along the thin scars on the underside of where my breasts used to be. It is as if he is creating a memory of my flesh. Blake leans down, brushing his lips, tracing with his tongue, the map he has drawn with his fingers. I shiver, and my skin tingles beneath his mouth. He draws his tongue upward flicking the tip against my right nipple, then my left. As he pulls my nipples into his mouth, sucking hard, almost violently, I can hear his teeth clacking against my rings. It is a sound I have imagined countless times.

I slide my fingers through his hair, clenching them into tight fists, thrusting my chest into his mouth. The crotch of my jeans is soaked. I tell myself that I should feel betrayed by my body, but I don't. I welcome this wetness. I want us to drown in it. My clit throbs and suddenly, I need to feel his body with my mouth. I slam him against the back of the futon, and desperately bite his throat, scrape my teeth down to his navel, and lower, moving to the floor. Quickly, I undo his slacks, and pull them off. His cock is thick and hard, red. I slide my tongue from between my lips and circle the tip, letting my tongue dip inside the wet slit. He tastes salty, a little sour, and I groan, loudly. I explore every inch of his surface with my lips and my tongue, sliding one hand around to grab hold of his ass as I take his balls into my other hand, enjoying the warm weight of them. The pale skin of his upper thighs are stretched taut. I want to swallow him whole, so I relax the muscles of my throat, wrap my lips around the head of his cock, and lower my mouth until I can feel hair against lips. I struggle to breathe but I tighten my cheeks. As if he is finally able to decipher my desire, he gently places his hands against the back of my head, and guides me along his rigid length.

I squeeze his balls between my fingers, harder, as he shoves his hips towards me. He holds my head more firmly, and my mouth now feels raw. My lungs are burning, and I feel as if my chest might explode. But then Blake stills me and his cock falls out of my mouth. I look up at him, confused. He pushes me to the floor, and removes my jeans. I can feel postcards sticking to my sweaty skin. He moves to mount me, but I shake my head, and roll onto my hands and knees, spreading my thighs, my ass high in the air. His hands start from my shoulders, move down my back, again slowly, as he creates another memory. I can feel his shaft against my ass cheeks, throbbing, insistent. Blake's hands pass over my ass, and I rear against him, then freeze, as his fingers dance along my wet inner thighs, my pussy lips. His tongue tastes the small of my back, the dark shadow just above my ass. He flicks just one finger against my clit, and I hear a sound that I cannot recognize until I realize that it is me.

"You are stunning," he whispers, letting one finger slide inside my cunt.

I clench myself around him, and spread my thighs wider. A creature inside of me begins to beg, pant, plead for him to treat me like his slut, his whore, his bitch boy. And I realize that I can say these things to him, because he understands. He removes his finger from my cunt and slides it into my mouth. I suck eagerly, tasting me, his cock, his cigars. I reach through my legs for his cock, pulling the head to my ass. I need him to take me like this. I need him to be the first. I hear him rustling with his pants, then foil ripping, latex rolling. He dips two fingers inside my cunt, then smears my juice against the wrinkles of my asshole. Carefully, he places the tip of his cock against me and moves slightly. I gasp. My thighs quiver and I scrape the floor with my fingernails.

"Take me," is all I can say. "Just fucking take me."

He grunts, and slides his cock, inch by inch into my ass. I spasm around him. I feel stretched, torn. I cannot control anything. He pulls back, and it feels like all of my internal organs will come pouring out of my body. Sharp twinges of pleasure spiral directly from my ass to my cunt. He slides forward again, deeper. He holds my body between his hands and begins a sensual cadence of his hips, slapping against mine, then emptiness, then his body pressed against mine again. My face is burning. My clit is burning. And then he is thrusting into me hard. I fall to my elbows. My ass grips him tightly. Up until now, he has been controlled, but now, I can feel the frenzy in his skin. He is telling me he loves me. His right hand slides around my torso, over my mound to my most sensitive place, and he presses with two fingers, circling with each thrust of his cock. I have no experience in my life to compare this to. I begin shaking uncontrollably. I am unable to form words. Instead harsh, guttural sounds fall from my mouth. There is a tiny part of me that wants to wrench myself away. Run somewhere. Hide. So I tell him not to stop. I tell him to fuck me harder. I slam my body against his. His other hand is on the back of my neck. He holds my head to the floor. I open my eyes, and I can see our reflection in the glass of a painting resting against the wall. I like the look of us.

I can no longer keep myself tight around his shaft. As I loosen, widen to him, he is fucking me faster. There is no more rhythm between us. We are reaching for something. I am really crying now and I have no idea when this flood of tears started. I think he is crying too. My body shudders, just once, and then I feel my skin crawling as if it is trying to escape my bones. With a scream, I come and with a final thrust, he falls on top of me. There is a wet, sucking sound as his chest heaves against my back. We don't have the energy to move, but eventually, his body drifts to the side, and I wrap myself around him.

My jaw is tight as I try to speak, but I need to fill the silence between us, find something to hold on to. "I don't know what to say."

"You don't have to say anything," he says, kissing the top of my head.

"I'm still not quite…"

"Neither am I."

I try to smile, but I am too tired. "I made you wait so long."

He is quiet for a moment, then brushes his nose across mine. "That is but a small consideration."

According to some self-proclaimed Experts On The Subject, it's only men who enjoy that "great perversion" of taking on an opposite-sex role in order to make sex extra-hot while simultaneously enjoying the fun and funk of genderfuck. And then there are those of us who know better. Fortunately, it's every bit as hot either way, and this little vignette about two boys and a bike (which makes it a threesome in our book) proves it.

Raven Gildea lives in Seattle, Washington. She is a butch dyke who is also multi-gendered, bisexual, ambidextrous, non-monogamous, and a switch. She's not quite sure how that happened, but finds it nice to have so many options. Her inner fag is a Harley-riding Tom of Finland icon with very big boots.

Wild Ride

Raven Gildea

W hat I love most about riding my motorcycle is that the thrill never wears thin. On warm summer or crisp fall days, motorcycling is as enthralling as it was the first time I straddled an engine.

The best of all possible motorcycle rides is when my boy rides behind me, clinging to my back with determination to be a good passenger and make his Daddy proud. I feel him pressed against me, his thighs behind mine astride the black and silver machine that smoothly carries us around each curve in the mountain road. His arms encircle my torso, his hands rest on my belly. The leather of his gloves is a dull counterpoint to the shine of my jacket. Although I can't see it, I can picture the gleeful smile on his face. I feel as if we could ride forever like this, off into the sunset, never having to return to real life.

It's a warm September day and I unzip my leather jacket, letting the wind ruffle my T-shirt. The boy slips one hand down until it rests just above my belt buckle, then lets the other drop casually into my lap. As he brushes his hand over my fly, my dick begins to stir. He thinks I'm not on to what he's doing, but my cock knows him too well to be fooled. Sure enough, a moment later his fingers slide gently along my leg, then stroke the length of my stiffening meat. I reach down to cup his little hand in mine, pressing him against my crotch. If he thinks he can tease his Daddy, he's about to be reminded that Daddy can tease back.

I tip my body forward slightly and rub myself against my boy's hand. I can feel him shiver behind me, but my teasing him backfires, increasing my own desire. A moment ago all I wanted was to ride like this forever: now I can't wait to find a place to pull off the road.

I turn off onto a dirt road. Bumping along it creates a friction which only makes me hotter. Parking under some trees, I order my boy off the bike. He waits respectfully while I cut the engine and put down the kickstand. He doesn't know what's going to happen next, but he has a pretty good idea as to where it, and he, are going to end up. His eyes reflect fear, excitement, and anticipation. I lean back against the seat of my bike, slowly removing one glove, making him wait.

"Come here, boy."

He responds immediately, stepping forward and dropping to his knees before me. My heart surges. He is such a good boy. I am such a fortunate Daddy. "Take a look at how horny you just made me," I tell him. My boy hesitantly reaches up to touch the tented front of my pants, then gently undoes my buttons. His eyes widen when he sees the size of the boner pushing against my shorts.

"Go ahead, take it out," I instruct him. He hears the stern tone in my voice. His hands tremble just a little as he slides my cock through the opening in the crotch of my underwear. My dick springs free and points directly into his face. "See how hard you made my dick, touching me like that?" I demand. "Don't you know that we could get into an accident if I'm not paying attention to what I'm doing?

"Yes, Sir." He replies sheepishly. He drops his gaze to the ground. I put my gloved hand under my boy's chin and lift his face until he is looking into my eyes again.

"You look at me when I'm talking to you, boy."

"Yes, Sir." He looks directly up at me. I reach into his vest and grab a nipple between my thumb and forefinger, squeeze and twist. My good, hot boy's gaze never drifts from mine, but his eyes glaze as that ecstatic look I love so much takes over his face. His lips part, and I slide my leather-gloved thumb into his mouth. Sexy boy that he is, he immediately begins sucking on my glove as if it were his only link to life. His eyes drift closed, but I am feeling indulgent at the moment and I let it pass. For now.

I release his nipple and pull a condom from my pocket. Touching the wrapper to his cheek, I watch with amusement as his eyes fly open.

"I know you don't want your Daddy to get into an accident, so you just suck me off like a good boy, and then I'll be able to concentrate."

Opening the condom wrapper with my teeth, I touch the rubber to his lips. My boy's eager mouth leaves my glove, now shining with his saliva, and his tongue flicks out to take the condom. I grip his chin and pull his face into my crotch.

I can feel his lips and tongue working as he slips the condom over the tip of my dick. The heat of his mouth brings a groan of pleasure up from somewhere just below my belt buckle. I drop my hands against the seat of the bike and lean back to let my boy's hunger take over. No need to pull him onto me: in moments he has me down his throat.

"That's right, boy," I moan, "swallow your Daddy's meat. Take it all, you dirty little slutboy. This is what you wanted, isn't it? Don't try to tell me any different. You're nothing but a hungry little bitch, begging to get your mouth around your old man's tool. Well, now you've got it, so show me what my boy can do."

He puts his hands on the backs of my legs and gulps down my cock as if it were his first meal after a week in the wilderness. I'm glad to have my motorcycle propping me up, because I wouldn't want to have to depend on my legs just now. The sight of my boy's bobbing head is every bit as sweet as the sensation of his lips stroking my shaft. I run one hand through his rumpled hair, pet his downy cheek, tell him how hot he is, how hot he gets me. My climax seems to start at my rubbery knees, surge up to my balls, and whirl there like a tornado before exploding out the tip of my cock. I shudder and shake as my jiz pumps into my sweet boy's waiting mouth.

I'm reluctant to pull him off me, and he's reluctant to let me go. As I remove the condom he looks up at me and smiles, clearly pleased with himself. I pull him to his feet. "Get out of those pants," I tell him, "and bend over the bike." I snap my handcuffs off my belt. "I'm gonna show you what happens to boys who don't let their daddies focus on the road."

Wriggling out of his jeans, he stands before me in his boots and vest. His boydick stands at attention. I point to the motorcycle, and my boy obediently places his hips against the seat and bends himself over the machine. His toes barely touch the ground. He offers his sweet, round ass to me, and I think my heart will break. I doubt my boy realizes just how hot the sight of his luscious little butt gets this nasty, perverted fagdaddy. But he's about to find out.

I snap the handcuffs over his wrists, locking him to the bike. "Don't want you to burn yourself on the hot pipes if you get distracted." Kicking his legs apart, I run my hand over his succulent cheeks, down to stroke his boycunt. He lifts his ass up to meet my hand, and I smile broadly. My hungry boy, always eager to please his Daddy. And please me he does. My heart swells with pride. My dick swells with lust.

I pull off my leather glove and replace it with one made of latex. Feeling the caress of this new substance, he moans in anticipation. But I'm not ready to fuck my boy: not yet. I bring my bare hand down with a resounding smack, leaving a glowing red hand print on the sweet white asscheek in front of me. He exhales sharply at the impact but is too well trained to protest. He knows his Daddy will never give him more than he can take. He knows what I do to him is always for his own good. His own good, and my pleasure.

Right now, it's my pleasure to spank my boy. I tell him what a slutty boy he is, trying to seduce his Daddy, that he has to learn to think beyond his dick. I know that's hard for a boy to do, but I will help him learn this lesson. He can't just reach for my cock whenever the urge comes over him. My hand snaps down again, the sound of the smack punctuating my words. He wriggles in the pain that follows the impact, then holds still, ready for the next blow. Instead I caress him, letting my gloved hand brush over his asshole and pubic hair. I bend down and lick the smarting hand print I have just made, tell him how I love it when he takes his spanking so bravely.

Now that I've made my mark with two hard smacks, I begin warming up my sweet boy's butt. I spank him lightly, teasingly, talking to him all the while.

"You're a dirty little whore, aren't you, boy?"

"Yes, Sir, I am."

"You know you deserve this. You know you want it. You want your Daddy to spank your nasty little ass, don't you? You were playing with my dick just so you could get me to spank you, weren't you? You're nothing but a sick, perverted little boy who doesn't know what's good for him. You're lucky to have a strong Daddy to take care of you. That's right, Daddy's gonna give you what you need. Daddy will make you a good boy. You need your Daddy to make you be good, don't you?"

"Yes, Sir, I do. I need my Daddy to take care of me."

As my blows get stronger and sharper, my gloved hand strays down to play with the open cunt my boy presents to me. He is shameless, dripping with desire. I can't really blame him. This spanking is getting me as hot as it's getting the boy's ass. Before long I need to leave off hitting him so I can take my swollen dick in my hand.

Stroking myself slowly up and down, I slide one finger into my boy's waiting hole. He opens to take me. He is soft, slippery, eager. I slip a second finger in and start pumping rhythmically. The rosy crown of my dick rests against my boy's smooth skin, my fingers fill his cunt. He is rocking back and forth, rubbing his erect boydick against the black seat of my motorcycle.

"That's right, boy, hump it. Hump Daddy's machine. But don't you come, boy," I tell him sharply. "Don't you come all over my bike. Don't you let your sticky, perverted boycome mess up my seat cover." I add a third finger and increase my tempo. I've got him between a cock and a hard place now: he won't be able to keep himself from coming, and we both know it. Good boy that he is, he starts to beg.

"Daddy, please let me come. I don't know if I can help it. I need to come, Daddy, please. *Please!*"

I love to hear my boy beg. I can never hold out for long against his sweet pleading. But I pretend I'm not going to give in, just to hear him continue.

"Don't you dare, boy. If you come without my permission, you're gonna be in big trouble. You don't want to be in trouble with your Daddy, do you?"

"No Sir, I don't. But I want to come. I need to come, please let me, please say it's okay . . . ."

I feel my own orgasm rising to the fever pitch of my boy's urgency. Pressing my cock hard against his asscheeks, thrusting my fingers deep inside him, I give him the release we both want.

"Go ahead, boy, give it to me. Come for your Daddy. Come all over the place, let go."

He throws his head back and cries out, his pleasure taking him over completely. I grasp his tousled hair in my fist and pull his wriggling body against my crotch, my dick, my hand. His toes leave the ground, only the motorcycle and my two hands keep him from falling. He yanks back hard against the handcuffs that anchor his convulsing body.

The sight, the sound, the feel of his pleasure sends me over the edge. My come sprays over his tender ass, and our rigid bodies shake against each other. Slowly we relax, slumping over the metal curves of the motorcycle. I release my grip on his hair and rub my jiz into the still-red skin which bears the imprints of my hand. We gasp for breath, feeling the blood pounding in the places where our bodies connect.

At last I pull my hand from my boy's glistening cunt, remove my glove, and unlock the cuffs. He slides to the ground at my feet. I pull him to me and pet his head. I am so proud of my hot boy. He looks up into my eyes, and the adoration on his face melts me.

Sliding my dick back into my pants and buttoning up my fly, I instruct my boy to clean off the seat of my motorcycle. His hot, eager tongue immediately gets to work, lapping up the mess he's made. I lean down to kiss the back of his neck. He's getting to be one hell of a passenger.

Ah, penis size, a problem so worrisome to most men that doctors amputate too-tiny penises on intersexual baby boys and have them raised as girls... because, of course, no self-respecting man could manage to be happy and well-adjusted without a whopping Hebrew National salami-sized schlong. Some of the folks we know who get along just fine with their magnificent microphalli could teach those doctors (and any other men who look worriedly at their endowments!) that as everyone in the know knows already, it really isn't the size of the wand that matters... it's whether a lover can get the whole thing into their mouth and still keep breathing. Priorities, priorities, priorities!

Matthew Kailey, a gay transman living in Denver, Colorado, is a public speaker, educator and writer on trans issues. His writing has appeared in The Gender Identity Center of Colorado Journal, The Equal Times, Transgender Tapestry *and* San Francisco Frontiers. *In his spare time, he holds down a conservative day job, plays bass, facilitates an FtM support group, works out and sleeps. His tireless research for "Teeny Weenies, Inc." consisted of looking at a lot of men's magazines. He can be reached at FtMatt@aol.com.*

Teenie Weenies, Inc.

Matthew Kailey

He made quite an entrance. No one had ever walked into a T.W., Inc. meeting with such confidence before. I had been attending the monthly support groups for almost a year and it had taken me six months before I could lift my head upon entering. Most new guys slowly shuffled in, examined the carpet, then took a chair at the edge of the circle. Sometimes the door would pop open a crack, then close abruptly, meaning whoever peeked in had changed his mind. It's not surprising. I haven't yet met a man who wants to admit that he is, at least by certain standards, microscopically endowed.

Maybe it's even tougher for a gay man. I could watch a night of porn or flip through any gay-oriented newspaper or magazine and come away feeling doomed. I had endured it for twenty miserable years before I found T.W., Inc., which stood for Tim Williams, Inc., the founding father of the support group that members had immediately dubbed Teeny Weenies. I found Teeny Weenies on a website—a stroke of luck, because I never would have called. Tim Williams, a 40-year-old gay man with a teeny weenie, was tired of all the pomp and circumstance surrounding big cock worship. He decided to found a group dedicated to the few, the not so proud, the invisible. I had e-mailed Tim immediately, excited that I was not alone in Lilliput. He responded with an invitation to a meeting, which it took me two months to work up the courage to attend. Perhaps whatever cruel joke of nature caused our cocktail weenie proportions also caused us to be intimidated in all other areas of our lives. But not the new guy.

He bumped open the door and charged through as if he were a corporate CEO late for a stockholders' meeting. He made immediate eye contact with everyone in the circle as he looked for an empty seat. I have to admit that I was pleased when he chose the one next to mine. His confidence was attractive and the rest of him lived up to that initial promise. He was short and slender, with small but well-defined muscles outlined by a fitted black T-shirt. As he strode across the room to his chosen chair, a shock of dark hair fell across his forehead and into his eyes. He sat and pushed the hair from his face, pausing to catch his breath.

Then he said, "Sorry I'm late. Couldn't find the place." His eyes swept the group as he smiled apologetically.

"Not a problem," Tim Williams said from the head of the circle. Tim appeared slightly amused himself at the newcomer's boldness. He had apparently grown used to the stealthy slinking of the new attendees. "If you'd like to introduce yourself, you can. It's up to you. You don't have to say anything—"

"I'm Greg McIntyre." He leaned back in his chair and extended his legs, causing his pelvis to thrust forward and out. None of us wondered what was in his pants. If he was here, we knew... not much.

Several of the members murmured, "Welcome, Greg," or "Nice to have you." I just gave him a sideways glance and the hint of a smile, admiring the shadowy growth of beard along his jawline. He winked. I yanked my eyes toward Tim, then silently chastised myself. *He was flirting with you, you idiot*, I thought, but the entrance, the full name given so directly, the wink, were too much for me to handle. Sure, the guy was good looking, but why was he so cocky when we all knew he wasn't cocky at all? There were several attractive men in the group, but they seemed to know their place. Good looks don't necessarily go very far—usually only to the zipper of your jeans.

Not that I would know. Small children didn't run screaming from me on the street, but I was far from handsome. This was one of several discoveries I had made in my youth. At 14, I discovered I was gay. At 16, I discovered that cocks larger than four inches when hard were decidedly more attractive. At 21, I discovered that mine was not going to grow any more. And, throughout my adulthood, I discovered that I was "a nice guy," "sweet-looking," and "funny." I would smile but cringe inwardly at these kiss-of-death compliments that were always followed by the promise of a phone call that never came. So I had spent the most recent years of my life in the gym, developing a muscular body which, to my dismay, only served to make my cock look smaller. My hair started thinning, too, just because it was my hair. A glance in the mirror never failed to reflect a balding bodybuilder with a miniscule member, so I quit glancing. The mirrors in my house were getting as lonely as I was when I made my most important discovery—Tim

Williams, Inc. And now I was sitting next to a brash, attractive man who seemed to have few qualms about his missing link.

"Would you like to say anything more, Greg?" Tim said. "You're not required to. You can tell us why you're here, if you want."

"I think I'll just listen tonight, if you don't mind. I'd like to get a feel for the group."

"No problem." Tim looked around the circle. "Anyone?"

"I'll talk," said Jerry, surprising no one. Jerry was a regular at the group and always had a pity-me story about his latest sexual failure. "I went to the bathhouse Saturday and met this great-looking guy. He was huge, too, hung like the proverbial horse. Well, he had rented a room and we went in. I still had my towel on, but he had been strutting around showing off his stuff all night. Man, I wanted him bad, really bad. Anyway, I took off my towel and he sort of looked at me. He didn't say anything and we actually had a pretty good time. But I gave him my number and he never called. It's Thursday now and he hasn't called. He won't call. He was polite about it and everything, I mean, he didn't say anything, but I know." Jerry shook his head and examined his hands. "I know."

"Wait a minute." My head turned sharply at the sound in my ear. Apparently, Greg had changed his mind about just listening. "Are you saying he didn't call because of your cock? Come on, man, you don't know that. It could have been any number of reasons—"

"No," Jerry interrupted. "It was that, I'm sure of it. He was huge, he was great looking, what would he want with me?"

"Superficial," Aaron piped up from the corner. "If he cares about the size of your cock, he's superficial."

"But you don't know that," Greg said. "You have no idea. If you think every rejection is because of your cock, you'll make yourself crazy. I mean, it was a bathhouse, after all. Not exactly the place to find undying love. And, anyway, speaking of being superficial..."

"Yeah," I chimed in, suddenly catching Greg's drift and wanting to join up with him, impress him. "Who's superficial? All you mentioned were the guy's looks and the size of his dick."

"Right." Greg looked at me and nodded. "Exactly."

Greg didn't seem to notice the bemused stares that I was getting from some of the members. He couldn't know that I rarely talked and even more rarely confronted anyone. I surprised myself a little, too. Whatever he had going for him was tangible; I could pick it up and make it my own. It felt good, and I secretly plotted to save him a seat every time.

Jerry could not be persuaded from the certainty of his inadequacy. Greg and I had formed a silent bond. I imagined a chill from some of the others for standing up to Jerry's whining, but, if it were there, Greg did not seem aware of it. The meeting continued without me as I played out scripts in my mind about asking Greg for his phone number

afterward. Mark either had a new boyfriend who was a cop or he had
been arrested and frisked; Sam had recently vacationed in Mexico and
had sex on a beach, or at least had read about it. I couldn't be certain
and it didn't matter. The base of my brain was processing the threads
of conversation, but my more cerebral self was scrambling for a plan.

When Tim announced the end of the meeting, panic set in. Greg
stood up immediately and moved behind my chair as if to leave. I
thought it was already too late when I felt his warm breath next to my
ear.

"Let's get the hell outta here," he whispered.

I blushed with pleasure and anxiety, wondering if my thoughts had
been so strong as to be obvious. He was halfway to the door before I
was able to stand. I scampered after him, not wanting to delay so long
that he changed his mind.

Once outside, he said, "Whoa. Some unhappy people in there."

"No kidding," I said, shaking my head in pity for the others as if I
had stumbled into the meeting by mistake. "Oh, I'm Steve, by the way.
Steve Abbott. You missed the introductions."

He shook my outstretched hand. "So I did. Okay, Steve Abbott. Nice
to meet you. You know, I live just a few blocks from here. Want to come
to my place? We could have coffee or a beer or something."

I agreed, trying not to get too excited. I had taken his side at the
meeting; he was just being a nice guy. He probably had a boyfriend at
home—one with a real man-sized cock. It soon became evident,
though, that he lived alone. His apartment was a studio, plain but
clean, with barely room for two of us as we bumped around digging
for beer in the refrigerator. He didn't apologize or make excuses for the
size, just chuckled at our Keystone Kops routine and took my arm to
propel me into the living room.

Once we had settled on the futon couch, which obviously doubled
as a bed, I asked, "Why did you come to the meeting?"

He laughed. "Well, because I have a little dick." His smile was like
the room, plain and clean. It enlarged the space while minimizing the
distance between us.

"It doesn't seem to bother you."

The smile faded into an expression of agreeable amusement. "I
can't let it bother me. You'd go nuts if you worried about stuff like that
all the time. But I was interested. I wanted to see how other guys dealt
with it."

"And?"

He adjusted himself on the couch so he was facing me and draped
an arm across the back. His fingers were almost touching my shoulder,
and he still wore the half-smile. "Well, it's still different for me. Being
a tranny and all."

"A what?" I turned my body towards him, which caused me to
back up slightly on the couch. I was instantly self-conscious because it

appeared that I was backing away from him and I tried to casually re-
adjust myself.

"I'm a transsexual," he said, ignoring my clumsy wiggling. "You
know, born a woman, didn't have no say, however that stupid song
goes. I really don't have any dick to speak of. I mean, if you wanted to
speak of it."

Now I like to think I'm a man of the world, even though my world
tends to consist of my familiar neighborhood, my boring job and a
lifetime of loneliness that I like to blame on my unfortunate genitalia.
Greg was sitting next to me talking about his virtual nothingness, and
the reason for it, as if he were mentioning that his car broke down. He
was so smooth that, even with this revelation, I wanted nothing more
than to impress him with my open-minded coolness.

In order to do that, I opened my mouth and squeaked out, "What
do you have?"

He laughed again and took a long swig of beer. "If you're still here
in an hour, maybe you'll see. Do you like chess?"

I nodded enthusiastically, although I had limited knowledge of the
game. This was evident when I was checkmated early in the first round.
After he won the second with ease, he got up to put the chessboard
away, then sat down next to me, sliding his arm around my shoulders.

"You're still here, I see," he said. His fingers moved in small circles
on my shoulder and across my back to my neck.

"I thought I should stay until I beat you at something," I said, then
silently complimented myself on being rather witty.

"I'm sure we could find something you could win at." His face
moved closer to mine and I felt his breath against my cheek. He
smelled of beer and patchouli and a hazy thickness that I couldn't iden-
tify. His other hand touched my knee and began the small circles there.
I remembered trying to pat my head and rub my stomach at the same
time when I was a child. I couldn't do it. Maybe he was equally inept
at multiple hand movements. I didn't mind.

I was hard, and annoyed, as usual, that only the hint of a bulge
showed at my zipper. Then I remembered that he had nothing there.
Had he chosen me because he could not get anyone more attractive,
someone better looking, someone, well, bigger? He leaned closer and
kissed me, teasing his tongue into my mouth until I could feel it
against my teeth and gums, running along the edges then exploring
more deeply, sliding against my lips as he pulled out. I looked at him
as he slowly closed his mouth and realized that he could probably get
anyone he wanted.

"Why me?" I asked.

"Because you understood what I was talking about."

His hand was at my shirt collar now. As the buttons came open, his
fingers moved lightly across each section of chest that was revealed. No
circles this time, but a soft back and forth motion that tickled and

chilled me. When his fingertips feathered over my nipple, I looked again at my crotch, certain that the tiny bulge had grown to porn-star proportions, and was almost surprised to see that it was still barely visible. His hand moved to my stomach, tugging at the hair that grew up my abdomen and around my navel.

"You have way too many clothes on," he said to my belt buckle.

"So do you." I yanked at his T-shirt, embarrassed by my clumsy attempt, but he lifted his arms and wriggled out. Shirtless, he quickly slid his arm across his chest.

"What is it?" I said.

"Oh, nothing really. I didn't scar well here." When he moved his arm, I could see the thin white strips of scar that ran under his pecs. He pointed to an inch-long place near his underarm that bulged out awkwardly.

"You're kidding," I said. "After all this, that's what bothers you?"

"Hey," he said, with a mock-wounded look. "We all have our cross to bear."

"Let's forget about that." I was suddenly emboldened by the knowledge of his Achilles' Heel. "You said I would get to see."

His smile returned. "And you shall. But to warn you—I haven't had surgery. Hormones produce miracles, but sometimes they're small miracles. Just call it enhancement of my natural charms."

He stood and undid his jeans. His body writhed slightly as he pushed his jeans and boxers as one down his hips and legs. Even in his thinness, his hips were wide, his thighs slightly fleshy. Voluptuous was the description that came to mind, and, although I had never associated that word with a man before, it became instantly desirable as my eyes roamed his body. A pleasant tangle of brown hair rested between his legs and, as if struggling to free itself from the dense thicket, a tiny dark pink head, like a cock for a Ken doll, pushed its way through. A warm sensation began in my chest and moved down to my groin. An uninvited smile broke out on my face.

"You're laughing at me," he said, but he was smiling, too.

"No. No, it's… amazing," I said, still grinning like an idiot. I wanted to bury my face there, to lick and suck on his tiny cock. I started to move towards him, still seated, at just the right level to indulge.

He backed up. "Uh uh," he said, putting out his hands. "If this is show and tell, then it's your turn. You still have way too many clothes on."

He again sat beside me, all skin and nakedness. Suddenly, my hands and mouth could not be controlled and I lunged at him, sucking and biting on his shoulder and neck as my fingers roamed his chest.

"You're not making this easy," he said as he struggled with my belt.

I didn't want to let go of him, but I felt my cock straining against the confines of my jeans. It was my imagination, of course. My cock had never strained against anything in my life, but it didn't matter. I wanted out, I wanted him to see and touch what I had tried to keep hidden for so long. I got myself out of my jeans, and, finally freed from its denim prison, my four-inch cock sprung up straight and tall, as if pointing to something on the ceiling.

"Oh, man," he said, thrusting his face into my lap and taking it into his mouth. He sucked it as if he had been waiting forever, as if it were the grandest thing he had ever seen. I started to think it was grand myself. I moved my hips, matching his rhythms, shoving my cock into his mouth and fantasizing that it was hitting the back of his throat. A few minutes of this and I was ready to come. I almost stopped him, wanting to prolong the experience, until I saw his hand move to his own cock. In a moment of detached fascination, I watched him begin to jerk himself off, his thumb and forefinger gently tugging on the diminutive piece of flesh. While my mind took it in with intellectual interest, my body reacted far less clinically; I came without warning. As the last spasms of my orgasm subsided, I felt his body shudder with his own coming. I panicked. It had happened too quickly; I wanted more.

He raised his head and swiped a forearm across his mouth. As he sat, his hand moved automatically into position over his scar. "Stop that," I said, gesturing towards his chest.

He looked down, then dropped his arm. "Oh, sorry. Habit."

"Yeah, I'm familiar with those habits," I said, eyeing my rapidly deflating dick. He kissed my shoulder, then moved his hand to rub the back of my neck.

"So," he said, "are we going to see each other before the next meeting?"

I closed my eyes and relaxed, enjoying the gentle massage. "Why do we have to go back to the meetings?"

"Umm... because we have teeny weenies?"

"You don't need to go to those meetings," I said, opening my eyes to take in his body once again.

"Neither do you." He pulled his hand from my neck and rested his head on my shoulder.

"Hey," I said, "maybe we can start a new group—B.S.S., Inc."

"And that would be..."

"Bad Surgical Scars." I started to chuckle. He smacked my chest with his palm.

"Okay, smart ass," he said, standing. "If we're not going back to the meetings, you better just spend the night now. Get up, I have to make the bed."

I rose reluctantly and watched him pull on the futon until it enlarged into a reasonably sized bed, taking up most of the space in the miniature living room. As soon as the bottom sheet was on, he plopped down on his back and stretched out his naked body. The tiny pink cock had retreated into the depths of his hair and the folds of his skin. I would see it again. With any luck, I would see it many times.

Some transgendered folks find that there's a definite double-standard when it comes to body modifications—discussing transgender "body modifications" with even the most bepierced and inked-up folks often ends up with the trans-gendered person being perceived as the freak, the extremist. But what would it be like to live in an era where not only piercings or tattoos, but skin, anatomy, organs, and even sex and genitals were just more parts to be designed and bought for a price? What sort of cultural changes would it engender, and what would happen when sexual identity met up with the panoply of variation possible among such these wild new bodies? Speculative, vivid, eerie, and enveloping, Allison Lonsdale's vision of this kind of world offers us a mesmerizing glimpse into one possible future.

Allison Lonsdale has always suspected that we have more sexes than our languages recognize. Her first fiction publication was "The Symbol for Intensity" at www.cleansheets.com; go look, it's still in the archives. A science fiction fan and optimistic technophile, she is also a poet and guitarist. She can be found in San Diego coffeehouses singing "geeky music for geeky people"—her original lyrics use metaphors from math, physics, programming, genetics and virology to explore desire and suffering. This is her first appearance in a real paper book, and she is enormously pleased, particularly since "Tangaroa" was rejected for being too weird by another anthology... which ended up including work by Thomas S. Roche and Poppy Z. Brite!

Tangaroa

Allison Lonsdale

He staggered to the bathroom, got the box from the hidden compartment, and thumbed the print lock. Reflected in the lid, his face was drained of life, and his pale hair was dark with sweat and matted to his skull. He took out the translucent blood-colored sphere, hesitated a second, then pressed the fifth stud on its glossy surface. The largest variation, which he had never used even in his most depraved moments, afraid of the pain.

Discipline built character. He needed that pain now.

The sphere unfolded into a phallus as thick as his wrist. The base anchored itself to the wall where he placed it. Tiny beads of lubricant welled up on the surface. He peeled off his sticky trousers and kicked them aside in disgust. Kneeling, his pulse hammering in his skull, he pressed himself back against the toy.

It split him open cruelly as he pushed, its surface giving just enough that he did not tear. The agony drove up into his belly, blurring his vision. Tears ran down his face and dripped to the floor. He forced himself to take more, pushing back into the pain, determined to teach his unruly body that it didn't want what it thought it wanted.

Then he imagined for one second that the phallus splitting him open belonged to her, and it stopped hurting entirely. His empty balls contracted in an agony that was not pain as he climaxed, blind, helpless, shooting nothing at all across the bathroom floor.

He collapsed onto the tiles, the toy sliding out of him with a muffled pop, and he wept.

It began with an express mail delivery to his office in Victrix. At his deskware's chime, he jacked out and examined the package. The source was a corporate address in Freeside, which housed several legitimate code mills and an anonymous remail center... never mind how he knew that. Inside was an unlabeled memory spike. It was just conceivable that this was legitimate; some industrial code was too bulky to move by net without risking corruption or piracy—but he knew it was something else. He had been covering his tracks very well, but he had always known there would be a price for bending the rules. His life as a professional of his clade was narrow and colorless; his life as Faber, shadowmarket coder of the Gray Area, had been worth the risk. His designs under that name, interfaces of shocking beauty and strangeness, would be labeled "degenerate" in Victrix. So would he, if anyone knew. It appeared that someone did. A cold knot of fear grew inside him, but he gave no sign. Years of practice at concealing his real self were paying off.

He pocketed it and finished his shift. At home that night, he slid the spike into a reader whose insides were off-spec and possibly illegal. He jacked in, loaded wares he had no legitimate reason to own, and probed the data. It was a sim, so big it had to be full-sensory and very hi-res, in a shell of code so tight he couldn't extract anything meaningful. It carried no viral sign his wares could recognize. He disconnected, grinding his teeth in frustration.

He should destroy it. But he could not bring himself to choose safety over finding out what it was. He had to know.

He ran the simulation.

Darkness. Ocean smells. A tattered glyph of sea-green light that resolved into the word "Tangaroa." Sand under his feet, moonlight on waves, a warm breeze in his face.

Nude, he strode down to the water's edge. This body was massively solid, a stark contrast to his slender real-world form. The skin along his sides was ridged and sensitive. The tissue between his fingers felt complicated, and his feet more so. This was an aquatic reconstruct: someone who loved the sea more than his own humanity, and had taken that love into the nano tanks. Faber had seen these in the diving media and read some of the design specs, but had never met one. The reconstructed were not permitted citizenship in Victrix. He was both fascinated and repulsed. The body walked out into the surf; it was warmer than he expected. The gills along his sides opened slightly and began to taste the water, though he was still breathing with his nose.

A dorsal fin broke the water, and his muscles tensed. It went under and a woman surfaced, dark and glistening in the moonlight, ugly by Victrix standards. The hair was short and dense as black velvet, the nose broad and flat, and the eyes alien, hooded by deep epicanthic folds and showing almost no white. Huge and dark, they looked more animal than human—based on seals' eyes, he realized, an optical design suited for both water and air.

"If you can't take the pressure," she said, "don't swim in the deep water." He felt her webbed hand on his groin, and a wave of heat washed through him. He heard himself say, "I can take it," in a voice not his own.

She grinned, showing teeth "Let's go deep." Releasing his achingly hard cock, she turned and dove. He followed.

His nostrils sealed and his gills opened wide. With the first movement of his arms that told his body swim now, webbing slid out between his fingers and his feet spread into fins. His eyes closed as he went under, but he was not blind. Not eyelids, then, but membranes protecting his eyes from the salt. He could actually see through the water, not with the familiar crisp view of his diving mask but with surprising clarity nonetheless... and he could see into the infrared. The woman's body was a luminous beacon, massive and streamlined. Her legs bore exaggerated curves of muscle, ending in broad fins.

The water on his gills tasted deliciously clean. He guessed that in daylight, the sea here would be clear as glass. As he drew closer to her, he caught another flavor, hard to distinguish at first from the baseline sea-taste. It grew stronger: smoky, musky, almost sweet. He realized it was the taste of her arousal. His cock was still rock-hard from her earlier touch, and the water moving against it like warm silk as he swam had brought him close. Now her flavor on his gills almost made him come.

He followed her down into the cooler water, towards a mound of sand that read strangely to his IR vision. As they passed over it, his buoyancy changed, pulling him down onto her. Clever editing, or a gravitics pad under the sand? Had this been recorded from a wired actor, or scripted and run through a sensory compiler? Her body against his made him lose his train of thought.

She was a perfect balance between hard and soft. Dense, rock-solid muscle underlay her insulation of fat, yet even that lush padding was firm. Her mouth opened to his and her fingers traced the sensitive edges of his gills, making him groan against her invading tongue. His cock flexed against her belly and suddenly the water around them tasted even more strongly of her cunt. Her webbed hands traced his back, making his shoulders tremble and his nipples ache, and then her fingers dug into his ass. Faber started to panic.

He hit the exit-override. It didn't work.

Rage, fear and disbelief tore through him. As his body writhed in her grasp, as one of her fingers inched closer to his anus, making him buck against her and whimper into her mouth, his mind withdrew and battered at the walls of this illusion. He tried to block out the sensations, but he had spent his life learning to treat simulated environments as real, and these stimuli were too intense to ignore. This was unbearable. This was…

Oh God.

His cock had been sliding against her stomach, where the skin was getting slicker and slicker. Now her finger pressed against his anus for an unbearably long second, and slid in to the first knuckle. He convulsed in orgasm. Red light hammered behind his eyes as waves of pleasure ripped through his body. He could hear his groans against her neck, distorted and ugly through the water. Her arm, a thick cable of muscle sheathed in silk, held him close, careful not to block his gills. He caught the taste of his own semen on the water. Heart racing, he held onto her through the aftershocks.

Her finger pulled out of him with a tiny pang that he felt through his entire cock. He slid down, nuzzling her breasts; they were firm, streamlined, held close to her rib cage by webs of muscle. Her nipples hardened under his teeth; her groan sounded like distant whalesong. Her taste in the water grew stronger. She dug nails into his scalp and arched, pushing her breast against his mouth. He slid a hand between her thighs and stroked her swollen lips, slick where he had expected the fluid to wash away. Of course, he thought, her design would compensate for that. One finger slid inside her, then two, and her muscles clamped down so hard he could feel his knuckles creak. He sank his teeth harder into her nipple and she bucked, pulling his fingers deeper. He moved his thumb up and found her clitoris, big as a grape, hard and slick as a pearl, straining the limits of its hood. Each stroke against it produced an answering clamp inside of her. His cock was hard again, and the itch left by her finger seemed to be moving deeper inside his ass.

She pushed him off her and shifted, kneeling on the sand. She spread her mons with her hands, and he watched her swollen clitoris flow outward, burning with hot blood to his IR vision. It unfolded into a curved shape that was both phallic and profoundly feminine. When it stopped growing, it was bigger than his own cock, nameless colors of heat rippling across its surface. No veins, no head, a perfectly smooth form like some exotic sea creature. It writhed gently, flexing at him with a rhythm he remembered from her cunt. He took it in his hand. The surface was incredibly slippery, and had the same strange balance between hard and soft as her body. It felt nothing like his penis. It moved under his fingers as he stroked it, surging to meet his caress. She trembled and bit her lip. Finally she seized him and pulled him towards her.

His legs wrapped around her waist, and she gripped his thighs and pulled him down. He was burning with desire and fear. The tip of that alien organ nudged slickly at his anus, and he felt his cock flex and his nipples contract into points of almost-pain. Finally it slid into him in one long exquisite press of sensation, impossibly smooth but so damnably thick. He began to move against her, completely lost in the sensation of that alien heat inside him, and then it started squirming.

He dimly realized that she could control it, that it was prehensile.

She found the right spot inside him and began fluttering against it, and he gripped her shoulders and cried out as her mouth found one of his nipples and his cock was pressed between their bodies. She fucked him with profound hunger, driving his body down onto her phallus. His universe contracted to her moving inside him and the dull red pulse, rising through the spectrum to blue-white, of his cock sliding between their bodies. The orgasm started at the base of his spine and burned its way up until it blew through the top of his head. The sensation was so intense that he lost consciousness.

That part, it occurred to him as everything went dark, had to have been done with a sensory compiler.

Faber came back to himself, drenched in sweat, the front of his pants soaked with semen. He pulled out the neural jack and then fumbled at the reader until it ejected the memory spike. He threw it across the room.

Discipline. It was because he lacked discipline...

He lay on the bathroom floor, shaking. He had been naive to think his shadowmarket coding was the worst thing that could catch up with him. Someone knew his tainted secret, infinitely worse than his activities in the Gray Area.

He should disappear and create a new identity. Not easy in a clade as punctilious as Victrix, but Faber knew he might be good enough to get away with it. But would she find him again? Too likely, given what he knew she could do.

He showered in the hottest water he could stand and scrubbed himself raw. He made coffee and put too much brandy in it. Then he ran a search on "Tangaroa."

It came back as the Maori word for "water-dwelling"... and as a signature on posts to the deep-water thread of a sporting board. She was posting from Liberty, but that was meaningless; their data laws were the laxest on the net. She used that name for business as well; it appeared in articles about the transclade consulting group that held her contract as a market profiler. Nothing about a career in coding. So who had worked on that sim? No mere hobbyist could have done it.

One last find: a tiny file dated yesterday, crypted, on a public server in Freeside. Faber took a copy and cracked it in half an hour. It was audio, matching the voice in the sim.

"We need to talk. I'll see you in the Gray Area."

★

Normally, Faber was in the Gray Area every night. Now he stayed away, losing shadowmarket clients and not caring. He ran the sim twice more before finally destroying it... and regretting it immediately.

She haunted his dreams: that alien, designed body, female but with...

He lost sleep. He lost weight. He drank.

He went back to the Gray Area.

He considered going under a different identity, but suspected it wouldn't make a difference. He wore his usual icon, the one he had designed with such careful precision. From a distance it looked gray, and some people thought he was part of the Gray Area's wares. But up close he was black and white: all the shadings of his fine-boned face and his archaic suit were delicate crosshatch lines. For this meeting, he disabled the icon's expression transfer. He would not give her the satisfaction of seeing how badly she had shaken him.

He sat at the bar trying to pretend this was business as usual. Within minutes, a message bot crawled up and sparkled at him. It was a metallic cockroach covered with antique circuit-board patterns: one of his early designs. He tapped it to receive. It contained one word in her voice: "Now." He palmed the cockroach and made a knocking motion. The Gray Area's wares pulled him into the private room.

"Faber. It's a pleasure to meet you." Her icon matched the body in the sim, all fluid curves and padded muscle. In this light her skin was a dusky caramel. Her garment covered her from shoulders to crotch like a layer of paint; it would be considered obscene in Victrix. The "fabric" was a video of bright tropical fish. It left her sides bare, exposing her gills. She looked wet—not the slick shine from a cheap image filter, but well-rendered water that beaded on her hair and skin, trickling down.

"The pleasure is all yours." He had his wares run a signal trace. It would take time; nobody showed up in the Gray Area without a few layers of crypt. "What do you want?"

She smiled, looking predatory. "I've examined your work. You write beautiful code. I want to meet you in person. Outside the Net."

"This is highly improper."

"Improper? You're writing your clade on your icon, Faber. I thought you were subtler than that. Your code is subtler." She started to reach for him.

"Don't touch me."

"Are you frightened of women?" She said it without the venom he expected, the implied accusation of unclean tendencies. Had she disabled her own expression transfer? He couldn't imagine a woman saying that so neutrally.

"I'm not used to reconstructs."

"I like diving. I don't like suits and breathers. I know your clade disapproves of tankwork, but you still use it. You just don't admit to it. I've seen your women; natural-borns don't look that much like a Pre-Raphaelite painting."

"No clade is free from hypocrites. But it's wrong to meddle with nature." The irony of this struck him as he spoke, unnatural as he was.

"Humans are natural. Our tools are natural. I think my use of medical nano for functional reasons is less ridiculous than using it for aesthetics, pretending you don't, and acting self-righteously superior."

"Did you come here just to attack my clade for hypocrisy?" He was stalling for time. A few more seconds and he'd know where she was from.

"I've told you why I'm here. I know what you are, and I'm offering you a chance to run with it, not away from it."

"Stop talking nonsense. Make your demands and get this over with."

"Faber. I am not a blackmailer. For one thing, nobody in Victrix would believe me. Outclader and reconstruct—zero credibility."

Faber's wares reported back. "Her" node of origin was in Bifrost clade. The Rainbow Bridge. He flinched. Unnatural, unclean—exactly what he was, his conscience reminded him. Suddenly the cues in "her" conversation made perfect sense.

He tried to log out. He couldn't. His skin went cold and his ears rang. That was a damned high-level override; how did "she" get away with that? Part of him said that this was exactly what he deserved.

"Now we're even," he said. "I know what you are too. Sodomite. Filthy degenerate."

"That was a fast signal trace. Did you code the tracer? I'd like to buy a copy. When you're done wallowing in your prejudices, run your icon gestalt wares—I'm sure you have some loaded. This is my real body, Faber. Go ahead, check it."

Gender match, 96% probability; appearance match, 74% probability. He told the wares she was a reconstruct. The appearance match jumped into the nineties.

"This isn't making sense." He was numb. This disaster was failing to unfold according to his expectations.

"Your clade has such narrow definitions! I told you, I know what you are. And that's not gay. Just as I'm not male. You're something much more rare. So am I. Gender isn't as simple as they tell you, Faber."

"You can't—" he began helplessly.

She snorted. "Can't what? Know what you are? Have overrides in the Gray Area?"

He was silent for a long moment. Then, the inevitable question: "How did you do it?"

"The overrides? Very good coders owe me favors. Some better than you." He raised an eyebrow. "Crossovers," she said.

"Undead?" His eyes widened.

Tangaroa sighed. "I am not going to debate the nature of transfer sentients with you. Where I come from they're full citizens, and it is both bad manners and stupid to treat them otherwise."

This was stranger than he had imagined, but he had to learn how the pieces came together. That was what he lived for, knowing how things worked. "Then how did you...find me?"

"Synthesis of patterns from incomplete data. I do it for a living; I've got a wetware boost. The Bifrost mainframes run crossovers, not AIs. One of them is very old. He canced and went cryo in the teens, and transfer was the only option. He taught me about a field of social engineering from his past that overlaps my work by a huge margin, but applied to individuals, not economic trends. My boost made me very, very good at it."

"I don't understand."

"The threads you post to. Your designs. You've been so careful to make sure nobody in your pristine little clade of hypocrites would discover what you are. But to me, it shines out even through the innocent things. I knew it before I found out about that toy you bought in Freeside." Faber flinched at this, though his icon did not. "I can taste it on your data like blood in the water. You are what I live to hunt."

Then she was pressed against him. Her icon carried tactile coding for slick and cool. She growled, "Your desire is stronger than your fear. I can feel it coming off you in waves. I am going to have you, Faber." Despite everything, he liked the way she said his name, like she was naming a food from childhood that she longed to taste again. "You know what I am. I am going to fuck you, and you are going to beg me for it."

Faber knew he was lost because, pinned between her and the wall, he felt more safe than trapped. He started crying. With his icon's expression transfer shut down, his reflection in her dark eyes looked perfectly calm, despite the ugly noises coming from his mouth. Through his sobs he heard her call him by his real name and tell him things about himself that he could have sworn nobody knew. "You have a choice," she said. "Believe the lies your clade has told you about desire, or find out for yourself." And she told him a date, a time, and coordinates, and made him repeat them back to her until she was sure he knew them.

He wept and did not tell her no.

This was insane. This could not possibly be happening.

This was happening.

Faber was two klicks off the coast, ten meters down, having burned heavy power on his suit jets to get here by an indirect route. He had tampered with his GPS ware; it was still checking his position against satellite signals, but was no longer rebroadcasting on the patrol band. If something happened to him, he might never be found.

Something was going to happen to him, he was certain. And he did not want to be found; every second brought him closer to being irrevocably lost and he was not turning back.

By the readouts in his mask he was within meters of the right place and five minutes early. His breather's rasp blended with distant clicks and pings as he waited. His suit flexed, helping him breathe against the press of the water on his chest.

Tangaroa came up from below, a sleek shape that seemed too dark until he realized he was remembering how she looked to IR vision. Nude except for a sheathed knife and a utility terminal bonded to her skin, this was the body he knew from the sim, from her icon. Her hands were fully webbed; her feet spread out into wide fins. Her nostrils were clamped shut, giving her face a froglike smoothness, and the gill-slits along her sides opened and closed rhythmically. He felt his cock harden. He had an instant of panic before he was caught in her arms. Feeling the strange texture of her flesh, he calmed. This was just like the sim, like his dreams of the last few weeks. The waking world and its rules seemed very distant now.

He had to use his jets to keep up with her. Their destination was a floating arcology; the huge column of shadow beneath it was threaded with beams of light and spangled with nude and suited swimmers. Huge cables led down to a heat-exchange installation on the seafloor, invisible in the murk. Thoughts of the thermocline brought him back to the sim, her body burning bright in the water, the light of her hot blood visible in her alien phallus. Watching her powerful legs move as she swam ahead of him, he remembered having gills, and tasting her cunt in the water. Above them brilliant patches of open water interrupted the dark plane. Within that vast shadow, he felt claustrophobic, as though they were diving in a cave. She led him upwards and a quicksilver square opened to meet them. Closer to the underside of the city, its scale became even more monstrous for a second, then suddenly shifted into the ordinary. This was her neighborhood, her block, her front door.

They broke the surface. He saw the nictitating membranes retract from her eyes. Thankful for an easy gesture to hide his reaction, Faber peeled the breather and mask off his face. They folded into a compact egg of polymers in his palm and he filled his lungs with the air of her home, which carried the faint, familiar scent of neglected laundry and strong coffee.

The front door was in an enormous bathroom, lit by pale green panels in the walls. Tangaroa rolled out of the water, her feet shifting to walking shape. Faber heaved himself out gracelessly, sitting with his legs in the sea while he got his bearings. The floor under him was tiled with coppery triangles that felt like wet silk over closed-cell foam. He could feel the arcology rolling with the waves like a vast ship, but he knew it had to be his imagination. The place must be designed to compensate for that. Then he noticed that her toiletries were webbed into wall pockets, and revised that estimate.

"Welcome to Bifrost's offshore arcology." She sounded exactly as she had in the sim, in the Gray Area...but now there was the scent of her mouth, a sea-muted musk of rice and seaweed and papaya. This was real. Her breath smelled like what she'd eaten for breakfast, and it didn't get much more real than that.

"Come on," she said, touching his shoulder. "Get out of this thing." Standing, he set his suit to retract. It flowed into a thick disc that he peeled from his chest and stuck to the wall, along with the mask and breather. She unbonded her gear, leaving knife and terminal on the sink. Over her shoulder he saw his nakedness in the mirror, contrasting with hers. She made him seem as frail and porcelain as the women he had courted in Victrix. Beside her black velvet and caramel bronze, his blondness was intensified. He looked like a watercolor from a fairy tale, the sort that involved snow and magic and a hundred-year sleep.

She turned to face him. "You're handling this well." He nodded, his mouth dry. Her eyes were huge, dark, looking more animal than human—the seal's eyes he remembered from the sim. He remembered a fairy tale about seals coming onto land in human bodies to find human mates. He wanted to touch her hair, that strange dense texture where jewels of sea water clung. After a long moment, he realized that there was no reason why he shouldn't, and he reached out and stroked the sleek shape of her skull. If velvet were alive, he thought, it would feel like this. Then she pulled him to her and his nerves burned with memories of the sim. She picked him up as easily as if he were a child and carried him to the shower, a sunken pool in the corner where nozzles came out of the wall. "Let's get clean," she said. "I love salt water but I hate the feel when it dries."

She had him wash her gill ridges with a soft brush. He traced them with his fingers and she arched her back and made a low noise in her throat. He got down on his knees, grateful for the cushioned tiles, and began to lick at the gills where they began just above her hips. She turned so his face was buried in her side. His right hand slid up the back of her thigh, exploring the solidity of her flesh and the sensitive crevice where thigh met ass, while his left stroked her stomach, tracing the line of velvet that ran south from her navel and suddenly broadened before the cleft. As he slid a finger to the swollen mass of her clitoris, hard as wet stone under his touch, she hissed and her gills fluttered wildly against his mouth. A smell, a taste, was coming from their rosy depths, and it made his balls ache. It was somewhere between the sweat of her skin and the taste of her cunt in the water.

Then her clit began to unfold into that alien phallus, and he found himself hunched at the other end of the shower saying, "No. No."

"You have come this far and you can't handle it? I don't think so. You could have turned back a long time ago." She took his shoulders, lifted him to his feet; her strength frightened and excited him. He reached up to push her away but his arms went around her instead, and when she sank sharp teeth gently into his shoulder, he felt his nipples tighten and ache. But that unnatural body part was pressed against him, next to his own, and his head was spinning. "I want..." he got out through the knot in his throat.

She looked into his eyes. "Tell me what you want." He had thought her irises were brown; this close, they were dark amber streaked with burgundy. She was so powerful, and so alien, that his knees went weak. None of his discreet adventures with the fragile ladies of his clade had prepared him for this.

"I... want to lick you. Not this. What you—what you were before."

"What I was before hasn't existed since I went into the tanks. Or are you expressing your reluctance to suck on this?" And she flexed her cock, pressing it into him. He flushed and nodded. "No matter to me," she said. "It's not your mouth I want this in." His face burned.

She carried him to the bed and threw him down. He landed hard on the mattress, gelfoam deforming from the impact and then oozing back into shape. Then she was on top of him, and he could feel his heartbeat hammering in his skull. He pulled her tight against him and they rolled across the bed, biting and tasting each other. Faber slid down her body, rubbing his face against her stomach, reveling in the texture of her flesh. She took fistfuls of his wet hair and pushed him further down.

Her clit was a hot stone under his tongue, beating like a heart. Her velvet crushed against his nose and he struggled to breathe. She clawed at his scalp, rocked her hips up to push at his mouth. Her breathing was ragged. He slid two fingers inside her. She was so hot he nearly pulled them out, but her strangled cry persuaded him to keep them inside, and then to curl them and push against the firm spot in the ridges of the upper wall. "More," she hissed. He worked a third finger in. She made a noise like the whalesong groan in the sim, and he could feel that sound in his cock where he ground it into the bed.

Then her clit was unfolding, surging to fill his mouth, and he tried to pull away. Her fists, clenched in his hair, held him in place. No. He could not do this. He thought, If I bite down she will have to stop. He tried to make himself bite her. But he wanted her too much, wanted even this, as much as it terrified him. Through tears, through the fear that something inside him had broken and he was drowning, he let her in. Tangaroa made incoherent noises and pushed deep into the wet heat of his mouth, and he opened for her, feeling the pressure of his own fear like the pressure of the depths as he struggled for breath. Her cries came to him with the dense clarity of sound under water. He lost his sense of time and place; this was the sim, was his dreams about the sim, was real, was false, was everything. His universe contracted to the hot slick alien shape moving in his mouth and the tidal surge of Tangaroa's body arching against him.

When she finally stopped, he was red-eyed and gasping. "On your knees," she said hoarsely. He turned and braced himself, cold with fear and rock-hard with unbearable hunger. Then it was pressed to his ass, slick and pulsing, and with a single relentless push it was buried in him to the hilt. It was so intense he could feel it in his palms and the soles of his feet. She started to move and the intensity unfolded into panic. He tried to fight her. He never had a chance. She was growling, a low, terrifying sound in the back of her throat, holding his waist in an iron grip and slamming her hips into him. Inside his ass she flexed and pulsed her phallus, pushing it deliberately into the root of his burning erection with every stroke, and he was losing himself, pulled beneath the surface, overwhelmed by sensation. The rhythm of her moving in him grew until it filled the entire world with need and pain. She pounded him down through layers of shame and hunger, terror and longing, into the cold silence of the deep water. He could not breathe. The pressure was killing him. His lungs were burning; his vision was going dark.

He took the pressure. He pressed back.

His throat unlocked and he said yes, he could see light again, he cried out yes into the face of his fear, he threw his head back and shouted YES and the orgasm hit with the merciless intensity of an electrical storm. He was at terminal velocity but he was falling up.

His ass clamping down pushed her over the edge. Her nails dug into his hips and her phallus seemed to swell to an impossible size, stretching him to the limit, and then she started slamming into him viciously, driving even harder against that perfect burning core of intensity inside him. He heard her cry out in release, joined by his own scream as each wave made his ass clamp down even harder on the suddenly huge thing impaling him. The spasms wracked them both, tossed them around like charged particles in an unstable field, then slammed them back into their bodies and left them shaking, drained, luminous.

Her weight crushed him against the mattress. He tried to speak; failed; realized that he didn't have words for this. Eyes squeezed shut, face pressed into the pillow beneath her, he listened to her breathing. She was making a tiny, hoarse noise each time she exhaled. Her pulse, beating slow and hard, echoed in his body.

That was the language he was looking for.

✳

Faber came up from sleep. She was awake, watching him. The question came out almost without his volition. "Before you went in the tanks. I have to know. Were you male?" He rode the edge of panic as he spoke.

"I should tell you I was, just to shake you up. But no. I was born XX."

"Then what are you doing in Bifrost?"

"You talk like this is a gender-separatist clade. Didn't you notice that the traffic under the city was mixed?"

"But everybody knows…"

"Do they? Tolerance is the foundation of Bifrost. I was born in Labrys clade. They threw me out. Bifrost let me in."

"I don't understand."

"You think Victrix is narrow?" She laughed. "In Labrys, wanting a penis was sick. Wanting to fuck men with it was unforgivable. They said I was rejecting womanhood in the ugliest way I could, and they wouldn't listen to me for a second. I was told that I could stay if I got a personality scrub. I left. I heard later that my mothers declared me dead."

Faber squeezed her hand. He could barely imagine it. She had survived the exile he had been fearing his entire adult life. "How old were you?"

"Sixteen. It was hell. But I got lucky. I went to Liberty. They fell all over themselves to help me, an individual wronged by an oppressive state. I finished school there and got my tankwork done. I did some contract work in Freeside, where I met a family from Bifrost. They treated me like I belonged. Even so, I didn't really trust the clade at first. In Labrys they believe gay men don't even see females as human. That's why they were so angry; they thought I wanted to be a gay man. But the more I saw of Bifrost, the more I realized that Labrys is as twisted as the patriarchies they hate. I finally understood that in this clade, I am a person before I am a set of desires, and those desires will never be considered a threat to the community unless they hurt someone. That's when I applied for citizenship."

There was life after the unthinkable… and her unthinkable had been so much worse than his could be. If his clade had told him at sixteen: psych mods or exile—he would have stayed, believing it was the only choice. "What will happen to me now?"

"You can run back to your clade. You can pretend this never happened. A memory wipe helps."

"No." He rolled towards her, buried his face in her breasts. "No."

"Shh. I know you won't do that." She held him close, speaking into his hair. "Remember what I'm boosted for. I can see where you're going. I've broken you for your clade. You won't go back. You don't belong in Bifrost... not yet. It will take you time to adapt, and right now the culture here would drive you crazy. But you will find a home, more than a home, in some sane community—Freeside, Liberty, maybe Starseed—where you won't be told that you are sick or evil."

"I'm drowning. This is too much." He shuddered in her arms.

"Faber, you were a misplaced line of code. A perfect line, but in the wrong app. I code. But people, not data," she said. "You won't drown." She rolled on top of him, taking him inside her for the first time, beginning to ride him up the face of a mounting wave. "You're learning to swim." And his body believed her, believed that he would make it to shore, that she was not the undertow pulling him out, but the tide carrying him home.

The lives of transgendered people are not all strutting about in sequins or leather. In fact, most of us live rather ordinary lives, where we have to cope with rent, utility bills, clogged toilets, pets that wet the carpets, shoveling snow, heartburn, and the common cold. This charming story manages to put a sexy, funny, warm twist on an ordinary slice of life.

Simon Sheppard is the author of Hotter Than Hell and Other Stories *(Alyson Books) and the co-editor, with M. Christian, of* Rough Stuff: Tales of Gay Men, Sex, and Power *and the upcoming* Rough Stuff 2. *His work has appeared in many editions of* Best Gay Erotica *and* Best American Erotica, *as well as over fifty other anthologies. Simon's syndicated column "Sex Talk" appears in queer newspapers and on the Web, and he's hard at work on his next book,* Kinkorama. *He lives, unsurprisingly enough, in San Francisco, and thanks D.H. for the inspiration.*

Pinkeye

Simon Sheppard

He looked in the mirror. His left eye was inflamed, past inflamed, gross. What had been white was now bright red, gelatinously swollen around a pale blue iris, the eyelid puffy, caked with crud. There was crap on his lashes, a discolored bag under his eye.

"Highly contagious," the doctor had said. "Some sort of virus," the doctor had said. "Nothing to do but wait." Oh shit. At least it didn't feel as bad as it looked. Small consolation.

Everyone he knew had had pinkeye at some time or other, mostly when they were kids. Which should have made him feel better but didn't. He felt like some lousy horror movie. Virus-laden tears rolled down his cheek, drying in crusty little streaks.

The telephone rang. Not rang, really. Beeped, chirped, burped out an electronic hiccup.

He blinked twice, redly, and went to answer it.

Buzzy's reedy voice was on the other end. "How are you, Ric?"

"Not so well, I'm afraid. Conjunctivitis."

"What's that?"

"Pinkeye."

"Oh, I had that when I was a kid."

"So how are you, Buzzy?"

"Horny."

Ric dabbed at his cheek with a wadded-up Kleenex. He knew what Buzzy was inviting him to do.

"Listen, Buzz, I'd love to, only my damn eye is a mess."

"I'm a big boy, Ric. I think I can handle it."

"You have no idea. It's a real bad case." It was. Even the doctor had been impressed.

"So I'll keep my eyes closed."

"It's real contagious."

"So wear a condom over your head." Buzzy had an answer for everything.

"Shut the fuck up. I'll be right over." Ric felt his cock beginning to swell. He hung up the phone and grabbed his jacket.

"Yuck. That is ugly." Buzzy made a funny kind of face.

"Listen, you asked for it. Kiss me." Buzzy did, deep and hard. Ric reached down and grabbed the short boy's ample butt, pressing Buzz's hips into his hard-on. The boy tried to wrap a leg around Ric's waist, but the balance wasn't right and the two of them tumbled, laughing, onto the bed.

"I'll try not to cry on you."

"Is that one those famous lies like 'I promise I won't come in your mouth'?"

Ric rolled onto Buzzy, clenching one arm around the boy's neck and rubbing his other hand over Buzz's bulging crotch, while the boy unbuttoned his jeans. Then Buzzy had Ric's hard dick out, playing with the long foreskin, pinching it over his dickhead.

"Doesn't that hurt?" Buzzy asked.

"Huh? No, it feels good."

"I mean your eye."

"Not really, surprisingly."

"And you can see okay?"

"Well enough to be able to still be able to tell that you're cute as shit. Especially with that new goatee of yours. Forget the eye. Let's get your shirt off."

The boy's torso was just slightly pudgy, his belly covered with dark hair. Ric rubbed his hand over Buzzy's flat pecs, down over the fur, heading south for the waist of Buzzy's sweatpants, pulling the pants down to the boy's thighs. Buzzy was showing basket through his Calvin Klein briefs. Ric grabbed the boy's wrists, pinning them to the bed, and started dry-humping.

Slightly breathless now, Buzzy said, "Glad you could come over."

"Not as glad as you're gonna be."

"When your dick is inside me?" Buzzy strained against Ric's grip, but not very hard. Not hard enough to escape.

"Yeah, when my big, fat dick is inside you."

Buzz smiled. "Wait, loosen up on my wrists. I want to get this out of the way first." He pulled one hand free, reached into his briefs, and pulled out the rubbery bulge that had padded his crotch, tossing it onto the bedside table.

Ric, still pinning one of Buzzy's wrists to the bed, shoved his free hand between the boy's thighs. The crinkle of pubic bush through the thin cloth. The lips of the boy's pussy. He used his middle finger to spread the lips while his thumb played with the... the clit.

"Mmm. You do that well."

"Beginner's luck."

"Nah," Buzzy said, "I bet you were a heterosexual in a former life."

"Yeah, well stranger things have happened. After all, you were a dyke. In this one."

"A leatherdyke, at that. And now I'm one-hundred-percent gay boy. Want me to suck your dick to prove it?"

"Why don't I go down on you for a change?" Ric couldn't quite believe he'd said it, but he had.

Buzzy was already tugging down his briefs. "Protection?"

"Yep. Call me consistent, but..."

Buzzy was on his back, legs spread, pussy wide open. "There's Saran Wrap in that drawer. You've got your choice of clear or festively colored."

"I'll take the clear. This is already too much fun."

When Ric had spread the plastic between Buzzy's legs, he said, "Be patient with me, boy. Never done this before, you know."

Half-taunting, half-inviting, Buzz said, "Well, you're never too old to learn. Get on down there."

"Honey, you are one pushy bottom."

"You should have seen me top my girlfriends when I was a big butch dyke."

"There are some things, maybe, that it's best not to know," Ric teased. "Or even to think about."

"Get down there before I find me a straight boyfriend."

"Straight guys like to eat pussy? That's not what I heard." Ric lowered his head between Buzz's hairy thighs. Sure, he'd finger-fucked that thing, cock-fucked that thing, but he'd never been so close to it, face-to-face. Contrary to fag myth, it wasn't scary at all, especially not when it was attached to a boy as cute as Buzzy. He stared at the pussy. And saw, reflected in the shiny plastic wrap, an eye staring back. His eye, swollen, red and wet. He blinked. Another virginity to lose. It didn't seem like such a big deal, though, not any more. *Thanks, Buzzy,* he thought, and stuck out his tongue. He licked tentatively at the pussy lips, then loosened the wrap so he could push his tongue in there a ways. It must have been more fun, he figured, in the days before safe sex. Buzzy was moaning, maybe for his benefit, but moaning in any case. Encouraged, Ric moved his mouth up to Buzzy's clit, tonguing it through the wrap while he stroked his own stiff dick.

"Oh fuck, that's good. Now suck at it," the boy said. Ric did. He got the slippery, swollen nub between his lips and gave it his best shot. Just like it was a tiny dick. Instinct. Apparently instinct worked. Buzz started bucking his hips and thrashing around like crazy. The excitement was contagious; Ric's cock began dripping with pre-come.

"Man, I want you inside me," the boy said.

Ric could have gone on eating Buzzy out, but *What the hell*, he figured, *I'll save it for another day.* He backed away from Buzzy's pussy and, struggling to his knees, reached for the rubber lying on the bedside table, right next to Buzzy's dick.

"Here, let me do that," Buzzy said. "It's one of the first tricks I learned when I became a gay man." He tore open the little foil packet, positioned the tip of the rubber over Ric's dickhead, and, leaning over, used his mouth to unroll the latex over the throbbing shaft. It was one of those make-safe-sex-fun gimmicks that Ric usually found rather silly, but every time Buzzy did it, it didn't seem silly at all. Ric pumped his latex-clad cock into the boy's slippery mouth, grabbing the back of Buzzy's head, skull-fucking him good.

"Sure you don't want me to come this way?" he asked.

Buzz's mouth was off him like a shot. The boy threw himself back on the bed. Threw his legs in the air. "Fuck me," he panted, a thin trickle of drool running down his cheek. "Fuck me good."

Ric reached for the lube, spread it all over his hard fuckshaft, then rubbed a palmful into Buzz's pussy. He leaned over the eager boy, pinned his wrists to the mattress again, and slid inside. Give or take a sphincter, it was pretty much what he was used to. *Tastes like chicken*, he thought, and chuckled.

"What's so funny?" Buzzy asked, but Ric just smiled and pumped, pulling out, teasing the swollen lips with his wet cockhead, then plunging back in again. Buzzy thrust his hips, straining to get all of Ric inside.

"Oh man, you sure are one hot fuck," the boy gasped, breaking free of Ric's grasp, reaching down for his clit. "Make me your boy, Ric. Make me your pussyboy."

Ric leaned down and stuck his tongue in Buzzy's mouth. Buzz frigged himself faster and faster, kissing Ric more desperately while Ric fucked away, until, mouth to mouth and dick in pussy, they both came, noisily, explosively, definitively.

When they'd caught their breath, Ric pulled out, and nuzzled his face against Buzzy's hairy belly, condomful of come draped lazily across one thigh. Ric directed a swollen, sidelong glance upwards to where, in a nod to gay whorehouse-decor sensibilities, Buzz had hung a mirror on the ceiling. It reflected back an image of the two of them, naked, improbably together.

"So am I?" Ric asked, stroking the scar on Buzzy's chest. When they'd first met, the scars had been the hardest thing for him to deal with, more difficult than what was below Buzzy's belt. He wasn't squeamish about them anymore, though; it was just another thing about the boy. "Am I really?"

"Are you what?"

"A hot fuck."

"I've given up lying," said Buzzy with a grin. "To myself, to every-body."

"And you didn't mind my eye?"

"Did I look like I minded?"

"No, but..."

"There's no problem so big you can't work around it."

Now it was Ric's turn to grin. "Well, I hope you don't come down with pinkeye."

"I'm sure I won't," Buzzy said.

And he never did.

Part of the reason why we transgenderfolk have always had an uneasy time in the gay and lesbian community is because those labels are based on people being clearly male or female, and those of us who switch back and forth keep screwing up the nice little boxes. How do you class the sexual preference of a couple in transition? This story explores the intricacies as how two halves of a couple learn to become different people in the same relationship.

M. Christian's stories can be seen in Best American Erotica, Best Gay Erotica, Best Lesbian Erotica, Best 2000 Mammoth Erotica, *and over 100 other books and magazines. He is also the editor of the anthologies* Guilty Pleasures, The Burning Pen, Rough Stuff *(with Simon Sheppard) and others. A collection of his gay men's erotica,* Dirty Words, *is out now from Alyson Books, and a collection of his lesbian erotica,* Speaking Parts, *will follow next year.*

Evolution

M. Christian

The First Year

Sundays were the best. Sundays when the sun rose hot early, when the hard rays came through their bedroom windows and turned the cool darkness to a golden sauna of light.

Rocky was always awake first. She wasn't one of those fragile sleepers, liable to shoot from dreams to consciousness at the tiniest sound, but she suspected that she never dropped into deep dreams at all. When night fell, and Willow curled into a tight ball next to her, Rocky had a feeling of floating just above the surface of the bed. It was as if sleep was just a thin gauze curtain between day and night, and not a clear cut to a dreamy landscape. Since sleep and not-sleep were so close, Rocky felt the sun's climb as a slow, methodical progression of warmth and light. She would lie in bed, letting the bath of morning creep slowly up her body, enjoying the building suspense of the day—especially Sundays.

Willow was the softer of the two, the one more bent towards poetry and trying to raise orchids in the backyard. She slept like she died and was reborn each morning. She snored gently as she slept, a fact that Rocky had never told her, enjoying the joke that this little, flower-like woman could produce such a harsh sound. Willow seemed to be able to sleep forever, snores sawing between her plush lips—so absorbed that occasionally Rocky felt a stab of jealousy, as if her lover was being unfaithful, having a dream relationship with which she could never compete.

Most of the time Rocky would let Willow start to emerge from the depths of her sleep before waking her. But Sundays were different, Sundays were the best. On Sundays when Willow's snores changed pitch and the room became a glimmering bathtub of light, Rocky would slowly kiss her girlfriend's neck and shoulders, her cheek, and even those plump lips, drawing Willow out of her dreams and into their special Sunday morning.

Rocky also liked Sunday mornings because Willow's deep sleep screened her from Rocky's transformation. Rocky had always been self-conscious about it. She wasn't really ashamed; it was just that when Willow's eyes (or anyone else's) watched her little dance from the everyday Rocky to the Rocky she'd rather be, it sort of ruined the illusion for her, as if someone had peeked behind the magician's curtain.

As Willow grunted and groaned her way out of her dreams, Rocky carefully rolled over and reached for the wicker basket under the nightstand. There, without looking, she wrapped a large hand around her favorite. She'd had many over the years, but they often failed her in one way or another. One had been an ugly color that just looked too… well, artificial. Some popped free at embarrassing times to fall with a sticky plop to the floor. It had taken some time, but she'd finally managed to find just the perfect thing, the ideal object to help her feel so much more comfortable. More herself.

Strapping it on, she curled up beside her lover, pressing her stocky body up against Willow's plump ass, the plastic toy slipping neatly between her lover's thighs. It just felt right, those kind of Sunday mornings; it felt good.

As always, Rocky had slept in her sports bra. It was easy to forget about that part of her body, bound and hidden behind the tight black fabric. Laying next to Willow, her cock pressing between her lover's thighs, Rocky felt still inside, free from the conflicts that always seemed to push or pull her all over her emotional landscape. Rocky was Rocky, firm and hard, comfortable with herself… himself.

"… morning…" Willow whispered, voice thick with sleep. Rocky, gently moving her plastic extension between Willow's thighs, moved up and leaned over until their lips brushed. Still kissing, lips touching ever so gently, tongues making quick, electric contacts, Willow dropped a hand down between her legs to feel the thrusting firmness that was the tip of the dildo. "Someone's horny this morning."

"…woke up next to you, didn't I?" Rocky countered, breaking the morning kiss to speak.

Willow could do nothing but moan softly as Rocky slipped a narrow, callused hand around her waist to cup one of her breasts, rubbing the nipple into hardness between her thumb and forefinger. Finally, after a few long heartbeats while they kissed, Willow said: "Yes, Sir."

"'Yes, Sir,'" Rocky quoted, nuzzling Willow's neck as her plastic dick slowly moved between her thighs. "You sure know how to be romantic."

Willow responded with a deep, long moan, and shifted herself so that Rocky's insistent dick moved closer to her quim. Her hand, which was still between her legs, relishing the tapping of Rocky's cock, pushed in to find the gently pulsing tip of her clit. There, there it was... and with a gentle tap, tap, tap, she rode one wave after another of tense excitement building up her spine. She paused just long enough to reach down again and feel the hard plastic head of her lover's cock. As her excitement grew, she pulled her lips away from Rocky to whisper: "You're the best girlfriend I've ever had... Sir."

The Second Year

The fuck was a long, lazy Sunday morning one. It had started slowly, with the sunlight warming the room, and had stayed with a comfortable rhythm as Rocky rode her from behind. His mastectomy was recent, bandages still wrapped around his chest, but the liberation was so fresh that despite the pain, he still gripped her tight, pushing his cock in and out of her.

Rocky's hand snaked around, gently grazing Willow's breasts, her nipples. Rocky gently tickled them the way Willow liked it, through her tight white bra. As he did it, and he felt the hard points of Willow's excitement, Rocky felt a bittersweet surge—an echo of the way he'd felt about his own nipples until the surgery. But it was a special day, a warm Sunday, and he hoped that Willow understood that the little touches were part of their play; he wasn't trying to draw attention to a sensitive part that Willow sometimes wished she didn't have.

The morning grew warmer, and Rocky pushed his cock in and out faster and faster with a steady escalation. Willow moaned more deeply with each thrust. "Thank you, Sir; thank you, Sir; thank you, Sir—" she began to mumble at the withdraw phase of each stroke. The respectful masculine address rang in Rocky's mind, settling him deeper into his comfortable self. It was a little gift, one that caused him to bend slightly and leave a sweet kiss on Willow's shoulder.

Increasing... Rocky's own excitement sent a shiver up from his old genitals, the ones he'd retained behind the dildo. He didn't know what a man would have felt, but this was good, and it propelled him to buck harder, slapping his thighs against Willow's plush ass, pushing harder, faster.

"Thank you, Sir; thank you—" a special mantra. No longer a game between them, but now a verification, a spell of summoning and strength.

Feeling Willow entering that panting quiet time that was close before a teeth-rattling come, Rocky backed off of his strokes, lowering Willow down from her orgasm. He kissed her on her shoulder, a lingering kiss he knew tickled and scratched from his recent, boyish beard.

Knowing what was happening, Willow turned her head to look at him. "Bastard," she said with humor. "You're a real bastard."

"You bring it out in me," Rocky said, kissing her cheek and tickling her again, still fucking her, but not as earnestly, more like a gentle rocking that a full-blown driving fuck.

"You're the best boyfriend I've ever had… Sir," Willow said, a gleaming tear starting to form at the corner of her eye.

The Third Year

Their rocking continued, the slow, methodical in and out between them. Outside, a morning rain had ceased; only the still, cool air remained after the pattering storm. It was trickier, but not impossible, between them. Plastic passing plastic: Rocky's sliding between Willow's, dildos grazing between their thighs.

Trickier, but still wonderful on a lazy, cool Sunday morning. At first it had created tension between them. But their love and desire had pushed the uncomfortable feelings aside; they worked it out. After all, it was just logistics. More than anything, they wanted, needed, to spend their Sunday mornings lazily fucking in their great big bed.

Rocky was still on top, more from experience than anything. He knew what his cock felt like, knew the right amount of in, the precise degree of out. He knew how to fuck, knew how to lay next to Willow and work his hips this way and that for the best effect. Willow was still just a boy; hadn't lived long enough as a man to know all the tricks, so he was at the receiving end.

"You're so handsome," Rocky said, his voice gravelly and deep. It still sounded a little strange to his ears; the wonder had yet to wear off. The movements between them were still new, so they tried not to think too much about what, exactly, was happening. For Rocky it was slightly easier: his cock was fucking, sliding in and out of his boyfriend, his handsome fag-boy. But when Willow thought about it a slight shiver of dissociation raced up his spine: fag boys don't have vaginas. Fortunately the pleasure of Rocky's fucking was too good, and the uncomfortable reminder of his cunt faded to simple pleasure. Then there was the grin he couldn't suppress with the wicked thought, "it's an asshole, it's an asshole, it's an asshole… or a helluva lot better than an asshole."

It was also harder because Willow's surgery was recent, the bandages still wrapped around his chest under a T-shirt. He had a new, deep voice, and hair in places he wasn't quite accustomed to yet, so Rocky was careful to support Willow's masculinity.

They needed those Sunday mornings. Those hot mornings when they'd been dykes, warm mornings when they'd been as close to straight man/woman sex as they'd ever been. Now this overcast-with-rain morning, when they were boyfriend and boyfriend. Yes, Willow needed to be one of the boys, needed to feel rough, gruff and hard—and Willow also needed Rocky.

It might now be an asshole, or it might be a reminder of Willow's original gender, but it was also a link between the two of them. Rocky and Willow, Willow and Rocky, fucking on a cool Sunday afternoon.

"Such a good boy," Rocky whispered in Willow's ear as his dick slid in and out of his cunt, a slow, steady fuck. "Such a sexy boy. So hard—" Rocky's hand reached down and gripped Willow's plastic erection "—so fucking hard. You like your dick, don't you, boy? You like to fuck and you like to get fucked, don't you? You like a nice hard dick up your tight, wet asshole. That's right, that's right: you love it, ache for it, starve for it. Well, that's what I'm here for, boy. I'm here to suck that dick, to fuck that dick, and to fuck you right up your tight… so tight… asshole."

In and out, slow to faster, but not fast yet. As he worked Willow's tight hole, Rocky kept up his steady, rough voice. His words were as rough as the thick beard that scratched Willow's cheek and neck. "Yeah, slut-boy, yeah; you want it, you want it bad. You crave dick, need dick. Well, slut-boy, my dick's balls-deep in you right now."

Faster, but still not fast enough. In and out, arms carefully wrapped around Willow's bandaged chest, Rocky held him and fucked him. "Such a slut-boy, such a tight, hot slut-boy. God, how I love to fuck you! Feel that? Feel my dick slide in and out of your hole? Isn't that great? Isn't that hot? Oh, yeah, it is—oh, yeah…"

Now, then, fast enough: in and out, in and out, quick but not frantic, Rocky fucked his boyfriend, slid his plastic dick in and out of his body. He heard it then: the quiet oasis he knew so well, the absence of sound that marked the coming thunder of Willow's come. He fucked him, fucked him hard and rhythmically as he passed through the eye and into a sudden storm of orgasm.

"Oh, yes, oh, yes, that's so good, isn't it, boy? That's it, that's it, let it out, scream for it, yell for it, slut-boy—roar it out!" Rocky grinned as he fucked his boyfriend, pushing him over the edge.

The bellow turned into a roar which rolled out into a near-shriek; Willow came hard and good and wild. It was good. It was so damned good. But what was the best wasn't the come, or the return to the special ritual of good Sunday mornings, but the few simple words that Rocky whispered into his ear: "You're the best boyfriend I've ever had."

"There's boy cock, and girl cock, and then there's magic cock!" a friend once said, and butches know it in their bones. Butches have always had a hard time of it, from the repressed fifties when they were shunned by society, to the politically correct seventies when they were shunned by their own women's and lesbian movements. It's especially hard being butch and having both your manhood and your womanhood validated at once. As this story proves, it takes a special kind of person to truly celebrate all the aspects that a butch possesses—and a powerful butch to inhabit them all with wit, lust, and grace.

S. Naomi Finkelstein, a.k.a. Max, spent the time since writing this piece six years ago "transitioning" from a bad boy feral street butch to a grown-up butch, almost tame but not quite. Max writes: "My work has been published in GCN, Bridges, Sinister Wisdom *and* Real Change, *and spend my time working with a popular education school (UrbanAction.org) doing economic literacy classes for poor women, sex workers and queer youth, finishing my paralegal degree and starting an indexing business as part of a micro-credit loan group. In between I visit the girl who lives too far away and write about the transgressions of desire and the making of 'home' in all its guises—endless sources of fascination for me."*

She'll Always Own A Piece of Me

S. Naomi Finkelstein, a.k.a. Max

I have memories of last winter without her imprinted in my bones, the time that I waited for the light to return, making do until I gathered the strength to go on. But she still has my cock.

I tried to get another. I did. I got a black silicone one, and a wooden one, made out of sustainably forested wood, of course, and turned to smoothness on a lathe. Then there's the lavender one and one that's squat and hot pink. There is an aluminum one, too, and one made of blown glass that is just beautiful. I keep that one on the coffee table as a conversation piece. I don't, as a general rule, use those pinkish "flesh" colored ones for the same reason I don't use that color Band-Aids. I mean, shit, who the hell wants white imperialism hiding in their pants?

I found a cool black and white one that's marbled, in a swirl pattern—it's pretty fly. It's slim, has a nice head, and it's ribbed along all eight inches. I liked that one. I even tried to pack with it but it just ain't the same. I feel like I can't get it up, ya know? So now I have this collection sitting on a lawyer's bookcase that I crafted with my own hands, all these dildos in a line above my law books, marching over the heads of labor law, immigration law, intellectual property, contracts. They all stand there, purple, beech, black and marbled. I have stands for them all. And I stare at them, yearning to have my cock back.

She says don't write, don't call. I hadn't planned to, I really don't want to. Except that she has my cock. I want it back.

But after all, she bought it. She said she got from a baby butch who was living on the edge, making a living by creating porcelain shafts, firing and glazing them for the queer nation. Apparently the kid goes from leather show to leather conference, Pride march to Pride march with these cocks in his backpack. A damn sight better than the job I had at his age, working for the UPS.

It was porcelain but it wasn't delicate, the cock she got from that butch kid. It was sturdy, long, wide and handsome, a real beauty. And though she bought it and it was technically hers, it became mine when I used inside her. Hollow inside, it stayed cool and its glazed surface easily became slick with her juices. It stretched her lipstick-covered mouth way wide when I fucked her with it, too.

She was a good cocksucker, gave real nice head. She sucked and strained over the girth and length of it. She liked me to fuck her until she gagged. She'd get a look in her eyes, climb down over my big body, over my large belly and to my cock, grabbing my asscrack for balance. I'd hold her head as I pumped into her, and she'd hold on. The need to jerk my hips was intense. I felt her lips on me, felt the warmth of her mouth, listened to her slurping and groans and gags as she sucked me off and I'd come that way, with that big, nasty cock of mine in her mouth.

Then she'd set back on her heels, eyes soft and submissive. Good thing that my cock stayed hard after I came. Shit, that's what makes butches such good lovers, our staying power. That and we know our girls' bodies like no man ever could. Good thing I stayed hard , cause she wasn't satisfied yet and that's when I'd slide my cock into her cunt, wet and ready. Mouth free, she'd say, "Daddy, it hurts."

"Then you'd better open for me because I want fuck you and whether you're open or not, I'm sliding my cock back as far as it needs to go," I'd growl.

"Please let the play with my clit," she'd beg, and of course I would let her. Playing at being a selfish brute is one thing, but it was pleasure—hers even more than my own—that we were after. And that cock was so smooth, so easy to slide in and out in, so big and hard, yes.

I'd always have to hold back just a bit so she could take it. I was used to being with other butches, wrestling and pushing and testing our strength against one another. She needed it softer, though still not all that soft. I rode that girl damn hard, using the same muscles I banged a hammer with all day long, the same muscles I used climbing scaffolding and carrying five-gallon buckets of joint compound up flights of tenement stairs when I did rehabs. I'd feel the inside of her cunt contracting around my cock and grit my teeth from the tightness. She'd arch herself to meet my thrusts and I'd bite on her nipples. "Daddy, oh Daddy!" she'd yell then.

"You are daddy's dirty little girl," I'd growl in her ear, "you like my big cock in you, don't you?" And I'd make her say she liked it or I'd stop until she begged me to begin again. I'd agree to go on but assured her that I would have to spank her for being such a bad girl. I'd pick up the pace as she told me how full she was, and her fingernails would dig into my shoulders as she whispered "stay still" and we would both hold position as she began to moan that she was coming.

You'd think that would be it, but my baby loved to come twice. The second time, she'd shoot. I began again as she teetered on the brink, pumping her up.

"Daddy, I am going to pee," she would cry, anxious, hopeful.

"If you pee the bed, Daddy will spank your bottom red," I would warn, reassuring her that I was going to force her to come again, give her exactly what she wanted.

"No, Daddy, no, please don't spank me, I have to pee!" she'd whimper, and with short sharp thrusts inside her my baby would come again, her come shooting further than mine ever could.

"Don't spank me, Daddy!" she'd beg. I'd smile my evil daddy grin. "If you don't want a spanking, you know you have to please daddy." She'd nod. So I'd continue. "Do you know what you have to do to please daddy?" She'd nod and begin.

She'd draw long fingernails down the side of my shaft, raising goose pimples all over my body. Then she'd close her hand around it, working it up and down. It stayed hard even as she turned me over to fuck my ass, stayed hard even as I'd tell her I'd spank her ass until it glowed red unless she rimmed my asshole and used her little girl hands to work my ass open. I'd feel her red, lipsticked lips touch themselves to my anus, her tongue going deep inside me, fucking me open, and I'd relax into an almost meditative state. Next came the lube.

Most times it was her long-fingernailed hand encased in a glove, stretching me until I broke out into a sweat, but sometimes it was another cock, not one she ever wore, but one she knew how to use well, just the same. She'd push inside me, saying, "Daddy, I am such a dirty little girl… I like playing with your asshole." That girl definitely knew how to fuck her Daddy, and daddy would come and come that way, his nasty girl inside of him.

Afterwards I'd spank her anyway (evil Daddies don't keep the deals they make, you see) just because I loved to see her gorgeous fat ass shake in front of me, my belt landing again and again on her rump, making her red and swollen and hot. "Please, Daddy," she'd plead, "please, you're hurting me," but I'd keep swinging because I loved to hurt her so. My cock was hard even then, especially then, as I told her to push her rump out to me to show how obedient she was. And she would, holding herself open as I spanked her cunt and the inside of her butt crack, holding herself for the touch of my belt under the cheeks of her ass. My cock stayed hard as I punished her for how much I needed her hand in my ass. I'd punish her because punishing her made me hard with want all over again. And I would enter her again and lay down next to her, her crimson, sizzling bottom against my fat gut. We'd lay there, joined by that cock of mine inside her. And for days it'd be hard for her to sit, hard to keep from squirming around as she sat in her power femme outfits doing her professional job, well fucked and well punished by a working stiff bad boy with a hard cock she'd do anything to get inside her.

She didn't give back the thick silver anklet I had my friend, a silversmith, make for her. I traded nearly two damn weeks of painting—three coats a room, semi-gloss on the trim, plus installing cedar shelves—for it. "Wear it and be mine." I had offered. At the end when she no longer wanted me and I no longer wanted her she had spit at me, saying she was glad to give me back the damned thing, but she never did. She often said things she didn't mean. Things like "I love you" and "We'll be family always, no matter what, I promise." Things that wounded me more than the anklet ever could. You'd have thought I'd've known when she was bullshitting me by then. But I waited for that anklet. Three months later, at Rosh Hashanah, I threw my need for her and for that anklet into the Hudson River along with all my other sins, all the ways I had missed the mark. I'd have to end being her top without the anklet, have to grieve being her bottom differently. I'd have to mend the wounds of her broken promises for a long time.

Ah, but that cock. My cock, so handsome and strong, black with lightning streaks all over it, made by an edgy butch. For a while the only thing I could do to please the womyn I loved, but whom I myself could not seem to make happy, was to use that cock well.

You see, I never felt before that in order to be a butch I needed a femme. Not when I did karate or construction, not when I was a bouncer at a bar or when I put on leather or a tie, not when I shaved or when I walked down the damn street. Not ever. I knew my own strength, counted on it. But no womyn I have ever been with before, not in the nearly twenty years I have been a queer, not even the womyn I have bent over and opened my ass for or been tied up and whipped by, had ever seen me so vulnerable as she had, standing there naked with my cock on. And though she was careless with so much else of my heart, she held that piece of me as sacred. She gave life to a part of me by witnessing it and believing in it like so many other femmes have done for so many butches. It is a shaman's dance we do.

Before her I had never told anyone before that as a kid I knew I was a girl but believed that I would grow up to be a man, that I knew it like I knew winter followed fall. I never told any of my dyke friends that I had, in fact, grown up to be a man. No womyn had ever seen through so clearly to the boy that was me.

No womyn had ever acknowledged that I had a cock and that my cock was a part of me as my breasts were a part of me. No womyn ever needed my cock as fiercely as she did. Her fierce want was her magic and it still holds a spell over me.

She'll always own a piece of me. I think I'll try the wooden one again, but it's just not the same.

Do you see? It won't ever be the same.

Oh, come on, doesn't part of you thrill to the idea of kneeling at the feet of a six-and-a-half-feet-in-high-heels goddess who doesn't care what pointy-haired boss you have to report to at your weenie job? "I'm sorry, Boss, I just can't make it in today, I'm all tied up taking care of a sick friend—ow!" Hell, it makes us want to take an office job just for a week so that we can brag about getting fired for it. Fortunately you won't have to—just read and enjoy.

Dominic Santi is a former technical editor turned rogue whose erotic fiction is available in Best Gay Erotica 2000, Best Bisexual Erotica, Friction 2-4, The Mammoth Book of Historical Erotica, Penthouse Variations, *and dozens of other smutty anthologies and magazines. Santi recently edited (with Debra Hyde) the sex and politics anthology* Strange Bedfellows.

The Audit

Dominic Santi

It's not easy being an auditor. Everyone hates the IRS. Even I hate the IRS, and I work here. But I especially hate my boss. Lyle L. Lipton. He's one of those idiot managers whose "subordinates" send his memos to the guys who write comic strips.

L-cubed was still ticked at me for winning the Superbowl pool the week after I transferred in from Omaha. That, along with what he sarcastically referred to as my "impeccable performance record," put me on top of his shit list. So, when the decision was made to audit The Lady again, I suppose I shouldn't have been surprised when old Lyle made a bee-line for my desk. I looked up to see him smiling down with payback in his eyes and a large expand-a-file manila folder in his hands: Gerald Randolph St. Michaels, III. He dropped his present on my desk, said, "Tuesday, 10:00," and sashayed back into his glass-walled domain.

I felt the blood drain from my face. Gerald Randolph St. Michaels, III. I'd heard the stories. He, or rather, she was officially self-employed as an escort service. I'd even seen her business cards:

Mistress Sheila, Dominatrix
Accepting both experienced and novice submissives.
Will train to suit.

She was the most beautiful drag queen in all New Charleston. And her reputation, well, let's just say it preceded her. Even a newbie like me knew that our entire department quaked in their boots at the sound of

Mistress Sheila's name. No one had ever audited her more than once. The veterans either came back to the office terrified, or they disqualified themselves from future audits because of what they called "conflict of interest." I wasn't sure what that meant around here. I didn't think I wanted to know. I opened the file and started to read, wondering in the back of my mind if I could go into business with my brother, grooming cats—in spite of how the stupid furballs make me sneeze.

Tuesday morning came all too soon. I was nervous about meeting Mistress Sheila, but I'd been pretty surprised by her file. Everything seemed in order—straightforward, no previous penalties. There was nothing to indicate why they'd audited her every one of the past 15 years. I had the feeling that fact alone wasn't going to predispose her to liking me.

I wore my usual gray flannel power suit, though, this time, I added my Looney Tunes silk tie. Maybe not in the best of taste from old Lyle's perspective, but I already had an inkling that the audit was going to go in Mistress Sheila's favor. I figured I'd at least try to take the edge off of what had probably become a major annoyance for the lady.

Her home was a large Tudor mansion, set well back from the road on a walled, wooded property. My Honda Accord looked totally out of place. This was a driveway meant for Rolls Royces and limousines, both of which would have been well within the means of her reported income if she'd decided to have them. I parked at the end of the white gravel drive at 9:55 and let the smell of roses waft in through the open window while I admired the intricate stonework on the main building.

At exactly 10:00 am, I squared my shoulders, walked up the path to the carved mahogany door, and rapped on the brass knocker. Then I stepped back and waited for a servant to answer.

Mistress Sheila opened the door herself. She caught me completely off guard. Not that I'm interested in chicks, but this man was the most beautiful lady I'd ever seen. Her wavy brown hair cascaded over her shoulders. Her full red lips looked naturally soft and wet. She was wearing a red leather mini-skirt—smooth and flat and rounded in what I assumed were all the right places for a woman. Her black silk blouse showed real cleavage where the curves of her skin disappeared into the rise and fall of the tight red vest. The supple lambskin seemed to breathe with her. Even the jeweled collar that covered her Adam's apple was made of the same flowing red leather. I squirmed, shocked to feel my dick jump when she swallowed.

It was a total mind fuck. Visually, my mind was recording her as female. But her scent was very masculine, like when you kiss a lover's balls in the shower and he still smells and tastes like himself, even over the scents of the soap and shampoo and the water on his skin.

Apparently, my confusion showed in my face. Her lips framed the ghost of a smile. I looked into her velvety brown eyes, and I completely forgot everything I'd been going to say. I just stared at her, completely smitten.

It took me a minute to realize I was being rude. I shook my head and stammered out, "Ah, Mr. G-Gerald Randolph S-St. Michaels? The Third?"

One perfectly sculpted eyebrow shot up, but she just stood there, calmly resting her fingers on the ornate doorknob, watching me while I wiped my hand on my pant leg. She glanced down and I blushed as I realized she was looking at my tie. Her lipstick shimmered, like she was trying not to smile.

I licked my lips and tried again. "Excuse me, um, Mr. St. Michaels?"

This time the eyebrow flicked up a bit more sharply. Her fingernail tapped on the doorknob, but right about then I figured out what I was doing wrong. The sweat trickled down the back of my neck. I cleared my throat and said, as politely and courteously as I possibly could, "Excuse me. Mistress Sheila, Ma'am? I'm Albert Smith, from the IRS."

I was rewarded with a smile.

"Good morning, Mr. Smith."

Her low, husky voice reverberated against my ears. My whole body relaxed in relief. She held out her hand to me. Without thinking, I lifted the delicate offering to my lips and kissed the smooth white skin. "Pleased to meet you, Ma'am."

This time, the smile went all the way to her eyes. "I'm very pleased to meet you, young man. Come inside." With that, her grip tightened, and she pulled me gently but very firmly out of the warm sunshine and into the cool shadows of her house.

Mistress Sheila was considerably taller than I. She would have been, I realized, even without the three inch heels on her black leather boots. I tried to convince myself that her height was the reason I kept looking at her legs. And why my cock was swelling. I liked tall men. I liked the way her silk stockings curved into her knee-length boots. I especially liked how her long brown curls reached almost to where the soft red lambskin clung to her lean, narrow hips.

And I liked my job, or at least my paycheck. I concentrated on being professional, getting myself pretty much back under control while we walked. My nose still twitched as we entered her study. The room smelled of warm leather and books. I appreciate good taste, and Mistress Sheila's private domain was exquisitely appointed. I had no doubt the Picasso over the desk was authentic.

"Would you like something to drink, Mr. Smith?"

Two crystal goblets rested on the conference table. Mistress Sheila took one and motioned me to take the other. Needless to say, that's not the way I'm accustomed to being treated during an audit. I lifted the

glass to my lips. It was raspberry lemonade, my all-time favorite drink.
I tried not to gulp as I drained my glass.

"Thank you, Ma'am," I said, setting my goblet back down. "That
was delicious."

The sweet-sour taste lingered on my tongue. Trying not to think
about sex always makes me thirsty. When I licked my lips, Mistress
Sheila laughed and waved me towards a small serving cart near the
window.

"Help yourself, Mr. Smith. We have a great deal of work to do, and
I'd prefer that you be comfortable."

I hurriedly poured myself another drink. As I was setting the pitch-
er back down, I looked at her glass and noticed it was only half full.
My hand froze in mid-air.

"May I refill your glass for you, Ma'am?" I asked politely.

Mistress seemed immensely pleased with my request. Nodding ever
so slightly, she held out her glass to me. Her red nails curved sensu-
ously around the crystal. I was surprised to see my hand shaking as I
poured the pulpy pink liquid into the sparkling glass. Then her warm
strong fingers closed firmly around mine. Her touch was electric.

"Sit down, Mr. Smith, and take off your jacket. It's going to be a
long day."

The audit was over at 1:00. It was apparent right from the start who
was running the proceedings, and Mistress Sheila is very efficient. I
said, "Yes, Ma'am," and "No, Ma'am," handing her the appropriate
receipts and records when she demanded them. Not that some of the
deductions weren't a bit out of the ordinary: whips, vibrators, leather
restraints. But the supporting paperwork couldn't have been more perfect if somebody from my office had prepared her statements for her.

I was careful to put everything back in the order I found it. In fact,
I only made one mistake. Everything was going so smoothly that as the
sun moved across the table around noontime, I started getting sleepy.

"Mr. Smith!" Mistress Sheila's voice cracked through the quiet of
the study.

"Ma'am?" I jolted upright, confused and suddenly very awake.
Mistress Sheila picked up her little wooden ruler and pointed to where
I had accidentally put an envelope on the wrong pile. I immediately
realized my mistake.

"I'm sorry, Ma'am." I moved the offending item back into its proper place.

"As well you should be," she snapped. "Give me your hand."

Without thinking, I did. She took my wrist. The next thing I knew,
I was yelping as she stung my palm a half dozen times with her ruler.
Then Mistress lectured me sternly for a good five minutes about the
importance of keeping accurate records. Usually I'm the one giving

that speech during an audit. This time I sat there, opening and closing
my burning hand and nodding profusely while I promised not to make
the same mistake again. I was mortified—more at my unprofessional
behavior than at what she'd done. After that, I paid close attention to
what I was doing. And I kept her glass filled with raspberry lemonade.

I also found myself watching her a lot out of the corner of my eye.
Mistress Sheila fascinated me. As the sting faded from my hand, I realized my fingers were itching to touch her hair. I could feel myself sliding into a fantasy as I thought about brushing those silken strands into
a thick curl and running that curl slowly over her cleavage....

I shook myself awake. Yeah, right—me and cleavage. That was certainly enough to wake me up! I put my pen down and leaned way back
into the comfortable leather of my chair.

"I don't understand, Ma'am." I stretched my arms high over my
head. "With everything in order like this, why do they audit you every
year?"

Her laughter was followed by a wry grin. I sheepishly lowered my
arms, watching the leather band move across her throat again.

"You seem a bright young man, Mr. Smith. Perhaps if you recon-
sider my profession, you'll be able to figure it out."

Of course by then, I had. "I'm sorry, Ma'am," I blushed. "I forgot."

"Oh, did you?" This time the laughter was different, full-throated,
but huskier—definitely a man's laugh. I felt my balls tingle at it. And
of course I was blushing again.

But before I could stammer out any kind of a reply, an elderly man
in a black suit walked through the open door and announced that
luncheon would be served in 45 minutes.

I sat up quickly and started gathering papers. "I should be going,
Ma'am. Thank you so much for your time. I apologize on behalf of the
IRS for any inconvenience this audit may have caused you."

"I'm inviting you to stay for lunch, Mr. Smith." Her statement was
more along the line of a command. I stared at her in surprise. Nobody
invites an auditor to lunch!

"I, ah, really shouldn't, Ma'am." I was trying to bring order to my
now rather sizeable mess, but through the open door I suddenly
smelled Italian spices and some sort of garlic sauce cooking. My stomach growled loudly. I flushed to my hairline.

Mistress Sheila laughed again. My cock twitched against my underwear, and this time, it kept swelling. I was getting so hard I was going
to have to resituate myself, soon, and I didn't want to do that in her
presence. I was sure she'd notice—and most assuredly take offense. It
was a losing battle.

"But you are hungry." Her voice slid over my ear. My stomach
growled again, this time more loudly.

I opened my mouth, thinking I should insist on going. Then I
looked into her eyes. They were twinkling, the warm brown sparkle

sending a shiver crawling all the way up my spine. All I could do was let my papers fall to the table as I gave up on trying to control both my stomach and my errant cock.

"Yes, Ma'am." I smiled helplessly back at her.

She nodded. I felt like I was basking in her warmth. I jumped when she turned abruptly to the servant and said, "Leave us, Charles. Close the door behind you."

As soon as I accepted Mistress Sheila's invitation, Charles broke into a wide grin. As the door clicked shut, I found out why. Mistress looked me up and down once, quickly. Then she snapped, "Stand up, Mr. Smith. Now!"

Surprised, I stumbled to my feet, tripping on the table leg in my hurry. Her hand moved to her lips, like she was trying to hide a smile again, but I was so embarrassed I couldn't tell for sure. When I'd righted myself, she walked over to stand in back of me. She put her hand firmly on my shoulder, purring right in my ear, "I like a man who responds quickly."

I hoped she couldn't see how quickly the rest of me was responding. Her voice felt like it was sliding over my skin, pulling the blood straight down from my brain. I tried to move my hands surreptitiously in front of my crotch, so she wouldn't see how hard I was getting. I gasped as she dragged one of her long, sharp fingernails slowly and decisively over the curve of my butt. I knew right then I was going to have to untangle my cock or do real damage to myself. I just don't bend that way.

"Um, Ma'am." I tried to keep my voice steady. "I need to excuse myself for a minute…"

My breath caught when her hand gripped my butt cheek. "No, Mr. Smith, you don't. You will take your clothes off right here."

I jumped as she smacked me, hard, connecting full on my butt just before her palm started rubbing away the sting.

"Ma'am?" I tried to turn back towards her, shocked. My backside more tingled than hurt, although my cock certainly didn't have any complaints about the stimulation.

The next swat wasn't so gentle. "You heard me, Mr. Smith. Everything but your underwear. Off!" *Smack!* "Now!"

The last one really stung. I didn't wait around to think any more. I said, "Yes, Ma'am!" as I yanked my tie loose and over my head. Then I stripped off my shoes and socks and shirt, and undid my belt and the front of trousers. As my pants dropped, I reached into my shorts and untangled my poor cock from where it was caught in my fly. The sudden freedom was such a relief that for a second, I closed my eyes, rubbing myself. Then my eyes flew open and I looked up, mortified, to realize I was standing in front of Mistress Sheila, wearing only my boxers, holding my cock in my hand.

"Excuse me, Ma'am…" I choked, trying to step out of my pants without tripping. I was so embarrassed I could feel the heat flushing across my face.

Before I could stammer out an apology, though, Mistress Sheila started to laugh. In fact, she was laughing so hard she put her hand to the corner of her eye to keep her mascara from running. And as I followed her gaze, I remembered what else I was wearing.

"Looney Tunes, Mr. Smith?" she gasped. "You are wearing Looney Tunes boxers to an IRS audit?" She leaned against the table, laughing so hard I was afraid she was going to choke.

"Yes, Ma'am," I said sheepishly, trying not to blush or smile and failing miserably at both. Unfortunately, neither reaction was making my cock one iota less hard. "It sort of goes with my job, Ma'am. I didn't think anybody would see them, and I like the way they let me breathe and all."

"I see," she said, carefully wiping the tears from the edges of her eyes. She took a deep breath and reached over to cup the front of my crotch. "You do have quite a handful here to let breathe."

"Oh, Ma'am…" I moaned, leaning into her touch. I was already leaking so badly the silk felt cool on my hot skin. Odd little mewls escaped from my throat as her fingers squeezed and stroked my cock and balls. She looked like a lady, but the strength and the touch of her hands were all man. I shivered when she pressed another drop from the head of my dick and into what I knew was the general vicinity of Bugs Bunny's fur.

"You understand, Mr. Smith, that before we do anything else, we must first take care of the little matter of my displeasure with your employer, whom you represent."

"Yes, Ma'am," I whispered. I wasn't paying much attention to what she said. Her hands were caressing me, her long nails snaking up the open leg of my boxers to scratch delicately over my balls, her fingers reaching through my tenting fly to tickle up the underside of my shaft. My cock jumped at her touch, leaking as she teased the precome from me.

She led me, unresisting, over to the straight-backed chair near the bookcase. With her free hand, she pulled the chair away well from the wall. Then she sat down and drew me to her side. Her hands were stroking me again, one hand rubbing over my tingly bottom, the other open palm moving in large sweeps up and down my crotch. The sounds coming from my throat got louder with each stroke.

"You understand that your employer has taken up a good deal of my valuable time."

"Yes, Ma'am." I arched forward into her hands. Without thinking, I reached out for balance and rested my hand on her luxurious hair. It was silky soft. She shivered as my fingers caressed her scalp.

"You're a very polite young man, Mr. Smith."

Her voice vibrated in my spine. It was difficult to think with her hands touching me.

"Thank you, Ma'am," I whispered.

"You understand that I shall be taking you to task for the actions of your not-so-nice employer."

"Yes, Ma'am. Whatever you say."

I had no idea what she was talking about. All I noticed were her hands and her hair, and the smell of her perfume and the mansweat in her leather clothes. My balls tingled so much I could almost feel the sperm wiggling their way towards my dick.

With no warning, she tipped me over her lap. One second I was standing at her side, the next I was hanging face down over her knees, my cock pressed firmly into her thigh, my bottom up in the air, and Mistress Sheila's hand resting firmly on my cartoon-clad posterior. Her hand smacked sharply over my right cheek.

"Ouch!" I lurched up in surprise.

She rubbed her hand firmly over the tingle. "Pay attention, Mr. Smith."

"Yes, Ma'am!" I nodded vigorously. I was trying to concentrate on what she was saying. But in spite of my precarious position, I was totally distracted by the friction of my cock rubbing against her leg.

"For the past fifteen years, your employer has wasted my time with these ridiculous audits. A minimum of three hours every year for fifteen years! That's a total of at least forty-five hours of my valuable time!" She emphasized her displeasure with another sharp smack. "Do you understand that, Mr. Smith?"

"Ow! Yes, Ma'am!"

That firm hand was starting to worry me. I could still feel the sting from the last couple of swats, although my cock was telling me rather loudly not to pay attention. But Mistress definitely sounded annoyed. I wiggled my pelvis against her skirt, sighing as the dampness of my boxers warmed against my skin.

"Fifteen years, Mr. Smith," she said again, although this time I thought I detected a bit of humor in her voice. "And this year, they send me a polite young man with a Looney Tunes tie and boxers." She smacked me again, not terribly hard, but enough to emphasize her point.

Then her hand rubbed over my bottom. "Mr. Smith," her voice held the husky sex of her amusement, "because you are such a likeable young man, I will give you a choice. You may either remain over my lap and let me exact my standard retribution from your department—in this instance, forty-five sound smacks from my hairbrush, during which time I will also attend most properly to that excited young cock of yours. Or you may leave—immediately—and never return. The decision is yours."

"Ma'am?" I asked, lifting my weight up onto my hands. I couldn't quite believe my ears. "You want to spank me?!" Nobody had ever really spanked me before, not even my parents.

"Yes, Mr. Smith," she laughed. "I intend to spank your round little bottom until it positively glows."

The idea made my cock twitch, but I was still a little concerned. Her earlier swats had stung, and forty-five seemed like an awful lot. "Or I have to leave?" I asked.

"Yes, Mr. Smith, unfortunately with that beautiful young cock of yours still unsatisfied and drooling into your now very wet boxers."

I blushed at that. I really leak when I'm turned on, though I wasn't sure I'd ever been this hot before in my life. Her hand was rubbing the sensitive crease where my butt met my thighs. I pressed my hips forward, wriggling my cock against her.

"But I don't want to leave, Ma'am." I whispered. Nervous or not, I knew I was horny.

"Then you are willing to take the correction for your department?" Her fingers gripped my buttcheeks firmly, emphasizing just exactly where that correction would be administered.

"Um, I guess so," I whispered, arching my butt back into her hand, feeling my cock slide back over her skirt.

Her hand stilled. "Yes or no, Mr. Smith." She swatted me again, this time sternly enough to get my attention. "A spanking from me is serious business. You either consent or you do not."

For a minute, I hesitated. Out of the corner of my eye, I could see the hairbrush resting on the edge of the bookcase. The brush was dark—cherrywood, maybe—and highly polished with a long handle. The oval-shaped business end looked thick and sturdy enough to be pretty intimidating. In spite of what my dick was telling me, for a moment, I seriously thought of leaving. After all, it was still working hours. I was a professional.

That's when I realized I wanted to please Mistress Sheila—and myself—not old Lyle-cubed. I didn't care if I got fired. Summoning all my courage, I squared my shoulders as much as I could upside-down and said, "I, um, consent, Ma'am."

I took a deep breath, letting myself sag forward across her lap. I was surprised to discover I was more than a little bit scared. I leaned my face against her leather-clad ankle. Her hand rubbed over my bottom, teasing me until my skin seemed to reach back for her hand. Then I felt the hard wooden surface of the hair brush rubbing against the warm silk of my boxers. I shivered.

"Count them, Mr. Smith. In groups of fifteen." Her voice was deep and reassuring.

"Yes, Ma'am." At the first smack, I jerked up, startled. "Ouch!"

That stung! But after a minute, I realized the swat had made my skin tingle more than hurt. I figured that meant the spanking wasn't going to be all that bad.

"One," I said, relieved, and lay back down over her lap.

By fifteen, it was hard to stay cooperative. I tried, I really did. But I was glad that her other hand was planted firmly in the small of my back, holding me down. I fought to hold back the tears. My bottom hurt so badly it burned! And for some embarrassing reason, my cock was harder than ever.

She stopped and started playing with my stinging cheeks, rubbing and touching. After the pain of the spanking, her hands felt good. When I'd caught my breath, she stood me back up. The front of my boxers tented out in front of me.

Then she did the most amazing thing. She pressed the brush into my hand and said, "My hair, Mr. Smith. It needs attention."

I'd been lusting after her hair since I walked in the door. I couldn't believe she was giving me permission to touch it now. Very tentatively, I stepped in back of her and ran my hands over the glistening silky waves. They were so very feminine, soft and warm from the afternoon sun. I could smell the lingering rosemary of her shampoo. Yet as the faint dampness of her perspiration touched my fingertips, I caught a hint of something else—something that reminded me of the heavy scent of clean men playing basketball on a hot day. I picked up the brush and started pulling it in long gliding strokes through the luxurious fall of her hair. With each stroke I started at her scalp and ended with the soft tips curled around my fingers, working the sweaty male scent out from the roots to blend with the fragrance of the rosemary.

We stayed like that for a long time, the grandfather clock ticking by the window. My bottom was sore and hot, the damp silk cool where the precome wetness pressed against my throbbing cock. Just touching Mistress Sheila made me so hard my balls ached, yet at the same time, I didn't ever want to stop. After a while, she reached up and gently yet firmly rubbing her thumbs against the insides of my wrists.

"That was exquisite, Mr. Smith," she said huskily.

She held out her hand. Without saying a word, I placed the handle of the hairbrush in her palm. I shivered as I did it. My bottom was really sore, and I knew if I just held onto that brush, she wouldn't be able to spank me again. But I didn't have the will to resist her.

She motioned me to her side. I jumped when her fingernail slowly scratched over the back of my shorts.

"Take them off, Mr. Smith. They're only getting in the way."

In spite of my trembling, my hands seemed to move on their own. I pulled my cock back from where the head had slipped through the fly and slid the damp silk over my hips. Then I stood naked in front of her, the afternoon breeze cooling my naked, burning buttcheeks.

"I'm sorry, Ma'am." I blushed, looking down at my cock. It jutted out at full mast.

"For what?" she laughed. Another pearl of precome seeped out of my slit in response to her voice. "Young man, this," my cock jumped at her touch, "is behaving exactly as it should. As are you."

I felt the frisson all the way up my spine. She used just the tip of her finger to smear the viscous fluid over my glans and down the shaft. Then, at the gentle tug of her hand, I was again lying over her lap. I moaned out loud, beyond embarrassment as my cock slid over the soft leather of her skirt. I barely felt her arm wrap around my waist.

The hairbrush smacked down hard on my left cheek. I yelped, my eyes flying open as I arched into her. The sting was a lot more intense on my bare skin, and she was spanking me much harder.

"Count, Mr. Smith," she said firmly.

"Sixteen," I groaned, shuddering at the rush of sensation where the swat had pressed me harder against her thigh.

Then she really started tanning me. I mean Mistress Sheila set my whole ass on fire. Each time she cracked that damn brush over my butt, my cock surged forward over her leather-clad thigh, getting hotter and fuller and so engorged I thought I'd burst. By the time she reached thirty I was yelling and crying from the pain, and the only other thing registering in my brain was that one more stroke and I was going to come all over her leg.

The next thing I knew, she'd pushed me off her lap. I lay on the floor at her feet, trying to keep my poor sore butt from touching anything. She set the brush on the bookcase. Looking directly at me, she put her boot in my hand and said, "My feet, Mr. Smith. Attend to them."

My vision blurred with tears, I pulled off her boots and rolled down her silk stockings. With her leg lifted that close to my face, I could really smell her crotch. Her leather skirt held in the heavy aroma of her cock and balls. I can't begin to describe the affect that her strong male pheromones were having on my poor leaking cock. I massaged her feet, letting all my energies flow into each deep caress as I pressed the tension from her straining arches. I soothed my way up her smooth ankles and over the strong ligaments and tendons of her calves, then back down, milking each individual toe. Every so often she touched a polished toenail to my shaft and stroked. I closed my eyes at her touch, shivering as the precome oozed from my slit. It was exquisite.

The next thing I knew, she was drawing me back up to kneel beside her. She picked up the brush. Ignoring my incoherent cries, she carefully and deliberately scrubbed the bristles over my blazing tender skin. I was still sniffling when she lifted the brush away.

"My lap, Mr. Smith." Her voice was quiet and firm.

It took me a minute to comply. I knew Mistress had said she'd take care of my cock, but my backside was burning so badly I really didn't know if I'd be able to hold myself still for the final 15. When she saw my hesitation, Mistress held out her hand to me. It seemed like I was watching myself in slow motion as I let her strong arm pull me back over that soft smooth leather and her hard, muscular thighs. She grabbed me firmly by my cock and balls.

"You needn't count the final fifteen, Mr. Smith. I very much doubt that you would be able to anyway."

"Yes, Ma'am," I whispered. "OW!"

The first smack was pure fire. Then Mistress Sheila rained molten flame on my butt. I cried and hollered, twisting and kicking my legs, straining to get away from the incredible pain. My ass hurt more than I could ever have believed possible. I tried to concentrate on just breathing, but even the air coming into my lungs felt hot. Every exhale came out as a yell. With each swat, Mistress spanked me so hard I felt the heat all the way through to my balls.

And with each searing crack of that hairbrush, she stroked my cock. I love the feel of a man's hand bringing me to orgasm. Mistress seemed to know just how to time her movements. I almost choked on my tears as her strong hand drew the boiling juices up into my shaft. I was beyond being able to control myself. As her husky voice purred "Forty-five," the final flame seared across my ass. I shot all over her leg. Even after she stopped spanking me, I kept rocking back and forth into her hand and the leather, sliding on my sweat and my come, my cock jerking like it would never stop.

At Mistress' direction, I didn't put my underwear back on when I dressed for lunch. I gingerly settled my poor blistered behind onto the hard wooden chair and fidgeted my way through three helpings of angel hair pasta and marinara sauce. I even had dessert—homemade spumoni ice cream so sweet and creamy that I only thought for a second about how nice it would feel on my scalded backside.

Over coffee, Mistress explained about L-cubed and his campaign of audits. They'd had a run in a while back, 15 years ago, to be exact, when she'd refused to take on ol' Lyle as a client. So he'd set out to get his revenge. Even I had to smirk at that. He'd sure shown her who was boss!

Mistress Sheila said she knows she'll be audited again next year. My inability to sit still at work tomorrow will be duly noted. The wrath of Lyle L. Lipton will carry over into year 16, and I'll still be at the top of his shit list. However, I won't be doing the next audit. Since Mistress Sheila and I will be seeing each other rather frequently from now on, it would be a conflict of interest.

Ever have the feeling that somehow, somewhere, the earth must've slipped a degree on its axis? One of those days when things just aren't quite right... they're strange, revealing, mysterious, but you can't quite put your finger on it, the leaves on the trees seeming to be at a slightly odd, almost imperceptibly weird, angle to the ground? Todd Belton has, and in this story, takes us through exactly that kind of change in the lives of a pair of lovers, a metamorphosis which leaves them both irrevocably changed. Whose transformation is more remarkable? We'll leave that decision up to you.

Todd Belton is a writer by avocation and a hacker by necessity. He lives and writes in the wilds of Greater Boston, and comments on sex and gender news regularly at www.mouthorgan.com.

Doppler

Todd Belton

The irony is that we met at all.

I consider this proof of disaster. Proof that the ending was inevitable. After all, it was never supposed to—no, no, I can't say that. It was supposed to happen, that's why it was such an oddity. It went the way it went because that was the only way it could go.

I hate thinking that.

I don't go to clubs. Or bars, or discos, or any of those places where the idea is to roll smiles like dice and see who gets to pass Go. Sure, I look. Everyone looks. But I hate the auditions.

I met him in a club.

I have a car. In the city it's not very useful. I get groceries in it. But my friends know I have a car. They know I don't go out much. This is why I get the phone calls. They know I don't go out much. So I get to be the taxi. Lorraine was drunk three nights out of four and it disgusted me. I don't know why I agreed to go rescue her. Something helpless in her slurred words, barely audible under the noise and music.

It took me twenty minutes to go, ten minutes to park, and fifteen minutes to stand in the line at the door. I looked around the obvious places someone would wait for a ride. She wasn't there. I sighed and started to push my way through the bodies. I was looking at faces in one direction, scanning the room, while still walking forward in another direction which is how I nearly knocked him over. Or more accurately, nearly knocked myself over. He caught me.

"I'm sorry," I said. He didn't seem to be paying much attention, seemed lost in space. He waved it off and I continued on my patrol, still not watching where I was going.

A complete trip around the club and a hunt across the dance floor I never want to repeat and I was back where I started. He hadn't moved. He turned to me and I realized that it wasn't that he didn't pay attention. He was definitely looking right at me. But his eyes always seemed focused on a point a few inches further away than whatever he was looking at. Like he was always thinking about something else.

"You're looking for someone," he said.

I nodded. "And I don't think she's here." It turned out later that Lorraine had met some friends and, oblivious, gone home with them. "I'm giving up on her. I want to leave."

"Would you like a cup of coffee?"

I would like to say that by now I understand, after the fact, why I said yes.

"What am I doing here?" I asked, once we had Formica in front of us and my ears had stopped ringing from the noise of the club.

"You're having a cup of coffee," he replied. "Would you like to order some food as well?"

His name was Paul. He had hesitated before giving the rest of it. "You forget your last name?" I asked him.

"Did you ever have trouble," he asked, "remembering your phone number because you never call yourself?"

"That's different, though. You can't forget your name. It's like forgetting your birthday."

"I have an even harder time remembering my birthday," he said. It seemed strange at the time, but I can't remember his last name anymore myself.

He had a very slight build, long graceful arms with very light hair, long fingers that hunted and encountered the coffee cup like he was reaching for it blind. Maybe he really was unable to focus. No, no, I reminded myself, he'd had no trouble walking.

"Why did the club upset you?" he asked.

"I don't know," I replied. He just looked at me. Or through me. Blue-gray. "I guess it's the people," I said. "They're all trying to find something and most of them aren't going to get it. Most of them don't even know what they want. It's a rotten system. You end up in bed with someone for a night and you hate yourself the next day but you liked the feeling, so a couple of nights later you go out and hit yourself with it again. And you wonder why you stay empty. Does that make sense?"

"But some people don't want breakfast," he said.

"What?"

"Not everyone sees it that way," he said. "Some people don't want any sort of entanglement, any sort of romance. They don't want to be served breakfast the next morning."

"They're kidding themselves."

"That's narrow. You've never been with someone just because you needed sex?"

"I think I have the opposite problem."

"I don't understand."

I sipped my coffee. But I couldn't stay silent with those eyes on me.

"I'm looking for breakfast," I said. "Lots of breakfasts. I don't care about the sex."

"That's interesting."

"You don't believe me."

"Halfway." He didn't even have the grace to look abashed. "When someone tells me they're not interested in sex, it always means they haven't done it well." No repentance, no apology, but also no accusation. Just a fact, by his rules.

I realized then that I was dealing with one of those people who has never mastered the idea that tact requires lies. What should I have done? I should have gotten up right then, walked away from the table. Maybe poured coffee in his lap. But I went home with him. I guess I wanted to prove something.

He proved something to me. He didn't have an erection when we started. The rest of his skin was as pale as his arms, the hair just as white. I watched his body as he touched me, testing with his long fingers the way he'd searched the air for his coffee cup, finding what was there without looking. I watched his body. I didn't want to look at his eyes.

He examined every inch of me, feeling the soft skin on the side of my neck or the insides of my thighs, the knobby skin on my knees and elbows, the slightly sticky-sweaty skin between my breasts and under them. Feeling the grooves left by my bra and the tiny bumps in my areolae. And though he had not yet once put even a finger up between my legs, not so much as a touch, I was getting aroused. Excited, I think, by the idea of this focus, the idea that he was concentrating on me and nothing but me, studying me, memorizing me with his fingers. Then he started using his mouth, covering the same trails, brushing his lips against my skin, once in a while darting his tongue out, tasting, finding out. What I found out was that those small noises were coming from me.

"Mmm," he said, nodding as if the noises were a signal. Lowering his face below my hips, he moved my legs apart with his hands. He explored for my clit, sometimes probing around it and tickling it with his tongue, sometimes squeezing it lightly, experimentally, with his fingers. He was watching me for reactions, I was sure. I didn't know. My eyes were closed. I wouldn't have been able to stand the idea that with all that focus, his eyes were still somewhere else. Somewhere beyond me.

"Please," I said, and it was a gasp.

"Keep going like this? Or—"

"You."

He straddled me, still playing with me with one hand. He didn't move for a little while. I didn't dare open my eyes. Then, as I was about to wonder aloud, I felt his penis enter me. Carefully. Like asking permission to intrude. He had me so worked up then that that was almost all it took. He put his arms around me. One thrust, two, three—and I don't remember the rest.

I am ashamed to say I don't even remember if he came. I slept then, slept the way men are supposed to sleep after sex. And in the morning, waking up still blissful, I knew I was in trouble. He had been right. Not only had he been right, I wanted breakfast.

I wondered all day, wondered if I was going to be able to forget it. Wondered if I was going to be one of those pathetic lust cases from the clubs, always chasing the next thrill. Wondered if I'd been ruined. Nowhere in the wondering did I consider the idea that I'd see him again. It hadn't been in the deal, it seemed to me, if I had read the conversation correctly.

But as I was getting ready to leave work, he called. "Come after dinner if you like," he told me. It was thrown out in such a casual way, it made me want to turn spiteful and reject it. But even then I knew better. I can't sustain my lies to myself.

By the third night, I was ready to ask the questions. Is this all that will happen? Are we becoming something else? Will we? But it was only the third night. And I didn't want to be the woman who picks out curtains too soon. I didn't want to sound ungrateful. I didn't want it to stop.

It was always after dinner. No excuse for socializing, no conversation really, just his body and mine. We would part in the morning with a kiss, having barely spoken all night. I did listen to the part of my brain that was going unsatisfied. And ignored it.

I knew—I suppose I always knew—that it was temporary. I think that kept me from being afraid. One morning while he showered, I went into one of the closets he didn't use, in his way-too-big-for-one-person house. It was full of women's clothes. So maybe I was expecting her to arrive at any moment.

He was soft. On a man with a skinny frame like that you expect to collide with a protruding bone, or run into a mass of muscle, tense and solid. But neither happened. He was soft, even on his face. Men's faces are never really soft, there's always a little scratchiness, even just after they've shaved. I never saw him shave.

He got me in the habit of exploring with my fingers, finding his face by Braille, moving along the hollow of his neck. "You're the only man I've ever met with no Adam's apple," I said.

"It happens," was his reply.

Two weeks. I didn't ask what he did during the day, I didn't ask about the woman in the closet, and most of all I didn't ask what he wanted from me.

"Did you always wear your hair long?" I asked him one night, running my fingers through it slowly. I had always thought "cornsilk hair" was a cliche. It was so fine, it felt like it wanted to wrap around my fingers, surround them and entangle them.

"It's simpler that way," he said.

"I don't like keeping up with mine either. That's why I keep it short."

"Do you want me to cut my hair?" he said.

"No. It's wonderful like this," I said, coaxing out another tangle. I wasn't sure if that had been the right answer. Even though I'd been telling the truth. It was so hard to tell what bothered him, or whether anything did.

Two nights later, I got to his house and no one answered the door. I figured maybe he had been at work late. If he worked. I waited for a while—half an hour maybe. He didn't show up. I worried, but not for the right reasons. I wasn't scared he'd died in a car crash somewhere. I don't think it would have occurred to me, not for him, but I don't know why. When I got home, I called the number. I'd never used it. He always called me. I let it ring forty times.

I went back the next night and he wasn't home again. But there were lights on in the house that hadn't been on before, and his car was there. I sat in my car for a long time. I don't know. Hoping he'd see me, maybe, for no useful reason. He knew who'd been knocking.

I let myself call in sick for a day. Then I clenched my teeth, put concealer on the circles under my eyes, and went back to the world. I lasted another three days. The fourth day I watched his house, concealed on the opposite side of the street, telling myself the whole time how psychotic it all was. But I knew he was there. I waited until three o'clock, when he opened the door to get the mail. After he'd gone back inside, I came out, shaking a little, and crossed the street and knocked on his door.

It took him a long time to answer it. His face was just as unreadable as always. "I thought it might be you," he said.

"You owe me a rejection."

"I suppose I do," he said. What was different about him? He gestured to me to follow him inside.

I had to see him from behind, the shape, to really get it. It doesn't take long to get in the habit, you know, of seeing people a certain way and just throwing out any new information that doesn't fit. That's why we have so many conversations that start, "Something about you has changed." We should know automatically when someone has cut their hair or gotten a new pair of glasses. But our brain takes shortcuts.

"Take off your shirt," I said. I was a little surprised that he actually did it.

He turned around. The startling thing was that they didn't look out of place. I suppose if they had, I'd have known what was wrong right away. But they were exactly the kind of breasts you'd expect to find on that body. Small, soft, but definitely there. His nipples were bigger, of course, but still the palest red they could be. The same pale red as his lips. As the tip of his penis. I wanted to touch them.

"What you really owe me," I said, "is an explanation."

"I don't have one."

"But you knew it would happen."

He nodded.

Should I have screamed? Should I have tackled him, pounded my fists against him until I'd gotten the frustration out? Slapped him across the face? I sat on his sofa and crumbled. Just let it all pour out of me, hot water into my hands. I wiped my eyes and looked up at him.

"You wouldn't have believed me," he said.

"Strip." I wished so badly that I could make my eyes as unreadable as his.

He undressed, matter-of-fact, no attempt to be sexy about it. He stood in front of me, hands on his hips. His much more prominent hips, prominent enough that it was his penis that looked out of place. It was the part that didn't belong now.

"What are you?"

"I'm myself. I'm never anything else."

"And these are just special effects." I walked over and squeezed one of his breasts gently. It was as I had expected it to be. Definitely real. I felt the nipple with the tip of my index finger, over it and around it.

He shrugged.

I grabbed him by the shoulders and pushed him, shoved him like a bulldozer all the way into the bedroom and backwards onto the bed. I sat astride him, holding him down, his legs dangling off the side. "You are," I said, unbuttoning my blouse, "the most frustrating man— the most frustrating person—I have ever met."

That was when those blue-gray eyes showed the only obvious emotion I ever saw in them. "You still want me," he said. Nothing in his tone of voice told me he was surprised. It was the one and only time his eyes ever gave him away.

I lowered my mouth and licked one of his nipples. I felt it stiffen on my tongue and I smiled. I wasn't about to tell him that I had surprised myself. He didn't deserve to know.

His skin felt the same. His penis felt the same. And he didn't make any more noise than he ever had. Then a thought occurred to me. "It doesn't stop there, does it?" I asked, as we lay beside each other, cooling down.

"No."

"How long does it take?"

"Maybe another week. Maybe two."

"I'll be back tomorrow night," I said.

"I know."

When I knocked on the door the next night, he was wearing a dress. Loose, with a low hemline and no sleeves and a cheerful print. He was barefoot, and his hair wasn't tied back.

"I'm not sure if I can think of you as a 'he' anymore," I said.

"Then don't," she replied.

Her voice hadn't changed. But, like so many things, it hadn't been so masculine before. She still had pale hair on her arms. How far into this process had I arrived? Had the hair been dark once? Had her voice been deeper?

Part of me insisted I should react more, that I should be more surprised or frightened. But the touch of her skin was still the same, and her fingertips along my skin still made my head tingle. I ignored that voice in my head. She wouldn't have answered my questions if I'd asked them.

Now that I was watching for changes, they were easier to see. Her testicles vanished very fast—the way I remember it now, one day they were there and one day they weren't. But I'm sure I must be remembering it wrong. Her penis, on the other hand, got shorter very slowly. I knew she knew, and she knew I knew. But I didn't say anything. You don't say things like that. Men get very unhappy just thinking about that kind of thing. Of course, she wasn't a man.

"I'm sorry," she said, when I lay beside her one day and saw that there really wasn't much more than the tip, just a red nub with maybe a tiny amount of shaft.

I moved down by her hips. "Is it still sensitive?" I asked. I put my lips over it, tasted it. She wriggled a little, so I smiled and teased her with my tongue. I would have put my hands on it, but there was nothing to grab. So I put my hands on her hips, steadied myself, and lay there, licking and sucking pleasantly. Never so pleasant to do before. And when she tensed, and a very small amount of warm salty taste landed on my tongue, I felt a weird satisfaction. Like 'see, I knew I could make you do that.'

I lay beside her, the taste still in my mouth. She rolled onto her side, sat up, moved down between my legs, and without a word began exploring with her tongue. Maybe I should have told her that she didn't have to reciprocate, that there was no obligation. But I just closed my eyes and smiled.

By the next night, the red bump had receded further, continuing to retreat inside her, and the furrow below it was getting deeper, its folds more complex. My tongue was fascinated. Every night there was something new to explore. She didn't really ejaculate anymore, I noticed; on the other hand, she had started to make lubrication when she got aroused. It was the best science experiment I'd ever seen. I didn't tell her that, though. I wasn't sure she'd take it the right way.

"How do they handle this at your job?" I couldn't resist asking one night.

"I don't have that kind of job," she said.

"But you do go out of the house?"

"Most days."

"Do you notice people react to you differently now?"

"Of course," she said.

"Which is better?"

"That's not the right question," she said. "There isn't a 'better.' It's just different. To them."

"But what about—"

"Sex is different, yes. Orgasm is different. But not better. Not worse, either."

"I'm sorry. But you know, so many people wonder what it's like on the other side—"

"That's the problem. Not the wondering. The idea that it's the other side."

It didn't seem like there was a response for that.

Gradually she changed, and one night with my fingers inside her, I realized that her visible parts, at least, were as female as they'd ever be.

"You're sad," she said.

"Just a weird thought," I replied. She waited. "Well," I said finally, "I think I was wishing that I could have changed too. To play with this properly." I wiggled a finger.

"Don't wish that," she said very seriously.

"Sorry."

She looked like she was about to say something else. But she kept it back, and then I started licking her clitoris and that ended the idea. Whatever it had been.

Two nights later, I arrived at her door and she was more dressed than I'd ever seen her. Oh, her dress wasn't evening wear or anything, and her shoes were completely ordinary sandals. But she was wearing a bra, for one thing, and her hair was pinned up, and her face made up very subtly.

"How many times have you done this?" I asked.

"Have you eaten?"

I nodded.

"Then let me take you for coffee."

We sat facing each other across the Formica. One of her hands rested gently over mine, long fingers touching the beginning of my arm. "Did you ever have trouble," she asked, "remembering your phone number because you never call yourself?"

I smiled, with difficulty. "I think you've asked me that one before."

"Did you have any problem with my name, the last few weeks?"

I shook my head. "But I hardly ever use it, I guess."

She nodded. "It's not important. You don't always see what's important, but you do better than most."

"Are you telling me goodbye?"

She looked through me. "I have never actually changed, you know. It's a perception. 'Only visible to the stationary observer.'"

"But are you telling me goodbye? Because that's what this feels like."

"Is that an important question to you?"

I nodded.

She considered for a while, sipped her coffee. "Not yet," she said.

"What do you do here?" I asked.

"Not much," she said. "Look. Watch. I'm really just passing through."

"I don't want you to go."

"I know," she said.

Sex that night was especially frenzied. I think I was trying to make her scream. I know I was ashamed of myself when she finally did make a noise, as she arched her back from the climax.

The next night she was gone.

The house was empty, the front door unlocked. Completely empty. No clothes, no furniture. No note. Nothing.

"Not yet," she had said. Not yet, but only barely.

She couldn't have stayed. I think she wanted to.

I didn't go to work for three days.

I don't always see what's important. I may do better than most, but in this case I missed the most important thing. Gender wasn't it; that was just a perception. A perception by a stationary observer. Watching a moving object. That was the most important thing.

When a car passes you, the noise of the engine changes. It doesn't really change, it just sounds like that to you. She was always the same gender. I don't know what gender that was. Maybe one we don't have. And by the time I knew that, she was already gone and the universe had removed her. She'd been moving the whole time. I just didn't know what to look for.

It was supposed to happen, I tell myself again, that's why it was such an oddity. It went the way it went because that was the only way it could go.

And I still hate thinking that.

There's a particularly offensive Star Trek *episode that features a race of androgynous beings who all look and act like clones, a culture of androgynes that refuses to allow their members a choice of gender identity. We're pretty damned sure that whoever wrote that episode hadn't ever been in a room full of actual androgynes, or it would've been evident what a motley crew the non-conventionally-gendered really are. There is no one way to be a transwoman, or a transman, or a genderqueer; each of us choose our genders from a hundred different styles and needs. What's true for one is not always true for another. That said, there is that strong thread of experience that ties us together, as this story explores.*

Corbie Petulengro has been published in Zaftig: Sex for the Well Rounded *(Cleis Press) and other random places, and spends her time gardening, listening to her neurotic friends, lusting after transsexuals, and feeling entirely too old for her actual age.*

No Charity

Corbie Petulengro

Brian met Faith at a fundraiser for the homeless. She was sitting behind a table, taking tickets for the raffle. She wasn't the sort of woman who stood out. Unlike some of the other females present in business power suits, she wore a flowered skirt and blouse and her ashy hair was cut short in a shoulder-length pageboy. It was the kind of grey-blond that could have either recently silvered, or been that way since a mousy childhood.

Brian liked her on sight. There was something about her quiet demeanor and slight smile that attracted him. He wasn't drawn to flashy types, and despite the recent crumbling of his 16-year marriage to another mousy woman who had suddenly announced that she was leaving him to study ecology in China, he had found it hard to date the kind of women one met in bars.

Respecting the space of reserve that the woman kept around her, he pulled up a chair a few feet away and offered to help.

He watched her out of the corner of his eye until he felt that she was comfortable enough to allow conversation. She was thin, very thin. Her hands were bony, spinsterlike, he thought. No rings. He wondered if she was still a virgin at her perhaps fortyish age. The thought excited him a little, but he brushed it away as impossible. No one over sixteen was a virgin these days.

Her eyes were light hazel, and her features a bit bony, but not unlovely. Her voice, when she spoke to the people fumbling for their wallets, was low and modulated. When he finally engaged her in conversation about the homeless activism work that they both shared, her eyes lit up with subdued animation and she became much less quiet. He discovered that she had a master's degree and lived with a roommate and three cats. After four hours, when the raffle drawing was over and only cleanup was left, he proposed a hesitant date, later in the week. Looking him straight in the eye, she offered to come home with him that night, still in tone so quiet and classy she might have been discussing an article she had read earlier. However, she told him, she would have to leave no later than midnight and he would have to pay her cab fare.

It wasn't like she was desperate, he thought as he watched her survey his messy apartment with detached amusement. He got the distinct feeling that he was a whim she was indulging. Is that what spinsters did in this liberated age, he wondered? Picked up random suitors, got their urges dealt with, and then went home to their cats and their neat apartments, avoiding the mess and fuss of dealing with men on a regular basis? Whatever. He was still too attracted to her to feel hurt or used just yet.

One thing he knew: she was no virgin. There was nothing tentative or inexperienced in her kisses, but there was still a kind of reserve to her, something held back even as she undid his trousers and took his cock into her narrow-lipped mouth and proceeded to give him the best blowjob he had ever had. Afterwards, when he entered her, she guided his hands to her small breasts, just teacup mounds on her thin chest, and seemed to get a great deal of pleasure when her rolled her nipples between his fingers. She moaned, at least, for the first time.

They lay curled together in the bed for a while afterwards, discussing various safe topics that were better suited to breakfast conversation than to the smell of semen and sweat on the sheets, and at eleven-thirty he offered to drive her home. As she stood up and brushed her hair, one foot curled behind the other ankle so that its pale sole reflected in the semi-dark, he found that he was already thinking about when he would see her next. He worried that he was falling in love; worried so hard that he missed a stop sign on the way home and forgot to actually ask her about a second date.

Her apartment was neat, as he had suspected. The cats were curled in a multicolored heap in the floral-print couch. The surprise was her roommate, who emerged from the back room in a six-foot swath of scarlet satin bathrobe clutched around her, long dark hair in rampant curls past her shoulders, and her face heavily made up. "Faith," she said in a tone that sounded as if it was trying not to be accusing and failing miserably. Her accent was Hispanic, and her voice was deep. "Where have you been?"

"I left a message," Faith said lightly. "This is Brian." She took off her coat, not meeting anyone's eyes.

"You didn't tell me where you were going to be, just in case... I was worried sick."

Faith sighed. "Esperanza, it's all right, I was fine."

"I drove her home," Brian said inanely, feeling that he ought to say something to prove that he wasn't an axe-murderer. Faith turned to him with a small smile and put a hand on his arm.

"It's all right," she said. "Esperanza worries about me. There are crazies out there, you know."

Her tall roommate snorted and left the room in a tall scarlet huff. Is that a woman or...? Brian thought, but really, he realized, he had more important things to think about.

"Can I see you again?" rushed out of his mouth in a hurry. Just in case she might say no.

Faith stood for a moment, considering. Brian began to get very worried. He straightened his shoulders, trying to look like someone with honorable intentions. Finally, she nodded. "I suppose it couldn't hurt," she said slowly. "I'm free Saturday."

Brian was happy enough to hear it that the "couldn't hurt" part barely touched him. He promised her a walk in the park if it wasn't raining, and then went home with his heart full of hope. Once in his own bed, he discovered that her perfume was still on his pillow and he couldn't sleep until he had beaten off twice to the thought of sucking on her small pink-candy nipples.

It did rain, but they walked in the park anyway, and Brian managed to get her to laugh once or twice, breaking through her reserve. They went to dinner, and he vetoed the idea of going back to his apartment, telling her that things had moved too fast last time and he wanted to get to know her better. Women, he figured, liked that sort of thing. Anyway, it was better to wait before making love to her again than to lose her due to her thinking he only wanted her for her body. She looked at him quizzically, and then shrugged. "Have it your way," she said.

He blinked. Faith never reacted like any of the women he'd known in the past.

So he ended up taking her home anyway, and they made love again. Her body was hard and slender under him, and she smelled nice, and her mouth was wicked on his flesh. Afterwards, however, as they lay together, she told him that she wasn't sure she could see him again.

It hit him like a blow to the chest. "Why?" She was silent. "Is there someone else? Are you involved with someone?" So much for spinsterhood.

"Yes," she said. "Esperanza. She's my lover." Her fingers trailed across his skin. "She's not happy with me doing it with you. We're not exclusive, but... she doesn't like it."

He had seen Esperanza again that afternoon; a tall, resentful shadow in the neat kitchen, in tight jeans and a low-cut blouse that showed off both sizeable cleavage and a sizeable Adam's apple. "She's a man, isn't she?" he said, some of his own resentment creeping into his voice.

"She is not." Faith's voice was suddenly as cold and distant as a schoolmarm's, and she pulled away from him. Brian cursed himself and tried to recapture her, but she was sitting up and reaching for her stockings.

"Please," he said, hoping that his emotion came through in his voice. "I just want to see you again. I'll do whatever you want... I won't ask for monogamy, or even first place; you can be with Esperanza or whoever. I'll make peace... I just want to..." He trailed off and then finished the thought with an effort. "I just want you."

Faith paused and looked at him, her face unreadable in the dark. "I can't promise anything. You'll have to talk to her, if you're serious. She means a lot to me. If you can convince her, I'm yours."

"Convince her of what?" he whispered.

"Ask her."

He called their apartment and Esperanza answered. No, they weren't free tonight. They were both speakers at a shindig down at the Fenway Health Center, and he if he wanted to have any further dealings with either of them, he probably should come. She hung up, and he got his coat.

The topic was Transgender Life Stories, and Esperanza had just gotten up to talk when he finally slipped into the back of the room. She wore a tight black dress that showed her large breasts, and high heels. *Aha,* he thought. *Gotcha. I knew you were....whatever.* She talked about getting thrown out of her house as a teen, about being a sex worker on the street... a working girl, she called it. How a program set up by Faith had rescued her, got her off drugs and into a job, onto legal hormones instead of black market ones.

All right, Brian thought to himself. *She's a rescue case.* Faith felt sorry for her, pulled her out of the gutter, and took her into bed. Sweet Faith. And now she thinks that she owns her, but she'll never have half the class that Faith does. He experimented for a moment with the idea of the two of them in bed together, but couldn't picture it.

Then Faith got up, and her first few words turned Brian cold. She talked about how she, too, had been born a boy, and had transitioned years ago, got her surgery, and had decided to help her sisters who were not as fortunate as she had been. As she talked abut her life, Brian's stomach did flip-flops. He had fucked her; it hadn't seemed artificial. Had she come? He couldn't remember. His mind frantically reconstructed her naked body in his memory, trying to scrutinize it for tell-tale signs. Unlike Esperanza, with her broad shoulders and big hands, you couldn't tell at all with Faith. Or could you?

After the meeting he walked and walked, ending up walking around and around the edge of the park where he and Faith had walked before, only now it was pitch-black and pouring rain and he was soaked. The circles he walked grew tighter and tighter, until he was just circling the big monument in the middle over and over and he had pared everything down to one thought: He still wanted her. Whatever she had been, he wanted what she was now. It mattered, yes, but not enough to change his mind about that. He had not gone to bed with a man. Of that he was sure.

"Damn straight boys," Esperanza snarled at him. "Have to reassure themselves that they aren't screwing men. So what if you did? Not that Faith is," she added hurriedly, changing her tone and glancing at her lover.

Faith sat on the chair next to the flowered couch, examined her hands, and said nothing for a moment. "I'm a little sorry you had to find out that way, Brian," she said.

"I had intended to break it to you a little gentler. Esperanza thinks I was wrong to go to bed with you without telling you."

"Esperanza's right about that," Brian said, gaining a surprised look from his opponent, who glowered at him from where she leaned against the bookshelves. "You should have told me. But it doesn't matter now. I meant what I said. If there's any way I can still see you…"

There was an electric exchange of eye contact between the two women that he couldn't read. Then Faith said slowly, "Esperanza has to feel comfortable with you. She thinks that you won't treat me right now that you know."

Brian opened his mouth in indignation, but Esperanza held up a hand and cut him off. "Listen to me. Sure, right now you're saying, 'She's all woman', but sooner or later you're going to start looking at her trying to see how she used to be a man. You won't be able to help it. And you'll run up against her past; that she used to have a different name, one you wouldn't want to be calling out during moments of passion. And she has a whole history that she can't disown. You'll run up against that, too, and you'll want her to pretend it didn't happen, to never talk about it, and that's not fair. And pretty soon, it'll start to get to you."

Brian was silent. Faith kept her eyes on her hands.

"Here." Ruthlessly, Esperanza pushed a photo into his hands. The young man in it was clean-cut, with silver-brown hair in a wave across his forehead, obviously a graduation picture. His belly fluttered, and he looked back and forth from Faith to the photo, until he realized that he was doing exactly what Esperanza had predicted, and flushed red to the roots of his hair. Looking up, he saw the tall ex-hooker's dark eyes like gimlets on him. "Can you still fuck her now?" she asked harshly.

"Love…" Faith reached out a hand and Esperanza took it, but cut her off, not taking her eyes off of Brian. "No, dear heart," she said. "He has to know. Really know. No lies, no fantasies. He can't be constantly reassuring himself that he's straight, or you'll both lose."

"What was his name?" Brian asked, looking at the picture. He supposed it was a rude question, but he figured he was already in pretty deep.

Faith twitched. "Charlie," she said quietly.

The ludicrousness of the moment suddenly hit him and he smiled. "Well," he said, "at least you didn't call yourself Charlene or something. I always thought that sort of thing was pretty cliched."

Getting up, he crossed over to her and kissed her, ignoring her hand still hanging onto Esperanza's. "I like Faith a lot better," he said. "And I still want Faith."

She kissed him back, pulling her hand away from her lover. When she finished, Brian was on his knees, looking up at her. He looked up even further, to Esperanza's dark eyes, which were unreadable, but not hostile. "What do I have to do to prove to you that it's all right?" he asked.

For a moment she looked taken aback, and then she smiled evilly. "Do it with me," she said.

Brian stood up hastily. She was still taller than him. "You mean... have..."

"Yeah." Her smile vanished. "Sex. Any way I want it. I'm not quite like Faith, you see. I haven't had any surgery down there. But I'm not a man." Her eyes narrowed. "If you can suck me off and still see me as a girl, then I know you won't pull a homophobic snit on us someday."

All the blood seemed to be rushing around in his head. This is crazy. She wasn't his type—too brash, too colorful, too ethnic, too assertive, too... masculine? He looked at her breasts and wasn't sure about that. But he'd said that he'd do anything. "When?" he croaked.

She stared at him, and he realized that he'd called her bluff, and she had been sure he wouldn't.

Faith laughed gently. "I told you, Ranza," she said. "He's worth the effort."

Esperanza recovered quickly. "Now," she said, unzipping her tank top and exposing her red lace bra. Brian swallowed.

"I'll be in the kitchen." Faith got up and Brian caught her, desperately, by the shoulder.

"Couldn't you at least be there?" he asked hopefully.

She laughed again and kissed him on the cheek. "No. You two have to work this out between you. Let me know when you're done." Her silvery chuckle followed her into the next room, and it was just him and Esperanza.

"Bed's in there," she said. "Let's get it on."

She stripped the clothes from his body so fast that he felt as if a sirocco had hit him. Unlike when he was with Faith, he felt uncomfortably self-conscious about his paunch, his lack of muscles, his receding hairline. Pushing him down on the bed, she shucked her shirt and jeans and knelt straddling him in her scarlet lace bra and panties. He couldn't help looking down at the bulge there, but then she was unsnapping her bra and dangling her breasts in his face. "Look at these tits," she crooned, brushing her brown nipples against his lips. "Who would ever have thought that a beanpole like me would have grown pillows like these? 'Course, my mama's got knockers like Dolly Parton. Come on, suck them."

She stroked her breasts seductively and cupped them, overflowing, in her hands. Brian wanted to protest, to say that this was all too fast and he didn't want to be pushed around, but then one nipple was in his mouth and it was so like his masturbatory fantasies about Faith that he got hard in spite of himself. He sucked one and then the other, and she hissed and growled with pleasure and ground herself against his pelvis. His cock slid between the cheeks of her ass and rubbed back and forth, but just as he was wondering whether the sensation would go anywhere, she pulled away.

"I'm gonna give you something else to suck on now," she said, her eyes shining surprisingly bright. In spite of her brashness, he heard a slight hesitation in her voice. "I know you haven't done this before, so I'm gonna be gentle with you, but I expect at least some effort."

She raised herself up and pulled her red panties down, exposing her cock and balls in the nest of her dark pubic hair. Brian, tense as a wire, was perversely relieved to see that it wasn't bigger than his own. It was half-hard, and was colored slightly differently than her olive skin, so that it looked quite out of place on her body.

She inched forward, her knees trapping his upper arms, until the head of her cock bounced right over his face. "Open up," she said. "You're gonna suck this big clit. This is boy pussy, baby. This is girl dick. Show me you want it."

Strangely enough, her calling it a clit helped. *Just a big clit*, he thought. *Funny how you can think of things differently if you try.* He opened his mouth and the head slid in, silkily smooth. She didn't thrust the whole thing in, for which he was grateful, but just let him suckle on the tip for a while. He wondered if Faith had a clit. He hadn't looked, just assumed. As he grew more comfortable with the motion, she grabbed the headboard of the bed with her hands and leaned forward into his face, putting more of the shaft into his mouth. He watched her breasts bounce overhead and his hand stole to his own cock, fondling it. It was amazing how erotic that in-out feeling could be in your mouth, he thought, surprising himself in the process.

Then she was suddenly pumping hard, and it was all he could do not to choke, but he tried to breathe between thrusts as she fucked his face, and cried out, and a small amount of salty come poured into his mouth. He swallowed reflexively, and then worked his jaw around as she lay down beside him.

"Faith's right," she said, her voice much more mellow than it had been. "You are a decent guy. That was a good try, for a beginner." Her voice was rough and hoarse, a man's voice, but he had ceased to think of her as man or woman, just Esperanza, the force of nature. She stroked his cheek. "You're a good sport, Brian."

He shrugged and smiled weakly. "It got you off," he said. Then, suddenly, he said, "I'm glad you came. It means you weren't treating me like a trick."

Her eyebrows went up at that, and she grinned. "Guess we'll have to take care of you, now," she said, and dove for his cock, devouring it. He gasped and arched his back as she took it all the way in to the hilt. Did Faith teach her, he wondered, or was it the other way around? Or did they both learn on their knees in some gay bar somewhere? His hand flailed about and found her bare ass, and bravely slid down between her spread thighs until it cupped her genitals. Her nuts were soft and squishy, instead of being firm like his, and her cock was soft. He flicked it and she moaned around his erect organ. Then his hand trailed, fascinated, up between the cleft of her asscheeks again.

"Yes," she moaned, and he teased her hole, watching her hips wiggle. Like a girl's. She lifted her head from his crotch and said, helpfully, "There's lube on the table next to you."

There was, and he lubed a finger and slid it in. He'd never done this before; he'd only been with about five women in his life, not counting Faith, and none of them had been interested in exploring that particular hole. She thrust back onto his finger, and soon he added a second one, and soon she pulled him up to his knees so he could take her with his cock. And then he had Esperanza on her hands and knees, spreading her pale ass with his hands, banging her from behind, feeling her scrotum swinging against his thighs as he came. Her ass squeezed rhythmically against his cock as she fingered her own nipples; her cock never got hard, but he could have sworn that he felt her sphincter tighten in an orgasm at one point. He had the distinct feeling that allowing him to fuck her was a seal of approval, that he had passed a test.

Afterwards, Faith climbed into bed with them, with warm wet washcloths, and cleaned everyone's tender spots fastidiously, which created a good deal of giggling from both Brian and Esperanza. She snuggled down between the two of them, facing Brian, with Esperanza's arms around her from behind, and said, "So I guess you can sleep here tonight, hon. If you don't mind sharing the bed with two trannygirls who snore."

He kissed her, feeling fine and relaxed, and then kissed Esperanza over her shoulder, which startled the Hispanic woman. "Oooh," she crooned, making a mock-hurt face at him. "Weren't you supposed to do that first, before you put it to me, stud?"

"Are you going to get surgery, Esperanza?" he asked, and then berated himself for the far-too-personal question.

Her eyes narrowed and turned away. "I don't know," she said. "It's pretty expensive, beyond my range right now anyway. And it doesn't always work so well. Sometimes you can't come with it. What I got works now; I think I like orgasms too much to risk it."

Faith buried her head in Brian's shoulder. "There are other compensations," she murmured, her voice muffled.

He met Esperanza's eyes, and she stroked Faith's shoulder. "Faith doesn't come with her pussy," she said. "She didn't want to tell you, because she didn't want you to think of her as defective."

"It's not a big deal," the silver-haired woman said, her voice firmer. "I couldn't come that way since I started estrogens and couldn't have erections any more, and frankly I don't miss it. I could never use that… thing… the way it was supposed to be used anyway. I'd rather have a pussy that doesn't come than a cock that does. To each his own, I guess."

"We're very different," Esperanza said, "for all we've got in common. It's amazing that we're able to get along so well."

Very different, Brian thought, *and it's amazing that I can feel desire for both of you. But I can.* He moved forward and kissed them both again, and then Faith was wriggling against him in a way that made him hard for the second time that night. He put a hand between her legs, and then stopped. "If it doesn't work for you… which I wish you'd told me…"

"Nonsense." She reached for him. "I love feeling you inside me. And there are other feelings—not like the way you come, but oh, they're still good."

Brian looked up at Esperanza for permission, and she reached around and spread Faith's thighs with her big hands. "Go for it," she said.

So he tried to slide into her, only she needed more lube—her pussy didn't make it naturally, she apologized—and after he had lubed her, he passed the bottle to Esperanza behind her, and slid in with a sigh that synchronized with Faith's. He felt Esperanza's slippery fingers probing in the hole next to where he was gently thrusting, then Esperanza positioning herself and sliding into Faith's backside, Esperanza's big clit separated from his own cock only by thin tissue, her balls rubbing against his, and Faith spreading her legs as wide as she could to accommodate them both.

And it seemed to him, as the three of them strained against each other, he reaching around Faith to get to Esperanza's nipples, she cupping Faith's breasts, that they were just three ordinary people together, nothing exotic. Faith with her silvering hair and the wrinkles around her eyes; Esperanza with her Adam's apple and big-boned frame, and him, balding and paunchy. Three ordinary people caught in a very sexy situation.

After he came, Brian held Faith while Esperanza tried to finish and then declared that she couldn't do it again. Faith cleaned them all off again, and climbed back in between them.

"I could get used to this," Brian mumbled into her hair.

"Yeah, but can you get used to doing dishes after dinner's made?" Esperanza quipped. "We don't allow any stupid ideas in this house about what's men's and women's work. Everybody pitches in."

"No gender exemptions," Faith said, and the two of them giggled, contralto and baritone. "Everybody does dishes, shovels snow, and gets fucked."

Esperanza reached around and patted Brian's backside. "Speaking of which," she said teasingly.

Brian flinched and captured her hand just as the long fingernails crawled into his crack. "No," he said firmly.

"Not yet, anyway," she corrected him, grinning evilly. Then she sat up and stretched. "There's butter almond ice cream in the freezer, Faith. Want to come?"

"Sure." Faith bounced up and out of Brian's arms and grabbed her robe, wrapping it around her slight figure. Esperanza, still gloriously naked and unashamed, put an arm around the shorter woman, tossed back her long black curls, and looked over her shoulder at Brian.

"You'd better keep up," she said as they left the room. "Or you might get left behind."

And Brian did.

They say that Eros rules love stories, but Thanatos triumphs in myths, which explains the mythic quality of this gritty, sexy, bloody noir story. "Up For A Nickel" is like a classic black-and-white film that you've seen a hundred times, and even though you know you'll cry at the end, you watch it anyway. It's queer Bogart at its best. Here's looking at you, kid.

Thomas S. Roche's writing has appeared in many antholo-gies, including the Best American Erotica *series, in which this story was previously published, and the* Mammoth Book of Erotica *series. He is the editor of the* Noirotica *series of erotic crime-noir anthologies and is currently at work on a series of crime novels. He works at San Francisco's Good Vibrations as the editor of their web magazine at www.good-vibes.com. He can also be found on the Web at www.thomas-roche.com, and you can join his newsletter mailing list by emailing*
      thomasroche-announce-subscribe@yahoogroups.com.

Up for a Nickel

Thomas S. Roche

Icruise the streets smelling cheap tacos and junkie vomit, searching the faces of whores. Searching. I drink rusty water at the Darkside, some of the old guys remember me from the neighborhood, but no one gets my name right. I slip down 20th and pay a visit to Mama Lamia the Palm Reader in her curio shop, stalking the shadows among shrunken heads, ritual daggers, voodoo dolls. *No shit, Jakey, you ain't a little boy no more...* She has to be fifty years old but she never stops coming on to us young bucks. No one's ever been sure if she's Cuban or Haitian or Puerto Rican or what.

You're nice and big, Jake....where you been? "Listen, Mama Lamia, I need a little heat, could you help me out?" *Sounds like you got enough heat of your own, pretty boy....was it hard time?* I smile. "Hard as it gets, Mama. You know what I mean. Some hardware." *Foreign or domestic?* "Either one." *Preferred caliber?* "Thirty-eight'll do, short barrel if you got it, nothing too heavy." *How about .38 special? Detective Special?* "Better still, I always wanted to be a detective."

Mama L. takes me into the back room, hands me the piece. It's a simple weapon, black as death, nothing pretty but it'll do the job if it comes down to it and the job needs doing. Mama L. lets me check it out, roll the cylinders, check the action. The grip and trigger are wrapped with that porous tape that won't take prints. Nice touch, Mama L. carries only the best.

"How much?" *I could set you up for a dollar, with one of those shoulder holsters like in the pictures and a nice box of shells.* "A dollar? Damn, Mama, where'd you get this piece?" *Took it off my thirty-sixth husband when I took a cleaver to his* head last night, OK, Jake? I should know better than to ask Mama Lamia dumbass questions. I give her two fifties, strap on the holster, slip the gun into it. I put my old jacket on over the rig.

She pushes me up against the back counter, her hand groping my crotch. She kisses me hard and I let her tongue sink into my mouth. It feels good after these years and she knows it, she feels me getting hard. She puts her hand down my pants and feels my cock, stiff. *Slot number thirty-seven's open, Jake, care to step up to the plate?* "Thanks, Mama, I've got some business to transact." With a glance down her arm: *Sure looks that way.* She takes her hand out of my pants, straightens her hair. *That business gets transacted, or not, you come back here and let Mama Lamia show you a little business of her own, complimentary. You take good care of yourself, Jakey. I don't want a pretty boy like you to end up with central air conditioning, if you know what I mean.*

"Thanks, I'll be careful. Listen, Mama L., I'm looking for a girl from the neighborhood. You remember her—Consuela? Connie? Sweet girl, half Puerto-Rican?" *Jake, she's not...* "Yeah, yeah, Mama L., I know, I know. I know. Where is she?" *She's got some powerful relatives who don't like her much, Jake. You know her mama was....* "Yeah, I know all about that, Mama, I know all about it." *I hope you're not—* "I'm not, Mama. I would never hurt this girl, I just want to talk to her. Just tell me where she is." Mama Lamia thinks about it a long time, slips her hand into the windbreaker, pats the butt of the .38. *All right. The Uptown. You know the place?* "I know it. She still dancing?" *Uh-huh, that's what I hear. Dances under the name Banana Flambé.* "Banana Flambé? Oh Jesus Christ." *I know. But I hear it's a good act.* "She have a guy?" Lamia shakes her head this time. *No.*

"Thanks." I kiss her on the lips. *Watch your back, pretty boy. You know what they're saying.* "What's that, Mama?" *They're saying you whacked that guy upstate. Jimmy decides he thinks it's true, things could get ugly.* "You don't worry about me and Jimmy, Mama L. I didn't whack nobody. Yet."

I drop by one of those discount stores on the main drag. I get myself a dark suit and some new wingtips. I head back and get a room at the Ambassador. I set the .38, loaded, on the edge of the sink as I shave my beard into a Van Dyke. I want to look good for her. I wonder if Connie will recognize me right away or if she'll have to think about it, remember how I looked, remember who I was, what I meant to her once upon a time. I put on a black tie and slick my hair back. Day burns slow and steady into evening. I sit down at the tiny table, cheap wingtips propped on the windowsill, watching the world through the open window and the jail-cell matrix of the fire escape. I light an unfiltered Pall Mall and watch things go blood-red, shit-brown, grey, dark grey, black. I get up and put on my hat.

The guy at the counter says Banana Flambé doesn't hit the stage until after midnight. I get myself a nice dinner up the street, sit there reading the paper, looking for word about the body. Nothing. Have a drink, have two, feeling the bulge of the .38, keeping my eyes out for trouble. They can do me in public and never get taken for it. It just ain't fair.

I'll tell you what ain't fair. I mean, I'm up for a nickel and I don't open my goddamn trap to tell the fucking pigs Jimmy Silver's fucking shoe size, for Christ's sake. So the parole board, they hear about how I'm an uncooperative prisoner, no matter how many times I scrub the fucking floor of my cell. Five fucking years. Who ever heard of serving five years on a nickel? And what's the word I get from Jimmy Silver's people inside? Jimmy can't associate with me, I'm too hot. All because I went up on a drug violation.

So Jimmy let me rot, and he never once said so much as thank you, Jake, for doing your time and keeping your fucking mouth shut.

That doesn't bother me half so much as it will if the cops get an ID on that body. I killed a made man without getting an OK from his boss first. Not only that, but Jimmy and Frank shared blood. I'm fucked.

The only thing that kept me alive through five years in the joint was that the body was never found. So what? Fucking goddamn lousy timing for them to find it now—if I hadn't been up for a nickel I could have driven up and taken care of the body when I heard they were building that housing development right where I'd whacked him. I could have kept it under wraps, just like it had been for five years. Jimmy never knew what happened to his brother that night, and if it wasn't for me serving the whole goddamn nickel he never would have known.

Too fucking late now. Now Jimmy will figure out what happened, figure out who did his half-brother, and there's some sort of poetic justice in that.

Frank. Fucking prick. That son of a bitch deserved to die for what he did to Connie. It still made my trigger finger itchy thinking about how she must have felt—

So I did him, wearing the hat of the pale rider, as the bringer of divine retribution, but funny thing, I don't think Jimmy will see me as the hand of God. How could that son of a bitch let his brother treat a beautiful, innocent girl like that and think he can get away with it—

Easy, I tell myself. Nobody knows a fucking thing—yet.

I finish my second drink and walk up the street to the Uptown.

It's close to two when she takes the stage. They have one of those silver balls that flickers multicolored lights all over the room. Connie appears up there in a gentle caress of half-dark and the mist from the smoke machines. She wears a thin silky thing of a tiny white slip-dress, virgin pale contrasting with her rich light-brown skin, as always. Her eyes are painted dark, so moist and sad. Her black hair spills over the gown and past the swell of her breasts.

She enacts her erotic danse macabre, the badly-recorded music a tragic Latin dirge, every verse another button coming undone. She looks down and sees me and doesn't miss a movement of her intricate dance, even though I know she recognizes me right off. She wriggles out of the slip as the song grinds to a halt, and it seems to hover after her in the smoky darkness as the spotlight follows the subtle curve of her back. She looks back just in time to vanish into darkness, looking over her shoulder, her eyes glowing sadness, with a purse on her blood-red lips. The spotlight illuminating just enough of that beautiful ass, bare except for the tiny g-string, to bring a thundering round of applause and a hail of bills onto the stage. She floats back out like a seductive ghost, smiles and licks her lips, clutches her white slip in front of her, arches her back just so as she bends down to pick up the bills, so that each movement shows off the swell of her breasts. Then she's gone.

She spots me coming back. Big guy tries to stand in front of me, puts his arms up like logs blocking my path. Connie touches him on the shoulder.

"It's OK, Louie. Let him come back."

"The other dancers ain't gonna like that—"

"Look, just forget it, Louie. Jake, give the guy a tip." I slip him a five. He backs off. "Jake, close your eyes."

She pulls me backstage, holding my hand, kneading my fingers gently. "Keep them closed," she tells me as she takes me into her dressing room. She turns me toward a wall and I hear her fidgeting around as she changes clothes. I smoke a cig, wondering what she looks like getting into her clothes—I want to see that more than I want to see her taking them off. I smoke another cig. It's taking a real long time, but I didn't expect anything different from Connie. "All right," she says. "You can open your eyes now." She presents herself to me, raising her arms. She's changed into a tiny red minidress that comes down over her shoulders, and carries a handbag that matches the red perfectly. She's got a rhinestone choker on and her lipstick's a darker shade than before. Her long earrings match her necklace. Her black hair's pulled up in a bun, just a few strands dancing around the curves of her neck and shoulders. She looks beautiful. "We'll go out the back. Do you have a car?"

"Afraid not," I tell her.

She smiles at me. "All right then, we'll walk. It's a nice night out. I think the only place left is the Darkside."

I shrug. "Sounds about right."

"You think about me while I was gone, baby?" *All the time, Jake.* "Then how come you didn't come visit me?" *Jake, don't start. You know the answer to that.* "Yeah, I do. It was Jimmy?" *Mmmm-hmmmmmmm.* "Things going OK for you? You making money?" *I get by.*

The waitress comes with our drinks. Whiskey sour for me, Brandy Alexander for Connie. I tip the waitress five bucks and ask her to bring us an ash tray. Connie lights a thin, exotic cigarette and sips her Brandy Alexander, leaving an inviting lipstick kiss around the tip of the straw. I take a drink, hear the ice cubes clattering.

"How's your drink?" *Fine, Jake. I like them here. Nice and weak. I can't be too careful.* She laughs. "You got a man?" *I got someone I see.* "Cop?" *Night shift at the airport. Graveyard.* "Union man." *Yeah, sort of.*

"Look, baby, I can't get you out of my head. I want you so bad, but you know I'm hot right now." *I know that, Jake. Word on the street is they're digging up Frank's body. Word is you did him.* I stand up. "Who the fuck told you that?" *Don't pull that shit, Jake. I'm just telling you what you already know. I figure you did him because of what he did to me. I always wondered who had gotten him. I figured it was you. Now I know.*

The waitress floats by with the ash tray, puts it down and slips away, looking nervous. I sit down and light a cigarette with shaky hands. Connie leans close, touching my arm. *Jake. Jake, listen to me. Thank you for what you did. You have to hear that, Jake. I know it's wrong but I'll always be grateful.* "You're welcome but I didn't do nothing." *Yeah. Well, thanks anyway.* "I need to get out of town, Connie." Her rich brown eyes filling mine, spicy perfume clogging my nostrils, seducing my mind. *Jake, come up with me. I've got a place near here.* "Connie, I need the money." She pulls me close. Her tongue snakes into my mouth and she drops her hand down, under the table, scratching my cock through wool trousers with her sharp fingernails. She begins to knead it and squeeze. *Come on,* she whispers. *We'll talk later.*

Barely in the door to Connie's place, and the door's slammed and she's on her knees. She gets my cock out, starts suckling on the shaft while she works my balls. I don't know where the condom comes from but she's got it in her mouth and is rolling it down over my cock. Then she swallows my prick like it was nothing, taking the whole thing down her throat. Then she lets it slip out of her mouth and rubs it over her face as she pulls her dress down over her small tits. She slips up just enough to rub the head of my rubber-clad prick over her tits, over the pierced nipples, then pushes her tits together and wraps them around my cock as she works it up and down. Then I'm down her throat again, but she knows I'm coming close, she knows my body better than she knows her own even after all these fucking years. She stands up slowly, locking my eyes in hers. She goes over to the window.

The neon lights outside flash on-off-on-off, Liquors, Beer, Cigarettes. Naked Girls. Objects d'Art. All Nude Female Modern Burlesque. Wrestling.

Consuela pulls her skimpy dress down to her waist, then shimmies out of it like a snake. Her slight round ass wriggles back out of her panties. The shimmer of her thighs as she spreads them slightly, leaning forward over the windowsill with her hand slipped over her crotch.

"No hands below the waist," she tells me.

I know it. It's Connie's rule, ever since…

I come up behind her and crouched down just a little so I could get the head in between her smooth light-brown cheeks. I fit the head into her tight little hole and start to work it slow, taking my time, opening her up. Then I'm in, just with the head, and she lets out a luscious little gasp. I slide it home. She pushes back against me, putting her head back and turning her face toward me. She reaches back with one hand and touches my cheek, stroking it oh so lightly with her fingertips. Her tongue slips in and out of my mouth as I fuck her from behind. The night air is cool on my face and belly. Connie lets out a little whimper as I do her. For Christ's sake, I can't believe how bad I want to reach down and grab it with my hand. I guess it comes from the time in the joint, you know, it wasn't like this before. It probably wouldn't do much for her, but I just want to touch it, caress it, taste every bit of her. With her free hand she grips the windowsill, holding herself steady. She whispers my name as I let myself go inside her. Then I whisper hers.

Connie takes a moment to go use the can. She comes out naked except for a frilly pink robe with pink fur down each side, framing her luscious tits. She takes me in her arms, the robe bunched between her legs. We tumble down onto the bed, laughing like old times, rolling about. Connie curls up with me, one hand spread across her crotch in the dark. I light up a Pall Mall and Connie takes a drag or two. In the flare of the cherry, I can see her eyes forming big moist pools. A single tear drizzles out of one eye. If she's anything like she used to be, Connie spends about half her life weeping.

"The money," I tell her. "I've got to get out of town."

There's a key in the lock. I'm off the bed in a second, the rubber leaking come and dripping Connie's spit. I get my pants buckled and get down in a crouch, hiding in the dark, the .38 in my hand. I pull back the hammer and Connie looks at me, horrified. She sits up, clutching a pillow in her lap. The door opens.

A kid comes in the room, he can't be more than fifteen. He doesn't see me at first. He takes a look at Connie, disheveled and half-clothed. The guy's wearing airport blues, smoking a big fat stogie, but he's definitely not more than fifteen, sixteen years old. OK, I've got it figured. This is the guy Connie's living with. She always did have a weakness for younger men. He turns and sees me. I drop my hand to my side, still holding the .38 but out of sight. I stand up. "What the fuck is this?" says the guy, and his voice is as high as they get. He starts at me and I bring up the .38. He stops. Then I get it. She almost had me taken, the chick has practically no tits and this thin sleazy moustache. And that fucking cigar, it's bigger than my dick by a couple inches. She's not a bad looking dame, though, for a sixteen year old boy. She turns to Connie and looks like she's about to hit her. I grip the butt of the .38. Connie stands up, clutching the robe together in front of her. "Please, Mickey, take it easy. He's just a trick. Just a trick I brought back here after the show."

Mickey looks at me, her eyes stone butch rage. She takes the cigar out of her mouth. "I told you not to fucking bring them here," she growls.

"I know," Connie says, wriggling up against the dyke. "I just brought him here because it was so late. I didn't think you'd come home early, I figured it'd be OK, he just wanted a quick one and he was paying. I thought you'd be at work."

"I moved to first graveyard shift, Consuela, don't you fucking remember?"

"Oh, Mickey, I'm so sorry, I was gone when you left for work today, remember—look, he's just a trick, I didn't think you'd be here."

Mickey stares at me, shaking the cigar like an accusing finger. "Get the fuck out." She seems like an OK broad but I just stand there smiling for a second, floored by the whole weird scene. I take time to light a Pall Mall and then slip the .38 into its holster. Mickey's watching me, and if she's even a little afraid of me now that she knows I've got a gun, she doesn't give me a fucking hint. She's got balls, I'll give the girl that. I peel a Franklin out of my roll. I reach over and tuck it into Mickey's breast pocket. "You got a hell of a woman there. You treat that whore right. She gives some damn good head." I blow Connie a kiss. I straighten my tie on the way out and then stop to pick up my hat from where it fell by the door when Connie pounced on me. I look back at Connie and wink at her. She's crying, but then, like I said a minute ago she cries about half the time. The dyke watches me leave, her face carved out of rock.

I open my pants, pull off the used condom and toss it into the growing pile of matching condoms in the alley. I go out into the fog.

The sewer grates are steaming like Hell's ready to pay a visit. I know I can't sleep. I wander through the street-level clouds looking for something to keep me awake. Connie has her dyke, and that's the way things are. I'm not jealous. I'm happy for her. I mean, I'm up for a nickel, and Jimmy orders Connie not to visit me, with good reason. So that's the end of it. Five years later, she's found herself a dyke to keep her warm. No big deal, no one gets blamed by me. I just don't want to sleep alone—yet. There on the corner of tenth there's this cute Filipino girl turning tricks. She has this tight white minidress that shows everything. I like the way she looks and we trade a few jokes. I take her back to the hotel with me and do her long and slow from behind on the single bed with a half a tube of KY and one hand slid down between her legs, the other playing with her tiny breasts. I kiss her neck and then her mouth as I enter her from behind, she's got this stud piercing the center of her lower lip. It feels pretty bizarre and I kind of like it. She does good work for fifty bucks, and she's really cute, with nice tits. But she doesn't match Connie. Maybe it's because she lets me touch her. Maybe I'm just still in love or some such bullshit. Either way, I give her the fifty bucks and an extra twenty for staying till morning. And I can finally get to sleep when she takes off around dawn leaving cheap perfume on the pillow.

I wonder if the dyke has weekends off. It looks like they're just getting out of bed, or maybe getting back in. I crouch on the fire escape just outside their apartment. Mickey and Connie are going at it. I want a cigarette, real bad, but I'm too close to their window, which is open. They might smell the smoke and look out the window, and see me crouching there in the midday shadows. Then again, they're pretty distracted. Connie's down on her knees, wearing just her red slip and a pair of black lace-top fishnet stay-ups, and the dyke's standing over her, one of those weird contraptions hanging out of her jockeys, looks like she's got a strap or something underneath. Connie's going at it like it's a real cock, her mouth and tongue drawing wet swirling patterns up to the thick flesh-colored head and then back down to the balls again, which look unbelievably real. Connie moves her mouth up and gets her lips stretched around the head of Mickey's schlong, which is no small job, believe me. Then, with what looks like only a faint effort, Connie chokes the whole unbelievable shaft gradually down her throat until her lips are wrapped around the base. I shake my head, suppressing the urge to applaud.

Mickey rocks her hips in time with Connie's ministrations. Connie lets the cock slip out of her mouth, then rubs it between her firm tits. It looks like Mickey's ready to get down to business. Connie looks up at her man and nods.

Connie lays face-down on the bed and lifts her red slip up over her ass, spreading her legs wide and sliding her fingers up and down in her crotch. Mickey gets up behind Connie and puts the head in, bringing a breathy moan from Connie. She teases the girl for a long time, just the head pushed in. Then, inch by inch, she gives Connie the whole schlong, making the girl's full lips part wide, showing her white teeth as she whimpers "more... more....more...." with every tiny squirming movement of Mickey's hips.

She's loud enough that I can hear everything. I don't know if maybe Connie's putting on a good act to try to pay the dyke back for that scene last night, but either way it seems to be working. The dyke presses her meat home and gives Connie a long, hard bang on the bed, making her clutch the dirty sheets and choke and sob as she gets fucked.

Mickey lets go, I'm not sure if it's an act for Connie's sake or if she really gets off on this. But it sure sounds real, like she's shooting long streams of jizz up inside Connie's lush body.

Then Mickey curses, loud. "I'm gonna be fucking late," it sounds like she says. I shrink deeper into the shadows as Mickey races around getting on a fresh pair of jockeys and some blue jeans and a work shirt.

It takes a long time for the dyke to get ready, and I risk a cigarette, hiding back on the edge of the fire escape in the darkness between the buildings. I don't move until I finally hear the sound of a motorcycle far below and see Mickey pulling away on a Harley, wearing a backward baseball cap and a black leather backpack, with a big bunch of white roses hanging out. I go back to Connie's window.

It's still open a crack to let in the humid summer breeze. I lift it up, nice and easy, and slip inside.

Connie's still laying on the bed, sprawled out on her back. It looks like she's taking a little nap. She's got the sheets tangled around her body, bunched up between her legs. The slip's hanging off her body, revealing her delicate curves. I was always a pretty good second-story man, though I suppose you could say it's part of my moral code not to break in on girlfriends. But I guess Connie counts as an ex. I'm real quiet as I come up to the bed.

Like I said, she's still got her red slip on, but one strap's hanging over her shoulder and one beautiful soft-brown tit is winking at me. One long leg hangs over the edge of the bed, the torn black fishnet stocking, a lace-top stay-up, bunched almost to her knee.

Connie's eyes flutter open, and she gives a little gasp.

She moves to cover herself up. "Jake," she says, a little surprised. "What are you doing here?"

"What do you think?" I ask her.

Connie squirms over to the edge of the bed, just a little.

"Come here and show me," she says, parting her lips and reaching out with one long-nailed hand.

I could never say no to her. I come over to the edge of the bed and she gets herself laid out on her back so that her head hangs over at just the right angle. Her lips part, her tongue flickering out eagerly. She works my zipper down with her fingers and gets her lips pressed around my shaft. I don't know where it comes from, but there's a condom in her mouth again, and I don't even know it's going on until after she's got half of my rubber-sheathed prick in her mouth. Then she starts taking it down her throat. That angle she's at, on her back with her head hanging over the edge of the bed, means that it goes down easy, smooth, gentle, without a hint of hesitation. Connie always was real good at this. Connie starts to whimper, low in her throat, as she swallows me.

"Connie," I make myself say, "I need the money."

She moves back, easing my cock out of her mouth. She rubs it all over her face, smearing her spittle across her cheeks and messing her makeup. She looks somehow sexier with her mascara and lipstick all wet and gloppy over her face. "Business first," she whispers. "Then pleasure."

With that she takes me down again, working my cock down her throat, pumping it in and out. I reach down and touch her breasts, squeezing the pierced nipples. I play with them as she works my cock in and out of her throat. Next thing I know she's getting me off right in her mouth and then I'm falling forward, stretching out on the bed with her.

"Where'd your man go?" I ask her.

"Tomorrow's Mother's Day, remember? She went to her old man's place upstate."

I wonder about that for a minute as I light a Pall Mall. Then I let it go. I look into Connie's beautiful brown eyes and kiss the soft-pink lips with their red mouth painted on and skewed about a half-revolution across her chin and cheeks.

"I need the money," I tell Connie. "I've got to get out of town."

Connie's eyes get all watery, glistening with lush pain.

"You did him for me," she says.

"I didn't 'do' anyone," I tell her.

"You gave me that .22 that day, about a week before you went up the river. With the money from that airport heist. You told me to hide them both and get rid of the gun when it was safe."

"Connie, I need the money. Some people are after me. They don't want to talk."

Her rouged cheeks are streaked with black lines. "Jimmy. He's going to kill you because you did his brother. Where did you shoot him? I have to know. Tell me where you shot him."

"Connie?"

"Please, Jake, I have to know how he died."

I look at her.

"Back of the head, all eight shots," I tell her. "With a twenty-two caliber they take a lot of lead to die, even at that range." I'm speaking in a flat voice, like it's nothing, which it's not. "He and I went up the highway to do some gambling, maybe catch a few whores. We'd just made a big score at the airport and I had to go up the river on that latenight charge in a week. I knew what he did to you. I was just stringing him along. No one knew where we'd gone. We were drinking the whole way, talking like we were buddies. Frank had to take a piss. I pulled off the road and said I had to take one, too. Ba-da-bing."

Connie looks very sad. "I know I'm not supposed to feel bad about it. I love you for what you did, Jake, you did it for me. But Frank was my brother. Jimmy, too, depending on how you look at it...."

"He was your half-brother," I tell her patiently. "You and Jimmy aren't related at all, that's why he lets you live like this."

"I know. I hated Frank for what he did. I'm glad he's dead."

"Look, I'm sorry. I should have OK'ed it with you first." I kiss Connie, hoping that will make her stop crying, not that it ever did before. "I'm going to get whacked if I can't hit the road before Tuesday. Maybe even then." I take a deep breath, telling myself this is the last time I'll ask her. "Where's the money?" I ask, knowing the answer.

Connie takes my wrist, draws my hand to her face, kisses the fingertips with sticky lipstick-disaster lips. Slowly, she spreads her legs as she guides my hand down between her parted thighs. She presses my fingertips into her crotch, and I feel the slick wetness of her cunt, the full lips, the exquisitely-sculpted clitoris, the smear of lube that's dribbled down from where Mickey had fucked her ass. Gently, Connie prods my finger and I press it into her tight cunt. She gives a little gasp as I do, like her cunt's real tender. My eyes are the ones full of tears, this time.

"It's still itchy," she tells me. "And it hurts a little. But it's the best money can buy. I did it about six months ago. I'm sorry, Jake. I'm sorry. I knew you'd be back, but I just had this chance to be happy, is all... and I couldn't say no."

"Oh, Connie," I whisper sadly.

Then she kisses me, climbs gently on top of me, her body soft and open and her legs spread facing me for the first time ever. She nuzzles my ear and tells me softly "You get to be the first, lover, my very first, just like I'm a sweet little virgin. Let's pretend I'm sixteen or something, and we're both doing this for the first time.... You can be my boyfriend, Jake." And so she gets off the bed and floats across the room to the lingerie drawer, slips out of the stained red slip and puts on a new clean white one. "Take off your clothes, Jake." And I get off the bed and undress, leaving my clothes in a pile on the floor, and the two of us embrace in the slanted light from the window. We climb into bed together and make out for a long, long time, like we really are sixteen or something and horny as can be, and when we finally do it I know for sure it's for the first time ever. It feels different than anything I've ever done, like I'm a virgin, too, which maybe I am, technically. But Connie's weeping as I finish off inside her. She tells me, over and over again, "I'm sorry, Jake, I'm sorry, I'm sorry… I shouldn't have taken that money…." And even though I know Jimmy is going to whack me, smear my brains like succulent marmalade, I tell Connie "It's OK, Shhhhhh—shhhh, little girl, it's OK, it's OK, don't worry…." I can't get the thought out of my head, of what it's going to be like, when they finally come for me.

What's the fucking point in running? Hiding? It doesn't seem to matter any more. I've still got the room at the Ambassador. I'm drinking pretty heavy. I keep looking at the .38, wondering if it wouldn't be smarter to kill myself. Instead, when I hear the footsteps on the stairs, I empty the .38 and toss it out the window, into the garbage heap below with all the shells.

But they don't bust the door down. Something's really fucked up— they knock. Maybe it's the landlord. I answer the door in my underwear, not really giving a shit if it is Jimmy, not caring if he does it or if he sends one of his men, if they give it to me in the face or the back of the head. Who gives a rat's ass any more? But instead of one of those anonymous mob revolvers with porous tape on the grip and trigger, I see a different kind of silver, a shield.

The cop says my name.

"Maybe," I tell him.

He tells me his name and department—Sergeant Fitz, Homicide. "We'd like you to come down to the police station."

My ears are ringing. I know what it means. My whole body goes numb. I wonder how he'll do me in the joint. Piano wire? Hung in my jail cell?

"Just let me get my pants on," I tell the pig. I look out the window as I get my black suit on. Someone's rummaging around in the garbage heap in the alley.

They show me pictures of her, stretched out across the bed with two holes in her chest, wearing the white slip pulled down and soaked with blood. She's got a strange look of peace on her face, one of her sad, lush pouts on her soft-pink lips. Her arms are stretched out like she's on some kind of obscene cross. The rusty little .22 that did Frank Chambers is clutched in one of her tiny hands. I told her to get rid of that fucking thing when she could. I sit there, numb, I can't even feel a goddamn thing.

"You know her, Jake?"

"Can I have a cigarette?"

They get me one, a fucking Marlboro Light, for God's sake. I light it and blow smoke.

"Yeah," I say. "I know her."

"What's her name?"

"Connie," I say. "Consuela Rodriguez."

"Born Conrad Jesus Rodriguez Chambers," says the pig, reciting all of Connie's erstwhile names like a list of offenses. "Mama was Maria Consuela Rodriguez, a pretty Puerto Rican whore, just like her son turned out to be." The pigs laugh all around the room. "Mama OD'ed about six years ago in a shooting gallery in the Heights. His daddy was Rick Chambers, consigliori to the gods. With a taste for fresh PR whore-meat." Fitz is grinning, pushing me as far as he can push me. "Can't blame him, can you? Rick Chambers later started his own family, you wouldn't know anything about that, would you, Jake? Nah, I didn't think so. Anyway, Conrad changed his name early last year, legally speaking. We understand he was a fruit for a whole lot of years, turning tricks out by the wharf. Taking it up the ass, I guess. But then they say guys give pretty good head—you wouldn't know anything about that, would you Jake? We think he was killed in some sort of lover's quarrel. He had been down to the station to talk to some detectives the day before, saying some things about certain people in his life, saying that maybe his girlfriend wanted him dead. She was one of those women who like to slap guys around. You wouldn't know anything about that, would you, Jake?"

"Afraid not," I say. I can't stop crying but I'm not making a sound, just wet tears filling my eyes so I can't see straight. "Did you ask her brother? Jimmy Silver? Silver-Chambers, that is? Rick Chambers, Connie's old man, he was Frank Chambers' dad, married Martha Silver Chambers after Paul Silver got whacked, and adopted Martha's boy Jimmy. Sure as fuck you must know Jimmy Silver, right? I mean, they pay you to do something over here, don't they?" I'm looking right at Fitz, knowing I'm going too fucking far.

Fitz looks at me like he's going to smack me. Then he does. He hits me pretty fucking hard, my head rings through the hangover fog and I taste blood through the day-old whiskey coming up my throat. I swallow.

"We think she was killed in some sort of, you know, love triangle," he said. "So maybe you could tell me, Jake. What was your relationship with Conrad?"

I close my eyes. "We were lovers."

The pigs all mutter under their breath, saying shit about faggots and pansy-perverts.

"Seems she had another lover, do you know anything about that?"

"I think she was seeing some woman."

"A woman?" More chuckles from the pigs. "You know this dyke's name?"

"Mickey something."

"Michelle Dubois. Works up at the airport. Smokes big cigars."

"Sure. I never knew her."

"Do you think Michelle might have wanted Conrad dead? Might have been some sort of lover's quarrel? Some sort of sick—"

"Consuela confessed, didn't she?" I say. "She confessed to something, didn't she? Told you she had the murder weapon? And you fuckers sent her home, knowing she'd be whacked, leaked the information to Jimmy, fucking had her snuffed, all because it's easier and pays better than getting off your asses to prosecute her." I stop all of a sudden. I'm killing myself, and I know it.

The cop is stone-faced. He acts like he hasn't heard me at all, which is lucky for me.

When he does answer, he speaks very slowly, as if talking to a child. "Do you think this Michelle might have wanted her boyfriend dead? Some kind of lover's quarrel?"

Boyfriend?

I wait a long time, finish my cigarette and snub it out before answering that one.

"I wouldn't know anything about that, Sergeant. But Michelle didn't seem like the violent type. Even if she was a union man."

Mickey comes to see me at the Ambassador. She's still packing, all dressed up with a bulky jacket. I know she has my .38 under there. It was her baseball cap I saw bent over the garbage heap the day the cops picked me up. I wonder if maybe she came to kill me, that day or today. She did and didn't, in that order. The cops are looking for her, they've got her and Connie's apartment staked out. She's been wearing the same clothes for days.

"I thought you did her," Michelle tells me, sitting on the edge of my bed. "Who else could get to her like that? But now I figure it wasn't you who killed her."

"It wasn't."

The .38's out of her pocket like a quick whisper of death, pressed hard in the hollow under my jaw. Mickey's in my face, her teeth set, her lips curled back under the thin moustache.

"But you know who did." She's all stone butch shit and I know if I had done Connie I'd be dead by now.

I stare her down, waiting long seconds before answering her. When she doesn't say anything, I know she's going to let me live.

"It was her brother," I say, the .38 pressing against my throat. "Her half-brother. The only one left. She was taking the fall to protect—"

Mickey still has the .38 under my chin. "That bastard raped her, didn't he?"

"Not Jimmy," I say. "Frank."

"Frank? Who the fuck is Frank?"

"It was a long time ago," I tell Michelle. "A long, long, long time ago. Frank's dead. Jimmy's the one who got Connie done like that."

"Where does he live?"

I look at her, cold. She doesn't deserve to die like that, but then again, neither do I. Neither does anyone, with a few distinct exceptions.

I stare at the dyke, wondering just how much she loved and wanted Connie, just how much she needed her around to keep her warm in this city of fog and stone cold bullshit, how much her stone butch cojones, pencil-moustache bravado and stuffed-jean swagger are worth when it comes time to pull the trigger. Wonder what will happen if the whole fucking world gets blown up by one bullet from a .38, in the forehead of a scumbag who would murder his own sister for supposedly doing something that should have gotten done a lot more than five years ago.

I reach up and take the .38 out of Mickey's hand. "Tell you what," I say to her. "I'll take you to where Jimmy works. We're gonna go over there together."

Then I catch Mickey on the jaw with a good one, she's out in a second and I've got her stretched out on the bed. I've got one phone call to make, before I go, to Sergeant Fitz, telling him he was right, it was a lover's quarrel, but it wasn't Mickey. I did Connie with a .38 special, two bullets in her chest from about three feet. Sounds from his tone like I guessed right on the caliber and range. It's the only way to save the dyke, and Connie loved this woman so I suppose I might as well, too, and this is my parting gift.

"You killed Conrad Rodriguez. In a domestic dispute."

"That's right."

"And you're willing to sign a statement to that effect?"

"Well," I say, "I'll be a little busy for the next hour or so. But if I'm still around after that, I'll sign George Washington's autograph on your fucking grandmother's ass, flatfoot."

I cradle the phone, pocket the .38, get the keys to Mickey's bike out of the pouch of her airport blues. She's waking up but I'm gone before she knows what's happening. I figure her bike's probably in the alley. There it is, parked up next to the garbage heap, Harley 883 Sportster, beautiful. I fire it up and hit the clutch. Rubber spins and then I'm moving like hell. Mickey screams after me, hanging out the window of the Ambassador. Yelling for me to stop. "Put it on my tab," I mutter as I shift into third and lay down the rubber, skidding onto the main drag, screaming toward Jimmy's bar like a pale rider with the .38 heavy in my pocket and the bad taste of payback in my mouth. It's almost sunrise, Jimmy's always at work early, his muscle's gonna be light this time of day. The sky cracks open spilling fire overhead casting black skyscraper-shadows along my path. Two in the chest. Birds rise in flocks as I pass, screaming death-wails announcing my approach.

God put a lightning bolt in my hand, motherfucker, a lightning bolt in .38 special. Blood is thicker than tears you piece of shit. The city blends like nightmares into a soundless watercolor around me, painted in Connie's blood.

Jimmy's in his office, greeting me with a smile.

We've long thought that there's more than a bit of magic in those who play with traditional notions of gender, a special quality that allows the transgendered to play out their roles with a certain style and knowingness that they mightn't have otherwise. And of course transgendered people and roles have a long, distinctive history in theatre and opera too, where they likewise play out their functions with a certain particular élan. This well-textured period piece demonstrates what happens when the two collide... with one of England's most beloved monarchs somewhere in the middle. It's a midsummer night's dream to remember for a long, long time.

Sacchi Green writes in western Massachusetts but refuses to limit her imagination to any particular place, time, or version of reality. Some of the results can be read in Best Lesbian Erotica 1999, 2000, *and* 2001, Best Women's Erotica 2001 *and* 2002, *and the themed anthologies* Zaftig, Set in Stone, Below the Belt, *and* More Technosex.

A Dance of Queens

Sacchi Green

Midsummer's Night, the play safely done, and dusk sweet as a languorous touch on yearning flesh… and still I could not take my love into the greenwood and lay her on my cloak and be consumed in her fire.

I cursed my own impatience. We should have pressed on without pause, but Quenta had tormented me so, slipping a hand beneath my shirt and then down into my breeches until I could scarce walk, and must stop for a taste of the feast to come.

So the Queen's messenger had caught us. And truly, by the shimmer in the air at the instant she appeared, I knew there had never been hope of escape. In the Welsh hills and valleys we have tales, more than tales, of such creatures; I had thought the filth and disbelief of London must repel them. At another time I would have been glad that the green countryside along the Thames still held such folk. Glad or no, we had no choice now but to let the greenwood's promise fade into shadow.

Frustration pounded in my veins. I jerked away from Quenta's touch, the mere brush of her hand making me forget that I dare not even think of "him" as "her" until we could be blessedly alone.

I focused on the wide skirt sailing just ahead. Though the farthingale was not devised with a lady dwarf in mind, its absurdity was more than countered by the messenger's bearing and the Queen's crest embroidered on her sleeve. It scarcely needed Quenta's nudge to put me on guard against those keen, merry eyes, though they looked up at me from about the level of my belt.

Such danger should have chilled my ardor. But surely the Queen would waste little time on us, might have already forgotten her whim. At most there might be a gracious word or two, perhaps a small purse. Why, then, command that we bring our play-garb? A jest among her ladies?

But in the great bedchamber we found Her Majesty alone, a slim, pale figure whose aura crackled through the paneled room like heat-lightning.

Our diminutive guide swept a curtsey. "The player boys, Madam. Quentin O'Connor and Kit Rhys."

Bright, tired eyes assessed us. "Well enough, Gwen. Now keep us private for a bit." The attendant gave me a wicked sidelong glance as she went to sit between the great oak door and the carved screen before it.

Quenta elbowed me sharply. I joined her in an elegant stage bow, feeling the royal glance caress our snug-hosed calves. Her Majesty was said to have ever an eye for a well-turned leg. Perhaps it went farther than glances—but I had never heard so much as rumor that it did.

Her voice was cool enough. "So, Titania and Hippolyta. You played the queen's part well, each in your own way."

"Never so well as you, Your Highness." Quenta's green eyes gleamed wickedly, and I suppressed a groan. This was no time for her sly wit!

An answering gleam lit the Queen's eyes. "Ah, but I have performed the role far longer!" Her face seemed less weary now; it was hard to believe that she had more than twice our years. "Do you not think I could play Queen of Faery as well as England's monarch?"

I tried to break the manic current between them. "Yes, in truth, Highness, or Queen of Amazons, or any ruler ever conceived." I knelt with Hippolyta's tunic and gilded leather breastplate across one knee. Her gaze turned toward me, lingering on my long legs, and I felt as when Quenta would stroke me from calf to thigh and beyond, and my flesh would melt and surge in sweet torment.

"I have not your height, lad, to play the Amazon," she said. "You did well enough, though one could scarcely credit that you would ever yield to Duke Theseus, whether in battle or in marriage bed. But come, it was bravely played, if a slighter part than Titania's." She turned to Quenta with a thoughtful look. "Have you two played Master Shakespeare's 'Romeo and Juliet?' You would suit well as lovers."

Did she toy with us? What hope had we against the wits of one who played with envoys, kings, even the Pope, for her own and England's gain?

"Quentin is acclaimed as Juliet," I answered cautiously, "but to tell truth, Hippolyta is my first speaking part, and well may be my last. I am more like to play an accompanying lute, or rattle distant armor."

"It is an awkward age, I know," she said. "Your voice is nigh too low already for a woman's part. Indeed…" Those keen eyes scrutinized us closely. "I might think you both somewhat old for boy players."

I tensed inwardly, forcing my body to reveal nothing. To stifle Quenta's special genius would be a crime against art, against life itself! But if she were thought to be a woman… a woman appearing upon the public stage would cause such outrage that the penalty could only be imagined.

Quenta laughed, and in that instant the tilt of her head, the cock of hip and shoulder, were entirely those of a brash youth. "I can play you any age, Lady, any sex." She took on the bombastic voice and gestures of Bottom the Weaver. "I can play you a roaring Lion, or a most excellent Wall…" and then her voice softened, its husky purr making my flesh quiver with longing for the velvet touch of her tongue. "Or I can be the Lady Moon herself."

She stepped toward the high window, every motion, every line now utterly female, despite the padded trunk-hose muffling the sweet curves of her hips. Had I been a jot closer my hand would have slipped of its own accord between cloth and smooth, seductive skin. And had she turned, and my fingers found what waited between her thighs…

"Look you, Lady, how the new moon burns, no silver bow, but a crescent slit through which the passions of the sky pour forth. Can you not see in me that same bright fire?"

And she was in truth the very essence of the new moon, its tremulous yearning in her slim grace, its hot intensity in her smoldering eyes.

Then I stepped toward her and broke the spell, and it was not her madness but mine that gave us away.

"Sirrah! Do not force me to see that which were better kept hidden!" If the Queen sensed that we were lovers, she had no wish to bring it to an issue. I did not think that she had yet sensed more.

"But Titania may see what England's Queen may not." Quenta knelt, proffering her red wig, leaf-green draperies and silver half-mask. "On Midsummer's Night, the fancies of mortal and fairy alike may roam free. Come with us, Lady, to observe their merry frolics!"

Even through my outrage I saw what Quenta had known at once. Though the Queen might conceal it even from herself, it was for this we had been summoned.

A moment of hesitation; then she took the silver mask. "In truth, I have a fancy to see my host's estate by moonlight. You shall escort me, and together we shall see 'what fools these mortals be.'" She caught my eye. "Yes, lad, I know, none better, how mortal and therefore foolish even a queen may be. That is my own affair. Send Gwen to me, and wait behind the screen." But Gwen was beside her already, the sole evidence of her passing the twinge of a playful pinch upon my rump.

When the Queen was ready Gwen went sedately enough before us.
I could not discern how she bespelled each guard we passed, but it was
clear that none could see her mistress until we were well outside and
mingling with the crowd.

The Lord Chancellor's estate was alight as though to cancel out
entirely this shortest night of the year. Near the great house lords and
ladies strolled the torch-lit paths, or clung together in the shadowy
embrace of shrubberies. Farther off, where the village clustered around
the river landing, a bonfire flared and crackled, and smoke hovered in
the sky like a lecherous ogre.

Habitual command mingled with laughter in the voice that urged
me forward. "Come, they can have devised no cruder games than when
last I walked free on a Midsummer's Night, though it were half a lifetime ago."

Quenta, just behind me, slid her hand between my thighs, and I
had no choice but to move forward or turn and punish her as she
deserved. Two Quentas imprisoned me, both shimmering with manic
energy, both intent on torture. The green-draped lady on my right had
every movement, every gesture, even the voice of Quenta-as-Titania.
No actor could have surpassed her.

On my left pranced my infuriating love in full boy-mode, her rus-
set hair swept up under a jaunty feathered cap. At every step her hand
and hip and shoulder nudged and stroked me. The Queen might not
see, but Gwen, trotting behind, smiled slyly.

Much more of this and I would be unfit to walk at all. In the bedchamber, as we had waited behind the screen, Quenta's seeking hands
and mouth had maddened me until I grasped both wrists and held her
away. Then she flicked her mobile tongue at me, and I could only muf-
fle my groans in the hollow of her throat. This too Gwen had seen as
she came to fetch us.

My arousal was mounting all too close to pain. "Quentin, you
unmannered lout, take the Lady's other side!"

The Queen cocked a brow at my strangled tone, but held out a regal
arm, and Quenta moved to take it. A glance behind showed a grin on
Gwen's round face.

The Queen seemed drawn to all the most vulgar displays. She
cheered on village maidens belaboring the pale hairy bum of a hapless
stock-bound miscreant, and would have taken a switch to him herself
had I not diverted her attention to two buxom wenches admiring the
massive virtues of a docile bull while their blushing swains tried to
draw them onward.

A cluster of tipsy revelers drew us to the village square. I could hear
the clown Will Kemp's falsetto above the laughter; he was a noted player in our troupe, and always rare entertainment. Then I saw his companion, and hoped short Gwen would take no offense.

Will pranced in strumpet's garb across a rough stage, swinging padded rump, while Long Tom the tumbling dwarf somersaulted in mock pursuit. Another time I would have laughed at their antics, and later bought an ale for Tom and traded japes in Welsh; he was a good man, philosophical, adept at using what he had to earn his living.

What he had, besides acrobatic skill and a merry black-bearded face, was the largest codpiece I have ever seen and ample means to fill it. A stallion might have envied his endowment. Will crouched, and swung his bum into Tom's jutting cock, and Tom tumbled and bounced and vaulted back, and the crowd howled, and my face burned. I tried to back my party out of the throng.

We were almost clear when I heard a gasp of outrage. I turned, and saw whose hands clutched at Gwen, and perversely welcomed this vent for my frustration. It was that sniveling whoreson weasel's whelp Dick Fry, talebearer and eternal understudy! And he'd chosen poorly, grabbing Gwen by her small shoulders and heaving her carelessly 'round.

"Ho, Rhys," he hailed me. "Come help me toss this hobgoblin up on stage with t'other! What, no stomach for sport?"

Quenta gripped her dagger; Gwen narrowed her eyes, and Dick's ears and nose began to lengthen and grow hairy. It would have made a rare spectacle, but the Queen must not be found out.

"The lady is with me, you lout! Would you feel my fist smashing through that empty travesty you call a codpiece?" I moved so close he had to peer upward at me. "Do you wet yourself dreaming of my fist mangling your puny balls?" Fear flickered in his eyes, and rage, and something else; I pushed him away in disgust and led my company past the gawking bystanders.

"Lucky for that one you were here," Gwen muttered in Welsh, and spat in the direction Dick had gone.

A slim, imperious hand gripped my shoulder. "Enough, lad. You have done nobly, but the Midsummer's magic I recalled is gone forever."

"Nay, lady, there is magic still!" Quenta's eyes glowed cat-like in the torchlight. "Kit has found a place a fairy queen might lie, and takes me there this night. We shall see what magic three queens together may ignite!"

I could have wrung her slim white neck. The Queen, though, waved dismissively. "I doubt not such a tryst is meant for two alone. Only see me back to the Hall, and then be off wherever youth and Midsummer madness lead you." She took my arm. "You may divert me as we go. Is there indeed 'a bank where the wild thyme blows... With sweet musk roses and with eglantine?'"

"As to that, Lady, the scent was more of mint and fern. I saw daisies but no roses, though there were berry brambles aplenty. Perhaps by daylight you might view it."

"Ay, perhaps." Her voice was bleak.

"Now!" said Quenta. "Now, by moonlight, or not at all!" Her fierce eyes held mine, her meaning all too clear. When I turned toward the greenwood the Queen, a gleam restored in her eye, did not demur.

The way was not so far that the Queen might tire. Indeed, I recalled, Her Majesty was known to out-ride and out-walk her courtiers, and out-last them on the dance floor, too, however quick or subtly sensuous the steps.

Earlier in the day I had followed a stream upcurrent to a place where the waters split and merged again, leaving an islet in their midst. Wading across had been easy, cutting my way through brambles harder, but the reward had been a grassy glade spangled with flowers and hidden from all but the sky.

Here I could bring my love where the rush of water would drown the wild, raw cries her touches forced from me. Always in the city I must stifle my voice, and my pleasure. But here, alone...

To be alone! But, now, not to be.

I waded across with Quenta first. She resisted being carried, but I clung to that remnant of my fantasy despite the temptation to drop her in the deepest water. When she guessed my mood and clung, other temptations rose to nearly overwhelm me.

"It was you who taught me, love, that the magic must be shared," she murmured, and lay a trail of kisses across my throat.

"Between two, yes! Solitary pleasures are paltry trifles! But three? And one of these the Queen? Your madness goes too far!"

"Yours has ever kept pace before! Truly, Kit, you always know my needs, better than I know myself. Open yourself to hers!"

"'Open'... you cannot mean..." but she had slipped from my grasp and danced away, her torch flickering eerily through the brambles.

I hoped that the Queen might have regained some sense, until I saw the torch set into the stream bank reflect from eyes gone fey and feral.

"It is the Queen of Faery who goes abroad this night," she murmured, "and all she sees shall be no more than fairy-tale."

As I lifted her she leaned her head far back to watch the moon and trailed one hand into the stream, and I had to press her close for balance. She felt so like Quenta... or perhaps moonlight on the water dazzled my eyes and other senses... but when I set her on the bank my blood raced despite the water's chill.

Going back for Gwen did little to cool me. Anger played as great a part as arousal; both vixens would be well served to be marooned while I looked elsewhere for ease of my throbbing flesh.

I noted again how compact in form Gwen stood, her mouth scarcely above the level of my loins....

Gwen knew that look. "Nay, youngling, my taste is for meat less tender. Do we but get my Lady safe home before dawn, I am appointed to meet a certain short tumbler and countryman for deep conversation." She gave my thigh a shove. "Go to, distract the Queen from her melancholy. For once she shall be entertained by earthly pleasures on a Midsummer's Night. When she lies safe again in her bed both Tom and I will thank you; for now, I wait and ward here."

Across the water light flickered from the torches left in readiness. No doubt Quenta had also found my bed of heaped sweetfern and the basket of strawberries and flask of wine. Damn her capricious impulse! I ached so for the promised tryst....

Gwen whacked me urgently across the buttocks. "Go to, young fool, or they'll begin without you! And do not doubt that I shall see all!"

I went.

Such moonlight poured across the little glade that the slender crescent seemed to burn as fiercely as my desire. Pale daisy faces glowed with inner life, and fireflies' lanterns pulsed in shadowy bushes—or had Gwen provided fairy lights?

The Queen reclined on the cloak-spread bed, but I had eyes only for Quenta. Moonlight bathed her pale, smooth skin, flowing over every inch, as she stood, her back to us, naked and trembling and lovely before our eyes. When she looked over her shoulder her eyes were moon-glazed jewels.

"Now, sprite," said Titania, "now that your companion is come, you may reveal what you truly are, if you think I have not guessed."

I could scarce keep from laying hands on Quenta. There was no way now to play this scene save by whatever mad script she had devised, though my heart ached that my acceptance, my love, was not enough to allow her to accept herself.

"Some would call me hermaphrodite, Lady," she murmured huskily. "My mother named me son on scant evidence, and my father so wished to believe that he deceived himself. You will find me writ on the parish roles as male."

The Queen raised narrow brows. "I do not presume to question parish records, but I would judge of this evidence myself."

I held my breath as Quenta turned, all bravado fled.

For long moments the Queen surveyed her; the small tilted breasts; the slender waist curving into gently flaring hips; the small, dainty cock nestling amidst tawny curls above the woman's shadowed cleft.

When at last it came the royal voice held not shock but years of anguish.

"Had I shown evidence twice as scant, my mother's neck had escaped the ax! Could my father the King have believed me a son..." Her voice sank almost too low to hear. "How many noble souls might have been spared...."

I fell to my knees before her. That she should feel self-loathing, after all she had done to make England strong!

"Nay, Madam, never wish yourself other! What was't you said before the troops when the Armada threatened? That you had 'the body of a weak feeble woman...but the heart and stomach of a king, and a king of England too....' Such a heart in such a body serves England best of all!"

"It may be so...." She summoned up a smile and spoke to Quenta, who knelt now beside me. "Enough of idle speculation. I had guessed, of course, that you were no boy; I would not have come merely to witness love of Plato's Athenian sort." She turned to me. "You tell me, sir, is this eldritch chimaera male or female? I'll warrant your judgment can be trusted on that score!"

"She is my love," I said simply. "Her form is to me perfect and unique, but I would love her had she horns and a tail."

"You might well love me even better!" Quenta sprang up and twirled around the glade, her wild mood renewed. "Come, show how you love me!" She pulled me up and pressed tight against me, fingers busy in the lacings of my doublet.

"Show you? You know all too well!" I caught her hands. "Is it the audience you play to that quickens your blood? Best be sure she has a taste for such display!"

Titania's eyes were dark behind the silver mask. "Play on," she murmured, and in her tone I heard regret, and sorrow, and the yearnings of a passionate heart too long reined in.

"Nay, Kit, truly, you alone inflame me." Quenta's eyes held mine; my hold slackened and her hands slipped free to brush my face, my lips, my throat, and then my chest in quicksilver, fire-trailing strokes. "Please, Kit, please, touch me, let me touch you...." Her husky voice deepened, throbbing in resonance with the pounding of my blood.

I pulled her close to still her fingers, but the press of her firm breasts was yet more maddening. I ran my hands over smooth back and waist and hips, cupped them over pert, rounded buttocks and lifted her whole body tightly against my hunger. "Your skin is chilled, love...."

"Then give me your shirt." She laughed into my face and pulled open my doublet. When she drew up my shirt and worked her mouth across my chest I knew that I was lost, that not even the icy stream could quench this fire.

"And take off your hose and breeches, too, you are so wet against me!" One hand slipped far down between cloth and flesh and I felt myself grow ever wetter, and hotter too, despite the chill from the wading of the stream.

"Which will you bare first?" she purred, a wicked light flickering in her eyes as fireflies flickered in the grass around us and their throbbing points of light seemed to spark in my own depths.

It scarcely mattered. I chose what might by a fraction be the lesser shock. I tossed my doublet aside and pulled off my shirt, draping it around

Quenta's chilly shoulders while she tore at bindings grown unbearable and let my aching breasts surge free.

"Not Athens." My breath caught as Quenta's soothing strokes became a torment that made me ever fuller and more sore. "Not Athens, Lady, but Sappho's Isle of Lesbos. I may reject the constraints of a woman's body, but I rejoice always in its pleasures."

This, she had not foreseen. The mask dropped; her eyes were wide.

"Please, Kit, please…" Quenta tugged at my belt while her hot mouth drove my breasts and nipples taut and aching with the need for more. "Please, I must…" Her voice was muffled against my swollen flesh.

"Slowly," I soothed, though I could scarcely speak. "The slower the sweeter, love." As ever, she who had teased and maddened me for hours was now all desperate haste, while to me each stab of pleasure promised such further, keener pangs that I would not give up any part to leap too quickly to release.

I kicked off wet boots and wriggled out of breeches and hose, Quenta's hands more distraction than help. Then I half-turned that the Queen might see I had no such exotic equipage as my love.

Her gaze moved over me from head to foot, taking in my length and strength and the incongruous swellings of a woman's body. A fierce longing for her approval swept me; now I understood what drove Quenta to reveal herself.

"You are the Amazon indeed," the Queen murmured at last, "and you," to Quenta, "a most exquisite Queen of Sprites." Then she laughed. "Master Shakespeare had it skewed, to say Hippolyta dallied with Oberon and Titania with Duke Theseus. Yours promises to be the better play, in truth!"

"Not so much play as dance, Lady, with intricate and subtle steps." I gazed into Quenta's eyes, holding her to stillness as my hands devoured the sweet curves of her body. She tried valiantly to wait, to savor, as I put my mouth to her small pouting breasts. She trembled, and her breath came in quick, soft moans, as I licked and gently bit at her thrusting nipples.

Then her hips began to sway, and twist, and she clutched at me, and since the bed was occupied there was nothing for it but to lift her up along my body until that sweet seeking little dagger, no more in truth than a greatly inflated clitoris, pressed against my own.

She cried out, and clung to me with arms and thighs. I stilled, knowing her needs, that every movement must be hers now, every pressure, lest the rapture of her wondrous engorgement turn to pain. The lightest stroke of my hand, my tongue, could tip the balance.

As steadily as could be I endured the piercing stabs of pleasure. Rough moans escaped me as she arched and writhed against my mound, but from her there came only a keening so faint it might have floated from a distant world.

All at once she flung back her head, the moon mirrored in wild, half-closed eyes. "Now love, now…"

But already I had slipped one hand between our bodies and into her ready heat. Two fingers, deep and gently deeper, probing and pressing into her hunger; and now at last her cries burst forth, and her slippery depths clutched at me, and her great hard clit vibrated against mine; and my joy in her joy came near to overwhelming me.

Still there was more I must, would, have. I held her while spasms dwindled into trembling and her breath at long last slowed. Then I loosed my hold, and she slid gradually down my length, her mobile mouth teasing and caressing all the way until she knelt before me.

"Do you lag behind, love?" Her laugh was still unsteady. "Come, you will overtake me yet." She moved her hands over my hips until they pressed into my tingling buttocks, then pulled me toward her. My clit, still aquiver, leapt at the subtle flick of her tongue.

I tangled my fingers in her moon-burnished hair as she drove me to new extremes. Moans racked me as she nudged my thighs apart and thrust her long supple tongue up into my molten cunt. Deep inside me a bright slim moon seemed to pulse and swell into roundness.

Pleasure surged and pounded through me, and my own rasping cries seemed far away as I rode the waves, striving still for more, and more, needing something more with an incoherent desperation…

And then a warm body pressed against my back, and a voice murmured low into my ear, "Surely this figure can be danced by three!" Slim arms wrapped about me from behind and long clever fingers cupped and weighed my full breasts and made the aching pressure build and build; and when she curved her palms around my nipples and circled them so lightly that the hardened tips must strain and thrust into her touch it was the final stroke. My clit strained and thrust too, and my cunt clenched and swallowed at the firm flame of Quenta's tongue, and the moon exploded inside me in a roaring burst of tangible light.

Or perhaps the roaring was my own. When at last awareness spread beyond receding ecstasy I felt hot breath on my shoulder, and a voice, hesitant yet tinged with laughter, murmured in my ear; "And can you make me sing so, as well as dance?"

Her arms were tight about me as her body swayed and rubbed against mine, breasts stroking my back, soft belly pressed beseechingly into the curve of my buttocks.

"Yea, Lady, you shall sing as full and sweet as any!" Quenta toppled us both onto the sweetfern bed and sprawled atop us; and there indeed we tasted royal flesh and royal passion, and taught the woman within to sing, taught her most thoroughly the joys of the body fate had decreed.

We had no doubt that the spirit of Midsummer accepted our triple offering as graciously as that of any mundane coupling. As wave followed wave of pleasure my lovers took on a glow of celestial light, Quenta the silver of the moon, our Queen the royal gold of the sun; while I, the dark earth, absorbed and radiated back their overlapping aurae. Bright sparks like stars flashed and swirled above us, while a swooping comet bore the grin and wicked eyes of Gwen.

Much later we laughed together and soothed our throats with wine and berries. When Gwen's muted whistle sounded we looked up, bemused; the moon hung low and the first faint harbingers of morning streaked the sky. I thought of her assignation with Tom and felt some guilt, but when we had made our way across the water she only smiled at the sweetfern clinging to the Queen and made no reproach.

"Ah, Gwen," said her Lady, somewhat ruefully, "I doubt but that I have forfeited the name of 'Virgin Queen.'"

A faint shadow drifted across my residual glow. Had we added to her burdens?

But Gwen had the right of it. "No such thing, Madam," she said cheerfully, hurrying us along deserted pathways. "It is the Queen's English, after all, and can mean no other than what the Queen decrees."

Is there anyone who hasn't wondered—even once—what it'd be like to have their lover's else's genitals, to be able to feel what sex felt like for them? In this sweet, evocative tale of an imaginary sex exchange in a magical-sounding place-time, Magdalene Meretrix makes it deliciously possible.

Magdalene Meretrix is a musician, textile artist, web designer and writer as well as being a 17-years-and-counting veteran of the sex industry, having worked the full range of the field from phone sex operator to stripper to prostitute. Look for her book, Turning Pro: A Guide to Sexwork for the Ambitious and the Intrigued *(Greenery Press). She lives in Idaho with a cat, a rat, and a wonderful lover, and online at www.magdalenemeretrix.com.*

Mars Conjunct Venus

Magdalene Meretrix

She'd come to him countless times, aching for union. Joining, parting, joining again. And there was always that yearning, that wishing for something she didn't have and he couldn't give her. He, too, always seemed to be seeking, thrusting deeply as if he wanted to crawl back inside the womb and nestle there gently within her.

Tonight the moonlight angled through the window, clinging to his boycurves. For a moment, she was afraid to touch him—savoring instead the soft shadows from his eyelashes, fluttering in time with his heart. Finally, the ache of wanting him outstripped the pain of his beauty twisting inside her and she traced his profile with a trembling finger, her fingertip lingering on his full lips.

"Sweet," he breathed in a sigh, a trailing tendril of smoke. "I want you to see." She could taste his tortured nerve endings, the crackle of electricity snapping from his fingertips, extended like probing Tesla coils, entwined in her hair, making it glare with static like a child's sparkler. She could smell his sex growing. The metallic tang of his sweat was causing her to expand until she felt as if she contained herself, him, the room, the city—blood flowing through her veins in rhythm with the freight trains. Breasts flowing rivers of milk and his cock towering high above markets, temples, undulating fields.

She watched him through her fever-haze as he half-raised to kneel before her, taking his cock in his hand, a curious look on his face. "This part is always awkward," he apologized as he tenderly lifted his testicles like St. Francis bearing a wounded bird. She watched, fascinated. He lifted the sack all the way to his left then kept lifting at an impossible and frightening angle. She gasped in fear and sympathetic pain, eyes widening as he brought his balls over the hard-as-steel shaft of his cock, then around to his right. He paused in his meticulous ministrations to glance at her. A single tear was edging its way down her cheek, a second one caught in her lashes.

Carefully holding his penis in its awkward, terrifying position, he leaned forward and kissed her, first on one eye, then the other, her eyelashes tickling his nose. He settled back on his haunches, licking salt from his blossom lips. She trembled.

"Don't cry, it only hurts a little. You'll see in a minute—you will be everything." Her tears seemed to pain him, for he worked more quickly, wincing a bit each time he'd swing his balls around beneath his empurpled cock.

She couldn't move, but she heard a tiny squeak as his penis came loose. It took a second for her to realize that it hadn't made the sound, she had. It seemed as if it should've come from his cock, though, for now it sat patiently on the palm of his hand, testicles dangling to one side. A drop of wetness appeared at the tip, reflecting the cold white moon.

He held his cock up to her pelvis, resting it perfectly on the arch of her pubic bone. She looked down in awe as he twisted it onto her as casually as if he were closing a bottle. She could swear she saw it wink its gleaming wet eye at her as it spun around. With the final twist, she felt a clicking sensation near her perineum and his... her balls ached. She hissed her breath in sharply at the cold nausea in the pit of her stomach, sweat prickling out all over her.

"Just breathe slowly and deeply and the pain will pass," he said, a fey gleam in his eyes, his crotch startlingly bare, his long, long legs folded beneath him.

As the throbbing sickness passed, she felt her cock grow hard again and she began to feel more complete than she ever had before. Complete and completely aroused. She wanted to rub that hard cock everywhere through him—in his hair, in his mouth, deep inside his tight pink secret places. She held back, timidly, though, afraid this hunger in her would take over, afraid of hurting him, afraid of disgusting him, afraid he'd tell her no and terrified that he'd say yes.

Then he twisted to lay back on his side, propped on one elbow, calculatedly casual. "Use me sweetly," he purred.

Overwhelmed, she ran her hands along his body, starting with his glossy hair, brushing over his nipples to hear him moan, stopping at his waist to pull his dear body closer to her. The cock bounced between her legs as it bumped into his thigh. A jolt of sensation made her gasp and she rubbed the cock along his smooth skin, marveling at the heat.

She combed her fingers through his long, dark hair and pulled his head up toward her. The cock stood at attention, casting shifting shadows across his cheek. He lay sprawled beneath her, looking up with awe and love. She knelt, hips arching back and forth involuntarily, the musky rush of swollen cock almost more than she could bear. He parted his shining lips and reverently took the tip of her cock into his mouth, lips sealed around the shaft and tongue curved around the head. He held her there in his mouth and then gently slipped the slickness of his mouth down, down, down.

Her breath quavered with a trembling passion at the reality of dream sensations fulfilled. Had her clit swelled far beyond its most extreme dimensions, lavished by a score of eager tongues, she would not have felt so caressed, so enraptured, so engulfed as she did now. Half her cock was in his mouth and all her attention was between his lips.

She took his head in both her hands and thrust her hips forward, burying her cock in his mouth. Her body shook at the sweep of powerful sensations—his silky hair swinging against her thighs, the oven of his throat clenching and unclenching, his hands creeping up towards the small of her back, arms wrapped around her body as he suckled her. Savage wanton mingled with tenderness and she slipped from his mouth, taking his petal lips between hers, kissing him deeply.

When she lifted her head again, his gaze was upon her. Pupils dilated with desire, he allowed his eyes to travel slowly from her hair to her breasts to her cock, still wet with his saliva. In an instant she saw herself as he must see her and asked, "What am I?"

A tender smile played at the corners of his mouth. "You are my love," he replied and lay back, slipping a pillow beneath his hip. "You are my lover. Take me," he whispered.

She looked down again in wonderment at their gleaming cock jutting up between her legs, then watched his face as she slowly slipped inside him. His ass was golden hot tight oozing sweetness, and wet as a cunt. His eyes were huge and dark in the growing moonlight and his lips had reddened to a deep blood color. All else fell away from them, twin planets in mutual orbit. She pulled out of him then slid back in, interminably falling into the mystery of his sweet cunt, his ass. This hard cock no longer seemed to belong to him or her but rather to be a strange naked animal, offering eternal intercession between her passion and his sex.

Mindless, bodyless, she plunged into him over and over, hurting him, loving him, fucking him. He moaned and moved beneath her as she used his cock, owning it, joining him with him. His ass held her cock, squeezed it, pulsed against it, chipping the edges of her awareness until all that was left was this need, this cock, this sex. A sliding, a thrusting, a swelling. Nerves spinning in tightening spirals. Rising, becoming, coming.

She tried to hold back, make their pleasure last as long as possible but her balls contracted with a tickle-ache and she became a conduit with one source of relief, one path of release. Semen gushed up and out of her, from the tips of her toes, from the roots of her hair, gey-sering out the end of her cock as a hot white light that flooded his insides, searing him, branding him as her own.

As the golden rush of afterglow enveloped her, she looked down into his face, transformed through ecstasy and beheld... herself. His body was still that long, lean boybody she thirsted to embrace but he had stolen her face for his own. Startled, she put one hand to her head to see if he'd given her his in exchange.

Feeling none of the separation that normally followed a joining, she rolled alongside of him, holding him... her in his arms... or at least in someone's arms... at this point, she didn't think they could claim all these parts between just the two of them. For that matter, she didn't think that there really were two of them anymore. Her skin felt for the spaces between them, only to find him everywhere she was, every-where she was not. Her ass felt strangely full and hot and her penis lay against her abdomen, sleeping. He hadn't asked her to return it. She wasn't sure she wanted to part with it, nor even certain that she could.

He tilted his face to her and kissed her rosebud lips. "I love you..." he breathed into his own ear .

"I love you..." she breathed into her own ear, feeling it echo like an image in a carnival fun house mirror, from lip to ear, lip to ear, lip to ear, endlessly as they drifted into sleep.

Part of the female-to-male experience is being mistaken for much younger than your actual age; sometimes as much as twenty years younger. It made Raven profoundly uncomfortable when he transitioned at the age of thirty-five and teenage girls started making eyes at him. Then again, we suppose some people discover that youngsters are more hip to things tranny than their easily-freaked elders. This chickenhawk story (written by someone who is chronologically still quite young enough to be the chicken and not the hawk) suggests just that, as old punk meets young punk and finds that he can still dish out the surprises.

sam kling = stompyboy = queer as fuck; dykeboy; girl fag; bootlicker; Goth; James Cullen, Mr. Philadelphia Drag King 2001; porn fan; Irish music lover; pierced & tattooed & mohawked; friend to dominatrices, fetishy soccer moms, and felines alike; photographer; hellraiser. stompyboy loves cheese and dances all stompy-like (hence the name.) stompyboy has penisenvy@bombdiggity.com. stompy wants to thank VNV Nation for making hir less of an asshole.

Mallrat

Sam Kling

I saw him at the mall, one of those silly beautiful children who spends so much time engaging in petty dramas in front of the cineplex, sharing dollar sodas at the food court, primping for the dream lover who may never come.

"You're getting looks," my friend said to me, quietly.

I must have been at least six years older than even the oldest of the kids, but I remembered exactly what it was like to be in their position, to see an older person in 'the uniform'... all black, tall boots, leather jacket, piercings. We would always watch them carefully with awe and curiosity and sometimes contempt, mostly because we had contempt for everyone, even for those older versions of ourselves. We looked up to them, because they were living proof that we could get through the "dark pits of nothingness" that were our lives. At the same time we hated them because they were older and could do more: they could get into the clubs about which we only heard fairy tale stories, they could buy the drinks that we had to stealthily obtain from our parents' locked liquor cabinets, they could legally buy the clove cigarettes that we got through friends and chain-smoked, wearing the sweet smoke like shrouds, like dreams.

I felt them look at me, my blue hair and pierced septum, black army pants tucked into calf-high oxblood boots, faded Ministry T-shirt and attitude. Each one of the little mallrats looked at me, each one in baggy jeans and skater shoes and intentionally ratty haircuts and basketball jerseys, and none of them interested me except the one beautiful boy.

He didn't look a day over sixteen, but he seemed much older than that. His skin was the color of creamy coffee and smooth and soft as linen paper, naturally black hair falling in shiny waves over his forehead and into his eyes, giving him that delicious innocent puppy look. Silver jewelry glinted against his long, slender fingers, and a spark of light glinted off the ring of the bondage collar he wore around his neck. Our eyes met for only a brief moment, but in that instant, we exchanged much more than a look: his gorgeous eyes held me, and I knew that I must have him.

I could lure this boy child with candy and sweet wine and the promise of a warm bed, companionship, anything he could want. I could tell that this boy was lonely, desperate for human touch, and I knew I could give him just that. I promised myself that I would have him. I sat with my friend, and she told me about some fight with her boss, or something similarly insignificant, but all I could think was of how to get this boy home with me, how to own him, how to lead him into my bed so I could...

"You're not listening to me," my friend finally said. "You're think-ing about that boy in the black T-shirt."

I had to admit that I was.

"I'm sorry, Sarah, but he's gorgeous. I must have him. I want to take him home with me, I want to drive him mad. I want to rip into his gorgeous skin and taste his cock and fuck him for hours. I want to fuck him raw and..." I broke off in mid sentence as I saw him get up and leave his friends.

"God, why do you have to be so damned dramatic all the time?" I heard Sarah say, exasperated.

Damn, I thought, must be time for him to go home, off to meet mom and dad. I'd had to piss like mad, but I hadn't wanted to take my eyes off the boy. Now that he was gone, I told Sarah I'd be right back, and went in search of the restroom.

That damned mall was always under construction, and the bath-rooms were down a long winding hall, dark and dusty, the kind of place where you'd actually expect someone to jump out at you from behind any corner and drag you away to an uncertain fate. That's why it annoy me that I was so surprised when someone came towards me from the other side of a corner. I ran smack into him, and was almost pissed until I realized it was the boy. Before I could say anything, he put his head down and stammered an apology, holding his hands behind his back in a delicious submissive posture.

"Uh, sorry, sorry, so sorry..." he stuttered, seemingly afraid to look me in the face.

"It's okay," I said, trying not to grab him by the throat to push him against the wall. His obvious submissiveness and shyness and fear had me suddenly very aware of how desperate I was to have this beautiful boy, to press him face-up against a wall and grab hold of his painfully

sharp hipbones and break him in a million deliciously mean ways.
Without even thinking, I reached out and touched his beautiful skin. I
just barely brushed my finger over his cheekbone, and he was instantly quiet.

He looked up at me cautiously, and with the slightest tremble in his
voice, barely audible, obviously with all the courage he could muster,
he said, "Take me home with you? Please, Sir?"

I hesitated for a moment, and my mind spun with the possibilities.
It was what I'd fantasized, but I knew it could be a bad idea to just run
off with some random kid, just put him in my car and drive away
through the night, speeding down the glistening, rain slick streets. My
mind raced along, slipping at each curve of what could happen, what
could go wrong, then speeding up at each thought of what could go
right. I felt a warmth spread through my body, spreading outward
from between my legs through my chest and out to my fingers like
slow lightning, maddeningly slow in contrast with the speediness of
my thoughts. I felt drunk, and I couldn't stop myself.

I pressed the boy against the dusty sheetrock wall with my body,
pushing my cheek against his, my mouth right next to his ear. He
squirmed and let out a little groan, a tiny animal noise that made the
heat in my crotch even more insistent.

"Do you know what you're getting yourself into?" I growled.

When he didn't answer, I pulled away and left him standing there
against the wall. The corridor was narrow, and two steps backward
backed me up against the opposite wall. He stood for a moment, utterly still, his eyes closed. He drew in a long shuddering breath as he
opened his eyes, then dropped to his knees at my feet. Without thinking, I leaned back against the wall and grabbed a fistful of the silky hair
at the back of his neck, drawing his face closer to the seam of my jeans.
He ran his gentle hands slowly up the backs of my thighs to cup my
ass, then ran the tip of his tongue along my zipper, and suddenly I
remembered that it'd be pretty bad news to have someone walk back
here and get an eyeful. I could just imagine some poor soccer mom
with a sticky-faced toddler on one of those little leashes, Old Navy and
Nordstrom bags dangling from her arm, could almost hear her screams
as she caught sight of this beautiful boy going down on me right here
in the mall. I tightened my grip on the boy's hair and pulled him away
quickly.

He whimpered quietly, reaching for the bulge in my jeans. "Please,"
he begged, "I want to taste you…"

"Not here, boy," I interrupted, and pulled him up by the collar. In
my car, I told him to look through the tapes in the glove compartment
and pick out whatever he wanted. He pawed through them for a
moment, and I heard a quiet "oooh…" as he picked one out of the
pile. He popped the tape into the player and immediately turned up the
volume as I recklessly pulled out of my parking space. We rolled our

windows down and let The Smiths fly loudly out and behind us like
the tail of a comet as we rode swiftly through the cool drizzle.

"So," the boy started to ask, as he lit a sweet smelling clove cigarette, "where do we go?"

I thought briefly, but it was so hard to think with this beautiful boy
sitting so close to me, ready to fuck, ready to taste, ready to break and
tear and caress.

"My place…" he suggested, before I could answer. I revved the
engine in response, and let the engine match my racing pulse. The boy
kept reaching for my thigh, caressing gently, trying to inch his way
towards the warmth between my legs. It was pure heaven, my over-
sensitive nerves screaming for the feel of his fingers, sucking up the
sensation like a parched desert soaking up rain, but it was horribly dis-
tracting as I drove down narrow suburban streets that I had never seen
before, so I slapped his hand away. The third time he reached, I grabbed
his hand and squeezed.

"Do it again," I growled, "and I'm dropping you off right here.
Keep your hands in your lap. Got it?" He nodded timidly and obediently kept his hands in his lap for the rest of the ride. I could tell he
wanted to touch himself. It was hard for him to have his hands in his
lap, so close to the gorgeous erection he had. I reached over and moved
his hands, fondling the fabric around his rock hard dick. His head fell
back against the headrest as I touched him, and his breathing grew
quick. Just as I wrapped my fingers around the tip of his cock through
his jeans, he whispered, "This is my block… my house is right
there…"

I squeezed gently once, then let go. After all, I needed both hands
to parallel park.

His room was a sanctuary of the passage to adulthood, a combination of the comforts of youth and the darker emotions of a child on
his way through adolescence. His walls were covered with posters of
The Cure, Marilyn Manson, and morbid comic books. Liquor-bottle
candle holders stood upon every surface, half-finished drawings of Tim
Burton-like characters adorned the walls, black lace hung from the corner of a mirror marked with black lipstick kisses. Stuffed animals and
old GI Joes stood atop a bookshelf full of ratty, dog eared books whose
spines repeated the names Anne Rice, Poppy Brite, and Stephen King
over and over. Pages softened from constant reading, these books
would be folded over and tear-stained, favorite passages memorized
and taken to heart, highlighted over and over until the butterfly-wing
pages glowed faintly when under the black light fixture above the boy's
bed. The bed was surrounded by Jhonen Vasquez and James O'Barr
comics, stacked in fanatically neat piles next to dune-like drifts of battered spiral notebooks. If this gorgeous boy had as much in common
with me at that age as he seemed to, I knew those notebooks would be
full of late night ramblings, sonnets of unrequited love, bad goth poet-

ry and pencil sketches of his own black velvet utopia. This boy and I had a lot in common, and I looked forward to fucking this younger version of myself.

"Hold on just a sec…" he said quietly, and pulled the blanket off his bed. He crossed the room and wedged the blanket into the space under the door. "Don't want anyone to hear that I'm home."

Christ, I thought to myself, this boy's parents are gonna hear something going on and walk in on god knows what and blow my goddamned head off! "What, your parents don't approve of late night guests?" My tone was a bit more biting than I had intended, and the boy looked hurt—and more than a bit confused.

"Parents? What are you talking about?" He moved closer and pressed his fragile frame against my side, massaging my hip with his crotch. My fear of parental wrath grew as quickly as my lust, and I moved away from the boy.

"I really don't need to get arrested tonight, sorry…" I headed for the blanket-chinked door.

"I know what you're thinking," he said, a sexy defiant pout creeping into the edge of his delicious mouth. "But I'm not illegal." He slowly started removing his shirt, and I saw the edges of a fairly extensive tattoo peek out from under the black fabric, but still I remained skeptical. "I'll show you my goddamned driver's license, if that'll help."

I remembered being 18 and covered with tattoos, getting carded for cigarettes, always thinking to myself, "Who needs age ID with full sleeves and a face full of metal?" But carded for sex? What a horrible, terrible world we live in!

My head spun. The boy was so tiny, so fragile and fine-boned and hairless, how could it be? I quickly decided I didn't care. Come to think of it, wasn't I a bit of an impostor as well?

He stood in front of me, skinny, shirtless, pale and pouting, body language spinning off in a million directions of lust and hope and frustration. Skinny arms folded across skinny chest, one bony hip defiantly cocked in my direction, sparkly deep molasses-sticky eyes questioning, he finally tempted me. I had my fingers tangled in the hair at the nape of his neck before I was quite sure that I wasn't still going to leave. My closed fingers turned so quickly into a steely fist, pulling tightly on the spun silk, his skull tight against my knuckles. Not a single tiny noise escaped his gorgeously exposed throat, not the slightest squeal or whimper or plea.

And it pissed me off. I wanted to really rip into this boy, tear his little world apart and teach him what heavy flirting with strangers in malls would get him. Before I could even register what the soft clicking noise was, my knife was open and pressed against his throat. He went limp in my arms, and I looked into his eyes… there was no fear, just lust. "I never imagined that being this intimidated would get my dick so hard," he said quietly, the hint of a little cocky smile played itself across his trembling lips.

I flipped the knife over, pressing the dull side was pressing against his throat. After all, I wanted to fuck him, not kill him. With my other hand I reached down to unbutton my pants. I pushed him towards the bed with the back of my blade and he fell on to his back. He fumbled with the zipper on his faded black jeans, his slender fingers working the button, tugging on the zipper as it bunched and stuck. He yanked at them impatiently, working them over his jutting hip bones.

I'm afraid to sound like an asshole, but all I wanted was to fuck him. I wanted nothing else then… nothing more than to sink my cock in that beautiful boy's desperate ass. I didn't want to slow down this heat to take any time to kiss him, because to feel his hot mouth and searching tongue would only make me want to shove my aching cock in his mouth, and well, I had reasons for not wanting to do that just yet. I didn't want to slow down this passion to take the time to bite him, because to feel his paper-thin creamy skin between my teeth would only make me want to rip his flesh from his fragile frame, and as much as I appreciated Poppy Brite's stories of gore-encrusted vis- cera-fucking, I definitely wanted this boy alive and kicking.

I'd like to say that I had a little more class, that I made some attempt at foreplay, but there's no use in lying. I simply climbed onto the boy, and turned him onto his stomach. That was when I saw his tattoo. I unzipped my pants and wrapped my fingers around my cock, taking a moment to study his back as I straddled his fine young ass and stroked my dick. It was a collage of gothic comic book imagery on his right shoulder blade… finely rendered blackwork images of Death from *Sandman*, Shelly from *The Crow*, Mr. Fuck from *Johnny the Homicidal Maniac*. The images rippled as he flexed under me, straining his fine muscles to get my attention. I rolled off of the boy and stood behind him, up against the bed. I pushed myself between his legs and kicked his ankles apart, unbuttoning my jeans and pulling them down just a bit farther. He pulled his knees up just the slightest bit, giving me the most per- fect view of his sweet ass. I knelt on the bed between his spread legs and leaned forward just enough to rest my swollen dick against his hot flesh. Again, I wish I could wax poetic about the beautiful moments that I spent adoring and caressing and whatnot, but the truth is that all I did was spit into my hand and give my cock a quick lubricating stroke before rubbing it between his ass cheeks.

He balled the sheets up in his fists and braced himself as I made use of those wonderful hipbones. I grabbed onto him as I entered him, gently at first. As soon as I felt the head of my cock push into him, we were nothing but rhythmic primal energy. I was as deep in him as I could possibly be, grabbing his hips to pull him farther and farther down on my shaft as we settled into a deep, grinding fuck.

"Oh Christ. Just don't come in my ass," he pleaded halfheartedly, gasping.

"Don't worry," I whispered between strokes, "that won't be a problem."

"That's what they all say..." He sounded skeptical, but he didn't miss a single beat. He was pushing himself against me, grunting as he strained to meet my deep strokes. I became so entranced with watching his skin ripple over the subtle movements of all the fine muscles in his back that even my cock seemed much less important.

My hands began to wander over his belly, soft, finely haired skin so pliable under my searching fingers. I followed that wonderful trail of soft little hairs down, down to the base of his cock, harder than I could have possibly expected, and my lust suddenly went unchecked. One hand still pulling at his hip, I wrapped my free fingers around his dick and let him fuck my hand. He started moving fast, bucking between my cock and my hand, having his ass fucked, having his dick stroked.

It was all over too fast, before I could savor it enough, before I could truly start to memorize the movements and noises of this beautiful boy and his body. I felt his balls against the edge of my hand, and he shuddered under me as he let out an intense, animal groan. After a moment I brushed my fingers over his tip and felt the hot drops of come trailing off as I moved my hand away. I rubbed the sticky, sweet-smelling stuff on his ass as he slumped onto the stained black sheets, his breathing heavy and exhausted. He lay still for a moment and I pulled out of him, slowly, carefully. He whimpered, a little kittenish whine, and turned over to face me just as I had stuffed my cock back into my underwear.

"Wait," he whispered, reaching for my crotch as I pulled up the zipper. "You didn't come yet." He swatted my hands away, trying to get at my dick.

"What do you care?" I said, with a fake sneer. "You had your fun." The sneer turned into a smirk. He kept reaching, trying to get into my jeans, and I kept pushing him away, laughing. Before I could push him off again, he had me pinned, and reached right down into my jeans and tighty-whiteys and grabbed.

Time stopped. I felt my heart stop and my stomach lurch straight up into my throat. I think I even stopped breathing. The look on his face scared me almost as much as what he'd just done. The shy, submissive boy I'd met at the mall was a bit scarier now, as he all but ripped my pants off to see what it was that he had in his hand. Should I run? Stay and fight if it turned ugly? What now?

And there it was, in the light, pure as day... my cock in his hand, standing proudly through the fly of my underwear, all ten completely obvious silicone inches of it. Even worse, the stitched-leather straps of my harness were peeking through my briefs.

As I made a move to wrench myself away from this sanctuary-turned-nightmare, the boy put a hand on my chest to stop me. I glanced over at him quickly, ready to turn away from an oncoming fist. All I saw in his eyes was measured surprise... none of the twisted rage that I was expecting. Our eyes met and locked for a single second that felt like forever.

"Your cock is gorgeous. Let me make you come." I think I saw him whisper it more than I heard it, my eyes locked on his face, incredulous. I'm not sure that my ears and brain were even working enough to register an actual full sentence.

I remember watching his lips touch the head of my cock. It was still moist from fucking him. He kissed me there, and slowly parted his lips to pull me into his mouth. I remember watching his head bobbing slowly between my trembling thighs, his hands working the last few inches that he couldn't quite accept into his throat, the feel of his warm sticky spit trickling down onto my leg. His eyes would meet mine for brief moments, seeking approval, until his beautiful black silk hair fell into his eyes and he simply worked by feel. I remember coming for the first time, with another person, and it had been different from anything I'd ever felt on my own. When I came this time, with this boy's lips around my cock, it felt like something new yet again, a come that started deep in the folds of my brain.

We lay in bed together, tangled, sticky, sated, tired, still a little unsure of what had just happened. "So," I began with a tired smile, "what happened to that shy submissive young boy I picked up at the mall? He turned into a hell of an aggressive young man."

"Well," he purred, reaching for my cock, "we're not always what we seem."

When we put out the submission guidelines for this book, we were very clear about one of the things we didn't want—forced feminization transvestite porn with the same old ten plots. Don't send it to us, we said, unless it's so totally different that we can't resist it. This story was the only one that fell into that category. And how.

Alex Gino lives mostly happily in Philadelphia, PA. Ze is involved with the Transgender Health Action Coalition there. Hir self-identification meanders along the transgender continuum, but ze commonly refers to hirself by a combination of a few of the following terms: omnisexual, gender blending, nonaligned, femmey gay boy, female crossdressing, bouncing fag, female-towards-something, genderqueer, trannyboy, breast-touting, testosterone-pumping, bundle of righteous indignation. Ze welcomes all correspondence at: purplescissors@yahoo.com.

Becoming

Alex Gino

B ut I..."
Mistress glared at me. My eyes stung. I closed my mouth immediately, nearly biting my tongue, and lowered my head. Mistress
pulled off the black leather glove on her right hand, finger by finger.

"I know this glove is so old-fashioned..." The words dropped from
her lips onto my head. "So... Marquis de Sade. But it works ever so
well." Inching along, thumb, forefinger, middle, ring, pinky. Thumb,
forefinger, middle, ring, pinky. Thumb. Forefinger. Middle. Ring. Pinky.
"You're so cute when you tremble, love. And you do it so easily."

The glove struck my right cheek. I did not move my head. The glove
hit my left.

"See there," Mistress said, "That barely hurt at all, did it?" She
brushed the soft, cool leather of the glove against my cheeks, then rested her arms on my shoulders. "Now, as I was saying, darling, you're
going to learn tonight. You're going to learn to be a girl. A good one."

But I don't want to be a girl. I never did. Hadn't I worn my hair short since the first
time I found my mother's scissors in her bureau? Didn't I burn all my Barbie dolls? Wasn't
I the one who refused to wear a dress to graduation? Didn't I always pass, even with my
breasts? How could...

Mistress' nails seared into my neck. I concentrated on standing.
"Now that's pain, hon." Deeper. I screamed. "Don't forget it, dearie. But
what am I doing? I'm going to destroy your beautiful, feminine flesh
if I continue." I felt Mistress' nails pop out of their homes in my flesh,
and she licked the slits in my neck.

"Now, you will learn to be a good girl." Mistress picked up my leash from the table and latched it to my collar. "Right?"

I felt my stomach turn and my clit tingle. "Yes, Mistress."

"Good," she said. "Because your mother certainly didn't do a very good job teaching you the first time around." She looked almost startled at her own words. "Do you need to call Venus?" she asked. Calling Venus; that was my safeword to her. Just like she could always call Mars if she needed to calm herself. Could she still do that? Was I still Mars? Wasn't Mars a boy?

"No, Mistress," I said softly.

"Very good, girl. Now strip. I want to see your flesh." I began to unbutton my jeans.

"Top first," she said. "I want to see your breasts."

"Yes, Mistress." I slowly unbuttoned my blue shirt and pulled my arms through the sleeves, keeping my back tight. Mistress examined her fingernails, glancing up occasionally to meet my eyes. I folded the shirt and neatly placed it on the bed. I unclasped my binder, a tight piece of elastic, and laid it on top of my shirt. I pulled my white T-shirt over my head, shook it out, folded it and placed it on the pile.

"Very good," called Mistress, fiddling with a collar she had often used on me. "Now the bottoms." I finished unbuttoning my jeans and slid them off; then my underwear. I was so proud the day I'd walked into the men's department to buy them. BVDs. I'd felt so strong; so sure, so aware. I laid the underwear on the pile, then folded the jeans and placed them on top.

The air was cold on my skin; my nipples began to tighten and harden. I pulled in my ass cheeks and stood before Mistress; she stood over me. "Not bad. Not half bad. But you have a lot to learn. To begin, the proper panties." She held up a small piece of pink lace. "Put these on," she directed.

I took the fabric from her hands, fumbled to find the largest hole for my body; slid my legs through the other two large holes and pulled up. The fabric sat loosely about my middle and covered small portions of my ass.

"Lovely, my sweet," Mistress smiled. "How femme. So, how does it feel, little girl?"

I could feel my skin seeping through each hole. "Loose, Mistress."

Mistress' lips stretched into a thin smile as she chuckled. "Too loose?"

"N... no, Mistress," I stuttered.

"Oh good," Mistress said. "But fear not, this other piece will be tight. Do you know what I'm thinking of?"

"No, Mistress."

"Think, honey. What do girls wear?" She paused. "Well?"

What did girls wear? "Bras?"

Mistress tickled my side with her nails. I did not flinch. "Silly girl. The day I first went out dressed, what did I go out and buy? You were there. You remember." Mistress' smile grew. "Oh."

"Well, dearie, don't you remember? I was so happy. That guy at the store said, 'Miss? What size will you have?' I was so happy. I can only hope my corset can make you happy too. Hands over your head." I slowly raised my hands. I felt the leather against my skin. Mistress adjusted the corset. She tightened the back from the bottom, pulling, pulling.

"Stand up straight, little girl," she called. "We need to make you look pretty, or the boys will never like you. You want the boys to like you, don't you?"

"Yes, Mistress," I whispered.

She pulled, pushed her knee into my back, pulling tighter. "Breathe in, little girl." I did.

"Is your little girlie clit tingling yet?" Mistress asked. I nodded. Mistress walked, click, click, click, to my front and pulled my breasts up so that their flesh peered over the corset. Then she walked behind and finished tightening the top. I breathed lightly, feeling the leather tight about me.

Mistress knelt to my crotch and blew lightly. I shuddered from the cold. She stood and placed one of my hands on my hip.

"Bend your left knee, little girl." I did so. "Thank you. Perfect. Well, almost perfect. No girl is complete without a man. Wait here. Don't move." Click, click click, Mistress walked out of the room.

I stood in the cold and tightness. A man? Did she mean me? I doubted it. Mistress returned, minutes later, with Lynetta, a friend of hers. Lynetta wore a long blue dress and heels. She had her slave in tow; the slave wore nothing.

Lynetta laughed. "Look. My slut here is the only boy this room, and yet he's the one with a leash. Straight sex, eat your heart out." Adam, Lynetta's slave, rested on his hands and knees at Lynetta's side.

Mistress laughed as well. "Oh Lynetta, you're a riot." Her voice dropped. "But we have serious work to attend to. This little girl of mine has a lesson to learn."

"But of course," said Lynetta. She reached down and detached Adam's leash. "Boy," she said sharply, "pick up that girl and put her on the bed." Adam walked over to me and picked me up.

Mistress and Lynetta walked over to the loveseat and sat down, beginning to play with each other's hair. "You know what to do, slut. Begin," called Lynetta.

Mistress called over, "Where will you be, girl, top or bottom?"

"Bottom," I said.

"What was that, girl?"

"Bottom," I said more loudly.

Adam lay on top of me, his blue eyes looking to the sky. He pulled the piece of lace down from my crotch. He rested his dick against my labia and began to kiss my cheek.

Lynetta stood and strode over and whacked Adam's ass. "Did I tell you to kiss that girl? I'll do the kissing around here." She sauntered back to Mistress and kissed her deeply.

Adam put on a condom, added some lube, and began to rub his penis along my clit. I continued to breathe softly, feeling the corset at each exhale. I looked over at Mistress and Lynetta, now fingering each other's breasts, and I moistened.

Adam, above me, guided his dick towards my vagina. I could feel his push, not quite pain, not quite pleasure. That most revered sexual organ slid, popped, sank into its home away from home, then he began to pull out slightly, then in again. So different from a dildo, a full body attached to this prod. I looked over at Mistress. Lynetta's blue dress was on the floor and Mistress was intent upon her breasts.

Adam began a rhythm. I lay silent, feeling my nerves respond to the stimulation. I saw Mistress' dress lift. Adam rested his head on my shoulder, pushing and pulling. Lynetta's dick sunk into Mistress and they began to rock.

Adam started to moan, pushing more quickly now; Lynetta let out a shriek. Our rhythms were slightly off, Adam speedier than Mistress and Lynetta. He stopped suddenly and arched his back, pushing his dick into me deeply. I breathed out sharply as he did so, the corset restricting my skin. Then he pushed a few more times and dropped onto me; he rested for only a few moments before crawling out of bed to wait at Lynetta's heels.

I pulled the blanket over me and looked over to Mistress where she lay beside Lynetta on the couch. Both of them were smiling; Mistress' hand was on Lynetta's left breast. Lynetta giggled; Mistress joined her. They sighed together. Lynetta brought her hand down to tousle Adam's hair. "What a good boy you are."

Mistress sat up and said, "Well, Lynetta, it was lovely to have you and your boy over, but I'm sure you need to be going now."

"You're right," said Lynetta. "I need to bring him home." She thrust her head towards Adam. "He's got to get back to training. I just hope we didn't pamper him with your girl. Slave?" He looked up. "You don't think this means that you'll be fucking me any time soon, do you?"

"No, Ma'am," Adam said, "Not until after training."

"Good boy." Lynetta patted him on the head. "Now go get your leash." He trotted off to find the leash. He brought it back and lifted his head to bare his neck to her. She clipped the leather leash to the collar and cracked it on his back.

"I'll walk you out," said Mistress. "Girl!" She paused. "Girl!"

"Me, Mistress?" I said.

"Of course, you! Stand up!" I stood. "Legs together. Breasts out, girl." She placed an ice cube on either side of my neck. "Now stay, girl-slut! I wouldn't try pulling your breasts in if I were you. I'll know if you moved, and you don't want that."

Click, click, click.

Mistress left with Lynetta and Adam. The corset collided with my skin at every inch as I waited. My shoulders hurt with coldness, then grew numb; my back hurt from holding out my breasts. I felt a drop of water drip down my right breast. I didn't look at it, but hoped it was only one drop. I couldn't feel whether the ice cubes were still there. Still, I waited.

Click, click, click.

Mistress stood before me and nodded, brought her head down to my left shoulder and licked. Then she did the same to my right.

"You've done very well, my little one," she said. "Now stretch out those muscles." I raised my arms and stretched, then twisted at my waist to my left and my right. "Very good. Now close your eyes and stand still." Click, click, behind me. She loosened the corset, bit by bit, then let it slip to the floor. I breathed in and out deeply several times.

"Feel good, hon?"

"Yes, Mistress."

"OK, feet up, dearie," I walked out of the corset and she put it aside. I was naked. Mistress rubbed my back and massaged my shoulders; brought something to my crotch and snapped it in back. Then, she began to fiddle near my clit, adding a weight.

"OK, hon, open up." I looked down. A dildo. I had never worn a dildo before. This was the dildo we had seen in a sex shop just a few weeks ago. "You're not ready yet," Mistress had said at the time.

"It's yours, sweetie. Take me." She threw herself on the bed and, with full drama, threw her arms to out and onto the bed.

I walked forward and slipped the high heels off of Mistress' feet; then I crawled onto the bed. I kissed her, licking her lips, then her ears, then down to her breasts. I unzipped her dress and eased her out of it, licked her lips again, then kissed her. I nibbled at her earlobes, dragged my tongue down her chest to her thighs. I kissed her and she shivered. I brought my tongue down her left leg, kissed each toe on both feet, then licked back up to her clit. I wiggled my tongue about; quick flicks, then a long suck. I pulled her clit into my mouth and massaged it with my lips.

I brought myself up to kiss her again, then I took the lube and put some on my dick. I massaged her thighs and kissed her breasts, and then guided my dick into Mistress, feeling me inside of her. My dick went in as I pushed, went out as I pulled. I made small circles with my pelvis and felt my dick swirl in her vagina. Mistress began shifting her weight as we developed a rhythmic motion, in and out.

I slipped and the dick fell out. I giggled, but Mistress guided the dick back into her, and the rhythm picked up quickly. I sucked on her breasts and thrust into her.

Mistress began to breathe deeply. I continued to thrust, feeling my dick inside her. Harder. She moaned. I held my dick there, then pushed a few more times; Mistress moaned with each plunge. I slowed as her groans turned to sighs, and I rested on her, leaving my dick inside of her.

We breathed together. I twirled my finger through her hair as she rubbed her hands along my back. "Mistress?"

"Yes, my love?" Mistress asked, her nails grazing my neck. I purred as she scratched by my ear.

"Why... why did you make me a girl? You know I'm not, and you've always loved that about me. I just don't understand it."

"But darling, I knew one thing you didn't."

"What's that, Mistress?"

"The more of a woman you become, the more of a man you will be."

I felt my dick inside of her, and I smiled.

Mythology has always had its share of creatures that are somewhere between male and female—angels, daemons, gods, devas, incubi/succubi. Many are reported as slumming with human lovers… making many wonder just what sorts of secret perversions of submission an inhumanly powerful creature might have. Go ahead and find out. You might be a little sore afterwards, but we guarantee you won't regret it.

Gary Bowen is the creator of the scorchingly hot ezine Roughriders, *the FTM erotica site, which like a flame burned out altogether too quickly.* Roughriders *was the first place that FTMs could find erotica starring themselves in the spotlight, and is one of the direct ancestors of this book.*

The Coldest Light

Gary Bowen

I was coming out of the Harborplace Pavilion and heading for the bus stop when I saw him, looking like the star of a Hong Kong kung fu flick. I stopped dead in my tracks and stared. Oriens. I had almost convinced myself that he had been a dream, born out of the fear and anguish of the gay-bashing two years ago. But there he was, sitting on a bench, pitching popcorn to the seagulls, his long black braid wrapped once around his neck, his beautiful face intent on the birds at his feet. He wore a red satin shirt with a golden dragon embroidered on the front, black pants, and low black boots with pointy toes. He had bangs and a lock of hair in front of each ear in a style I had usually seen on girls in Japanese anime films, but the flat muscular body could not be mistaken for anything but male. My heart turned over in confusion.

He looked up and saw me and his pensive expression lit up; rising, he approached me, apparently oblivious to the stares of the tourists. Seen up close, he was six feet tall, a couple of inches taller than me. "Jim," he said in his excellent Queen's English.

"What are you doing here?" I asked.

"You said you wanted to see me again."

"Yeah, but that was two years ago!"

"I warned you that time moves differently for me than it does for you," he said quietly.

"Yes, but..."

"Should I go?" he asked.

"No! Not at all. It's just that I have a lover these days."

"I know. A leatherman, isn't he?"

I didn't ask him how he knew. Some things I didn't need to know. "Yes."

"I'm in a fey mood. Humor me?"

"Sure. What did you have in mind?"

"Sins of the flesh," he replied.

I remembered his body, his sleek, golden powerful body. I remembered how I'd called on him when my life had been in danger and how he'd kicked the asses of the guys who'd beaten me up. I remembered his mouth on my cock, my cock in his body... I was shaking, scared and attracted and worried. "I have to ask Dan. He's my master these days."

"Would he mind another player?"

"I, uh, well, you're a..." I stammered.

He smiled. "Think he'd like me?"

Who wouldn't? "Yeah, I think he would."

So we got on the bus together and I paid his fare because, naturally, he hadn't brought any money of his own. He tended to forget trivial details like that. He put an arm around my shoulder and I slid in next to him, propping one foot on the seat. I was wearing my leather jacket over my fast food uniform and I had Dan's chain around my right ankle. As few of the passengers glanced at us, but he met their gazes with serene confidence and they looked away again.

"Tell him my name is Lee and that I'm from Hong Kong," he remarked. "You can tell him that I used to make chop-socky movies."

"Did you?"

"Once. In another reality."

Another tiny piece of his personal past—a past that stretched back nearly ten thousand years, if he could be believed. I didn't want to believe. If I believed in Oriens then I also had to believe in heaven and Hell and a God that sat in judgment condemning my kind to eternal flames. "Does Hell really exist?" I had to ask.

He laughed. "Which one?"

"There's more than one?"

"They all exist. Every single legend you've ever heard is true, in one fashion or another."

"And God?"

"You know my duty."

Oriens, Archangel of the East, Guardian of Asia, one of the four angels charged with upholding the Throne of God. Oriens, the guy who was currently sitting next to me in the back of a mass transit bus with his arm around my shoulders. Waking up in bed with Genghis Khan would have scared me less. Genghis Khan had at least been human. But who could guess the mind of an angel?

✱

Dan wouldn't be home for an hour. I had time to prepare. My orders were explicit; he wanted to walk right into a well-prepared hole, get off, have a beer, put his feet up, and then torment me for a couple of hours before letting me come. So I left "Lee" to loaf in the living room while I showered and gave myself an enema. I shaved my crotch so that I was nice and smooth; Dan was hairy, even hairier than me, and he liked me to feel his hair on my naked crotch. When I finished preparing myself, I knelt in the hallway and waited, crouching naked in the front hall, black leather cuffs on my wrists and ankles. I held the collar in my hand.

At ten minutes before six I heard his key in the lock and braced myself. I grabbed my dick and pumped quickly, presenting him with the sight of my erection and submission as soon as he stepped through the door. He smiled when he saw me, teeth flashing beneath his thick salt-and-pepper moustache. Dan was a solid forty, stoutly built, with a barrel chest, lots of dark brown hair kept trimmed to just above his collar, and green eyes. He was dressed in full leather; jacket, jeans, engineer boots, studded gauntlets, the works. Blue-black chains swung jauntily from his left epaulet. Wordlessly, I held the collar up to him.

"Hello, slut. I'm glad to see you're ready for me." He took the collar and wrapped it around my neck, something that only he was allowed to do. I was his property. I pressed my face against his leather-clad thigh as he buckled it, and then said in a muffled voice, "I have a present for you, sir."

"What kind of a present?" he asked curiously.

"It's in the living room," I whispered, petrified.

He rose and stepped through the door into the living room, and I scooted to where I could see past his tree-trunk legs. There was Lee, kneeling on the floor, still dressed, his hands on his thighs. Dan stopped in surprise. "What's this?"

I crawled to his feet. "An old lover of mine. His name is Lee. He's from Hong Kong. He dropped by unexpectedly."

Dan walked a circle around Lee, who remained impassive. Lee knew that he was gorgeous; Dan would have no complaints on that account. "This is a surprise. Quite a surprise." His tone changed. "Do you suck cock?" he demanded.

"Yes, sir, I do," Lee replied.

Dan gripped him by his hair, and I saw the light in Lee's eyes as he felt Dan's fist. "Do you like getting fucked in the ass?"

"Yes, sir, I do, sir." Lee's voice was low and throaty. Always melodious, his voice took on an extra timbre that sent shivers along my spine.

Dan slapped him, and I saw a wary look cross Lee's face before he schooled himself to serenity. "Do you want to be used any way I feel like it?" Lee nodded. "Answer me!" Dan snapped.

"Yes, sir, I want to be used any way you want to use me!" His precise British accent was eroding to allow something older and more passionate to flavor his speech. My cock was hard as I watched him submit to my master. Maybe this would work out all right after all.

Dan turned to me. "Have you seen him get fucked?"

"No, sir, but I've fucked him myself. He's a good fuck," I added.

"How many men have fucked you?" Dan demanded.

Lee's eyes glazed. "I don't know. I haven't kept track."

"Guess. One, ten twenty, a hundred? More?"

Two points of color came up in Lee's cheeks. "More than a hundred. Many more."

"Have you been tested?" Dan was not careless. He cared too much about me and himself to play unsafely.

"Yes, sir. I'm healthy, sir."

Dan looked over at me. "Is he reliable?"

"Yes, sir."

Satisfied, Dan, released his hair. Still looking at me, he said, "All right, I'll accept your present. Take it downstairs and put cuffs on it. Take its shirt off first." Silently, I rose and tapped Lee's shoulder; he followed me downstairs.

The dungeon was Dan's pride and joy. He had painted the walls a battleship grey, and the floor, wooden ceiling, and peg boards were painted black. He had several floggers as well as clamps and clips and dildoes of various sizes. I moved around the room, getting things from the cabinet while Lee stripped off his shirt. He revealed a lean chest with perfectly sculpted pecs and two pert nipples. I wanted to fall to my knees and start gnawing his chest, but I didn't.

I was shaking as I wrapped the black leather around his wrist, and his eyes met mine with a hard flash of lust. Our mouths met, and his mouth opened to mine, and I thrust my tongue into him, feeling the warmth and the wetness that would feel so very good wrapped around my cock. Electricity sizzled through my nerves, carrying tiny shocks of pleasure to all parts of my being. He pressed himself hard against me, drinking pleasure from my mouth until we heard a booted step on the stair. We parted and I hastily slapped the second restraint on his other wrist, then turned and asked, "Sir, did you want him with or without boots?"

Dan came into the room. "Without."

So I removed Lee's boots and red silk stockings and laid them aside. I fastened the cuffs around his bony ankles, noticing that his feet were long and narrow with high arches. I suppressed the urge to suck his toes. That task completed, we both knelt and awaited Dan's pleasure.

Dan opened the cabinet and took out an old studded leather collar, and held it before Lee. "If you accept this collar, then I can do whatever I like to you for as long as I like. You can't remove it, and you can't say no to anything."

A shudder rippled through Lee's frame and he closed his eyes. The two points of color appeared high on his cheeks again, and he said, "I can't give you that. I belong to someone else. I can let you use me any way you like, but I can't give you something that is not mine to give."

Dan studied him. "All right, I understand. Let me put a time limit on it. I won't keep the collar on you longer than a week. When I take it off, you'll be free to go."

Lee shuddered again. I knew that Dan was fucking with his head by offering a week; our scene might actually last overnight or even all weekend, but not a week. But Dan wanted to see how hard he could push him. "Yes, sir," Lee finally replied.

The collar closed on the angel's neck and he exhaled violently, shivering as Dan worked the buckle and closed it tight. Then for an added measure, Dan clipped on a small brass padlock and snapped the lock shut. Lee's eyes were wide and staring, his lips parted. Dan put the key in his pocket. "I'm the only one who has the key," he remarked. Then he snapped a lock onto my collar, and I realized that I was shivering violently too. Dan owned me completely; for me the scene might end but I would not be released. Not ever. "You may kiss my boots. Both of you."

So we bent and each one of us kissed his boots. I lingered, lovingly slathering my tongue over the leather, but Lee delivered a graceful kiss and straightened up again. He was in control of himself again, face bland, his lust veiled behind a schooled expression.

"You're a cold one," Dan observed, walking around him again. Lee remained still under his scrutiny. "I suppose you think that because you're pretty, I'm all impressed to have you in my dungeon. Well, I'm not. I don't like useless boys no matter how pretty they are. I want you to get down there and polish your boots with my tongue." When Lee hesitated, he snapped, "Now!"

So Lee bent gracefully again and extended a pointy tongue until he finally made contact with the leather. He flinched, and I wondered what was going through his head. He said nothing, but began to lick with long smooth strokes. He worked carefully, covering every inch of the leather, but while he was obedient, he did not seem to enjoy it. Dan, frowning, glanced at me; I shrugged helplessly.

Dan walked away and threw himself down in his favorite beat-up overstuffed chair. The stuffing was leaking out the back, but it was the perfect size and shape for loafing. He crossed one knee over the other. "Maybe I need to stuff something up your ass to make you appreciate my attention." Lee looked wary again. "Jim! Come over here and play with his nipples."

So I scooted across the floor and grabbed his tits. Our eyes met, and again I saw the light blazing in them for just a moment before it was veiled. He wanted it, but he wasn't going to let it come easily. I squeezed hard; his lips parted and his breath became more rapid. I twisted and pulled them, and heard a small moan escape his throat. "Hurt him," Dan instructed. I pinched the nipples with my fingernails and he groaned, head falling back.

"Yeah, I know what you need. You need a little pain to teach you respect." Dan stood up and crossed to the pegboard, taking down a pair of clover clamps, and returned, clipping one to each of Lee's nipples. The bright chain hung across his chest in a smooth curve, and two brown nipples were squeezed up between the clips. I ran my hands over them and he quivered; I saw the wild light in his eyes again. Dan gripped the chain and pulled him forward. "Kiss my leather," he ordered.

Lee buried his face in Dan's crotch, rubbing his face against his basket and slathering his tongue across the leather bulge of his balls and dick. He gobbled that leather willingly, and Dan said, "That's better. Now let's see you show my boots the same enthusiasm."

Lee bent lower, and Dan said, "Fasten his hands behind his back." I did, and the angel bent over, licking those boots, knees spread, body arched over to service my master's feet. "That's a better job," Dan commented. "I expect your enthusiasm for every order I give. Now sit up."

Lee sat up, nostrils flaring wide, his eyes wild. What this was doing to the inside of his head, I had no idea. I hoped he wouldn't crack; not in a bad way, at least. Dan put his boot against Lee's chest and said "Lay down on your back." He kept the pressure on as Lee unfolded his legs and rolled back, his bound hands under the small of his back. The cement floor would not be comfortable for him, but Dan stood with his boot across Lee's neck and told me, "Strip him the rest of the way."

This was the moment I'd been worried about, but I obeyed, removing his pants until his legs and groin were bare. Dan glanced down and said, "Holy shit."

Lee was an androgyne; he had the body of a man and the genitals of a woman. His muscular thighs were spread, revealing not the testicles and penis that Dan had expected, but a short furred crotch with a very large erect clitoris. Dan put both feet flat on the floor. "Did you know about this?" he asked me in astonishment. I nodded, and he smiled ruefully. "Well, that's quite a surprise. You didn't tell me that he was a hermaphrodite."

"I'm not," said Lee. "I'm an androgyne. The opposite. Hermaphrodites have breasts and a penis; I have neither."

"Are you angry?" I asked Dan.

"No, not angry. Just surprised. And curious. But I have some technical questions first." Looking down at Lee, he asked, "Can you get pregnant?"

"…No."

"Good. Because I'm too old to have to start worrying about rug rats." Dan reached down and dragged him up. We unfastened his hands, removed the clamps, put him in the leather sling, and locked him in. Dan didn't like his boys to be able to touch themselves; he liked total control. He snapped his fingers at me and I went to my knees. "Mouth," he commanded. "Make me hard to I can fuck this bitch."

He unbuttoned his crotch and his meat spilled out; I scooped it up, running my tongue around the circumcised head, sucking eagerly. I enjoyed making him hard for other men. He was my master; he could stick his dick wherever he liked. I turned me on to know that he could fuck whoever he liked, whenever his liked, but that I was dependent on him for my own sexual satisfaction. When he was nice and hard, he reached out and grabbed Lee's bubble-butt and spread his cheeks. "I'm going to take both of these holes, slut."

Lee made no reply, but I heard him gasp as Dan plunged into his cunt. Dan was rough; he grabbed Lee by the waist and banged him deep so that his balls were slapping against Lee's ass. The angel moaned and writhed, tendons standing up in his neck as he strained to meet Dan's violent thrusts, grunting, his face contorted in passion. Dan rutted in him, the wet slapping sounds of his thrusting loud in the narrow confines of the room. I smelled them both, male lust and something else, a faint metallic tang. I watched in fascination; fully erect, Lee's clit looked like a small penis, with the folds of the labia sweeping away to wrap around Dan's hard cock. His clit was as large as my thumb, a thick stubby organ, something between male and female. I reached out and touched it and he bucked violently. I pulled the foreskin back and rubbed my finger across his glans; he kicked and gasped and acted just like I did when Dan pulled back my foreskin and tormented the most sensitive part of my flesh. Dan pulled out abruptly, and using Lee's own lubrication, thrust into his asshole. The angel screamed, high and falsetto, and Dan waited a moment to see if he'd injured him. Then Lee thrust himself hard onto Dan's dick, panting and moaning. "Yeah, you want that hard cock, don't you, you little faggot?"

"Yes, sir, please, sir," Lee gasped breathlessly. "I want it bad."

Dan clenched his waist again and waded in, working his dick deeper into Lee's body until his balls were slapping against his ass. Lee kicked and cried out and the whole sling shook. "Please make me come, sir! I want to come with your cock in my ass!"

"Fuck you. This is for me. I don't give a flying fuck if you get off or not." He thrust with a long deep stroke, braced his feet, and then grabbed the sling and began to rock Lee back and forth on his dick, impaling him with each swing. My cock was rock hard and I wanted to wank desperately. Lee was a whole lot louder with a cock in his ass than he had been before; the noise made me want to bury my cock in his body and rut until I fountained inside him.

Dan noticed where my hands were and snapped, "On the floor!" So I knelt, ass plastered to the cold cement, knees spread wide. "You don't need that." He stepped on my cock and trapped it under his boot while he resumed playing with Lee's ass. I embraced his leg and began to lick his leather thigh, my face a few inches away from the hot, horny, wet musk of their intercourse. I had an excellent view of Lee's brown hole pierced over and over again by my master's dick, and I was jealous. I wanted to fuck that hole, or be fucked by that dick. My hard-on didn't relent.

Dan rested a moment, the tip of his dick pressed against Lee's fuck-hole. "All right, Jim. I wanna come now. Jack me off. I want my come all over this boy's holes." He braced his legs and I jacked him with expert strokes, pointing his dick directly at Lee's two pink swollen holes. I jerked harder, getting turned on by servicing my master, furtively humping my dick trapped between his sole and the concrete. Dan inserted two fingers in Lee's asshole, and inserted two more fingers in his pussy. He opened both holes and then said, "Make me come."

I worked him hard and fast, and a little bit later his dick erupted, spraying come all over Lee's captive crotch. I directed my master's cock so that his jism entered each of the holes, and then Dan let go of Lee, and I let go of Dan. "Okay, Jim. If you want my come you can eat it out of his body."

He settled back in his easy chair while I buried my face in Lee's butt. There were few things I liked better than eating my master's come out of one of his toys. I went after Lee's asshole first, running my tongue all around the wrinkled flesh, then thrusting my tongue into his hole. He arched violently, pulling away from my mouth, and I chased after him, catching him and trapping him with my hands and mouth. Lee was yelling wordlessly, trying hard to hump my face, so I switched to his other hole.

It was soft like velvet, and I remembered the last time I'd been here. It had felt surprisingly good that time too, and I felt a twisting inside me and knew I was starting to develop a fetish for androgyne sex. I licked his slit, then my mouth slid up to his erection and I took it in his mouth. I wanted to jam my cock into his asshole something fierce, but I didn't dare do it without Dan's permission, so I kept sucking his dick-clit, and worked my fingers into his holes, filling him with my hands if not my cock. Le cried out and fought violently, but he couldn't escape me, and shortly his body was arching and shuddering as he came.

My jaw was tired and my fingers were wet, so I sat back and looked at Dan. He rose and guided me to my feet, and wrapping his arms around me, asked, "Which hole would you like?"

"Asshole," I replied.

His hand on my cock guided me inside, and Lee's tight tunnel clamped on me. He pulled us tight, then pulled my hands behind my back. He kissed the back of my neck and whispered, "Who owns you?"

"You do, sir."

"What are you?"

"Your property."

"What are you good for?"

"Getting fucked."

He shoved his cock up my ass then, wet with Lee's lube. I bent forward to accommodate him, and for that one moment Lee was nothing more than the condom wrapped around my dick while my master fucked me. The sling swung with each thrust of his cock into my body; he was fucking both of us at once. I shuddered and shivered and he kept my hands pinned between my shoulder blades, fucking me hard, pushing me towards climax, until I finally burst into a million pieces.

He wasn't done then; he simply let go of my hands and let me gasp for breath as he kept fucking me. He built slowly towards his second coming, and finally, grinding hard, gave me the honor of coming in me.

After catching his breath he released us. Lee and I dropped to our knees before his boots, and the angel bent and kissed the toe of his boot, murmuring, "Thank you, sir. I needed that."

Dan bent and removed the collar from his neck. "All right. You can go if you want."

Lee rose gracefully, his face as enigmatic as ever. He dressed, then stopped beside me as I knelt at my master's feet. "You're very fortunate to belong to him," he said. "I don't think you'll need me any more."

My heart turned over. "Will we see you again?"

"Oh, I imagine so."

We did see him again, dressed in a black leather jacket and blue jeans, working as a bouncer in a leather bar. He still had his long hair, but he'd gotten his right ear pierced and was wearing a gold ring in it.

"Your ex has gone American with a vengeance," Dan said as we sipped our imported beers.

"I don't think it's a matter of going American," I said. "I think he's finally come to grips with the fact that he's gay and just can't live where he used to any more."

"You should go talk to him; see how he's doing."

I threaded my way through the crowd. He saw me coming. I looked him over carefully, but he didn't seem as imposing as I remembered him. In fact, he looked rather tired. There were faint lines at the corner of his eyes that didn't used to be there. "Hey, how's it going?" I asked.

He sighed and shrugged. "Long night. At least I have a job."

"What about... where you used to be?"

He bit his lip and looked away. "I quit."

"Meaning?"

"I'm not an angel any more, Jim. I've fallen from grace. I'll live out my life as a mortal man, and then that will be the end of me."

"It isn't fair! Sheesh, why did He make gay people or angels if that's not what He wants?"

He smiled crookedly. "It's not a matter of being gay so much as it is a matter of holding something worldly as more important than His Will. We're supposed to set our sights higher than that."

"So if you really believed that, why'd you quit?" I grumbled.

He asked me with a question of his own. "Do you know what the Moslems say?"

I shook my head mutely.

"That God made man from the darkest clay, jinns from the purest fire, and angels from the coldest light. I got tired of being cold."

I wrapped my arms around him then, and he was warm and human, with nothing more or less than the passions of a man. We embraced for a long time before I was able to let him go.

Raven writes: "I originally wrote this story for a proposed anthology that Pat Califia (now Patrick Califia-Rice, thank you very much) wanted to do as a sequel for her smoking-hot anthology Doing It For Daddy. *This one would have been called* Make Mama Happy, *but it never came about, and the story languished in my hard drive until now. I'd done a ton of Daddy-boy play, but nothing around Mama stuff, so I asked my then-boy what sort of a Mama he'd most like to submit to. The character of the enigmatic Elaine grew out of that conversation, and soon I found her insisting, in her indomitable way, to have at least part of her story told. It came out in the form of an old, old myth, as those readers who recognize the title quote will understand.*

As The Sparks Fly Upward

Raven Kaldera

Mama brushed her long hair as I sat on the edge of her four-poster bed and watched over her shoulder. It fell, coppery and smooth, to her waist and didn't have a single thread of grey in it. I wondered if she hennaed it. She was ignoring me, her boy, busy giving her hair the hundred-stroke treatment as I stared in fascination. She opened her jewelry box and fastened two dangling earrings onto her ears. I could see the soft skin of her throat as she turned her head.

"Now, do you have any questions about your list, dear?" she asked me, reaching for her lipstick. I started guiltily and shifted my gaze to the slightly crumpled paper in my fist, my evening chores written out in her fine, curly hand. *Do the laundry in the bathroom, fold the towels and sheets and put them away....* My rational mind asked itself, for the ninth time, what in the world I was doing here. It's a voice I have to constantly crush in order keep myself in scene space, especially for long-term scenarios.

"Yes, Mama," I said, wincing at the sound of it. She resumed her toilette, applying her rosy lipstick and pursing her lips in the mirror. Mama was going out with someone tonight, and it wasn't me. It was one of her gentlemen friends. I almost smiled ironically at the old-fashioned sound of that, but then the wave of resentment flooded back. How could Daddy do this to me? I wanted to call him and tell him to come and get me, not to leave his boy here in this fluffy feminine place. Mama lived outside of range of public transport, and I didn't even have cab fare, so I was stuck.

209

The scent of lavender wafted past me and I looked up to see her applying perfume with her little gold atomizer. The bedroom was all white and gold, so that Mama could be the only spot of color in it, I expected. She tried to fasten a string of pearls around her neck, struggled with the clasp, and then looked at me with a frown beginning between her eyebrows. "Would you come and fasten this for me, dear?" she asked sweetly. I got to my feet and moved awkwardly toward her, into the cloud of perfume. She leaned her head back as I took the necklace and brought it around her neck.

My heart pounded in my chest and my fingers felt suddenly clumsy in their attempt not to touch her skin. Her long hair brushed against the front of my pants, and the cock underneath the denim stirred as a hot flash of wetness seeped out behind it. I finally got the necklace fastened and stepped back, my face warm. "Thank you, darling," she said, flashing me a smile, and then she took her wrap from the bed and went out. "Don't forget to unpack," I heard her call before the door shut and left me alone in the big house.

"Get in the car, boy," Daddy had said sternly when I'd come into the driveway with my suitcase. At his request, I'd canceled all my appointments for an entire week and come to stay with him. I stood blinking for a moment, and then asked tentatively, "Aren't we going to the con, sir?" The science fiction convention I'd assumed he was taking me to didn't start for another five days.

"Get in the car," he ordered, and I got in with a sigh. When Daddy got that tone of voice, there was no arguing with him unless I wanted to turn around and go home. I got the distinct feeling I was in trouble, and I was pretty sure I knew what it was.

He drove for a while in silence, scowling at the road, and I got a chance to eye him furtively. I'd met my Daddy at a leather event a year ago. I had a different daddy then, my third in three months. It wasn't that I was a bad bottom or even a bad lover, it was just that I couldn't seem to stick to rules about who I could and couldn't play with. Especially with all the handsome butches that I knew. And then there was my secret vice, the one that I was still flirting with in my half-conscious mind. I was beginning to fantasize about breaking that utter taboo for a dyke. You know. People who weren't female... or not exactly female, anyway.

Oh, it wasn't straight guys on the bus I got a hard-on for, or the smarmy het tops in their suits. It was fags. I dreamed guiltily about being put on my knees to suck some big leather daddy's cock, or slipping under the sequined skirts of a drag queen. (That one really confused me.) I wondered if I should just come out as bisexual or if that would immediately entail every dyke in range leaving skid marks and being replaced by a crowd of leering straight guys that I'd be stuck with for the rest of my life. And then Trevor, my Daddy, caught me cruising him as he sat at the bar, and all my prevarications were over.

It wasn't as if he was hard to miss, in his long black leather Australian drover's coat and bush hat, hair past his shoulders and biker's gloves on work-roughened hands. He put his boots up on the other barstool and scratched his beard, and his coat fell aside to reveal the ring of keys with the big knife at his left hip. When he ordered, I was surprised not to hear a shrimp-on-the-barbie accent. And then those keen grey eyes shifted onto me, and I couldn't look away. A slow grin spread across his face while I blushed and then he gestured with one thumb toward the back door.

I remember being nervous enough to piss my pants as I climbed into his battered old van and got down on my knees to blow him, and I remember as well my utter amazement at discovering that his cock was as latex as my own, and that under it was a cunt with a clit the size of my thumb. I'd never been with a transsexual before, and I'd never been so turned on in my life. Trevor was a man, all right, no question, but he was a man who knew more about what it was like to be me than any fag in that bar, and who was guaranteed not to treat me like a girl. If there was such a thing as a third gender hag, I became one after that.

Which is how I found myself sitting there in the van, nervous and fidgeting. A whole new world had opened up for me once I realized what I really wanted, and I couldn't be expected to be faithful, could I? Of course, I'd tried. Luckily, all the other female-to-males were either straight and wanted femmes, or gay and wanted real guys, but then there was the femme half of the gender community! I'd never been much for genetic female femmes, but my cock was like a magnet for genderfuck.

Daddy never beat me with his evil Australian bullwhip when I'd been bad and flirted, he reserved it for a reward. When he was displeased, he ignored me, which drove me crazy. But then I'd been alone in a room with cute little Niccola, who was barely out of high school and still having her electrolysis, and I just couldn't help feeling her up. I mean, it wasn't as if she didn't want it. I guess sometimes I'm just a bad boy.

I heard him sigh suddenly, as if his anger was letting itself go. "So you're interested in the girls," he said, and his voice sounded almost tired.

I was taken a little aback. Was this going to be a scolding, or not? "I'm your boy, Daddy," I said, as fervently as I could. "That's never going to change."

"That's not what I asked, boy."

Deep breath. "Yes, sir. I am, sir."

Silence for a moment as he pulled up to the stoplight and nailed me with his stern grey gaze. "Those girls are just learning about womanhood," he said. "In a lot of ways, they're as vulnerable as teenagers, no matter how old they are. Some of them are also pretty desperate for validation of their attractiveness."

"I… I think they're very attractive, sir," I said in a small voice. This wasn't like the jealousy fits of my last three tops; I wasn't sure I understood where he was going. "And I… I try to let them know that I feel that way."

"That's not the point," he said curtly, turning his attention back to the road. "You're still taking advantage of them, and giving them very little in return. You have to learn to respect femmes, boy. They don't have an easy lot, regardless of their chromosomes."

I sighed. Daddy had the same strangely old-fashioned attitude that I'd found in many transsexuals, male and female, about girls and gallantry. I wanted to explain that I wasn't exactly a rapist, that Niccola hadn't exactly said no, but he caught my sigh and his eyes flashed with anger and I became really unsettled. I don't like it when Daddy gets angry at me. It's not that he yells and throws things, it's that he just turns away with a look of disgust. It makes me immediately terrified that he's already considering another boy, one that won't disappoint him. "I'm sorry, sir," I said, feeling at a loss.

"No, you're not," he said grimly, "but you will be soon. Have you ever tried to be a femme, boy?" he snapped at me so suddenly that I blinked in surprise.

I snorted and ran a hand over my cropped head. "Me, sir?" I asked in disbelief.

"I have," he said simply. "A long time ago," And don't ask any more questions, his tone warned. "I won't have my boy acting like one of those drooling admirers at drag bars. You'll learn to respect them if it's the last thing you do as my boy, you understand?"

"We're not going to the con, are we, sir," I said, looking at the toes of my boots.

"I am," he said. "You are spending the week under the custody of someone else." Out of the cloud of anger came a sudden smile, like the rain clearing. "I'm taking you to visit your mother, boy."

So there I was, left at the large and impressive house in Sudbury. Daddy even stripped me of my wallet on our way out of the van, although I pleaded with him not to leave me there. Then the door of the house opened and I shut up.

Mama was tall, six foot two, and gorgeous. Except for the slight Adam's apple and the musky timbre to her voice, she could have been an auburn-haired Marlene Dietrich at forty. She had a faint British accent that made me think of afternoon tea and the BBC. I stood there in her spotless living room with my mouth open while she and Trevor exchanged pleasantries. Daddy finally gave me a light smack across the back of my head and said, "Where are your manners, boy? Say hello to your mother."

"Good afternoon, Mama," I said in wonder. I couldn't imagine ever calling her Mommy. Ever.

She smiled at me. "So you do have a tongue in your head, darling. I'm glad to see that your father taught you something besides how to scratch your balls and spit on the sidewalk."

Trevor was completely unruffled, so I decided not to bristle at her for his sake. Instead I turned back to him. "Please, sir," I said in a low voice. "A whole week?"

"A whole week," he confirmed, and my shoulders drooped. Mama was apparently a crony of his, and it was clear that this whole thing had been planned a while ago. "You be a good boy for your Mama, now. I'll be back to pick you up next Thursday." He nodded to Mama. "Evening, Elaine." Then he gave me one quick, fierce hug and was gone, spurs jingling on the steps outside.

I slept in the guest bedroom that night, after having done nothing all day except chores and watching Mama dress up to go out with some other guy, and I sulked and masturbated for an hour before I could fall asleep in the immaculate bed. The next morning I got a new list of chores—take out the garbage, do the breakfast dishes. Mama was going out again, but with a twist. She asked me into her bedroom as before, but this time she was dressed in nothing but a lacy bra, a garter belt, and a pair of panties. I could see the outline of her genitals through the silk, and I caught my breath. "I'm running late for my date with Winston, darling. Would you help me get ready? There's a dear," she said.

How could I refuse? I gently rolled her stockings up her long, long legs and attached them to the garter belt. I helped her into her tight black strapless sheath dress and zipped up the back as slowly as I dared. I fastened on the pearl necklace as I had the night before, and handed her the mysterious makeup tools. She did her earrings herself and I was glad, because by that time I didn't trust myself to have steady hands. Then, just as I was sure that I was wet to the knees under my jeans, she handed me her silver-plated hairbrush and asked me to do the honors. "One hundred strokes, please. Start at the bottom and make sure you get the underside."

My hands did shake as I did it, but at least I was careful not to pull her thick glossy hair. It was all I could do not to bury my face in it, smell its flowery perfume, but I didn't dare. I was still too much in awe of her. Besides, I was half worried she'd take a slipper to my backside.

The final task was to get down on the floor at her feet and buckle on her red heels, which made her even taller. I wanted so badly to put my tongue on the shiny red leather that I think I actually whimpered, but she just patted my head, told me I was a very good boy, and left.

Day number three. I was interrupted in the middle of making breakfast for us by her announcement that I was going with her tonight to dinner. I almost dropped my spoon. "You do have a nice suit, don't you, dear?" she asked. "Did your father teach you how to knot a tie?"

I had to admit, through a blush of shame, that I lived in jeans and T-shirts and that Daddy was the kind of guy who'd never be caught dead in a tie, unless maybe it was a rawhide bolo tie with a rattlesnake on it. But I got the feeling she knew all about that already. "We'll just have to spend the day shopping, then," she decided, sounding not at all unhappy about the prospect. I was a little less sanguine about it, but I didn't want to be home again another night. I wanted to prove to her that I could be just as fine an escort as any of the guys she went out with, although I was having massive waves of performance anxiety at the thought.

Shopping. Butch hell. Mama sailing through store after store with me in tow, getting me a new suit—"We'll just put it on your Daddy's bill!"—and picking out the tie, dark blue with pseudo-collegiate crests on it. Then, of course, Mama had to go into the ladies' section and try on dresses. My job was to come into the dressing room with her, zip and unzip, take things on and off hangers, and admire her in each outfit. We went home briefly, long enough for me to change into my suit and help her get ready as I had the night before, only this time Mama was dressing up for me, not some rich middle-aged man.

She did my tie for me, carefully knotting a half-Windsor, and her long rose-colored fingernails brushed across my throat like little blades. I gulped, imagining those nails running across my bare back. I could look straight down into Mama's perfumed cleavage when she was that close to me, but all I dared was one glance at that forbidden thrill.

Dinner was in a large, chandeliered restaurant. I remembered to open the door of Mama's glossy black Bentley for her and to pull out her chair, but I was still sweating with the fear of screwing up. I don't think I'd ever been anywhere fancier than a Ponderosa since my high school graduation, and I was desperately trying to remember if there was something strange that you did with the silverware when Mama remarked, "I'll have the *poulet cordon bleu*, darling," and set her menu down in front of me. The waiter appeared at that moment like a bunny out of a magician's hat, but Mama was suddenly mysteriously silent, smiling at me. After about ten seconds she cleared her throat and I realized belatedly that I was supposed to order for both of us; I did it in a voice that cracked with embarrassment. She gracefully interposed her-

self and ordered the wine, and I could only give her a grateful, adoring look.

"I really hope I'm not doing this all wrong," I whispered after the
waiter left. It was the first discomfort I'd admitted to since my arrival
at her house, although I was sure she'd been completely aware of my
feelings of inadequacy from the beginning.

Mama patted my hand soothingly. "It's all right, dear. After all, what
could be expected with you running off after Trevor all the time?"
There was a curl of affectionate sarcasm to her tone. "I brought him
here once, you know. For a trustees' dinner. He came in full leather and
did his Crocodile Dundee thing for everyone. It was really quite amus-
ing."

Disrespectful as it seemed to laugh at Daddy, a most unboyish gig-
gle got out before I could stop it. "He's the best Daddy I've ever had,"
I said. "He keeps me in line."

Her perfectly plucked eyebrows arched. "He was always good at
discipline, I will say. Ah, here come the salads. You do know which fork
to use, don't you, darling?"

An hour later, I knew a little more about the mysterious Elaine. She was
from old money—very old—and had come here from England at the
age of sixteen. I was a little afraid to ask about her relationship with
Daddy, although I got the distinct feeling they had certainly once been
more than friends. Most of my tentative questions were gracefully side-
stepped in a way that was sure to make me feel like a boor for probing
closer.

When we got home, I helped her unzip and hang up her dress, put
away her jewelry, brush out her hair. She left her heels on until I got
down to unbuckle them, and then out of nowhere she lifted her foot
gently to my knee. "You want to do it, don't you?" she said teasingly. I
stared up at her, almost in shock. "You've been such a good boy today,"
she said. "I know it can't have been easy for you, but then that's the
point, isn't it? Go ahead." And she moved the shiny red shoe to the
floor directly between my thighs, almost but not quite touching my
crotch.

I was down on that floor in a moment, licking Mama's candy-apple
heels, massaging her toes through the patent leather, taking the high
heel into my mouth and sucking on it showily as if it was a cock. *She
likes me*, I thought excitedly. *I'm going to get what I want!* She smiled down
at me, which made me feel better. "My feet are so sore, darling," she
said. "Why don't you take them off?"

I carefully pulled the shoes off and set them aside; started to lick
between her toes, but she pulled away and stood, taking a burgundy
silk kimono from the back of the chair and wrapping it around herself.

"Well," she said, almost as if to herself. "I suppose we have to start somewhere. Get up, dear."

I got up, wishing I could have stayed there at her feet. I was sure that if she just gave me a chance she'd like my foot kissing, and maybe she'd want it someplace else. Mama had other ideas, however. "Let's see what your Daddy taught you," she said. "Saxon salute, please."

This I knew, and I was comfortable with it. I assumed the position, feet wide apart with my back straight and my hands locked behind my neck. Daddy rarely bothered with bondage. He believed that I should be able to take a beating without flinching, and stand tall throughout it. I could feel her behind me, watching me, and then something suddenly made a sharp, stinging slap on my ass. Her hairbrush! I could tell. "One hundred strokes before bedtime," she sang out, and then stopped. I waited. Nothing. Then I understood, "One," I said, and the next blow fell.

"Two!" I yelled. Whack. "Three!" It continued like that. perfectly timed to three seconds apart. I remember she stopped at fifty and I was panting, breathing hard, terribly grateful for a rest. I almost fell forward onto the rug at her feet.

"Are you having a hard time, dear?" she asked sweetly. I desperately didn't want to shame either myself or my Daddy, but I'd never known a little hairbrush could feel that heavy. Maybe it was the strength with which she swung it. Mama was a lot bigger and stronger than me, and she swung that thing as if it were a tennis racket.

"I'm all right," I gasped. "I just need to catch my breath. I can take more," I tried to assure her.

She seemed amused. "Well, I certainly hope so. I'd hate for the evening to have to be over before your bedtime."

I would hate that ten times more than you would, I said silently as I tried to adjust my stance and keep my back straight. But Mama took pity on me and let me lean against the four-poster bed, holding on to the posts at its foot. I was even more grateful for that small favor when she brought out a sleek rattan cane.

"I went to Balliol, dear, did you know that? There's nothing like a public school education to give one a real appreciation for caning." And with that she lifted her arm and proceeded to beat the hell out of my ass.

"Uh—ma'am, please!" I groaned. "Mama, may I have permission to scream, please, mama!" The blows were raining down, not spaced out like before, and I wasn't sure I could take it in stolid silence. Daddy had trained me to take pain practically on demand; for him, warmup consisted of grabbing me, shoving me face up against a wall, growling "I'm going to hurt you, boy!" in my ear, and then laying into me. But I knew and trusted him; I knew that if I screamed or cussed he'd be smart enough to keep going, to ignore my struggle. I didn't know Mama's style.

"Permission granted," she said in that same sweet tone, not even breathless, as if the caning was no more effort to her than doing embroidery. So I screamed—loud and long—and then hung there sobbing from my deathgrip on the posts while she finished the beating. Afterwards she turned me around and held me to her, cradled against her perfumed cleavage, and it was all worth it for that, every welt and stroke.

"That was very good," she said softly, and I swelled with pride. "You're a very good boy. Your Daddy taught you well in that, didn't he? Well, perhaps you'd like to please me in another way." And she pulled off the garter belt and stockings, unsnapped her bra, and lay down on the bed, half propped up against the pillows.

I was already wet from the beating and shoe kissing, and I wanted her so bad it rose in the back of my throat. I also had no idea what to do. I'd never actually had sex with any of the transsexual women I'd made out with or felt up. I knew that some liked their genitals touched and some preferred to ignore them. I also knew that it could be a very tender subject.

She beckoned to me and I came over as if on a leash. "Take off your clothes, darling," she said, and I shucked my jeans and Y-fronts, struggled with my boots, dropped my T-shirt to the floor. Then I climbed onto the bed beside her in nothing but my cock harness. She took my head and guided it to her breast, and there I lay as if back to the womb, sucking on first one rosy nipple and then the other. Back to Mama's breast. She made small satisfied moaning noises in her throat, and smiled at me when I raised my head. "Would you like to go down on your Mama, boy?" she said in the teasing tone she had used when I was at her feet.

"I… uh… do you, I mean," I stammered. "I mean, do you like to be touched… there?" I flushed as I said it.

She looked at the ceiling. "It is an erogenous zone, after all. We shan't ignore it. Go ahead, dear." She patted my head and I moved down between her legs. Gulping, I drew off her silk panties to see the little cock nested in her damp pubic hair. I put my head down and took it into my mouth.

It had been a long while since I'd been in high school and given head to live cocks, and I hadn't been particularly enthused then, nor tried to do a good job. I'd sucked dyke cock, of course—gotten pretty good at deepthroating Daddy's big dick—but that's a different thing; you just provide pressure and good visuals, and you can bite it if you need to in order to save your gag reflex. Daddy had even allowed me to suck his elongated clit, which fit comfortably in my mouth and which he only wanted hickeyed as hard as I could until he came in about two minutes. But this was different. Mama took a long time to get hard, and my jaw started to get tired, so I moved down to her balls and gently tongued them. What I really wanted, of course, wanted so bad that my cock was practically thrumming against the bed, was to fuck her. I wanted to get my dick into her and impale her on it, and to this end I got my tongue into her asshole and explored it. She moaned and circled her hips around my tongue, and I wet it down just as thoroughly as possible.

When I thought she might be ready I came up from her crotch and went to lay on top of her, so horny I thought I might burst if I didn't get some friction down there pretty soon. Mama frowned, and then she lifted me off her as if I was a child, setting me down on the bed next to her. "That will be enough for tonight, dear. Go to bed."

I was taken aback. "But—" I cried in disappointment.

She cut me off. "Go to bed. Now." Her tone could be just as stern and chilling as Daddy's. I disconsolately collected my clothing and went to the guest bedroom, climbing between the sheets with a heavy heart.

What had happened? I thought she was enjoying herself. Did she just not like to get fucked? I didn't understand at all. My libido was furious and the rest of me wanted to cry. Instead, I jacked off and then lay awake thinking. I wondered about Elaine and Daddy. Did he fuck her? I'd bet he had. I'd bet she didn't throw him out of her bed. A surge of jealousy took me by surprise, and then I felt even sadder. I didn't want to feel anything negative toward him, or for anything to come between us, even this magnetic, sensual woman in whose care he'd left me. Feeling bereft, I finally fell asleep.

The next day, while I washed and waxed her Bentley, I thought about what had happened. She was out all day, shopping again, so I had plenty of time and space to consider things. Obviously I'd been a pushy, spoiled boy and ruined her evening; perhaps she was enjoying the oral sex and didn't want it to end. Perhaps... and here I blushed. I had screwed up big, now that I thought about it. I had blown the cardinal rule of SM—that the top sets the rules. Of course, she hadn't given much to work with as far as rules went. Or had she? When Daddy wanted something from me, he ordered me and I did it. All that was expected of me was readiness, obedience, and focus on the task at hand. Perhaps Mama wanted something more. After all, her physical signals had been fairly clear as to when she was having a good time. I should have paid more attention, and not assumed that she'd want what I wanted.

I had hours to plan before she got back. That evening, as I helped her undress, I changed things a little. After I rolled off her stockings, I took her bare foot in my hand and began to massage it. After all, Mama would have been on her feet all day, shopping in those high heels. Maybe she'd appreciate this more than sex. "Mama," I said penitently, "I wasn't a very good boy last night, and I'm sorry."

Her eyebrows went up, but she didn't pull away. The sole of her foot relaxed in my hands. "And what did your Daddy tell you when he left, boy?"

"To be good for you, Mama," I said softly.

"Well," she said in a mock-stern tone, "you have one more chance to do that. Are you up for it, boy?"

"I'm yours, Mama," I said, looking up at her, and I meant it. She was like a goddess, like the Queen of Heaven, Cybele, Ashtoreth. I prayed for patience, and the skill to serve her properly, to worship at the altar of the Great Mother. I'd heard all that goddess spirituality crap in the lesbian community, but I don't think I really understood it until that moment.

This time, I watched every clue her body gave me like a hawk. I hunted down and pounced on every tremor, every swivel of her hips. I learned to respond, first slowly, then instantly, when her moans turned to silence punctuated with a heavy sigh. It took almost two hours, going back and forth between her genitals and her tiny puckered asshole, using my tongue and lips when my jaw was too tired. Finally, like a gift, she shuddered into my mouth with a long, silent convulsion. There was no ejaculate.

I knelt there between her thighs, exhausted, not feeling anything but gratitude that I had finally prevailed. I was still wet, though, the leather of my harness rubbing almost painfully against my swollen clit every time my cock moved against the mattress. I wondered what it would be like to have that much difficulty coming, and I wanted to take her in my arms as she lay there panting with her eyes closed, hold her close and assure her, over and over, that it was all right, I would love her and appreciate her, I would treat her right, I would give Mama as many orgasms as she wanted, no matter how tired I was. But she had other ideas. Her eyes opened and met mine, and there was a kind of fierceness in them, like a beast awakened and smoldering under her calm exterior. She grabbed me as if I was an inanimate object and flipped me to my back on the bed, straddling my thighs.

I lay there in surprise, breath catching in my throat at the sight of her towering over me. She reached for the bottle of lube on the night table and squeezed a pile of it into her hand; reached back between the cheeks of her ass to apply it. Then she smeared the rest on it on my erect cock, which pointed up like an obelisk between her thighs. I held absolutely still, just as I did when I would pose waiting for the first blow to fall.

She took hold of my dick and moved it back between her thighs, a little frown appearing between her brows as she slowly, carefully mounted herself on me. One slow inch at a time I sank into her, and not until every bit of that latex dildo had disappeared did I dare to move my hips. She opened her eyes and frowned down at me. "Hold still, boy," she ordered, her voice deep and throaty, and I obeyed. She proceeded to fuck herself on me, moving up and down, tossing her head of auburn hair back and forth, lost in her rhythm. Her breathing escalated into shrieks, and her claws dug into my shoulders. I was awed by the sudden wildness in her, like finding a vein of gold underneath a serene verdant field, and I had a flash of a goddess I'd seen pictured once on a throne, flanked by lionesses.

She seized me again without warning and rolled over, and there I was, on top of Mama where I'd wanted to be and having absolutely no idea how to go about it. I stared at her almost helplessly, but she grabbed my sore, welted ass and used it to move my cock into her in a long slow rhythm. As soon as I showed willingness to keep that beat, she let go and wrapped her legs around me, arching her pelvis up until I wondered if I would be lifted off the bed by it. "Faster!" she hissed suddenly.

"Yes, Mama," I gasped, and did it. I wanted to come so badly that it hurt down there, and I could have done it without losing my erection, certainly; that was the good thing about dyke cock. But even though I wouldn't have lost the ability to serve her, it might have impaired the rhythm she had ordered, and anyway I wanted to come when she did.

Her hands grabbed my ass again, and she slammed me into her twice, long and hard, legs clenching around me. My head swam and I felt myself coming in spite of everything. I tried to hold off, but she crushed my head down to her breast and I came, sucking on Mama's perfect breast, feeling her buck and thrash under me. It was like an earthquake, and I could only hold on for dear life.

I woke up to the sun coming up in my eyes. I had slept the whole night in Mama's bed with her, after carefully cleaning her off. My cock harness still lay in a heap on the immaculate rug I'd knelt on. My heart jumped in my chest as I lay there, remembering. The Great Mother had been generous to her boy. And to think I had not wanted to be here, I laughed to myself. Given half a chance, I'd stay here forever, taking her shopping, making her come, taking care of her. It was as if something in me had gone through a rite of passage and was just a little bit older. I knew what to do for her now; knew it better, I'd bet, than any man she'd been with. Hadn't she taught me herself, trained me, even created that part of me in a way? I was her boy forever, yes, Mama. Then I realized that I ought to be up making breakfast for her and got out of bed.

It was late; I'd overslept. The sun peering through the window was almost overhead. There were voices in the kitchen; one was Mama's, and one—I knew that one! Tearing out into the kitchen stark naked, I threw my arms around Trevor's neck as he sat there, boots up on the table.

"Thank you, Daddy! Oh, thank you for bringing me here!" I caroled, kissing him on the cheek. He nearly choked on his croissant, and untangled me in order to grab for his juice glass.

"Well, at least you didn't try to run for it and hitchhike back into town," he said, but his mouth twisted into what might have been a suppressed smile.

Mama sat, cool and serene in her burgundy silk kimono, like a presiding queen. "The boy has done excellently," she said. "We had a bit of a rocky start, but I'm quite proud. There's nothing more I need to teach. You needn't worry about the safety of all those little girls now, I don't think."

Daddy grunted his approval, and I suddenly noticed that his boots were getting mud on Mama's clean table. He caught my gaze, but didn't move an inch. Something akin to a challenge gleamed in his eye, and I backed right down. If Mama had a problem with it, she would handle it.

She was looking at her delicate gold watch. "I have an appointment by two, so I'm going to have to ask you to be out in an hour. I'll need to get ready and make a few phone calls." Her clear gaze settled on me. "It shouldn't take you that long to pack, dear," she said.

My stomach dropped like a stone being flung into a pond. "What?" I asked, my voice cracking.

"I'm taking you home," Daddy said. "Elaine called me over this morning. We'll hit a laundromat, and then go to the convention. You did want to go," he reminded me.

I didn't want to go. I wanted to stay there with Mama forever. "I thought you said it was going to be a week," I said, hearing my voice go flat and slow. He looked at Mama, lifted an eyebrow, and took another bite out of his croissant.

"There's no need for you to stay any longer, dear," she said, as if she was speaking of the weather. "You've learned everything I can teach you here. It's time to go." She got up and patted my cheek. "You were excellent," she repeated. "One of my best boys. Well, I must run a bath now. Another time, Trevor. Goodbye, darling." Her lips brushed my forehead and then she was gone.

I sat in the van with tears running down my face for the entire two-hour drive. Daddy didn't say a word, just squinted at the road and let me cry. All I could think about was the way those legends about the Great Mother and her son-lover always ended—he dies and she goes on to the next one, always widowed, always in control. I remembered the discussion of Robert Graves in college, the teacher talking about the symbolism of Attis, of Tammuz, of Adonis. "But that's a stupid thing to keep repeating!" a guy in the class had complained.

"That's just the way things are," the teacher had said mysteriously. She'd been a femme too. It figured.

After an hour I broke the silence. "Did she kick you out like that too?" I asked recklessly, not caring if it was a taboo subject.

He snorted. "I'm not a boy. And no. I left first." He looked over at me, and his gaze was steady. "The way you're going to leave me some-day."

I wanted to say *no, Daddy, never,* but I couldn't. Permanence was too far a concept from my mind at that moment.

"Daddy?" I said in a very small voice. "Is that really just the way things are?"

He pulled the van off the road then, put it in park and gathered me into his arms. I cried and sniffled for a few more minutes, but most of it was out of me. I rubbed my face against the leather of his coat, knowing his good familiar smell. "I'm not going to say yes to that," he said, "because I don't know everything in the universe. Contrary to rumors," he added, and I had to give him a shaky laugh. Then he pulled back out onto the highway, and we were on our way.

If you're loved enough, you're real, right? So much of our experience as transfolk in sexual relationships depends on our partners' ability to see us as we see ourselves, often in spite of our physical reality. This is true even of the briefest encounters; a grope in a bar or a clinch in a parking lot can reaffirm our true being or bite big holes in our self-esteem. Sometimes the hardest thing of all is just taking that risk of rejection, an issue which this story explores.

N. D. Hailey is a 20-something bi/trans/geek living in California. He spends too much time on mailing lists and writing porn. He considers medically transitioning, but doesn't think the computer is going to notice much of a difference.

The Velveteen FTM

N. D. Hailey

Watching, I see him in line for the bathroom. I catch the glint of light from his 10 gauge earrings in the dimness of the bar. He poses. His bright blue eyes scan the room full of men and a few women.

I've talked to Eric about cruising. Claims he's never done it before. We spent the day wandering around this queer tourist trap, showing and learning the body language of our fellow men. The ones who dress the same are coupled, they don't look. The ones who are by themselves in the daylight are too shy, they need the darkness. The ones who go around in groups look for things they never seem to get.

The dark, familiar confines of the bar gave off the comforting smells of alcohol, sun block, male sweat and salt. The balance of people to empty space was about right, here. Too few and you'd never make a pass at anyone for fear of too much attention. Too many and you'd get drowned out in the crush of humanity.

Gay sex is so new to me. I feel like I am on the outside. I've realized, for what I want, it's about passing. Passing is such an intricate matter. Does that shirt hide the binding? Do these shorts sit low enough to hide the waist? Is my hair cut short enough? The crash course in masculinity never ends. That used to bother me, until I found out that many of genetic guys have similar thoughts. Sometimes I think we are all trying to pass for men.

I watched another man look at Eric. I mean really look, take in his eyes, his piercings, his stance. So bold. I love that. The other man was hot, the sort that can't stand still and not be clocked for gay. He was slightly effeminate, not too much of a gym queen, twenties-ish. Eric noticed the other man's gaze and returned the inquisition with a lazy glance, catching his admirer with a raised eyebrow.

Eric feels like a student, or a child to me. Or a very large puppy. Or maybe a model from which I can paint myself.

"So, you here by yourself?" Eric said. I was stunned; I never expected him to be that forward (or that cheesy). He leaned back slightly and jutted his hips out at the slightest possible angle. I could almost focus on the words over the din. What I couldn't hear, I made up in my head—trying to get context from body language. Life is more interesting that way.

"Uh, yeah. I mean, nah, I'm here with my buddies over there. What about you?" The admirer said, and jerked his thumb "over there", where a group of entirely nondescript looking gay guys are talking with each other.

I took a better look at the admirer. He was shorter than Eric, but taller than me. His chestnut hair was only marginally mussed from the raging wind outside. I started to fantasize, what if I could fuck a real fag? (*What is a real fag?*) What if I could be masculine enough for the connoisseurs of maleness to take an interest? I felt a slight wetness from these idle contemplations. Images of cocks and muscles against one another, no softness or curves to disrupt all the masculinity. I work out, but I'm not on hormones. I can't get as hard as I want. Yet. I am trying to be patient.

"Ah, I'm with my g—uh, boyfriend. He's never been out to the Cape before. I thought I'd show him around. The scenery can be very beautiful around here," Eric said, with a visual grope of the man's crotch.

"Oh, yes, well, I've been up here a few times, myself, and I usually find it worthwhile," he said, and started scanning the crowd for the "boyfriend." His eyes lit on me after a bit. I smiled a half-smile at him before returning to my calculated indifference.

"So, you have a name? I'm Eric," my lover said, in his very friendly manner, and held out his hand.

"Pleased to meet you, Eric. I'm Rod," he said as they exchanged a manly handshake. Not bone-crushingly butch, just manly.

"Rod! How can you live with yourself with that name?" Eric said, and nearly lost his cool from laughing so hard. Rod looked a bit put off for a moment, but with the gracefulness of a queen, he recovered.

"You know the story, my mother did it to me," he said, winking at the old Freudian joke. I studied Rod some more. I liked his body language. I liked his open sexuality.

"Hah. I won't ask what else she did to you. Oh, it looks like that restroom is free now, see you in a few." Eric said and took off for the restroom, leaving a very bewildered Rod standing next in line. Maybe

Eric didn't want to pick up a bio-guy. My heart momentarily sank. I thought about trying to realize my fantasy without Eric's help.

I gave Rod a look and shrugged my shoulders, leaving him a shade more confused. I reluctantly turned my attention back to Eric's straight friends, Richard and Lisa. I couldn't stand Lisa. The whole day she had been referring to me with my birth pronoun, causing the cute boys to turn their attention away from me; after hearing that fatal "she," they dismissed me as a butch dyke. Richard was OK, he was just there for love. His big goofy hair and his silly laugh eased some of the tensions, but I was busy pondering how I could ditch both of them so Eric and I could go fuck Rod. However, in my mental wanderings, I had ceased paying attention to Eric and Rod's flirtations, and was surprised when I found Eric behind me.

"Hey," he said, grabbing my ass.

"Hey. I thought you were supposed to be fucking Rod in the bathroom," I said, one notch too loud.

"Andy! You're so crass!" he said in mock offense. I, unsubtly, readjusted my package. It was shifting too much. I needed something more realistic to put in my shorts.

Time passed. We watched tired queens, hot studs, and the rest of the usual flora and fauna at gay bars; I even managed to dance a bit while I looked for Rod. I found him on my way out; he was standing next to one of his friends. I wondered if they went out of their way to be stereotypical or if it was guys like them who make the stereotype. Like most, I gave up on this chicken and egg problem. Rod was much more interesting. I wondered if he had any piercings. Men with nipple rings give me a big hard-on.

"Rod, I was looking for you," I said, straining my voice to the lower edge. He looked up, no recognition in his face.

"Uh, yeah? Oh wait. You're that guy's, um, boyfriend?" he asked uncertainly, looking at me more closely.

"Yeah. Look, Eric and I are getting sorta sick of the straight-edgers we took up here from Boston. They are having issues or something. Would you like to come smoke out with us?" I asked. I made the internationally known joint-smoking gesture, and then smiled.

"Sure, but where's Eric?" he asked. I sighed. He was so transparent. However, Eric managed to appear a few seconds later. He gave me a short questioning look, then seemed to relax when he looked at Rod.

"Oh, hey. I was asking Rod to smoke out with us. You are coming, aren't you?" I said, and leered a bit suggestively at him.

"Um, okay," Eric said, still not looking quite pleased with me. We walked across the parking lot making inane conversation with regards to the weather, the straight tourists, the gay tourists, lesbians, and, unfortunately, Martha Stewart. I saw my little car under the yellow sodium light and sighed. I should have known better than to park under a light! Luckily there was a big green van and a bunch of over-grown sumac to the right of my car.

"Well, here's my car, let me get that weed," I said. Eric and Rod headed to the shadows. I got my box of weed out of my backpack, and managed to slip my "playing" cock into my shorts and take out the, um, packing material. I went around to the other side of the van. Shadows, darkness, and baggy clothing manages to hide extraneous information.

"Oh, Andy. I hope you remembered a lighter? Rod and I were talk-ing about how much it sucks when you forget a lighter," Eric called out.

"Don't worry, babe, I got it covered." I said as I was returning from the car. I walked up to Rod and Eric with the joint in one hand and the lighter in the other; held the joint up to Rod and lit it. He sucked. I stayed close to him, mostly to invade his personal space in a definitely sexual manner. We passed the joint around until it was gone, contem-plating the stars, or at least pretending to contemplate the stars. It gave me enough time to realize that people were still at the clubs, which eased my nerves considerably. The woods by the parking lot would be deserted for a time yet.

"Weed always makes me horny," Rod interjected. I tried my best to look surprised. I was glad my cruising efforts were being appreciated; I was starting to wonder if I should call up my best-fag friend Ryan and ask him for pointers. So, Ryan, how exactly do you ask a random bar guy to suck your cock? He never seemed to have any problem getting laid.

"Yeah? You wanna suck my cock?" I said, now drawing attention to my unnatural bulge and the desires that went along with it. I bet that's how Ryan does it, point blank. Okay, maybe not. Well, I never said I was smooth.

"Um?" he said and looked at Eric. I could see that he didn't think I was butch enough for him, that I didn't worship at the gym-queen altar, that my slight physique was far too effeminate.

"Don't worry, honey, you'll get Eric too," I said. Eric was looking somewhat shocked and intensely interested. I pushed Rod's shoulder down and he obediently sunk to his knees on the compacted dirt. The light was coming in from behind me; it highlighted his olive skin and sharp jaw pleasantly. The flickering brought exactly the illicit, exciting mood I desired. Eric had moved to about four feet behind him and was watching. I undid my zipper and brought my blue-and-white-swirled cock out.

"...But—I mean—it's not real!" Rod sputtered. Eric sighed and looked away uncomfortably.

"Honey, I don't want to get all existentialist on you. Come on, I know you are a good cocksucker. See if you can suck tranny cock. Just think, you can have a new story to tell to the queens at the gym," I said, only letting a restrained amount of cruelty into my voice. I didn't mean it. I was afraid I would get rejected. Then he smiled, and I could see that he'd decided.

He tentatively grabbed my cock and placed the head at his lips. His tongue darted out to lick around it, getting a feel for the texture and taste of silicone. I noticed that his grip at the base of my cock felt more sure, and my insecurities melted away as he got closer to me.

He took in an inch, then more. He closed his eyes. His mouth started working, as it had on many other cocks, I imagined. I started rocking slowly back and forth, testing to see if he liked getting his face fucked as much as I liked seeing him take my cock. He seemed to be getting into it, and those vibrations from fucking his mouth were hitting my clit so sweetly. I put my hands on his shoulders, I explored his neck and back. He felt so strong, so different from girls.

I almost didn't notice when Eric undid Rod's shorts. I definitely didn't notice until Eric took his lovely cock out of his own shorts. There it was, hard and natural, sheathed in latex, glistening with lube. A huge smile crept onto my face. I slowed my fucking of Rod, who looked up at me quizzically. I nodded to Eric, who, by now, had Rod's pants around his knees, and was touching Rod's lower back and ass. Rod was trying to stay focused.

"Rod, sweetie, Eric here is suited up and wants to fuck your ass. Now, I don't want to stop fucking your face. Is that okay? No, don't talk, just nod. Ah, good. Eric wants to see how good you are," I said. Eric knelt behind him and lathered more lube on his ass. Rod shivered a bit from the cold lube. By now I was completely wet under my harness, and I was starting to worry that the whole contraption might come undone.

Rod was sucking my cock like it was his anchor. He let out a muffled moan when Eric's cockhead pushed into him. I saw him struggle to widen his thighs, but his knees were restrained by his fallen shorts. His cock was glistening with precum. He looked beautiful, very well proportioned. Just the sort of cock I had wanted Eric to take.

I put that thought aside, and took in the scene before me. My lover and I had our cocks inside this one man. Rod slammed his ass further down Eric's cock, until he had taken it all, and then Eric started to fuck him in earnest. I didn't have to move any more as the motion from Eric was jamming my cock down Rod's throat when Eric jammed up his ass. I felt like I could come only from seeing that, but I wanted more friction. I started moving, ever so slightly, side to side. I looked at Eric. He had changed from the long, deep strokes to the fast, hard ones that he sometimes used before he came. I started moving again, in time to Eric.

Rod was a mess of gurgling moans. His hands were trying for purchase of whatever was near. I was so close to coming and I hadn't noticed Rod's state; when I looked down I saw he had one hand on his cock. He shot all over himself, and convulsed even harder against Eric, who looked up at me, mouth open, pupils dilated and his body taut.

I took a few last strokes down Rod's throat; my cock felt like it was channeling fire to my clit as I welcomed the flood of orgasm. Eric came as I was taking my cock out of Rod's mouth, and Rod grasped my thighs to steady himself and hold still; then Eric collapsed on top of Rod. All was quiet for a moment. I leaned down to Rod and kissed him hard; I felt like enough of a man to do it.

Pulling myself away, I went to the car and got a few towels from the trunk, removed my play cock, and put my regular packing one back on. I came back with towels and water; got everyone wiped down and cleaned up. I helped Rod back up and gave him a very chaste kiss on his forehead. Eric came around and put his arm around Rod. We were in that glowy phase; this time we looked up at the stars for real. Nobody felt like talking for a good ten minutes.

"Well, thanks for coming to smoke out with us, Rod," Eric finally said.

"Oh, well, um, it was, uh, different," Rod said, with a sheepish glance at me. I raised an eyebrow and looked over out past the sand dunes.

"You still worried about that cock being fake, Rod?" I asked.

"Nope. I could see you had a good time, Andy." He leaned over and kissed me, and then got up and stepped away, his body language saying that he wanted to go.

"Yeah, um, well, we should get back to our friends. Here's my email address; write us if you get down to Boston and, um, are bored or something. We'll try and entertain," Eric said and handed him a scrap of paper.

"Okay, will do. Thank you both… I should get back to my friends as well," he said, somewhat uncomfortably. I waved, Eric started to follow but I held onto his shirt until he got the hint that he was supposed to stay.

"So, Eric, did you like that?" I asked. I wondered how he felt about public sex, about cruising for sensations and live bodies.

"Yeah," he said, and paused for a moment. "Come on, we gotta go find Richard and Lisa before they start thinking that we were violently sodomizing some guy in a parking lot."

Watching. I return to watching, wondering what Rod will tell his friends. Wondering if Eric and I will ever do this again, wondering why it's such an issue that "it's not real." I have to remind myself that reality has no agreed-upon metric. All that matters is being real enough.

Is it a new sexual preference? People who are particularly attracted to transfolk are popping up like crocuses in springtime. One friend refers to them as "transfrienders"; I've also heard the terms "transhag" and the oft-scorned "admirer." Loving a transgendered person puts you into an odd camp with regard to sexual preference... are you gay? Lesbian? Straight? Or just Wandering Around With A Big Smile On Your Face? Even "bisexual" implies that there are only two genders. Either way, we need you all to come out of the closet—here's hoping it'll be as sexy as this story when you do.

Karen Taylor has been writing erotic fiction for the past 10 years. Her most recent work can be seen here and in The Academy: Tales of the Marketplace, *the fourth book in longest running SM erotica series featuring an FTM as the lead romantic character. Her short stories have also appeared in several anthologies, including* No Other Tribute *and* Leatherwomen III *(both ed. Laura Antoniou),* Friday the Rabbi Wore Lace *(ed. Karen Tulchinsky), and the 1997 Small Press award winner* First Person Sexual *(ed. Joani Blank). She is currently collaborating with her spouse, Laura Antoniou, on a short story collection entitled* Slaves of the Marketplace.

Wanting That Man

Karen Taylor

Almost from the first moment I spotted him, I wanted to suck his dick. I know, not appropriate behavior from a lesbian. But then, he wasn't an ordinary man, either. I knew that when I saw him that first time at the dyke bar, surrounded by women. And what women! I mean, I go to the dyke bar for company and to get laid, but a lot of these other women go there to get away from men. Years of anarchist politics, progressive city governments, and low-cost lands made the I-5 corridor a haven for lesbian separatists in the 70's and 80's. Although not many of the wimmin I hung with had been part of those early years, Seattle's lesbian social system was still influenced by decades of separatist politics. While I didn't mind men, most of the women in here would be steering away from anything with a whiff of testosterone. But there he was, surrounded by babes, laughing and drinking a beer just as naturally as if, well, as if he weren't the only man in a dyke bar.

I watched him carefully. He was handsome, in a boyish way. Lanky body, dark curled hair cut short in the back and on the sides, a mustache resting gently across his upper lip. The contrast between the dark hair and the flash of his white teeth when he smiled or laughed was a delight. His hands were delicate, with long fingers that caressed his beer when it was resting on the bar counter. He didn't preen, the way I see straight men preen when they're surrounded by women. His crotch didn't thrust out aggressively, the way gay men sometimes do when they're in unfamiliar territory. His hip remained cocked against the bar, one boot kicked on the railing. I watched, long enough to

233

enjoy the lazy shift of his weight from one side to the other, turning away from me, giving me a lovely view of a tight, hard ass. One of the women spanked it jokingly, and he laughed, twitching his butt back and forth a few times in rhythm to the music.

I think that's what did it. The flirtatious move of that ass had me transfixed. I wanted to spank him! I wanted to touch that ass, caress it, and move my hand slowly around to the front... and realized, in a flush of embarrassment, that I was in the midst of daydreaming about sucking a man's cock while I was standing in the middle of a lesbian bar. Fortunately I've never been afraid of my psyche. I decided I had to know this guy (and soon, whispered my hungry cunt), so, when she stepped away from the group, I asked one of my friends who he was.

"I knew him back in San Francisco, when he was still a butch dyke," she said, and I had a sudden sense of dizziness.

"You're telling me—" I started, and she laughed.

"Yeah, that's right, he used to be a she," my friend explained. I turned again and stared openly at the man at the end of the bar. Was he lanky, or slender? Was that smile pleasant, or sweet? Something about the face seemed feminine. Or was it? The body language was definitely male. Or maybe not. Lucky for me, I'm not shy. I introduced myself when it was convenient, and bought him a beer.

"I'm Kate."

"I'm Larry," he answered, smiling. I wondered what his name used to be. But when I shook his hand, I stopped wondering. His palm was smooth, his hands strong. Those fingers... I was sure those fingers would feel wonderful in my cunt. And with sex so strongly on my mind, I dropped my eyes briefly to his crotch.

Bad move. Because when I looked back into his smiling, inquisitive eyes, I felt something I hadn't felt in years about any guy. I wanted him. I wanted to take him home and fuck him. I wanted to suck his dick, feel him come in my mouth. I wanted that man.

You have to understand. I haven't wanted a man, not for years. When I get the urge for penetration, I use dildos or fists, just like any other healthy, horny dyke. I had separated my desire for getting my cunt filled from my desire for a penis. But Larry's presence made me remember the joys of cock sucking—the way a living dick pulses in a wet, hungry mouth, the hot, sucking sounds as my lips would tighten or loosen around a cock shaft, tugging on the head while my tongue would tickle a wet piss hole. And especially I remembered the tension in the flesh just before my mouth would fill with hot, salty come. I wanted that again. And the urge was so strong I could barely keep up my end of the conversation.

Lucky for me I can sometimes keep my cunt and my brain separated—or at least act like it.

"It's strange to see a guy so comfortable in a dyke bar, Larry," I said. "Most of these wimmin would rather spit at a man than invite him in.

You've got balls walking in here." I winced internally. Maybe I should have used a better term. But Larry just smiled back, ignoring my possible faux pas.

"I've got a lot of friends here," he said. "Some of whom have known me for a long time—back when I was still living in California. I'm up visiting for a few weeks."

"Good," I said recklessly. "I mean, good that you'll be here for a while."

"Is it?" he asked, still smiling. I noticed this close that his eyes were green, with gold flecks dancing in the irises.

"Yup," I answered. "Because, Larry, my new friend, I think you're very attractive." Larry chuckled, pretending great shock.

"How un-lesbian of you!" he said in mock horror. "Attraction to a man! Unless," he said, "you're thinking I'm not really a man." I saw that under his joking demeanor there was something else.

"Look," I said, "Seattle's grapevine is notorious the country over for its speed and viciousness. I got word about you within two minutes of walking into this bar."

He nodded, his eyes clouded. "Yeah, well, despite rumors to the contrary, I'm not the butchest dyke you'll ever meet, Kate. I've spent a lot of time and money to be something—someone—else."

The silence between us was growing, and I didn't want it to. But it was clear that this was not the place to continue.

"Larry," I finally said. "I didn't think you were a butch dyke. I still don't. And I would really like to see you. Would you be interested in having dinner with me tomorrow night?" He was surprised, but pleased. I gave him my address and phone number, he gave me his. By the time we parted, the clouds had left his eyes, and he was smiling again. And my level of horniness was back on the rise. Our date was at seven. Less than twenty hours away. Already I couldn't wait. I nearly rushed over to a group of friends to announce "I've got a hot date with Larry tomorrow." But suddenly, I didn't want anyone to know. I didn't want them to treat my date with Larry like it was just another edition of "Kate's Adventures with the Odd and Unusual." My date with Larry wasn't just another unconventional experience, another feather in my proverbial cap, was it?

Yeah, well, maybe it was. After all, I was the one who giggled with the drag queens and flirted the most outrageously with the butchest diesel dykes in the city. Those gender edges always attracted me. But this was more complicated. After all, Larry was a man in a dyke bar. There just isn't a place in our world for people like him. On the other hand, no amount of drugs or surgery could change the fact that he had been part of the dyke culture for several years before making this decision. I wonder how it felt, to make a decision that would always keep you on the fringe of an already fringe community. I wonder if he ever talked about it with anyone.

I lay awake that night thinking about Larry. Whether the skin on his face was rougher than mine. Whether his nipples were responsive to a light touch, or to a quick, sharp twist. Whether he clenched his toes when he came. And especially, whether he liked his cock sucked. I wondered if he had a cock. Or if he used anything in its place. I fell asleep dreaming of those freshly masculine hands caressing my body, that low voice murmuring in my ear. Spreading my legs. Larry fucking me slow.

The next day he came to place right at seven and I was waiting for him. I wanted to be as femme as I could be against his masculinity, so I wore a light rayon summer dress with a floral pattern, sheer stockings, and a lace garter belt that matched my bra and panties. Larry was handsome in his creased slacks, crisp white cotton shirt, and bright tie. We went out for Mexican, drinking margaritas and eating spicy food. I waited until we were near the end of the meal before I told him about my dreams the night before.

He smiled, but there was something else with it.

"You flatter me," he answered, his dark eyes bright and smiling at me. I smiled back, but pressed on in my usual, subtle-as-a-tractor way.

"This isn't about flattery, Larry. This is about attraction. I'm attracted to you. I noticed you as soon as I walked into the bar last night. Okay, okay," I said, laughing as he grinned. "It wasn't hard to notice the only man in the place. But what I mean is, I saw you and I thought you were hot! Who knows why? Because I'm attracted to "female" energy in men and "male" energy in women? Or is it simply because you have a cute ass?" By this time Larry was laughing with me. I grabbed his hand (oh! getting fisted by a man! my cunt clenched so hard I almost lost my train of thought), took a deep breath, and continued.

"Larry, you are so fine, I can't stop thinking about you. I don't know all the reasons why, either, but I do know you're the first man that's interested me in years. The more important question for the moment is whether you want me." He stared at me, a good long time. I refused to drop my eyes, challenging him back. When he smiled, I knew I had him. I was floating on air all the way back to my apartment.

I waited until we were inside before I kissed him. I had a feeling that his moustache would make my knees weak, and it did. I nibbled at it, testing the sensation against my tongue and lips, hoping Larry would taste my hunger for him. I let him undress me, wanting to feel his hands on my body, and I unbuttoned his shirt. He hesitated as I touched his collarbone, then sank back on the bed with me. I traced the scars that followed the line of his muscles on his chest, memories of his old life. When I asked, he told me the feeling in his nipples was duller, and then he rolled my nipples in his fingers lightly. I moaned as they grew under his touch. Larry licked and sucked them into hardness, my back arching as I clawed at his hair, pulling his face into my breasts. I begged him to fuck me and he answered "not yet," his mouth working its way down my belly. I shivered when his tongue opened me, flicking against my clit, then howled as he nibbled and worried the sweet inner flesh. His delicate fingers pushed gently into my cunt, then curved, rubbing the back of my clit. I felt the wave carry me into an orgasm, his mouth staying on me, fingers buried deep inside as I bucked and jerked. I discovered my fingers tangled in his hair when I finally stopped shaking.

Larry pulled himself up next to me, caressing my belly, my breasts, my collarbone, and I let my body respond wholly to his touch. I felt my arousal grow again, and I rested my hand against his crotch, feeling his bulge through the fabric of his slacks. I rolled against him, unbuckled his belt. His hand stopped me.

"I want to suck you," I said. He shook his head.

"It's not—they haven't perfected the surgery for a good penis, yet," he said.

"I don't care," I answered. "I only care whether you'll get off if I suck your cock. Will you? Can you get off like that?"

"I don't know," he answered. I sat up, surprised.

"Hasn't anyone ever sucked your cock before?" I asked.

"No. Not since the change."

"I'm willing to try if you are," I said, grinning at him. He hesitated, giving me time to open his fly and breathe lightly on the bush of hair I discovered hidden beneath. He moaned, and sighed. To me, it sounded like "All right, I give up."

So I pressed ahead, letting my fingers do the talking. There was a dildo, half-soft, resting in the bush of hair. Carefully I rested my hand over it. I wrapped my fingers around it through his pants, and squeezed gently, bearing down at the same time so he could feel the pressure against his crotch. His eyes closed and he let out a long sigh. I continued to rock my fist against his package until I could see all the muscles in his neck and shoulders relax. Then I made my next move.

I kissed his neck, gently, brushing my lips against his skin. "Larry, I'll suck this, I've sucked plenty of dyke dicks, but I'd really like to taste you, if you'll let me," I whispered, letting my breath tickle his ear. There was a slight tightening in his shoulders, but Larry didn't open his eyes. I kept my hand rocking against his groin as I increased the intensity of my kisses. He moaned a little, and I took his earlobe into my mouth and tugging on it gently with my teeth. That seemed to do it. Larry groaned and arched up against the bed, tugging his slacks off, and removing his packing dick. His eyes were still closed. Was he scared?

Of course he was, I admonished myself. If no one has sucked this man's cock before, he's probably nervous as hell. And while I wasn't exactly subtle about what I wanted—did I really know what I was getting into?

Without rushing too much, I started to move down his body, leaving a trail of hot kisses from Larry's neck across his chest (with some time focused on his nipples to get an idea of what he liked there), and down his stomach to his thick bush of hair.

He smelled different than I remembered men smelling. But at the same time, he didn't smell like a woman. There was a tang that was definitely not female. I used my hand to part the hair, and immediately discovered his dick, pushing up from between the two folds of skin. I pulled the lips slightly away from his cock, freeing it.

What can I say? It was a lot like a big clit, but not really. More fully developed, thick as my thumb, and there was even a head. My own clit was pretty small, and I'd never looked at it that closely, so I don't know whether Larry's cock was just a bigger version of what his clit had looked like. And frankly, I don't care. Because it looked like a great cock to me. A dream cock. The kind of cock I could suck and tug and tickle and never have to worry about whether he would choke me.

I breathed on it first, warming the skin. Larry shivered, and one hand opened and closed. I flicked my tongue quickly across the tip of his cock, and as he moaned, I covered his cock with my mouth.

I started licking slowly, the way I would to a clit, and played the length of his shaft, then circling it. I pressed my tongue at the base, pushing off toward his cunt lips. Then I hesitated. Licking, pressing, finding those spots that would send shivers up a woman's spine, I was starting that way without even thinking. This wasn't what I wanted. *Think, girl!* I told myself sternly. *You have your man where you want him. You've got his cock in your mouth. Work it!*

Oh, the ride that followed! When I closed my lips and began to suck the length of Larry's cock, it was like all of his fears melted away. I felt a hand drop heavily onto the back of my head, and when I looked up, I could see him playing with his nipples with his other hand. I found that a little nibbling around the base drove him to thrust hard into my mouth. When I tugged hard at the root, he arched his back, and I got my hands under him, cupping his ass and spreading his ass cheeks slightly. The hand on my head gripped my hair as I tongued the length of his shaft and tickled the head of his cock. He was pulling and twisting his nipples, which sent hot rushes to my cunt and made me suck harder.

We finally got into a rhythm that I knew would lead to his orgasm, and I let him take the lead, his hand tugging and pushing at my head. Cupping his ass cheeks, I pulled him toward me in the same rhythm, deepening his thrusts into my mouth. His moans had changed into animal grunts, and I could feel Larry's cock flexing, the way cocks do just before they come.

And indeed, he did come, groaning and thrusting hungrily into my mouth. I could taste his hot, bitter juices—definitely not the heavy saltiness of semen, but too tangy to be women's juices. I savored Larry's uniqueness, wondering if the tequila from dinner was adding its own essence to the flavor. I resisted the temptation to start sucking again, and instead disentangled myself so I could slide back up Larry's body and rest my head on his chest, listening for his heartbeat to slow down.

Larry finally sighed heavily, putting one arm around me. "Kate, that was... I mean, I never thought..."

"I'm giving you fair warning," I told him. "I'm lousy at making breakfast, but I grind fresh coffee every morning if I get fucked first."

"Lucky for you I'd do anything for a good cup of coffee," he laughed, and then kissed me, long and slow, the kind of kiss you know you're going to want every night and every morning right after you fuck your brains out. Yes, indeed, I wanted that man.

We're glad to know that we're not the only ones with a thing for Walt Whitman... or FTM bears. Two great tastes that, as they say, taste great together. It's a tricky thing to write a long blow-by-blow of an involved, extended sex session and not have it degenerate into something that sounds like sportscasting, but Ian Philips manages it adroitly, grabbing your most erogenous zones and not letting go until he's done. We like that in a person.

Ian Philips is a proud son of Sodom and a garden-variety bio-boy whose best friends really are trannies. In fact, this very story was inspired by a crush he had on one of their boyfriends. His literate filth has appeared in Best Gay Erotica 1999, 2000, *and* 2001 *as well as* Best of the Best Gay Erotica. *These and other wicked tales have been caged in his first book,* See Dick Deconstruct: Literotica for the Satirically Bent *(AttaGirl Press). He lives—not surprisingly—in San Francisco and can be contacted at iphilips@aol.com.*

Walt

Ian Philips

San Francisco. Saturday night. Almost midnight.

I was at The Hole in the Wall. Alone. I know, I know—I'm making it sound like a bad thing. And it wasn't. No way. I'm just trying to picture it in my mind so you can in yours.

Okay, Saturday night. So I wasn't bummed really. Or scared. It's just I'd never been there before without my roommates—the guys.

Okay, so maybe I was a little nervous.

Cuz I'm shy.

I mean it's not like I'm ugly or anything. Brown hair. Brown eyes. I keep my goatee trimmed real close. I've got a big mouth. Honest. And a big nose. I don't like it. But this hot guy told me it was "classical." He said I have a Roman nose. Makes sense. I'm Italian. Okay, my mom's dad and my dad's grandparents are Italian. So I try to remember what he said and how sexy he said it when I get self-conscious. Like Saturday night.

I know, I know—BFD. What's my problem? Especially when most guys just want you to have meat on your boner. No sweat, then. I don't mean to be bragging, but I gotta big, fat dick. What can I say, it came with the body. And when I used to fuck around with "most guys," I scored all the time. But what gets me hard, you know, dick-pointing-to-the-sky-rock-hard, is men with meat on all of their bones.

So? Shit. I forgot to tell you I'm real skinny too. So, I'm always thinking, since I am so skinny, those guys won't want me. They'll throw me back in the water just like my dad does with any fish he thinks is—his words, not mine—"a runt." Okay, it probably doesn't help that

243

that's his nickname for me too. And I'm not that small. It's just my dad's 6'1" and I'm 5'8". And, I guess, if you put only 130 pounds on 5'8" worth of bones, you gotta runt.

Whatever. By the way, none of what I just told you was to throw me a pity party. I swear. It's so you'll know why I didn't tell Walt to go fuck himself when he came onto me. Even if he did seem a little crazy. Hell, he is crazy.

Great. Now I want my men big and crazy.

Well, right now, I just want Walt.

No, he isn't one of the Naked Guys or that guy that barks. Though they were all there last Saturday night. But maybe you've never been. Sorry. I keep forgetting I'm supposed to see it so you can see it. Okay. The Hole in the Wall. It's like that bar—you know, the one in *Star Wars*. Honest. Except this time everyone's a fag and horny. They call it a biker bar. I guess it is. There's always a bunch of guys there who look like they're Hell's Angels. But, to say it's a biker bar, you gotta include mountain bikes with the Harleys.

Okay. Right. Saturday. It was packed. Two deep along the bar and three around the pool table. In the back—you know where that mural is of the great daddy bear riding a Harley and his boy into heaven— the one right beneath the sign that says "Booty Juice Rules"—back there, it was so thick with bikers and bears and boys it didn't take much to guess what was going on.

I looked across to the bar, then looked up front again to see if my guys had decided to show up after all. Nothing. Then I looked straight ahead again, and two blue eyes were staring back. Staring right through me. This blond bear—bear cub—was cruising me. Heavy cruising. No looking away. No blinking. But there was something odd about him. He had the cruise down, but, even though his thick lips never moved, I could tell he was grinning at me. With his eyes. You know. Like that cat in *Alice in Wonderland*. The one that had the shit on everyone and just smiled, driving them crazy cuz they all feared just how much he knew. Yeah, his face was a lot like that cat's. Then the eyes, the smile, the face, him—they all moved toward me.

His belly pushed guy after guy out of the way. Kinda like those big rocks in streams that water has to split itself in half to get around. Except the stream was men heading for the bar or the john. And the rock kept moving towards me. God, my eyes musta been bugging. I almost had to bite my tongue to keep from grinning back. I wasn't nervous anymore. Okay, maybe still a little. But, mainly, I was stoked to be singled out by such a hot man. All I could think was Please, sir, don't stop.

I braced my butt against the ledge that runs along the wall. I didn't want to start shaking. But I was getting so excited. *Omigod. He's getting so close. Is he gonna kiss me? Yes, c'mon, daddy bear. Closer. C'mon.* And he kept com- ing, until his thick gut was pressing hard against my belly-flopping stomach. He was only a few inches from my face. He leaned in. He's gonna kiss me. I closed my eyes, I dunno why. You're such a girl, I screamed to myself. But I didn't care. I waited for his bristles to poke my lips.

Then I felt them. On my ear! He was snorting in my ear. Okay, breathing. But he was a heavy breather. Like a crank caller. Like a bull.

My ear prickled and burned till my whole face musta been red. Then, his body gently crushed mine and he whispered, "I sing the body electric." And I felt it. The current coming from his fingers as he grabbed my shoulder blades. "The armies of those I love engirth me and I engirth them." His hands dropped slowly along my spine. I thought—I hoped—he was gonna shove them down my pants. But they kept going till he'd pushed my butt from the ledge and held a cheek in each hand. "They will not let me off till I go with them, respond to them." Then he pulled one hand from my ass and dragged it around my hip. If he was going for my dick, it wouldn't be hard to find now. It was making as much of a pup tent as it could in 501s one size too small. I breathed in. Closed my eyes tight. He found it. I had a raging boner by the time he crushed his palm into my crotch and said, "And discorrupt them, and charge them full with the charge of the soul."

After one hard, slow squeeze, he pulled his hand from my dick and up along my stomach—totally belly-cartwheeling now—and over my chest till he held my chin. I felt his breath now before I heard it. My lips grew warm. Please, kiss me. I waited. He waited. I opened my eyes.

"It's Walt."

"Hey, Walt. I'm Joe."

He laughed. A burst that softened as it fell down the register. God, he's cute.

"No, Walt Whitman. That was from a poem by Whitman."

I think I've seen just one picture of Walt Whitman. He was a really old dude. Probably sixty or seventy years old. Maybe not. Back then, life was rougher. He mighta been forty. But that Walt didn't look like this Walt. That Walt—Walt Whitman—he looked like Grizzly Addams' friend. You know—the old guy, not the bear. What was his name? You know. Well, it was the same guy that played Uncle Jesse on *The Dukes of Hazzard*. This Walt didn't look like either of them. Okay, maybe he looked like Grizzly Adams. But mine's a few inches smaller and so's his beard.

Now all that thinking I just did really happened in a second. Well, as long as it took to get one good look at his face. Okay, I'm not sure; it coulda been longer. I'd been drinking. Good thing too or I never woulda had the balls to do what I did next.

I leaned up to his ear and grabbed his dick. It's hard too. Then I said it. "Wanna go to my place and fuck?" I felt his whole body shake. He laughed till I thought it was the laughter lifting me in a bear hug.

We held hands the whole cab ride to my house. I didn't let go of his paw till we got to my room and I had to plug in the strings of pink flamingo lights on the wall above my futon. It was just them and the lava lamp across the room. Enough light to tell where the buttons in our jeans were.

I looked up from the outlet and there was Walt. He was grinning for real now. He'd propped all my pillows up against the wall. Then scooted his whole bulk into his new chair, pulling most of the blanket up under his ass. He was patting his thigh. His thick fingers thudded against his thicker leg. It was a drum beat I couldn't ignore.

I bent down and tore at the laces of my boots. Yeah, it was light enough to see a silver button, but there was no way in hell I was gonna untie a little black knot fast. I think I said one of those strings of "Shits" out loud. Finally, I got both boots off. I marched up and onto my bed, straddling Walt's legs. I tried to kneel down slowly but he grabbed my hips and tugged. My ass fell hard onto his lap but I didn't even knock the wind out of him. Nope. He wasn't even fazed. Just pulled me in closer and kissed me.

His lips were heavy and wet. Mine slipped around on them, scratching against the edge of his beard if I rolled too far, till he had my mouth and me anchored to his tongue. He tasted so good. Honest. Like really dark beer.

He slipped his hands up under my shirt. It wasn't difficult. It'd come untucked and it was a velour pullover anyway, a real deep purple. They were warm, his hands. He fanned them across my chest. "The curious sympathy one feels...." He slipped them under my arms. I jumped back. I couldn't help it. It tickled. But he kept talking, "...when feeling with the hand the naked meat of the body." He lifted my arms, then his, and, with it, my shirt up and over my head. One cool move.

"Was that Walt, too?"

He smiled. God, he must know every poem Whitman ever wrote! He didn't say anything—just placed a palm right on top of each nipple. Then he arched his hands so only his fingers and my skin were touching. I watched them and waited. They looked like they were gonna play the piano. He dragged them real slow down to my stomach. I was shaking. A big quivering shudder ran up and up then down my spine. He was getting closer to the rim of my jeans, to the buttons. And my dick was getting closer to rock hard. It was showtime.

Leaving one hand waiting at my waistband, he took the other and started fumbling with my top button. I sat up on my knees, sticking my butt up like a cat. Pop. One free. His hand slid under the denim. Pop. It was at the tip of my crack. My dickhead jumped out. Pop. Pop. Pop. His fingers slid into my butt crack, digging for my hole, while my dick sprung up to my stomach like one of those flowers in time-lapse that comes up outta the earth in full bloom.

Before my cock could cool in the open air, Walt had it in his grip. His hands were fucking huge. This one held almost three-quarters of my dick. He squeezed. I groaned. He squeezed even harder. His thumb stroked my sticky hole again and again. Quickly, it was sliding back and forth. He breathed more words in my ear. "Without shame," his thumb kept counting out the beat, "the man I like," back and forth, "knows and avows" back and forth, "the deliciousness of his sex."

I was "unnhing" by now. Which isn't bad. It sounds hot. It feels hot. It's just if he kept thumbing and I kept "unnhing" I was gonna shoot way too soon. So I grabbed for his dick. It was long and hard against his thigh. I tried to squeeze it real rough-like. Shit, this fucker's thick. He barely noticed. So I pulled on it. I couldn't tell if he was moaning or laughing.

I gripped it harder and yanked it. He got quiet. He stopped thumbing me but didn't let go of my dick. My other hand was still holding onto his ledge of a shoulder. I let go and made a grab for the back of his head. I pulled him in till his open mouth was on mine.

There's no better way to say it: we were sucking face. No shit. I thought he was gonna swallow my head like a Tootsie Pop.

Somehow I was able to keep up the tongue-wrestling match we had going while I unbuttoned the top three buttons of his flannel shirt. Plop. I broke the vacuum seal. I gulped down a breath and then dropped my face into the brush of his beard. His hairs pricked my lips and tongue again and again as I dragged them down his face to his neck. Walt's hand had long let go of my dick and joined its twin on my ass. He held each cheek tight while thumbing my butt crack. As I pushed my mouth down his neck, I inched my hole towards his thumbs. I was sitting on them by the time I got to his chest. His skin was smooth with sweat and sweet-smelling. Then, finally, I found it, that patch of dark blond hair. I matted it some more with my face. I was getting real close to his meaty tits.

Okay. I know the minute I said "meaty" you were thinking I meant the usual two sirloin steaks circuit queens either grow or have glued onto their chests. Nope. In fact, "meaty's" kinda lame since I'm a vegetarian. I just mean those big, thick ones you can totally suck on. Like the monster man-tits in Bulk Male. You know, they look like two huge mudslides on Pacific Coast Highway 1.

And Walt had them. We're talking El Niño mudslides. With the biggest, pinkest nipples I'd ever seen on a guy. I sighed in awe, and that got Walt's thumbs to wriggling at the edge of my hole. My ass sent a quick message up my spine to my brain. If I wanted any nippage, I was gonna have to totally scrunch down on his thumbs. Two holes filled in one move—yeah, it was a sacrifice I was willing to make.

I stuck out only the end of my tongue and moved in. I flicked it against his fat nipple. A butterfly kiss. Walt shook. The futon creaked. My asshole danced over his thumbs as they took turns jabbing it and each other to get in. I quickly locked my lips 'round the tip of his tit and the Waltquake stopped.

His thick knot stiffened between my lips. He growled and I sucked. Then I pulled away till I held the tip of his tit in my teeth. I bit down, real gentle-like at first, then not-so-gentle-like.

Walt belched out something that sounded like "Ah, shit!" My asshole was pulling around empty air. His thumbs were gone. He tugged at the back of my head with both his hands and pried me loose like I was some kinda tick.

I slipped free, dragging my tongue down through the trail of hair to the edge of his jeans. I kept expecting his belly to shake like that bowlful of jelly under the weight of my tongue, but it was one solid block of fat and muscle. I was leaking some serious precome now.

I reached for his belt buckle. My hands fumbled like I was a kid, up since 4am, tearing into his first Christmas present, finally, at 9am. Got it! Now for the button fly. Top button down. Then another. My whole body was shaking. I wanted his dick. Now. To let him know just how bad, I gripped it hard and squeezed.

Suddenly my face was swallowed in the palm of his hand. He tilted my chin up from his crotch till our eyes met. "Whoever you are holding me now in hand,/ Without one thing all will be useless," he smiled just like that cat again. "I give you fair warning before you attempt me further,/ I am not what you supposed, but far different."

I guess if I was listening to what the words meant, I might have stopped then and asked him just what the fuck he was talking about. But he used so many words. Some pretty. Some weird. Some really vague. They all sounded like what a genie in a fairy tale says or a fortune cookie. I didn't really care; I just wanted to see his cock and suck it. Talk later.

I shoved my fingers under the tight waistband of his black underwear. It was leather. A leather jockstrap. Kinky. I had to see his dick bad now. Please, let him have a Prince Albert. My asshole twitched. Amen, sister.

I kept pushing down. At some point I knew my hand would find that odd spot in the damp, wiry hair and soft fat of his mound where a hard, thick stick grew. But I kept pushing down. Where was it? It's supposed to be just south of the belly button. Then my fingers slid over another curve of fat and into this warm, wet crease. I panicked.

"Where's your dick?"

"You pushed it out of the way for my cunt."

"Your cunt?" I yanked my hand out of his pants as fast as I could. "How can a man have a cunt?"

"I just do."

My face was swallowed again by his hand. For a sec, I got scared he was gonna crush my head like a walnut. But, instead, he held it real tender, like I was this little baby bird that'd fallen out of its nest.

Then he let go and grabbed my hand. I started to wig when he tried to push it back down under his jockstrap. He just held tight and shoved my fingers into his sweaty and steamy bush. "Have you ever loved the body of a woman?" I watched him pull my wet hand up his stomach and onto his stiffening nipple. "Have you ever loved the body of a man?" My fingers were almost cold and he pulled them up and into his mouth. He sucked till they were warm, then dragged them out over his soft, wide lower lip. "Do you not see that these are exactly the same to all in all nations and times all over the earth?"

"Is that another poem?" He smiled again. "Could you just fucking stop with the poetry crap!" My dick was shrinking like a dying balloon and I was cold.

"Stop and listen to their words. Feel them. They're so beautiful—like you."

I forgot what I was gonna say. Then I blurted out, "You tricked me."

"You tricked yourself."

Okay. Reality check. Yeah, I thought right then about telling Walt to get the fuck outta my house. For a sec. Or two. Maybe a minute. I was kinda shocked. All right, I was pissed. But before I could say anything, my dick had to go and put in his two cents. Well, more like his eight-and-a-half inches.

Walt, my dick and I both agreed, was—even with a pussy under his dick—one of the hottest guys we'd ever seen. Honest. I wasn't that drunk. And, my dick reminded me, the last time we got laid was two weeks before finals and my last final was almost two weeks ago. Hell, that's a month.

I snapped outta my head just in time to see Walt groping around in his pants for his dick. "Here," he pulled it loose and it flapped up between us. "I'll keep it on the whole time. Okay? You just get it wet and I'll fuck you with it. All right?"

I stared at it. It was pretty realistic, for a dildo. You know. You could tell the head from the shaft. It had veins. Even smelled like skin from being in Walt's pants. But I knew it'd taste like silicone.

"He's hot," my dick shouted. "A month. Thirty fuckin' days and no one's touched me but you!"

Walt pushed me off and stood. Snapped his fingers and pointed to his feet. I scurried over and tried to make a go of it.

His dick was about eight inches long and six around. It was hard, and Walt knew how to face fuck like it really was his. In a few minutes, he was shoving it down the back of my throat. He was a rough, mean fucker and didn't care if I was choking and sobbing. I shoulda been happy. Real happy. It felt good. Honest. But something was missing.

I know you thought I was gonna say "a real dick." Wrong. It's just the more I sucked, the more I thought. And the more I thought, the more I knew that no matter what he did with that dick, he couldn't feel me and I couldn't feel him. I mean I'm pretty good with my tongue.

But it was wasted on his dick. I wanted Walt to feel how excited I was by him. And I wanted to feel, from the surge of his skin and blood, that he was excited by me.

You have to understand this. You just do. It's real important. Really. So you'll get why I did what I did.

Okay. First, I raised my hands off his cock and onto his belly, pushing it, pushing him, to lie back on the futon. I started to get up off my knees while keeping the dick in my mouth. Of course, now I can see it wouldn'ta withered in the cold air if I'd popped it out of my mouth. So, maybe it was outta habit. Or respect. Whatever. There I was crouching with his dick in my mouth and hoping he'd figure out what I wanted him to do next.

Maybe it was the luck of the first date, but he did. He laid back. All this time, I was still casually blowing him and waiting. He hadn't been on his back long before he was tweaking a nipple real hard and sliding his other hand down his heaving belly towards my head and his dick and his cunt. He stopped for one rough tug on my head to remind me to keep up the pace. And then, it was under the band of the dildo harness. You know, the leather jockstrap.

He grunted. Low. He moaned. Lower. He snorted. He sighed. Still, he was a long way from orgasm. But he musta been getting hard under there. Or flushed. Whatever he called it. I didn't care. I just knew each loud breath was a good sign. So I started "unnhing" again. I wasn't hard or anything. Walt wasn't even touching me. I was doing it cuz I thought if we're both making noises he won't hear me popping his harness open.

Snap. One down. I wasn't sucking his cock anymore. Just pushing on it so he'd think I was. Snap. Two down. I needed to get the dick out of the way now. I thought of pulling the harness up and over it. But I woulda had to yank the back side of it down and out through his butt crack first.

Not too subtle.

So I crawled up onto the futon alongside Walt. Then I tilted the dildo at an angle and pulled real gentle. You know like in the "Grinch Who Stole Christmas" when he takes the candy canes from the sleeping babies. And Walt didn't notice either. And me, all I was thinking was that I had to see his cunt. I had to touch it. With my hands. Hell, with my face. I don't know why, except, like I said before, I had to feel him getting it up for me.

I pulled back the leather triangle. And there it was. The first cunt I'd ever seen. Honest. Its lips were big, fat, wet, and pink, real pink. The pink of bubblegum. Not that hard, dry pink of Bazooka Joe, but the soft, squishy pink of Bubblicious before you bite into it.

I watched his fingers to find the clit. And there it was, under this thing that looked like the awning on some fancy apartment building. A little dick head with wings, no bigger than a thumb or a Vienna sausage, you know, a cocktail wienie. Honest. I'm not trying to be mean. That's just what I thought at first. I didn't think it looked gross. Just kinda weird, kinda different, kinda cute.

"Well, boy, whatdya think? Too small fer ya?"

For a sec, I thought it was my dad talking to me about some fish. Or me. Why is size such a big fuckin' deal?

"Well, boy?" A hand yanked hard on my hair. I snapped outta my head. This wasn't my dad. He never touched me.

"Hey," the hand let go and slapped my head, "you asleep?"

"No, sir. It's no runt, sir."

"That ain't no pig yer talkin' about. That's my dick, boy." The hand rubbed the top of my head, mussing with my hair. "Be more respectful."

"Yes, sir."

"Well, go on now. You kin touch it, boy."

You'd think touching a dick that was a clit woulda been weird to me. But it wasn't. I wasn't even thinking that. What I didn't get was why Walt was talking now like Festus on "Gunsmoke." You know, some old prospector or something. I guess cuz it made his voice sound deep, like Darth Vader's. It was odd but hot.

Whatever, I sighed to myself. He'd grabbed hold of my dick. "Ah, fuck," I said out loud. The thumb had found that magic spot right where the dick meets the dickhead.

Then he let go so I could scooch down. I put my face in and it felt like his cunt was giving me a big, slobbery kiss. My cheeks were sticky, but I kept going. I puckered and aimed my lips for where I thought I'd seen it last. I was gonna try and get it all in my mouth with one suck. Won't Walt be impressed with his pussy-eating virgin.

"Fuck!" He grabbed me by the back of the head and yanked me out. "Listen, boy. I may call it a dick and you may think it's a dick. But it ain't just like your dick. So don't be getting all riled up to tug at it like it's your teenage peter in a circle jerk."

"I'm sorry," I mumbled.

Good thing it was dark. I was blushing. I felt so dumb.

"First rule, tonight, no fingers. We'll work up to those." I suddenly got excited. He was already talking about a second date.

"Next rule, use your tongue. But think of my clit as a thousand times more sensitive than either of your nipples." He gave both a hard twist and I jumped. "Okay?"

"Okay."

"And five hundred times more sensitive than your cock." He stroked the underside of my dickhead lightly and I shook. "That's more like it."

I sighed and gave him this real goofy grin. God, I'm such a 'tard.

"Now, kiss me." I did. I went all out. What the hell, I figured. Might as well let him know that when I kiss I like to get my face wet and my lips sore. Minutes, maybe hours, later, he pulled out for air.

"You're a fuckin' good kisser," he gasped. "Now, do it again." I leaned in and bumped my lips against his finger. "But this time, my tongue is my clit."

I know my eyes bugged this time. Walt just laughed. "Geez, that sounded way too much like a paper I wrote in school." I think he was blushing. "Okay, I want you to pretend my tongue is my clit. And I want you to use your tongue to get it off."

I almost had "but" outta my mouth.

"Don't worry," he said. "I'll do a little old-fashioned operant conditioning to let you know when you're doing it just right. Trust me. Now, close your eyes." I couldn't even blink. "Trust me. Close your eyes and feel the force, Luke." I laughed. "Feel it." Walt rubbed his thumb beneath my dickhead. I closed my eyes. "Kiss me." I barely had a chance to mush lips or even get them wet when he goes and shoves his tongue into my mouth. So much for fuckin' foreplay.

I wasn't ready. I just poked his tongue with mine. Then his thumb pushed down from my piss slit. I poked it again. The pressure grew less. So I touched it lightly. The thumb was gone. Fine. I jabbed it from underneath. He left my dick waving in the air—alone. Oh-kay.

I was getting pissed, and panicked. Whaddaido? Then an idea.

I pulled my lips back from his tongue until I sucked only the tip. Walt stroked my dick. I kept sucking. Stroke. I prodded his tongue with as much careful force as he was using to rub my cockhead. Stroke. Then I got creative. I lapped at its underbelly as it curled away from me. I kept at it. And Walt repaid me by rubbing his thumb in circles below. I was gonna "unnh." His tongue pulled away.

"Good. Now git down there and suck my clit, boy." A final flick of his thumb, as if he hoped to get a spark from my dick.

I knelt into his cunt.

"Close your eyes."

I looked up.

"Close'em." I did. "Follow your instincts. Follow the heat." I inched closer. "Remember what I've taught you, Luke, and someday you may just become half the Jedi pussy-eater your sister Leia is."

I opened my eyes and gave him a look that said, "You are so weird." Of course, the longer I stared the more it said, "You are so weird, but so hot."

Walt was grinning back. He gave my hair a yank. "Okay. Close'em."

I leaned in towards the heat. The smell. Somewhere between microbrewed beer and musk deodorant in a really sweaty armpit.

"Now lick my lips. Go on." A few mouthfuls of hair and then I touched skin. "Now, suck my clit, boy."

I kept expecting to taste salt. You know how precum a lot of times tastes like when you're drinking a plain margarita and the rim's all crusty and you take a sip and all you get is that sting of salt with a little tequila? That didn't happen.

And I thought the first kiss from his cunt was wet! He drooled on the bridge of my nose, then all over my cheeks as I pushed my face in. I stuck my tongue out slowly into the hot, sticky-sweet darkness. Walt's clit didn't leap out to greet me like it had in his other mouth; I was gonna have to dig deeper. So I stretched my tongue till it bumped up against a hard, hot rock of flesh that wouldn't budge. But it sure did shiver. Then Walt's whole body, wrapped around my head, did the same. I thought he was trying to twist my head off with his thighs. *Captain, I believe we've just made first contact.*

I brought my tongue back to his clit. I pushed against what had to be the clithead. A steady pressure. Then pulled away. Then back, but longer. Walt shuddered. Now, I thought, time for the fancy stuff. I did an underbelly lap. Then again. Then a side-swipe. I knew I was doing something right cuz I couldn't hear a thing, his legs were crushing into both sides of my head that hard.

I got into a real pussy-eating rhythm after a while. Some slow and steady tonguing followed by spurts of tongue acrobatics. Not that different from cock-sucking. And I didn't hate it or anything. It's just after a while I got bored. My tongue can only feel so much. It was time to send in my hyper-sensitive probe. Just one thing—Walt had originally thought he was gonna fuck me. Now I had to let him know, real nice, that there'd been a temporary change in plans.

I dragged the tip of my tongue across his clit. I lifted my head and said, "Fuck."

"Fuck," Walt groaned.

"I wanna fuck you." I dragged my tongue back over the clit. It was getting so hard I was afraid it might pop.

"Fuck."

"I wanna fuck you." I wriggled my tongue against the head.

"Fuck," he grunted. I kept on flicking my tongue. "Fuck me." Man, I've seen guys with sensitive dickheads, but... if Walt had had balls, they'da been blue by now.

I pulled up leaving his cute little dick pointing into the cold, cold air. Then I really startled him.

"I said I wanna fuck you." I bent down and gave it a few laps of my tongue like a cat. "Right now. Here." I lapped one more time, hoping. "I've never done it before."

He pushed my head away and sat up. "Fucked a man?" He sounded nervous, hurt. I shook my head. "Oh, a pussy."

"Yeah. A real man pussy."

"A what?!"

"You know. Like in the personals. A man pussy."

"Asshole," he said, real serious.

"Huh?" I said back, real casual, but I was so scared I'd pissed him off.

"They mean asshole."

"I'll fuck you there if you want. But I'd really like to fuck you in your man pussy. Then you can fuck me anywhere." He laughed, then grew quiet as I put his hand beneath the super-swollen head of my cock. He gripped it hard till a bubble of precum popped outta my piss-hole. My dick head was red, bright red.

"Okay, but to get my cunt really wet, I need a lot of tit torture."

"Sure," I said. I couldn't wait to chew more on his soft, thick, hairy tits. I leaned forward. My chest bumped up against the palm of his hand.

"Oh, no, boy. Not mine. Yours."

He shoved both his hands into my armpits and heaved. In one move, he dragged my body up along his legs and held me in mid-air like a baby and plopped me down so I was riding his lap.

"Much, much better," he said. Yeah, for you, I thought. I was total-ly naked with my balls dangling in the wind.

It wasn't that cold, for a San Francisco night, but I was shivering anyway. Suddenly, I felt the warm, wet weight of his palms pressing into each of my asscheeks. He pulled me towards his mouth.

Okay, my nipples are nowhere near as big as Walt's. But they ain't the size of dimes either. Or "innies." But it still took him a few tries to get one snug between his teeth.

He bit, then licked the sting away. Another longer, sharper bite. Again. I sucked in my breath. He snorted back. I think he was laugh-ing. He moved over to slurp on the other nipple. And hard. So hard I started to freak he was gonna draw milk or blood outta it.

Then the heat was gone. The pressure was gone. Walt was reaching for his pants. He swung for something glinting in the shadows. A chain. Probably to his wallet, I thought. What's he want with that? Condoms? I've got plenty of those. He tugged and it slithered out of its nest in the jeans pocket. It crashed hard on the floor. It wasn't a wal-let. It looked more like two high-tech clothespins held together by a bicycle chain. I flinched from the back of my scalp to the balls of my toes. Tit clamps! They rattled as he dragged them across the floor. The heat rolled back towards me.

"I am the poet of the Body and I am the poet of the Soul." His broad tongue squashed one nipple then another. "The pleasures of heaven are with me…." He sucked in what I thought was my whole right pec, holding it between his lips while his tongue poked my aching nipple. I was wriggling. Then he did it all over again to my left tit. I was totally squirming and sighing now. He pulled away and his spit grew cold and my nipples harder. Like goosebumps. "And the pains of hell are with me," he hissed. Then I did. Something thick, heavy, bit into my nipples. Both of them. Not like a pinch. Not like teeth. Heavier. And it didn't let go. "The first I graft and increase upon myself, the latter I translate into a new tongue." He got his tongue up under one nipple, wetting it. It was one hot ache. I thought there'd be steam. Then he dragged his stinging beard over my tightening, shaking skin to the other.

At some point, he musta stopped again to talk. "Boy, you're getting your Uncle Walt real wet." He yanked the chain. My chest burned. "Now it's your turn."

He wrapped his fingers slowly around the chain and pulled it towards him. The pressure built, I threw myself ahead of it and landed on his face. Our tongues were pushing, then slipping in sync with the moving of his fingers between my legs. He pushed my dickhead into the tight hat of a condom. My skin was hot and dry while it was cool and wet. He tugged and rolled it down my boner. In my head, I kept jumping back from my tongue to my dick.

Somewhere I heard what sounded like a baby with the runs. He was getting the bottle by my bed to cough up some lube. I kept kissing as he greased up my dick, and I felt that odd, solid cold of the lube where the condom ran out and my skin started.

He guided me between his legs and I sank in. Slowly. The lips of his cunt—warmer and softer and wetter than any mouth that had ever blown my dick—were rising up on both sides to pull me deeper. He slapped my butt and pushed me in all the way. I pulled out and the warmth fell away. I pushed back and it thickened against my cock.

I wanted to start out slow. Go so far, so fast. Let my hips keep time. Really get into feeling my butt tighten then relax. Rock on my hips. Each thrust I'd dig a little deeper. I wanted to work up to slamming his cunt with the full length of my cock. You know, do his man pussy just like I like having mine done.

And it did start out that way. But Walt was up to something. He didn't sigh or groan or snort. He just smiled that cat smile. And it got wider and wider as I began to get a rhythm.

I was thrusting and thrusting and thrusting. The sweat was welling up at my hairline. Then the first trickle down my back, then my forehead. I was getting a pretty good fuck going, I thought. But Walt just smiled and looked so fucking content, so calm. Like he was coming onto X or something.

I was startled, but relieved, when he spoke.

"Ebb stung by the flow…" I closed my eyes. I was trying to feel the fuck, shut out the words. "And flow stung by the ebb, love-flesh swelling…" Then, outta nowhere, Walt arches his back, his belly, up, and I thrust down—bam—to the bone under my bush. I gasped, but Walt kept on talking. "And deliciously aching…" I heard his back hit the futon. At least the bed was groaning. "Limitless…," his fingers dug into my ass, "limpid jets of love…," and pushed me and my dick as far into him as we could go together. "Hot and enormous…," he squeezed my hips with his palms, "…quivering jelly of love…," and almost popped me back out, "…white-blow…," only to push me down again and pull me out again. "And delirious juice…," he blurted as he slapped my ass down into him.

Now I was pumping. Really pumping. It sounds stupid, but, at that moment, I am my dick. And I think I'm banging the hell out of Walt's cunt when he goes and really does it.

"What's that grimace fer, boy." He was panting. "Ain'tcha having fun?"

I grunted this deep wild moan. And bared my teeth. I was trying to smile. I think.

"C'mon, boy. Whoop it up." He reached towards me, my chest, and ripped the tit clamps off with one jerk.

I was stung. The air was cold. It felt like a sharp slap, the jab of a needle, then stinging hot. Like a sleeping foot waking up in one second. Burning. Breaking out in a cold sweat. I was choking. Couldn't swallow. I'd forgot how to breathe. I couldn't get air in or my scream out. Then Walt smacked my butt and I coughed it up. And somehow, I was able to holler and fuck at the same time. I was mad. Raging. I was gonna bang him till he broke in half.

Well, that's what I was shouting. Walt was getting pretty red-faced himself. And gushing sweat. Looked like he was gonna have a baby or something.

I almost jumped out of him when he reached down toward his cunt. I thought he was gonna grab my dick and get me to fuck him even harder. But, without looking, he stopped at his clit. He must have felt the heat. Hell, I could feel its heat. And it was as red as the end of a cigarette.

I was still huffing and puffing. Squinting all my tits' pain into the pounding of my dick. And I was gonna make sure he felt every inch of it. But I was also on auto-fuck. Kinda. Watching his hands, hearing his voice.

"Bridegroom night of love…" He was almost barking the words out. "Working surely and softly…" He pressed his finger down onto his clit and rubbed a circle 'round the head. "Into the prostrate dawn…" He never let the finger up. He was groaning now. "Undulating into the willing…" he dragged his finger up the under-belly, "and yielding day…" He pushed his finger back down. His fingernail was white. "Lost in the cleave of the clasping…" He ground his finger 'round and 'round and mashed it up and down. If that had been my dickhead I woulda come by now and hard. Hit the ceiling even. But Walt kept panting out more words. "And sweet-flesh'd day."

Under the flickering of his lids, I could tell his eyes were rolling. Like a mad dog. And all this show was getting my slip-'n-sliding dick so stiff I knew if I didn't come soon it was gonna snap.

"Ah, fuck." Another Waltquake had begun. This was gonna be The Big One. "Ah, fuck." The bed was rocking and creaking. He was thrusting his hips as high as he could and lifting me with him. "Sweet... fucking... day!"

And then, I think I'm still pumping. But I'm not. It's Walt. His pussy's yanking on my dick. I don't mean squeezing like some virgin butthole. I mean like a hand. A big man's hand. That does it. I shoot. And shoot and shoot, and his cunt keeps on squeezing all the come out of my dick. Like so much so that any part of me that isn't coming is freaking the condom's gonna explode. Next my arms are wobbling like some newborn colt's legs, then they finally give way and I fall onto Walt's chest, into Walt's arms.

"We two boys together clinging," Walt said over my panting as he gripped my butt. "We two boys together clinging,/ One the other never leaving...."

I kept my eyes closed and let my hands slide under and down his tree-trunk of a back till I could dig my hands into his ass. I pulled us together as tight as I could. Walt chuckled and kept murmuring, kept kneading my butt. And I kept repeating to myself, "We two boys together clinging,/ One the other never leaving...."

In every transsexual's sex life, there comes that moment of explanation, revelation, exposure, when you have to bare your body—and with it, much of your soul's desire, carved into its flesh—to the eyes of another human being, and pray with all your might for the right reaction. It's one of the most frightening things we ever have to do; far more frightening than the actual gender reassignment process. "Will anyone love me?" is the hardest question of all. Of course, true courage isn't being unafraid, it's being scared to death and doing it anyway.

Stacey Montgomery Scott lives by her wits in Boston's Jamaica Plain. She has been (among other things) a freelance geek, a sex worker, a computer game designer, and a writer. She is Femme Mommie to the Lesbian Avengers of Boston and has been known to get people into trouble. She still hopes to be a supermodel or superhero when she grows up. You can follow the adventures of Stacey, her partner Gunner, and their family on Gunner's website at www.butchdykeboy.com.

The Essence of Magic

Stacey Montgomery Scott

Careful", she said, "that salsa is very hot, you should treat it with respect." Her hair was exactly the same color as her eyes. I dug my nacho in like a blade. "What kind is it?" I asked, "What's it called?" She smiled at me from under her perfect bangs and shrugged, so I put it in my mouth. The taste was loud on my tongue, and by the time I had swallowed, she was gone.

What followed felt like epilogue. It was one of those parties where everyone was someone, if only by the standards of a small community, and I felt transparent in my obscurity, and overdressed in my prim gray skirt. I wondered if I looked sufficiently old-fashioned that I might pass as Goth.

But if it wasn't a welcoming atmosphere, it was at least rather safe. These were the kewl and the hip, and while they might smirk and joke from behind, no one would dare to be mean to a trannygirl. In some way that I could not fathom, trannygirls were in. Not very in, but somehow, just in enough.

So I drifted among the punks, the leathergirls, the bears, the cyber-hippies and the retro-hip, the post-ravers and the dotcommed (and of course, all six of the currently flourishing flavors of Goth) and the— well, whatever the other two were, I was never sure. I danced near them, and around the edge of their conversations, like an outer planet sliding uncharacteristically close to the sun, risking disaster for a taste of warmth.

I knew a few people. My friend Una had brought me to the party, and her circle of friends, like Andrea the hippie and Leo the tattoo col-

261

lector, were always friendly. Una herself was like a wind blowing through the party, she would sweep through a room, her dreads waving like some aquatic plant, and move from person to person, somehow drawing a thread that would link everyone together. She had a singular talent for social context.

Una was also a former exotic dancer and lately worked as an auto mechanic. Of course we were friends.

She and I had known each other back before my big change of life, but while that transition had cost me many friends, it had somehow caused my relationship with her to quicken and thrive. Recently she had taken on the personal mission of dragging me out of my apartment "to see people." I lacked her talent for crowded rooms, however—I can't think of any place lonelier than a crowded party.

A few times that evening I drifted back past the food table, but the salsa was always unattended, and somehow tasted quiet; its specialness had faded.

Una seemed to track me with radar. "Having fun?" she asked, and "Did I miss something?"

"Nothing I could give a name to," which was true enough. Eventually, Leo drove us all to our various homes and I consoled myself that I was finally getting out and meeting people again.

From my ragged balcony the neighborhood was a dark landscape lit from within by the frosty glow of televisions sets, as if the planet's flesh was threaded with unborn stars. Waiting. I drank jasmine tea and went to sleep in the cool solitude of my bed.

The next time I saw her it was raining hard, like the night itself had begun to melt and pour dark and heavy from the sky. I was with a bunch of artsy theatre folks. Her group looked more geek-ish. We passed each other on opposite sides of a rapidly growing puddle. I saw her first, so when she looked up and saw me, I winked at her. I could see her startled smile as her group pulled her off into the night. For once in my life, it seemed to me, I had successfully played the ingenue.

It was a good feeling.

I have never been much for dating or romance. I was always too solitary, too wrapped up in my own life. How can you share yourself with someone if you don't know who you are, what you would be sharing? How can you have sex when you and your body can't be in the same place at the same time? When I was a child, I had always assumed that some kind of spell, properly pronounced, would transform my body and make me right , and special, and worthwhile—like magic.

It turns out though, if you really want something, you have to work for it, and so I began the "gender journey." But since emerging from the solipsist hell that we call transition, I had found myself unsure how one proceeds. I wasn't sure where to go, how to dress, what to say. I had a lifetime of rules and nuances to catch up on. What did I want out of life? What sort of person had I been; what sort of person did I want to be now?

For one thing, I didn't want to be solitary and wrapped up in my own life any more. But dating seemed... unlikely. And sex... that seemed too much to even think about.

And besides, I couldn't really have sex anyway.

The third time, we were listening to women read lesbian porn out loud. The back of the bookstore was crowded, and the air was completely still. I was, once again, more or less welcome. It was a women's bookstore and men who came in could expect to receive a frosty reception. But if they didn't all think of me as a woman, fewer thought of me as a man. I suppose that to most of them I was a sort of honorary lesbian—after all, I only had long nails on one hand, and they were trimmed down to nothing on the other.

The women who read were butch, or femme, or androgynous, or not. They had pink or blue or burnt sienna hair, or not. Silver glinted from their ears, noses, and tongues. Their stories were tales of gender bent, submissives dominated, passions entwined, and taboos dispensed with. Or not.

I sat and listened, as if I was unaware that she was sitting just a few rows of collapsible metal auditorium chairs behind me. The woman who was reading had hair like spilled ink. Her story—a tale of anal discovery—was tediously written, but she read it with such honest passion that no one noticed or cared.

And it struck me that I didn't care what happened next. She and I were connected, somehow, and something might come of it, or not. Our interests might fade. Circumstances might intervene. A million possible futures awaited us. But it didn't matter, and it was somehow delicious to be balanced on the edge of sexual possibility; the outcome seemed entirely beside the point. To be here and now, it seemed, feeling—and perhaps sharing—a quiet sexual tension, perhaps a mutual attraction.

And so we sat and breathed the thick wet air, like the amphibious denizens of tropical swamps sucking air as heavy as water into our gills, and moving gently with the tide. When the readings were over everyone rushed up to get their books signed, or back towards the exit to escape from the various kinds of heat. She and I didn't really move toward each other, but somehow, the crowd and the room's geometry shifted so that we were standing close.

Her smile was as bright as blood. "I know all about you," she said to me, as if sharing a secret. "I know your name."

I nodded, but had no idea what to say. I felt suddenly new.

"I've been asking around about you. We know the same people."

I noticed that people were noticing us. We were just talking, but something else was happening, and everyone seemed aware of it.

People gave us room, and then looked back, as if hoping to catch a glimpse of something real.

I smiled, and let her talk, suddenly, inexplicably bashful. I wondered what she was seeing, what she thought she saw, who and what she thought I really was. How much of my life's complexities made sense to her?

That's when I noticed that she had long nails on one hand, and her nails were trimmed down to nothing on the other.

We talked about the readings. We traded compliments. We compared schedules. We made a date. It all had a sort of well-lubricated inevitability. Whatever was going to happen was already in charge, reaching back to us from the future and arranging everything.

And somewhere in there we kissed. One of us must have started the kiss—one of us must have acquiesced. But her lips were a little dry and a little warm and a little spicy, and her body echoed somehow, like she had never yet been filled. It was the kind of kiss that takes place at right angles to time.

"Aren't you going to tell me your name?" I asked, after, but she just smiled and shook her head.

But I was a liar. I had done my research too. I knew everything about her. Or I thought I did.

This is my secret: transsexuals don't "do" transition. People say things like "When you transitioned" and "when you made your change" and they have no idea what they are talking about. Transition isn't an active verb, but a passive one. You don't transition, you simply stop resisting transition, you just give in. You just stop fighting. You just let the current sweep you away. Transition is a sacrifice, like an act of submission, like going to sleep, like dying.

Maybe sex is like that too. Maybe everything is.

Preparing for my big date: I'm sure I was supposed to learn all of this, somewhere. I was supposed to go to pajama parties with my friends and I was supposed to work out with them how it's all done. We would have said, "Don't wear that," and "eew, too much eyeshadow!" and "Hey, isn't so-and-so dreamy?" We would have invented good taste between ourselves, and then traded with other bunches of adolescent girls, until we were all part of the way things were done.

That isn't what happened to me, though. I got beaten up in the boy's locker room instead, and ran home with nothing intact. Somewhere along the way I had begun to develop a little bit of taste, a touch of style, a dab of skill, but it all seemed insufficient to the challenge my mirror reflected.

I went to a big transsexual conference once. The women there were angelic divas, tall and proud, somehow hyper-feminine, their clothes artfully arranged, their faces skillfully applied and stylishly worn. They tried to take me aside, like a duck who just needed swan lessons: here, girl, these are the tweezers, this is the brush, hold them so, and oh my god, your ear looks like a spiral notebook, and what did you use to get your hair so green?

And I stood there in and my denim and lace and thought, I'm not going through all of this to be somebody else, but to be me. Like a teenager escaping her stylish society aunts, I ran and didn't look back. Much.

But I'm not a teenager, and gender revolution aside, there is a moment when you find yourself in front of the cracked bathroom mirror of your sad, verminous apartment wondering how to make yourself "beautiful enough." I picked up the brush and tweezers and suddenly I felt like I understood something deep, something that connected me to millions of women who had sat in front of mirrors and sighed this very sigh.

It struck me that the mirror was filled with me (one of me, anyway) and the closet was filled with my clothes, and yet, this all wasn't about me, it was about her. I wouldn't see her for hours, but she seemed very present in the room. I put on my face and did my hair like she was watching, like I was performing for her. I could feel the way her eyes followed me, the way the taste of her skin would change when she smelled me.

A proud drag queen told me once that all of her life was a performance, and I had thought smugly, that's the difference between you and me, you're performing, and I'm somehow real.

Now I knew that I had been totally wrong. I smiled at the mirror and got to work. Ready or not.

"You're beautiful," she said, and looked at me so brightly that I had to turn away, but for once in my life I let a compliment stand. I was rescued by the waiter coming to take our order.

Luckily for the universe's plans, we had things in common: bands, TV shows, political causes—enough to keep the conversation going under its own power. Did you see the cliffhanger at the end of the season? Are you going to that rally? It was comforting, it told us what we had in common—a culture, of sorts.

But mostly I noticed the barbed tattoo coiled on her arm, the way her eyes moved, the way she kept brushing her bangs back from her eyes, and the fire that shaded her voice when she discussed something she felt passionate about. She was prettier, I decided, but I was better dressed. Did that make me the femme?

"You know, that party wasn't the first time I noticed you," she said, while we ate our spicy dumplings.

"It wasn't?" I was somehow aware that the conversation was shifting onto more serious ground. "So when did you first notice me?"

"At the Pride Dance. You were wearing a lovely white dress, and I thought you looked pretty and sort of vulnerable, and that you must be someone very brave."

"Why, because I was a trannygirl at the big dyke dance?" I asked, and I had done it, I had said the word aloud.

"Well, sure. There were women there who didn't really approve of you, you know."

"I know. But it felt like it was my place to be. And mostly people were very nice. And you're the one taking the tryke out to dinner."

"The what?"

"The Tryke. It means trans-dyke. I can't be a transsexual lesbian, I don't make enough money to be lesbian."

"Oh. I didn't know the word for it."

"That's the word. Someone made it up, and now it's real."

She nodded soberly, as if she was agreeing to something profound. "Oh, yes. Names are the essence of magic, you know. Like Rumplestiltskin. 'Tryke' is definitely a word to conjure with." She smiled brightly. "So, hon, what's the word for fucking a tryke?"

I sipped my tea and thought, I may not be ready for this after all.

The problem with sex is that it's all about bodies—at least, it is when you're doing it right. And my body and I just hadn't been getting along. For much of my life I would wake up every morning and check my body, wondering what gender am I today? The answer was always a disappointment. But for some reason, I was the sort of person who wasn't certain, morning after morning.

Certainly, I had sexual desires, and fantasies. Who doesn't imagine a grueling girl-motorcycle-gang initiation sex ceremony when they're trying to go to sleep? I sure do.

But actually having sex with people was hard—their bodies always seemed so interesting, but my own body always seemed so alien. I could never believe that they were really interested. And nothing felt right.

It turns out that with sex you don't really have to be there—you can slip outside of your body and let it happen to someone else, like dropping a coin down a well—you hear the splash, but you never get wet.

Of course, you can die of thirst that way.

Her place: a familiar scatter of furniture buried in a sea of CDs, videos, zines, and books. Lesbian track lighting strung along the hallway, like refugees from Xmas decoration hell. The unmistakable spoor of absent or discreet roommates. In no time the door to her room was closed and the stereo was playing loud enough to shield us from the world.

Her futon was firm and the blanket smelled clean, and we kissed like we were inventing kisses, like we had been given a grant to perfect lesbian kissing but we had to have the secret by midnight to save the world, so faster, faster!

Some girls are fun to kiss because they're beautiful, and some are fun to kiss because they're so excited, or because you know what's coming next, or because they smell so good (we were both good

CFIDs-aware dykes, no perfume or fragrance, we just smelled like ourselves). She was fun to kiss because she knew how to kiss, because she took it seriously. We didn't hurry along to the next thing—we stopped to get our kissing right.

But when I felt her hands starting to slip through my clothing, I felt a cold wind moving through my safe-zones. I could slip away, I thought, I could just be here and do this and be somewhere else too, and that would be all right.

Instead I moved back slightly, gently disentangling us.

"What's wrong?"

"We need talk a little bit first."

"You want me to promise to respect you in the morning? If you're going to make me promise to marry you first, I should say that I usually refuse."

"Usually? What happens when you don't refuse?"

"Then we get married. Fast."

"Um. Of course. Actually, I just thought we should talk a bit before we, you know…"

"Before we got all nasty? OK, what's on your mind, babe?" She settled into the mattress so that our bodies were still gently touching, everywhere. I could feel the heat from her, the pull of her gravity. "I'll even promise to wear a condom if it will help."

I tried to recall anyone ever having called me "Babe"—no one had. I took a breath and a Ritalin moment to get back on topic. "Ah, have you ever been with a tryke before?"

"No," she said, a little more seriously. "I had never even heard the word before, remember? I guess I'm a virgin."

"Well, I'm a virgin too."

She squinted at me. "You're a virgin? I find that a little hard to believe. You don't kiss like you just got out the convent. Or come to think of it, maybe that's exactly how I'd describe your kisses."

Then she spoke more softly. "Look, I have sex with girls. That means I've been here before. I've known victims of rape and incest and you don't want to know what else. Anyone who really has sex with girls knows that there's sometimes stuff you can't talk about, or really have to. It's okay. If you didn't have issues, you wouldn't be human enough for me to mate with. You want to see the marks from where I cut myself? Look, we all have this fantasy that sex just happens, in the darkness, like magic. It isn't like that at all. It isn't so easy. We have to work for it. Girls have to, anyway."

She leaned over and kissed me, as gently as you would nuzzle a newborn kitten, and for some reason, I could feel myself blushing everywhere.

"Thanks. I guess I need to tell you, um, that I haven't really been with anyone since my transition. The last time I had sex with someone, she, well, she thought I was a boy. It was years ago."

"Oh. Oh . So I guess you really are a virgin then, aren't you?" I nodded; she got it. "That's ok hon, I'm a famous deflowerer of girls. I've been doing it since junior high. I was the one who beat the world record at the Bratmobile concert last year—maybe you read about it in On Our Backs? Don't sweat it. I'll be gentle-like."

"Um. Right. And maybe you don't really want me to get undressed right now."

"Girl, you were not getting undressed just then. I was undressing you. There's a big difference. And that should make my intentions clear enough." She was still smiling, sort of, but she was more serious now.

"Well, if this is your first time undressing a trannygirl, there's some stuff we should talk about…"

"Yeah, well, I figured it was like Christmas morning. I'd unwrap and see what I got. Surprises can be fun, you know. I do have one question though."

"Yes?"

"Does it always take you this long to get to the nasty part? How can anyone question your being a dyke when you process so much? They're just not paying attention."

Right.

"Okay," I said. "Here." I took her hand in mine and brought it up to my forehead. "This is my hair—Sunshine Yellow, by the way, but you probably knew that. This is my hairline—see the way I've styled it forward? That's because my hairline is a lot higher than it is on most girls my age. The effects of too much testosterone in my life. I hate it when people notice that, like on windy days. I wear hats all the time, like my beret. Eventually I suppose I'll get some kind of hairpiece or wig, though I hope I've stopped losing my hair." She traced my hairline gently with one finger, and nodded.

I guided her fingers down across my face. "This is my big, heavy jaw."

She scowled at me. "I hadn't noticed."

"This is where my facial hair grows. I used to have lots and lots of it. I've been having it electrolysized away for a year or two now, but it's slow going. What remains I try to cover with makeup."

"Electrolysis hurts," she said softly.

"Yeah, and it hurts more every time I go. I take female hormones every day. They make my skin softer, more sensitive. The electrolysis needle used to hurt, but now I can really feel it."

She ran her fingers softly along my jaw, and down my throat, making tingly trails wherever they went. "Your skin gets more sensitive?"

"A lot more. The hormones have really changed me—no, they've changed the whole world. It's a much more sensual world than it used to be, much more tactile. Men and women, I think, live in very different universes. I feel a lot more now, I think things smell different too. Everything seems more intense. The 'mones change other things—my sex drive, my moods. I've lost an amazing amount of muscle, and I was never the muscular type. They saying going on estrogen even improves your verbal scores."

She nodded. "That's a scary thought in your case, but go on."

"These are my broad, boyish shoulders. I'm always aware of them, all the time. They stop anything from fitting me right, and people always notice them."

She did not comment, but helped me take off my shirt, and my bra. Her movements were was careful and deliberate. "These are my breasts. They won't get much bigger than this, because I started, umm, late in life. But they're real. It took a while to get used to having them. They can be so sensitive, and they're always brushing up against things. I'll never forget that day I jumped down three steps and really felt my breasts as I landed."

She smiled, and traced the shape of my breasts with her hands, I shivered as if she were winter arriving. Then, leaning forward, she kissed each nipple gently. I could feel fire inside me, answering her. It flushed my skin pink like a banner, as if to signal for her to go on.

"You have beautiful tits," she said, and then her fingers were teasing at the catch to my skirt. She looked up at me, and her face was deadly serious. "Keep going."

"I can't do this if you think I'm a boy. I don't know why, but it matters. You have to understand that I'm a girl, or we have to stop."

"Look, I've been with boys, and I've been with girls," she said. "I prefer girls, because they have soft skin, like yours, and because they quiver when I touch them, the way you do. You are as much a girl as any girl, and even if you weren't I would believe it anyway, because you said so, and I believe you. I'll bet that's the real reason things feel so different, taste so different for you now. I think that before, your life was a kind of fiction, and now you've made it real. This is the real world. And you are a real girl. And I know it. Have you got that?"

"I've got it. Thank you."

"No," she said, gently caressing my stomach with her lips, moving slowly lower. "No," she whispered, "Thank you."

And I wanted to say: Now that I have said all of this, the rest doesn't matter. This has already been the most intimate experience of my life. You have already had me.

And there was so much more to tell her, to explain, secrets still not spoken, but I could feel her hands on my back, and her lips and teeth against my hipbone, and my body shook in response to her every move, and I was there. Completely there, my body and I together, somehow synched to rhythm of heartbeats and quivers.

I tried to speak but it was too late for both of us, and my skirt opened for her and our bodies were turning together on the "Xena: Warrior Princess" sheets. We pulled off her jeans and her shirt; she showed me her hairline, and the smooth skin of her jaw, and the curve of her shoulders, and the soft pride of her breasts, the secrets of her piercings.

And then she kissed me, and this was another kind of kiss altogether, a kiss filled with sharp white teeth. She covered me with those kisses, each one made my body thrash, and each one left a mark. I would look half-eaten for days.

There's a kind of embrace that never rests, never stops. Holding her was like that, like a river trying to grasp a torrent of quicksilver, lightning bolts conjoined. She was wonderful.

I explored every inch of her with my hands, and then with my lips. I tasted all of her. Her breath tasted like summer; the inside of her thighs was like autumn. I put my tongue deep inside her. She threaded her fingers through my hair, guiding me, urging me forward. I put found her clit and wrote "You are wonderful" on it with my tongue. Slowly.

She liked it. I wrote more. I wrote my life story on her poor clit until she cried and shook and kicked, and I wondered if she had gotten it all, if somehow all of my secrets had been inscribed subliminally into her soul.

She grabbed me, with strong arms, pushing me down onto the bed.

And I knew that if sex outside of your body is like a movie, a book, a problem to be solved, a treasure to be appreciated like great art on the wall, then this was sex from within your body: the endless flash of lightning, the eternal roar of continents grinding together, the howl of stars forever being born.

Then she was on top of me, strong and wet and demanding, and I knew that she was really her and I was really me and this was really fucking. I could feel us. I could smell us.

"You're wonderful," she said, and suddenly I just stopped fighting, and let go, and let it happen.

The rest was magic.

Acknowledgments

"The Gay Science" by Charles Anders previously appeared in *Black Sheets* magazine and on the Scarlet Letters web site.

"Wild Ride" by Raven Gildea previously appeared on the Roughriders FTM erotic fiction web site.

"Walt" by Ian Philips originally appeared in a slightly different form in *Best Gay Erotica 2000*, Richard Labonté, Ed., (Cleis Press, 1999). It was reprinted in *See Dick Deconstruct: Literotica for the Satirically Bent* (AttaGirl Press, 2001).

"Up For A Nickel" by Thomas S. Roche previously appeared in *Best American Erotica*, Susie Bright, Ed. (Simon & Schuster).

"The Audit" by Dominic Santi was previously published in *Hard At Work*, David Laurents, Ed. (Zipper Books, 1998).

"Pinkeye" by Simon Sheppard previously appeared on the Roughriders web site.

"Wanting That Man" by Karen T. Taylor was previously published in *Best Bisexual Erotica 2*, Carol Queen and Bill Brent, Eds. (Circlet Press and Black Books, 2001)

☾✦ Circlet Press
Celebrating The Erotic Imagination

Best Transgender Erotica, $16.00
Edited by Hanne Blank and Raven Kaldera
A ground-breaking 'best-of' collection, celebrating gender variation with erotic fiction. Twenty three stories by writers of every gender (not just two) represent many forms of "trans" identity. Includes Charles Anders, Thomas S. Roche, M. Christian, Raven Gildea, and many more. ISBN1-885865-40-6

Sextopia: Stories of Sex and Society, $14.95
edited by Cecilia Tan
Circlet Press brings its uniquely erotic treatment to Sir Thomas More's exercise of creating societies to illuminate the human condition. In a utopia, a perfect world, what kind of sex would we have? how often? with whom? and why? Veteran world-builders Catherina Asaro and Suzy Mckee Charnas join cutting-edge erotica authors like M. Christian and Renee M. Charles in providing the provocative answers. ISBN 1-885865-31-7

SexCrime: An Anthology of Subversive Erotica, $14.95
edited by Cecilia Tan
Taking its title from 1984, George Orwell's dystopian novel, Sexcrime explores the erotic heat and intensity that can ignite when love comes under repressive conditions. Underground love and subversive sex can flourish through the intimacy of secrets, the thrill of transgression, the sweetness of forbidden pleasures. ISBN 1-885865-26-0

Nymph, $16.95 hardcover
by Francesca Lia Block
The author of bestsellers Weetzie Bat, Dangerous Angels, and Violet & Claire now brings her sensual, dream-like fantasies full circle with this erotic work for adult readers. Following the interconnected erotic lives of young punks and poets and surfers, Nymph weaves a kaleidoscopic erotic fable. ISBN 1-885865-30-9

The Velderet: A Cybersex S/M Serial, $14.95
by Cecilia Tan
The long-awaited erotic adventure novel from one of today's top erotica writers. Can two people in a happy, stable society where they condemn "inequality" explore taboo sadomasochistic erotic desires without changing their world? Or is their world already changing, and can they save it? ISBN 1-885865-27-9

Ask for these titles at your favorite bookstore or online bookseller! Or order direct from Circlet Press:

Name: _____

Ship to: _____

City: _____ State: _____ Zip: _____

Phone or Email: _____

MasterCard/VISA: _____ _____ _____ _____

Exp. Date: __ /__ or send check or money order.
Add $4 shipping for first book, $2 for each add'l
within US/Canada. US$7 each overseas.

X_____